Thomas Francklin,   Sophokles

Plays

translated into English verse by Thomas Francklin - with an introd. by Henry

Morley. Second Edition

Thomas Francklin,   Sophokles

Plays

translated into English verse by Thomas Francklin - with an introd. by Henry Morley. Second Edition

ISBN/EAN: 9783337187156

Printed in Europe, USA, Canada, Australia, Japan

Cover: Foto ©Andreas Hilbeck / pixelio.de

More available books at **www.hansebooks.com**

MORLEYS
UNIVERSAL
LIBRARY

𝔅𝔞𝔩𝔩𝔞𝔫𝔱𝔶𝔫𝔢 𝔓𝔯𝔢𝔰𝔰
BALLANTYNE, HANSON AND CO.
LONDON AND EDINBURGH

THE PLAYS

OF

SOPHOCLES

TRANSLATED INTO ENGLISH VERSE BY

THOMAS FRANCKLIN

WITH AN INTRODUCTION BY HENRY MORLEY

LL.D., PROFESSOR OF ENGLISH LITERATURE AT
UNIVERSITY COLLEGE, LONDON

SECOND EDITION

LONDON
GEORGE ROUTLEDGE AND SONS
BROADWAY, LUDGATE HILL
GLASGOW, MANCHESTER AND NEW YORK
1890

MORLEY'S UNIVERSAL LIBRARY.

"Marvels of clear type and general neatness."—*Daily Telegraph.*

INTRODUCTION.

THE last of the Plays of Sophocles, brought out by his
grandson five years after his death, associates Œdipus with
the poet's birthplace, Colonus, on a little hill, with a temple
and grove sacred to the Furies, about a mile distant from
Athens. Here, in extreme old age, Sophocles, expecting his
own death, sang, with sympathy in every tone, the death of
Œdipus. "Far as my eyes can reach," says Antigone to
her father,

> "I see a city
> With lofty turrets crowned, and, if I err not,
> This place is sacred, by the laurel shade,
> Olive and vine thick planted, and the songs
> Of nightingales sweet-warbling through the grove."

Here, within sight of Athens, Sophocles was born about
the year 495 before Christ, five years before the battle of
Marathon. He was about thirty years younger than
Æschylus, whose extant plays have already been given in
this Library, and fifteen years older than Euripides, whose
plays will hereafter be given. These are the three Greek
tragedians whose genius laid for all Europe the strong
foundation of the poetic drama. Æschylus, whose fire
burned like that of an old Hebrew prophet, shaped his
conceptions broadly and grandly, with a force of nature that
creates the forms of art. Sophocles followed, and with
the fine touch of a poet working under influences of an art
already vigorous and true in aim, added new graces of his
own; in the clear light of his genius the Greek play
ripened to the fulness of its beauty. Then followed Euripides, perhaps more faulty than either of his predecessors,
but of the three most human, and to us moderns rich in
echoes of the thought of our own hearts; therefore Milton
loved him.

Sophocles was the son of Sophilus. He was trained
liberally, and learned to so excel in music, dancing, and in
exercises of the body, that it was he who was chosen, as a
youth of fifteen, to lead, naked and lyre in hand, the song
and dance of triumph for the victory at Salamis. About
twelve years afterwards, at the age of twenty-seven, on a

conspicuous occasion, when accident made the leading men in Athens umpires, Sophocles competed with Æschylus and won the prize, for a play which is now lost. Æschylus then withdrew for a time to Sicily, as has been told in the Introduction to the Plays of Æschylus. Sophocles remained at Athens in highest favour, until it was his turn, when veteran, to be overcome by a younger poet, and in the year 441 B.C. the first prize was won by Euripides. Of the Plays produced by Sophocles during twenty-eight years, from the time when he overcame Æschylus to the time when he was overcome by Euripides, not one remains.

But in the next year (440), when his age was fifty-five, he produced his Play of "Antigone," and for the wisdom in its poetic counsels, which accorded with the policy of Pericles, Sophocles was appointed one of the nine military leaders who were associated with Pericles in the war against a faction at Samos. Pericles said of him that he understood the making of verses better than the marching of an army. Military duty did not disturb his calm or spoil his dinners, and even in camp he gave good dinners to his friends. Æschylus had won special distinction as a soldier; Sophocles neither won it nor cared for it.

At Samos, Sophocles made acquaintance with Herodotus. The poet and the historian met afterwards at Athens, and were friends. For the last thirty-four years of his life Sophocles was a patriot in troubled times, assenting often to a next best policy where best was not attainable, and putting his heart rather into his Plays than into the wars of party that beset him. He stayed by Athens and by Colonus, with

the songs
Of nightingales sweet-warbling through the grove.

His Play of "Antigone" was followed by "Electra"; next came, probably, the "Trachiniæ," "Œdipus Tyrannus," "Ajax," "Philoctetes," and "Œdipus Coloneus."

Sophocles had two sons: one named Iophon, whose mother was a free Athenian woman; the other, Ariston, whose mother was of Sicyon. Iophon was legal heir, but Ariston had a son who was named Sophocles after his grandfather, and Iophon was jealous of the old man's tenderness towards his grandson, fearing lest the boy might get some part of Iophon's inheritance. Iophon therefore publicly accused his father of imbecility—said that, his mind being affected by his great age, he was not capable of making a will. The old man replied: "If I am Sophocles, I am not beside myself; and if I am beside myself, I am not Sophocles." He then read, as evidence of his sanity,

a chorus in sweet praise of his native soil, from the
" Œdipus at Colonus," which he had just written :

> Thou art come in happy time,
> Stranger, to this blissful clime ;
> Long for swiftest steeds renowned,
> Fertil'st of the region round ;
> Where, beneath the ivy shade,
> In the dew-besprinkled glade,
> Many a love-lorn nightingale
> Warbles sweet her plaintive tale.—&c.

The reader will find at p. 287 the chorus in the Play, which
caused the judges to dismiss the charge of imbecility with
acclamation of a genius still fresh. That Sophocles bore no
malice to his son is inferred from another passage in the
same swan song, where Antigone pleads to her father for
Polynices :

> Remember, 'tis thy child—
> Thou didst beget him ; though he were the worst
> Of sons to thee, yet would it ill become
> A father to return it. Let him come.
> Others like thee have base, unworthy children,
> And yet their minds are softened to forgiveness
> By friends' advice, and all their wrath subdued."

Sophocles was about ninety years old when he died : he
was dead in the year 405. The enjoyment of his Plays will
be heightened to the reader who recalls to memory the
course of events in the history of Athens during the fifty
years after the battle of Salamis ; for a large part of a true
man's life, and all his work, lies in the world that is about
him.

Robert Potter, the translator of Æschylus, also translated
the Plays of Euripides and Sophocles. He was born in and
graduated from Emmanuel College, Cambridge, took orders,
and was incumbent, first, of Scarning, and afterwards of
Lowestoft. He wrote poems of his own, which he collected
in 1774, and published, three years afterwards, in one quarto
volume, his translation of Æschylus. This was received
with very great favour, and was often republished, with
addition of notes, in two volumes 8vo. In 1781 Potter's
Æschylus was followed by the first volume of his translation
of Euripides ; the second volume followed close upon the
first, in 1782. In 1783 Potter issued a pamphlet meant as
vindication of Gray in "An Enquiry into some Passages of
Dr. Johnson's Lives of the Poets," and in 1785 followed
a translation of the Oracle concerning Babylon, and the
Song of Exultation from Isaiah, chapters xiii. and xiv. In
1788 he completed his work on the Greek Tragedians by

publishing his translation of Sophocles. He died in 1804. Potter's work was at its best and freshest in his Æschylus. His translation of Euripides was rivalled by that of Woodhull, which appeared at the same time; and his Sophocles did not surpass the preceding translation of Dr. Francklin.

The Rev. Dr. Thomas Francklin was an older man, whose whole life was contemporary with Samuel Johnson's. He was twelve years younger, but Johnson and he died in the same year, 1784. He dedicated to Johnson his translation of Lucian, and caught Johnson's fancy by defining man as a tool-making animal. Johnson he styled in his Dedication "the Demonax of the present age;" Lucian having described Demonax as "the best philosopher whom I have ever seen or known."

Thomas Francklin (whose name was and is commonly spelt Franklin) was born in London in 1720, son to Robert Francklin, printer of *The Craftsman*, and educated at Westminster School. He went on to Trinity College, Cambridge, graduated, and became a Fellow of his College; also Greek Professor in the University. In December 1758 he was instituted vicar of Ware and Thunderidge, and afterwards rector of Braxted in Essex. He proceeded to the degree of D.D., and he became chaplain in ordinary to King George the Third. As a Greek scholar he translated Lucian as well as Sophocles. His Sophocles, dedicated to the Prince of Wales, appeared in 1759. Dr. Francklin wrote also two tragedies: the "Earl of Warwick," borrowed from De la Harpe, acted with great success in 1767; and "Matilda," acted in 1775, also with great applause, and borrowed from Voltaire's "Duc de Foix." Francklin produced also, without success, a two-act comedy called "The Contract," founded on D'Estouche's "L'Amour Usé." He also edited, with Smollett, a translation of Voltaire, in which his own part was only a translation of two of Voltaire's tragedies: "Orestes," which was acted for Mrs. Yates's benefit in March 1769; and "Electra," in 1774. In his own day Dr. Francklin lost popularity by severities of judgment as a writer in the *Critical Review* when Smollett was its editor. This caused Churchill to say of him—

> Others for Francklin voted, but 'twas known
> He sickened at all triumphs but his own.

He is chiefly known to us now as the best eighteenth-century translator of the Plays of Sophocles.

H. M.

November 1886.

Ajax.

DRAMATIS PERSONÆ.

MINERVA.	AGAMEMNON.
ULYSSES.	MENELAUS.
AJAX.	MESSENGER.
TECMESSA, *Wife of Ajax.*	CHORUS, *composed of Ancient*
TEUCER, *Brother to Ajax.*	*Men of Salamis.*

ACT I.

SCENE I.—*A Field near the Tent of* AJAX.

MINERVA, ULYSSES.

MINERVA. Son of Laertes, thy unwearied spirit
Is ever watchful to surprise the foe ;
I have observed thee wandering midst the tents
In search of Ajax, where his station lies,
At th' utmost verge, and meas'ring o'er his steps
But late impressed ; like Sparta's hounds of scent
Sagacious dost thou trace him, nor in vain ;
For know, the man thou seekst is not far from thee :
Yonder he lies, with reeking brow and hands
Deep-stained with gore ; cease then thy search, and tell
    me
Wherefore thou com'st, that so I may inform
Thy doubting mind, and best assist thy purpose.
    ULY. Minerva, dearest of th' immortal powers,

For, though I see thee not, that well-known voice
Doth like the Tyrrhene trump awake my soul,
Right hast thou said, I come to search my foe,
Shield-bearing Ajax: him alone I seek:
A deed of horror hath he done this night,
If it be he, for yet we are to know
The certain proof, and therefore came I here
A willing messenger: the cattle all,
Our flocks and herds, are with their shepherds slain.
To Ajax every tongue imputes the crime;
One of our spies, who saw him on the plain,
His sword still reeking with fresh blood, confirmed it:
Instant I fled to search him, and sometimes
I trace his footsteps, which again I lose
I know not how; in happy hour thou com'st
To aid me, Goddess; thy protecting hand
Hath ruled me ever, and to thee I trust
My future fate.

MIN.   I know it well, Ulysses,
And therefore come to guard and to assist thee
Propitious to thy purpose.

ULY.   Do I right,
My much-loved mistress?

MIN.   Doubtless; his foul deed
Doth well deserve it.

ULY.   What could prompt his hand
To such a desperate act?

MIN.   Achilles' arms;
His rage for loss of them.

ULY.   But wherefore thus
Destroy the flock?

MIN.   'Twas in your blood he thought
His hands were stained.

ULY.   Against the Grecians then
Was all his wrath?

MIN.   And fatal had it proved
To them, if I had not prevented it.

ULY. What daring insolence could move his soul
To such a deed?

MIN. Alone by night he wandered
In secret to attack you.

ULY.   Did he come
Close to our tents?
    MIN.   Even to the double portal
Where rest your chiefs.
    ULY.   What power could then withhold
His mad'ning hand?
    MIN.   I purposely deceived
His sight, and saved him from the guilty joy,
Turning his rage against the mingled flocks,
Your gathered spoil; on these with violence
He rushed, and slaughtered many; now he thought
That he had slain th' Atridæ, now believed
Some other chiefs had perished by his hand.
I saw his madness and still urged him on,
That he might fall into the snare I laid:
Tired with his slaughter now he binds in chains
The living victim, drives the captive herd
Home to his tent, nor doubts but they are men:
There beats with many a stripe the helpless foe,
But I will show thee this most glaring frenzy,
That to the Grecians what thy eyes behold
Thou mayst report; be confident, nor fear
His utmost malice; I shall turn his sight
Askant from thee. Ajax, what ho! come forth,
Thou who dost bind in chains thy captive foes!
Ajax, I say, come forth before the portal.   [him.
    ULY. What wouldst thou do, Minerva? Do not call
    MIN. What should Ulysses fear?
    ULY.   Oh! by the gods
I do entreat thee, let him stay within.
    MIN. But wherefore? Thou hast seen him here
        before.
    ULY. He ever was and is my deadliest foe.
    MIN. Oh! but to laugh an enemy to scorn
Is mirth most grateful.
    ULY.   I had rather still
He came not here.
    MIN.   And art thou then afraid
To see a madman?
    ULY.   I should little dread
The sight of Ajax in his better mind.

MIN. He will not see thee be thou e'er so near.
ULY. Impossible ! his eyes are still the same.
MIN. But I shall throw a veil of darkness o'er them.
ULY. By powers immortal all things may be done.
MIN. Wait then in silence till he comes.
ULY.   I will ;
And yet 'twere better to retire.
MIN.   What ho !
Ajax, again I call thee; wherefore payst thou
So little reverence to thy guardian power ?

SCENE II.

AJAX, MINERVA, ULYSSES.

AJAX. Hail to the daughter of great Jove ! to thee,
Minerva, hail ! Thou com'st in happy hour,
For I will crown thee with the golden spoils
Which I have gained by thy assisting hand.
  MIN. Well hast thou spoke ; but say, has Ajax
      dipped
His spear in Grecian blood ?
  AJAX.   It is my boast :
I'll not deny it.
  MIN.   Did th' Atridæ feel
Thy vengeful arm ?
  AJAX.   They never will again
Dishonour Ajax.
  MIN.   If I understand thee,
They are both dead.
  AJAX.   They are ; now let them come,
And take my arms away.
  MIN.   But tell me, Ajax ;
Laertes' son, hath he escaped thy wrath ?
  AJAX. Talkst thou of him, that fox accursed ?
  MIN.   I mean
Thy foe, Ulysses.
  AJAX.   Oh ! he is my captive,
The fairest of my spoils ; I have him here ;
He shall not perish yet.

MIN.   What 'vantage then
Meanst thou to draw from his confinement?
AJAX.   First,
I'll have him bound to the pillar.
MIN.   And what then
Wouldst thou inflict?
AJAX.   His limbs all purpled o'er
With many a bloody stripe, he shall be slain.
MIN. Do not torment him thus.
AJAX.   In all things else,
Minerva, would I gratify thy will,
But this, and this alone must be his fate.
MIN. Since 'tis so pleasing to thee, be it so,
Nor quit thy purpose.
AJAX.   ·   I must to my work;
Thus, great Minerva, mayst thou ever smile
Propitious on me, and assist thy Ajax!   [*Exit.*

SCENE III.

MINERVA, ULYSSES.

MIN. Behold, Ulysses, here the mighty strength
Of power divine : lived there a man more wise,
More famed for noble deeds than Ajax was?
ULY. None, none indeed; alas! I pity him;
E'en in a foe I pity such distress,
For he is wedded to the worst of woes :
His hapless state reminds me of my own,
And tells me that frail mortals are no more
Than a vain image and an empty shade.
MIN. Let such examples teach thee to beware
Against the gods thou utter aught profane;
And if perchance in riches or in power
Thou shin'st superior, be not insolent;
For, know, a day sufficeth to exalt
Or to depress the state of mortal man :
The wise and good are by the gods beloved,
But those who practise evil they abhor.   [*Exeunt.*

CHORUS.

I.

To thee, O Ajax ! valiant son
Of illustrious Telamon,
Monarch of the sea-girt isle,
Fair Salamis, if fortune smile
On thee, I raise the tributary song,
For praise and virtue still to thee belong :
But when, inflicted by the wrath of Jove,
   Grecian slander blasts thy fame,
   And foul reproach attaints thy name,
Then do I tremble like the fearful dove.

II.

So, the last unhappy night,
Clamours loud did reach mine ear
And filled my anxious heart with fear,
Which talked of Grecian cattle slain,
And Ajax maddening o'er the plain,
Pleased at his prey, rejoicing at the sight.

III.

Thus false Ulysses can prevail,
   Whisp'ring to all his artful tale,
His tale alas ! too willingly received ;
   Whilst those who hear are glad to know
   And happy to insult thy woe,
For who asperse the great are easily believed.

IV.

The poor like us alone are free
From the darts of calumny,
Whilst envy still attends on high estate :
   Small is the aid which we can lend,
   Without the rich and powerful friend ;
The great support the low, the low assist the great.
But 'tis a truth which fools will never know ;
   From such alone the clamours came
   Which strove to hurt thy spotless fame,
Whilst we can only weep, and not relieve thy woe.

V.

Happy to 'scape thy piercing sight,
Behold them wing their rapid flight,
As trembling birds from hungry vultures fly,
Sudden again shouldst thou appear,
The cowards would be mute with fear,
And all their censures in a moment die.

VI.

Cynthia, goddess of the grove,
Daughter of immortal Jove,
To whom at Tauris frequent altars rise,
Indignant might inspire the deed,
And bid the guiltless cattle bleed,
Deprived of incense due, and wonted sacrifice.
Perhaps, sad cause of all our grief and shame !
The god of war with brazen shield,
For fancied inj'ries in the field,
Might thus avenge the wrong, and brand thy name,

VII.

For never in his perfect mind
Had Ajax been to ill inclined,
On flocks and herds his rage had never spent ;
It was inflicted from above :
May Phœbus and all-powerful Jove
Avert the crime, or stop the punishment !
If to th' Atridæ the bold fiction came
From Sisyphus' detested race,
No longer, Ajax, hide thy face,
But from thy tents come forth, and vindicate thy
fame.

VIII.

Ajax, thy too long repose
Adds new vigour to thy foes,
As flames from aiding winds still fiercer grow ;
Whilst the loose laugh, and shameless lie,
And all their bitter calumny,
With double weight oppress and fill our hearts with
woe.

ACT II.

SCENE I.

TECMESSA, CHORUS.

TECMESSA. Sons of Erectheus, of Athenian race,
Ye brave companions of the valiant Ajax,
Oppressed with grief behold a wretched woman,
Far from her native soil, appointed here
To watch your hapless lord, and mourn his fate.
    CHOR. What new misfortune hath the night brought
      forth ?
Say, daughter of Teleutas, for with thee,
His captive bride, the noble Ajax deigns
To share the nuptial bed, and therefore thou
Canst best inform us.
    TEC.   How shall I declare
Sadder than death th' unutterable woe !
This night, with madness seized, hath Ajax done
A dreadful deed ; within thou mayst behold
The tent's o'erspread with bloody carcases
Of cattle slain, the victims of his rage.
    CHOR. Sad news indeed thou bringst of that **brave**
      man :
A dire disease ! and not by human aid
To be removed ; already Greece hath heard
And wond'ring crowds repeat the dreadful tale ;
Alas ! I fear th' event ! I fear me much,
Lest, with their flocks and herds the shepherds slain,
Against himself he lift his murth'rous hand.
    TEC. Alas ! this way he led his captive spoils,
And some he slew, and others tore in sunder ;
From out the flock two rams of silver hue
He chose, from one the head and tongue divided,
He cast them from him ; then the other chained
Fast to the pillar, with a double rein
Bore cruel stripes, and bitt'rest execrations,
Which not from mortal came, but were inspired
By that avenging god who thus torments him.

CHOR. Now then, my friends (for so the time
    demands),
Each o'er his head should cast the mournful veil,
And instant fly, or to our ships repair,
And sail with speed ; for dreadful are the threats
Of the Atridæ ; death may be our lot,
And we shall meet an equal punishment
With him whom we lament, our frantic lord.

TEC. He raves not now ; but like the southern blast,
When lightnings cease and all the storm is o'er,
Grows calm again ; yet to his sense restored,
He feels new griefs ; for oh ! to be unhappy,
And know ourselves alone the guilty cause
Of all our sorrows, is the worst of woes.

CHOR. Yet if his rage subside we should rejoice ;
The ill removed, we should remove our care.

TEC. Hadst thou then rather, if the choice were given,
Thyself at ease, behold thy friend in pain,
Than with thy friend be joined in mutual sorrow ?

CHOR. The double grief is sure the most oppressive.

TEC. Therefore, though not distempered, I am
    wretched.

CHOR. I understand thee not.

TEC.   The noble Ajax,
Whilst he was mad, was happy in his frenzy,
And yet the while affected me with grief
Who was not so ; but now his rage is o'er,
And he hath time to breathe from his misfortune,
Himself is almost dead with grief, and I
Not less unhappy than I was before ;
Is it not double then ?

CHOR.   It is indeed ;
And much I fear the wrath of angry heaven,
If from his madness ceased he yet receive
No kind relief.

TEC.   'Tis so ; and 'twere most fit
You knew it well.

CHOR.   Say then how it began ;
For like thyself we feel for his misfortunes.

TEC. Since you partake the sorrows of a friend,
I'll tell you all. Know then, at dead of night,

What time the evening taper were expired,
Snatching his sword, he seemed as if he meant
To roam abroad.   I saw and chid him for it;
What wouldst thou do, I cried, my dearest Ajax?
Unasked, uncalled for, whither wouldst thou go?
No trumpet sounds to battle, the whole host
Is wrapped in sleep.   Then did he answer me
With brief but sharp rebuke, as he was wont:
" Woman, thy sex's noblest ornament
Is silence."   Thus reproved, I said no more.
Then forth he rushed alone, where, and for what,
I knew not; but returning, he brought home
In chains the captive herd, in pieces some
He tore, whilst others bound like slaves he lashed
Indignant; then out at the portal ran,
And with some shadow seemed to hold discourse
Against th' Atridæ, and Ulysses oft
Would he inveigh; or, laughing loud, rejoice
That he had ta'en revenge for all his wrongs;
Then back he came.   At length, by slow degrees,
His frenzy ceased; when, soon as he beheld
The tents o'erwhelmed with slaughter, he cried out,
And beat his brain; rolled o'er the bloody heaps
Of cattle slain, and tore his clotted hair,
Long fixed in silence: then, with horrid threats
He bade me tell him all that had befallen
And what he had been doing.   I obeyed,
Trembling with fear, and told him all I knew.
Instant he poured forth bitt'rest lamentations,
Such as I ne'er had heard from him before,
For grief like that, he oft would say, betrayed
A weak and little mind, and therefore ever
When sorrow came refrained from loud complaint,
And, like the lowing heifer, inly mourned.
But sinking now beneath this sore distress,
He will not taste of food or nourishment;
Silent he sits, amid the slaughtered cattle,
Or, if he speaks, utters such dreadful words
As shows a mind intent on something ill.
Now then, my friends, for therefore came I hither,
Oh! if ye have the power, assist me now;

Perhaps ye may; for oft th' afflicted man
Will listen to the counsels of a friend.
    Chor. O daughter of Teleutas! horrible
Indeed thy tidings are of noble Ajax,
Thus raving, and thus miserable.
    Ajax [*within, groans*].   Oh!
    Tec. Louder you'll hear him soon; marked ye, my
      friends,
How deep his groans?
    Ajax [*within*].   O me!
    Chor.   He seems to rave,
Or mourns, reflecting on his madness past.
    Ajax [*within*]. Boy, boy!
    Tec.   Alas! he calls Eurysaces.
Where art thou, child? What would he have with
    thee?
    Ajax [*within*]. Teucer, 'tis thee I call; where art
    thou, Teucer?
Still must he chase his prey, whilst Ajax dies?
    Chor. He seems of perfect mind—open the doors,
Let him come forth. Who knows but sight of us
May keep him so.
    Tec.   I'll open them—now see
      [*The doors are thrown open and* AJAX *discovered.*
Your master there, and judge of his condition.

SCENE II.

AJAX, TECMESSA, CHORUS.

    Ajax. My dear companions, who alone deserve
The name of friends, ye see the dreadful storm
How it o'erwhelms me.
    Chor. [*aside to* TECMESSA]. What thou saidst, alas!
Was but too true; he seems indeed distracted.
    Ajax. My fellow-sailors! whose assisting hand
Plied the tough oar, and led me through the main,
From you alone can I expect to meet
Or love or friendship; therefore show it now,
And kill me.

CHOR.   Talk not thus, nor thus increase
By added woes thy dreadful malady.

AJAX. Dost thou behold this once intrepid Ajax,
The brave, the mighty, long for strength renowned
And dauntless courage in the bloody field ;
Dost thou behold him ? Oh ! what laughter now,
What vile reproach must he sustain !

TEC.   O Ajax !
My lord, my master, do not talk thus sadly.

AJAX [*to* TECMESSA]. Wilt thou not home ?   Wilt not
    be gone ?

TEC.   O me !

CHOR. Be patient ; by the gods let me entreat you,
Be more composed.

AJAX.   Wretch that I was, to let
The curst Atridæ 'scape, and shed the blood
Of harmless cattle !

CHOR.   But why sorrow thus
For what is past, and cannot be recalled ?

AJAX. How will that subtle instrument of ill,
Laertes' prying son, insult me now,
And smile at my misfortunes !

CHOR.   That must be
As seems most fitting to the gods ; from them
Or grief or joy must flow.

AJAX.   Oh ! would to heaven
That I could see him ! wretched as I am !

CHOR. This is no time for boasting : seest thou not
How very weak thou art ?

AJAX.   Almighty Jove,
My great progenitor ! oh, grant me this !
Grant me to slay that hateful, talking slave,
With the proud princes ; then well pleased myself
Should perish last.

TEC.   Oh ! if thou prayst for death,
Pray too for mine ; for wherefore should I live
When thou art gone ?

AJAX.   O darkness ! my best light
And hope ! oh wrap me in your friendly shade,
A willing guest ! I dare not look for help,
Or from the gods above, or men below :

The powerful daughter of eternal Jove
To death devotes me.   Whither can I fly,
Or where remain, my fame and glory lost
In this sad frenzy ?   Left without a friend,
And the whole army bent on my destruction !

TEC. Alas ! how dreadful 'tis to hear such words,
Which Ajax never would have spoke before !

AJAX. Ye well-known floods that roll into the main,
Ye caves and forests by the rocky shore !
Years heaped on years fast by the walls of Troy
Have ye detained me, but no longer now
Amongst the living shall ye ever see
The hapless Ajax ; this remember all :
Nor shall thy neighbouring waves, Scamander, still
To Greece beneficent, behold me more :
Troy never saw, forgive the boastful word,
A braver, nobler foe than Ajax was,
Though now dishonoured thus, and thus oppressed.

CHOR. I would not have thee thus lament thy woes,
And yet I know not how to chide thee for it,
So hard thy lot.

AJAX.   Who would have thought my name
Would e'er so well have suited my condition !
Oh ! I have reason to lament indeed,
For sure there is not such a wretch as Ajax !
Long since at Troy my valiant father fought,
And to his native land, with glory crowned,
Bore back the meed of his distinguished virtues :
Nor less renowned for gallant deeds was once
His hapless son, though now he perish thus
Inglorious : yet Achilles, well I know,
Were he alive, and to bestow his arms
On him who best deserved the prize, to me,
And me alone, would 'judge, the great reward :
But little deemed the Atridæ worth like mine,
And therefore gave them to that vile impostor,
Author of every evil work, Ulysses.
Had not my mind been wrought on by some power
Superior, and my eyes averted from them,
They had not lived to give another sentence ;
But Jove's great daughter, the invincible,

The dreadful Pallas, turned my arm aside,
Just raised against them, and inspired me thus
With horrid rage to dip my murd'rous hand
In blood of guiltless cattle: they meantime
Smile at the danger 'scaped, and triumph o'er me.
But, when the gods oppose us, valour bends
To cowardice, and strength to weakness yields:
What then can Ajax? hateful to the gods,
By Troy detested, and by Greece forsaken?
Shall I go leave the Atridæ here alone
To fight their cause, and seek my native land?
But how shall I appear before my father,
How will he bear to see his Ajax thus
Spoiled of his honours? he who ever crowned
With glory sits; it must not, cannot be.
What if I rush amid the Trojan host,
And with my single arm oppose them all,
Do something noble, and as nobly perish!
But that would please th' Atridæ, therefore never
Shall it be done: no, I will do a deed
To show my father that I still deserve
The name of son, and emulate my sire:
When life but teems with unremitted woes,
'Tis poor in man to wish a longer date:
For what can day on day, and year on year,
But put off wished-for death, and lengthen pain?
Of little worth is he who still depends
On fruitless hope; for it becomes the brave
To live with honour, or to die with glory.
Ye have my thoughts.

    CHOR   Thoughts not unworthy of thee,
Ajax; but quit, oh! quit, thy horrid purpose,
And yield thee to thy friends.

    TEC.   My lord, my master,
My dearest Ajax, dreadful are the ills
Which cruel fortune brings on human kind:
Of noblest race (a better, Phrygia boasts not)
Tecmessa was, and from a father sprung
Happy and free, though now a wretched slave;
For so the gods and thy all-conqu'ring arm
Decreed: but since partaker of thy bed.

Thou know'st I ever have with tend'rest care
Watched o'er thee : therefore, by domestic Jove,
Here I entreat thee, by the sacred tie
That binds us, let me not with foul reproach
And bitter scorn be taunted by thy foes,
When they surround me, as I know they will :
For oh ! when thou shalt die, that very day
The Greeks with violence will seize on me ;
Tecmessa then and thy loved son shall eat
The bread of slavery.   Then some haughty lord,
Insulting loud, shall cry, behold the wife
Of Ajax, once the pride of all our host,
How is she fall'n ! from envied happiness
To servitude and woe !   Such vile upbraidings
Oft shall I hear, on thee and on thy race
Casting foul shame.   Oh, then relent, my Ajax !
Think on thy father in the vale of years,
Think on thy aged mother, who with vows
Incessant prays the gods to send thee back
Safe to thy native land !   Pity thy son,
Without a father in his tender youth
To form his mind, left to the unfriendly hands
Of those who love him not. Alas ! what woes
Wilt thou bequeath to me and to thy child !
I have no hope, no stay but thee alone.
Thy hand destroyed my country and my mother ;
Death snatched my father to the realms below.
Deprived of thee what country will receive me,
Or where shall I subsist ?   Thou art my all,
My only safeguard : do not, do not leave me !
Nought so becomes a man as gratitude
For good received, and noble deeds are still
The offspring of benevolence, whilst he
With whom remembrance dies of blessings past
Is vile and worthless.
  CHOR.   Oh ! that thou couldst feel
Pity like mine for this unhappy woman !
Then wouldst thou say her words deserve thy
   praise.
  AJAX. And praised she shall be, if she but perform
What I require.

TEC.　　　　In all will I obey thee,
My dearest Ajax!
　　AJAX.　　　　I would see my child:
Let him be brought.
　　TEC.　　　　I hid him from thy sight
Because of——
　　AJAX.　　　My distemper, was it not?
　　Tec. It was: I feared indeed thou mightst destroy
　　　him.
　　AJAX. And well thou mightst: a deed like that
　　　became
My sad condition.
　　TEC.　　　　Therefore, to prevent it
I kept him from thee.
　　AJAX.　　　　I approve thy caution.
　　TEC. What wouldst thou have me do?
　　AJAX.　　　　　　Let me behold
And speak to him.
　　TEC.　　　　He is not far from hence;
The servants have him in their care.
　　AJAX.　　　　　Then why
May I not see him?
　　TEC.　　　　Boy! thy father calls thee:
Let some one bring him hither.
　　AJAX.　　　　　Is he coming?
Doth he not hear thee?
　　TEC.　　　　They have brought him to thee.
　　　　　　[*Enter Servants with* EURYSACES.

SCENE III.

EURYSACES, TECMESSA, AJAX, CHORUS.

AJAX. Bring him this way: for if he be the son
Of Ajax, the fresh blood that hangs about me
Will not affright him; he must learn like me
In earliest years the savage laws of war,
And be inured to scenes of death and slaughter.
Mayst thou, my boy, be happier than thy father!
In all things else it will be no disgrace

To copy me: I envy thee, my child,
For that thou seest not thy own wretchedness;
The happiness of life is not to know.
Thy ignorance will keep thee free from pain,
Till time shall teach thee what it is to grieve
And to rejoice; then must thou show thy foes
From whom thou art descended.   May the breath
Of life meantime nourish thy tender frame,
That thou mayst prove a comfort to thy mother!
I know there's not a Grecian that will dare
Insult thee when thy father is no more;
For I shall leave thee to the best of guardians,
The faithful Teucer, who far from thee now,
Sent forth by Greece, repels the invading foe.
Of you, my friends, companions of the war,
The only boon I ask is, that ye urge
This last request to Teucer: say, I begged
That straight to Telamon and Eribœa,
My aged parents, he would bear my child,
To be the joy of their declining years,
Till death shall call them to the shades below.
Let not my arms by Greece, or by that plague
Ulysses, e'er be made the prize of glory
For rival chiefs; but do thou take, my boy,

                 [turning to EURYSACES

The sevenfold, vast impenetrable shield
Whose name thou bear'st; the rest be buried with me.
Take hence the child with speed; nor in the tents
Let there be wailings.   Women ever love
To brood o'er sorrows, and indulge their woe.
Shut to the door.   The wound that must be cut
No wise physician will attempt to heal
With incantation, elegy, or song.
   CHOR. I tremble when I hear thee threat'ning thus
With sharp and piercing voice.
   TEC.   Alas! my lord,
What wilt thou do?
   AJAX.   Guess not; inquire not of me;
Be silent, and be wise; it will become thee.
   TEC. How am I tortured!   By the gods I beg thee,
By our dear child, do not destroy us both.

AJAX. Thou dost perplex me ; why revere the gods ?
I am not bound to 't, for I owe them nothing.

TEC. Be not so impious.

AJAX.   Talk to those will hear thee,

TEC. Art thou resolved then ?

AJAX.   'Tis too much ; thy grief
Grows troublesome.

TEC.   Alas ! my lord, I fear——

AJAX [*to the* CHORUS]. Will ye not take her hence ?

TEC.   Oh ! by the gods
I beg thee, be persuaded.

AJAX.   Thou art mad
To think thy words will ever change my purpose.

                                [*Exeunt.*

ODE.

CHORUS.

Strophe.

Oh, happiest, best abode, my native isle,
    Fair Salamis, encompassed by the sea,
On thee whilst gods and men indulgent smile,
    My country, oh behold and pity me !
      A long, long time on Ida's plain
      Thus doomed inglorious to remain,
While circling years roll o'er my wretched head ;
      New terrors still affright me here,
      Still is my heart appalled with fear,
Lest I should visit soon the mansions of the dead.

Antistrophe.

The woes of Ajax, too, embitter mine,
    The bravest leader of the Grecian host,
Untimely visited by wrath divine,
    And in the desp'rate cruel frenzy lost.
      There was a time when sent by thee
      He gained the wreath of victory,
Though now his weeping friends lament his fall :
      The ungrateful chiefs revere no more
      The virtues they admired before ;
His gallant deeds are now forgotten all.

Strophe 2.

Weighed down with years, when thou in hoary age,
    Unhappy mother, shalt these tidings hear
Of thy dear Ajax, and his cruel rage,
      How wilt thou weep and wail with grief sincere !
      Not like the plaintive nightingale
      That warbles sweet her tender tale,
But with loud shrieks of horrible despair :
      With sharpest anguish sore opprest,
      Then shalt thou beat thy aged breast,
And in deep sorrow rend thy wild dishevelled hair.

Antistrophe 2.

'Tis better far to die than, hopeless still
    Of cure, to languish under sore disease ;
When mortals suffer such distinguished ill
    The silent tomb is liberty and ease.
      Ajax, the pride of all our host,
      His ancient fame and glory lost,
Sinks down at last o'erwhelmed with foul disgrace;
      How will hapless father bear
      His son's distressful fate to hear,
E'en such as never fell on Æacus his race !

ACT III.

SCENE I.

AJAX, TECMESSA, CHORUS.

AJAX. Still are the secret things of man revealed,
And what is known again in darkness hid
By endless and immeasurable time ;
And nothing is there but in length of days
May come to pass ; e'en sacred oaths are broken,
And the fixed mind, perverse and obstinate,
Subdued by time : I, who like hardened steel

Was late inflexible, am softened now
To pity and remorse by this dear woman;
I cannot bear to leave her here a widow
Amidst her foes, or to forsake my child,
A helpless orphan. No; I will retire
Along the shore, and seek the running stream,
Avert the wrath of angry heaven, and wash
My crimes away : there haply shall I find
Some unfrequented spot where I may hide
This fatal weapon, this destructive sword :
Oh ! I will bury it deep in earth, that none
May see it more, but night and Erebus
Preserve it still from ev'ry mortal eye.
E'er since that hapless day, when from the hand
Of Hector I received this dreadful boon,
Nought have I had from Greece but pain and woe :
True is the adage, " From the hands of foes
Gifts are not gifts, but injuries most fatal."
Hereafter will I yield me to the Gods
And the Atridæ; since they are my masters,
'Tis meet that I obey them : all that's strong
And mighty must submit to powers superior :
Doth not the snowy winter to the bloom
Of fruitful summer yield ? and night obscure,
When by white steeds Aurora drawn lights up
The rising day, submissively retire ?
The roaring sea, long vexed by angry winds,
Is lulled by milder zephyrs to repose,
And oft the fetters of all-conq'ring sleep
Are kindly loosed to free the captive mind.
From Nature then, who thus instructs mankind,
Why should not Ajax learn humility ?
Long since I knew to treat my foe like one
Whom I hereafter as a friend might love
If he deserved it, and to love my friend
As if he still might one day be my foe :
For little is the trust we can repose
In human friendships. But to my intent :
Go thou, Tecmessa, and beseech the gods
To grant what I request : do you perform
The same kind office ; and when Teucer comes,

Tell him, the care of me and all my friends
I leave to him : whither I must, I must.
Obey my orders : wretched as I am
Soon shall ye see me freed from all my woes.   [*Exeunt.*

SCENE II.

CHORUS.

Strophe.

Now let sounds of mirth and joy
Every blissful hour employ :
Borne on pleasure's airy wing,
Io Pan ! to thee we sing :
Thee, whom on the rocky shore
Wreck-'scaped mariners adore,
Skilled the mazy dance to lead,
Teach, oh teach, our feet to tread
The round which Cretan Cnossus knows,
At Nyssa which spontaneous rose ;
Pan, oh ! guide this tuneful throng,
While to thee we raise the song,
From Cyllene's snowy brow ;
King of pleasures, hear us now !
From thy mountains, oh, appear !
Joy and happiness are here :
And do thou, O Delian king !
Now thy aid propitious bring !
Oh ! from the Icarian sea
Come, Apollo, smile on me.

Antistrophe.

All our sorrows now are o'er,
Grief and madness are no more :
See, the happy day appears,
Mighty Jove ! that ends our fears ;
Let us, free from every care,
Gladly to our ships repair :
Ajax now in sweet repose
Sinks, forgetful of his woes ;

Humbly to the gods resigned,
He devotes his better mind :
Time that withers can restore
Human pleasures.   Now no more
Must we say our vows are vain ;
Nought unhoped for should remain,
Since, beyond our wishes, see
Ajax from his madness free ;
'Gainst th' Atridæ all his rage
See how milder thoughts assuage,
Bitter strife and quarrels cease ;
All is harmony and peace.

Scene III.

Messenger, Chorus.

Mes. My friends, I bear you news of highest import :
From Mysia's rocky mountains hither comes
The noble Teucer ; know, e'en now I saw him
Amid the Grecian host, who, as he came,
Surrounded, and on ev'ry side poured forth
Reproaches on him.   Not a man but cried
" Behold the brother of that frantic foe
To Greece and to her council."   Such their rage
That they had well-nigh stoned him ; swords were
　　　drawn,
And dire had been the conflict, but that some
Among the aged chiefs by calm advice
Appeased the strife.   But where is Ajax gone ?
That I may tell him : from our masters nought
Should be concealed.
Chor.　　　　　　　He is not now within.
But just steps forth, as if on some new act
Intent, well suited to his better mind.
Mes. Alas ! too late did Teucer send me here,
Or I am come too slowly.
Chor.　　　　　　　　　Why regret
His absence thus ?

MES.   'Twas Teucer's strict command
He should be kept within the tent, nor stir
Till he arrived.
     CHOR.   But, to his sense restored,
He went to deprecate the wrath divine,
And expiate his offence.
     MES.   Thy words are vain
If Chalcas prophesy aright.
     CHOR.   What then
Did Chalcas say? Dost thou know aught of this?
     MES. Thus far I know, for I was witness of it:
Chalcas, retiring from the assembled chiefs
Apart from the Atridæ, gently pressed   .
The hand of Teucer, and in tenderest friendship
Besought him that by every human art
And means to be devised he would prevent
Ajax his wandering forth this fatal day,
If he did ever wish to see him more.
This day alone, he said, Minerva's wrath
Would last against him. Oft the mighty fall
In deep affliction, smit by angry heaven,
When, mortal-born, to human laws they yield not
As mortals ought, submissively: thus spake
The prophet, and long since was Ajax deemed
To have a mind disturbed. When first he left
His native soil, " Be conqueror, O my child ! "
His father said, " but conquer under God."
Impious and proud his answer was : " The worst
Of men," he cried, " assisted by the gods
May conquer ; I shall do the work without them."
Such were his boastings ; and when Pallas once
With kind assistance urged him to the fight,
Dreadful and horrible was his reply :
" Go, queen, to other Grecians lend thy aid,
'Tis needless here ; for know, where Ajax is
The foe will never come." By words like these,
And pride ill-suited to a mortal's pow'r,
Did he offend the vengeful deity ;
But if he lives, we may preserve him still,
The gods assisting. So the prophet spake ;
And Teucer bade me say, you all should try

To keep him here; but if that cannot be,
And Chalcas judge aright, he is no more.
    CHOR. [*to* TECMESSA *within*]. What ho! Tecmessa,
        most unhappy woman!
Come forth and hear the tidings that he brings;
They wound us deep, and all our joys are gone.

SCENE IV.

TECMESSA, MESSENGER, CHORUS.

    TEC. Scarce do I breathe from still repeated woes,
And now again thou call'st me : wherefore ? Speak.
    CHOR. This messenger hath brought us dreadful news
Concerning Ajax : hear him.
    TEC.   Oh ! what is it ?
Am I undone ?
    MES.   I know not what thou art ;
But if thy Ajax be gone forth, my fears
Are great for him.
    TEC.   Alas ! he is ; but why ?
How thou afflict'st me !
    MES.   Teucer hath forbade
His wandering thus alone.
    TEC.   But why forbade him ?
And where is Teucer ?
    MES.   He will soon be here :
He fears this fatal day.
    TEC.   Undone Tecmessa !
Whence are his fears ? who told him 'twould be fatal ?
    MES. Thestorian Chalcas did foretell this day
To life or death would fix the fate of Ajax.
    TEC. [*to the* CHORUS]. Assist me, friends, in this
        distressful hour.
To Teucer haste, and bring him to my aid ;
Some to yon western mountain bend your way,
And some to th' east ; find out which path he went,
Unhappy wanderer ! Oh ! he has deceived me,
His former love forgotten all and gone !
What must we do, my child ? I must not sit

Inactive here ; no, wheresoe'er I can
I'll go to search him. Let us haste, my friends.
Quick ! fly this instant, if we mean to save
The wretched Ajax, rushing on destruction.

    CHOR. Behold us ready, not in word alone,
But bent with speed to follow thee. Away ! *[Exeunt.*

ACT IV.

SCENE I.

    AJAX. There stands my sword, and fixed as it may
      best
Perform its office ; 'twas the gift of Hector,
My worst of foes, whom I detested ever :
The steel-devouring stone hath sharpened well
Its keenest edge. Buried in Trojan earth
It lies, and now in kindness seems prepared
To end my wretched life. Thus far is well.
And now, O Jove !—for first to thee 'tis fit
We pay due honours—I address my prayer.
I ask not much : I ask thee but to send
Some passing stranger here to bear the news
Of my unhappy fate to Teucer's ear,
That he may first behold, and take me hence,
Lest, by my foes discovered, I be cast
A prey to dogs and birds. Forbid it, Jove !
Thee too, great leader of departed souls,
Terrestrial Hermes, thee I call ! oh, hear me !
With easy steps, and swift, conduct me safe
To my abode, soon as this fatal sword
Shall reach my breast. And you, ye virgin powers
From whom whate'er befalls of human ill
Cannot be hid, ye goddesses revered,
Swift to pursue the guilty, oh, behold,
The wretched Ajax by th' Atridæ fall !
O seize the murd'rers ! By my own sad hand
As I shall perish, let my foes be slain

                                 B

By those whom most they love! Quick, fly, begone,
Ye vengeful furies! Gorge yourselves in blood,
Nor spare a man of all the Grecian host.
And thou, O Sun! who driv'st the flaming car
Along the vaulted sky, when thou shalt see
My native soil, oh! stop thy golden reins;
Tell the sad story to my hapless sire
And my afflicted mother. When she hears
The mournful tale, her grief will fill the land
With dreadful lamentations. But 'tis vain
To weep my fate: the business must be done.
O Death! look on me, Death; I come to thee—
Soon shall we meet; but thee, O glorious day!
And yon bright charioteer the sun, no more
Shall I behold: e'en now thou hearst my last,
My dying words. O light! O sacred soil
Of Salamis, my country, and her gods!
O noble Athens! O my loved companions!
Ye rivers, fountains, and fair fields of Troy!
And you, my honoured parents, oh, farewell!
'Tis the last word Ajax shall speak on earth:
The rest be uttered to the shades below.

[AJAX *falls on his sword and dies.*

SCENE II.

CHORUS.

SEMICHOR. 1. Labour on labour, toil no toil! Oh, whither
Have we not wandered? Yet no place informs us
Where Ajax is. But soft, I hear a voice.
SEMICHOR. 2. 'Twas ours, your friends.
SEMICHOR. 1. What news?
SEMICHOR. 2. We've searched along
The western shore.
SEMICHOR. 1. And is he found?
SEMICHOR. 2. Alas!
We met with nought but toil; no sight of him.
SEMICHOR. 1. We from the east return with like success;
For none have seen or heard of him that way.

SEMICHOR. 2. Who will inform us? who will say
    Where cruel Ajax bent his way?
Will not the watchful hind, who, void of sleep,
    Hangs laborious o'er the deep?
From high Olympus will no pitying god,
    Will no kind Naiad of the flood,
If chance they see the cruel Ajax stray,
    Tell us where he bent his way?
For oh! 'tis dreadful, wearied thus, to rove,
    Whilst all our pains successless prove
To reach the destined goal, or find the man we love.
TEC. [*from within*]. Alas! alas!
SEMICHOR. 1.   Hark! from the neighbouring grove
I heard a voice.
SEMICHOR. 2.   It is the wretched captive,
The wife of Ajax, the poor sad Tecmessa.

SCENE III.

TECMESSA, CHORUS.

TEC. Oh! I am lost, my friends, undone, destroyed!
CHOR. Ha! what hath happened?
TEC.   Ajax lies before me,
Slain by the sword which he had buried here.

CHOR.   Fatal sure was our return,
    Thy untimely death to mourn.
    Me, and all thy faithful train,
    Cruel Ajax, hast thou slain.
    Sad event, alas! to me!
    Sadder, woman, still to thee.

TEC. Oh! I have reason now to weep indeed.
CHOR. What hand performed the horrid deed?
TEC.   His own
Doubtless it was; the sword he fell upon,
Here, fixed in earth, declares it must be so.
CHOR. [*approaching towards the body*].
    Alone, without one pitying friend,
    Cam'st thou to this dreadful end;

Was I not myself to blame,
Who neglectful never came ?
Bring him, Tecmessa, to my eyes,
Tell me where thy Ajax lies.

Tec. He is not to be seen.   This folded garment
Shall hide the horrid sight—a sight no friend
Would wish to see : whilst from his nostrils streams
The black blood, more still issuing from the wound
Made by his own destructive hand.   O me !
What must I do ?   What friend will raise him up ?
Oh ! where is Teucer ?   He should have been here
To pay his last sad duty to a brother.
O wretched Ajax !   But to think, alas !
What once thou hast been, and what now thou art.
Thy very foes must sure lament thy fate.

Chor. Ajax, long since in thy obdurate mind,
          Thy sad purpose was designed ;
Long since wert thou resolved to seek repose
          From thy never-ceasing woes :
This from the daily sigh, the nightly tear,
          This from thy sorrows did I fear ;
This from thy hate which nought could e'er assuage ;
          And 'gainst th' Atridæ all thy rage :
For never did thy soul contentment know,
          But still with fiercest indignation glow,
Since great Achilles' arms were given to thy foe.

Tec. O me !
Chor.   Alas ! I know the wound must pierce
Thy inmost soul.
Tec.   Unhappy, lost Tecmessa !
Chor. Oh ! I believe thou art indeed unhappy,
Bereaved of such a friend.
Tec.   Thou but believ'st it ;
I am too certain, for I feel it here.
Chor. I know thou dost.
Tec.   What servitude, my child,
Must we endure ?   Who will protect us now ?

Chor. Doubtless thy fear of future pain
          From the Atridæ all are vain,

For never can they mean such ills to thee ;
    Unfeeling they of human woe,
    Nor love nor piety could know ;
May heaven avert the sad calamity!

Tec. The gods ordained it, and it must be so.
Chor. But he hath suffered more than he deserved.
Tec. Jove's dreadful daughter Pallas so decreed
His fate, to gratify her loved Ulysses.

    Chor. Ulysses, ever pleased to see
       His madness, now will smile at thee,
    Will laugh at Ajax's woes nor pity thine :
       By him the curst Atridæ led
       Perhaps will triumph o'er the dead,
    And in the cruel mirth with pleasure join.

Tec. Let them rejoice, let them insult him now
With savage joy ; but when the dreadful day
Of battle comes, whom living they despised
When dead they shall lament. Fools never know
The treasure's value till the treasure 's lost ;
But far more bitter was his death to me
Than sweet to them : to Ajax it was most welcome ;
Death was his only wish, and he obtained it.
Then wherefore should they triumph ? By the hand
Of Heaven, and not by theirs, my Ajax fell.
Then let Ulysses smile : he is not theirs,
He lives not for the Grecians : he is gone,
And has bequeathed his sorrows all to me.

Scene IV.

Teucer, Tecmessa, Chorus.

Teu. Alas! alas!
Chor.   Hark ! 'tis the voice of Teucer
In mournful sighs lamenting our sad fate.
Teu. O Ajax! is it so ? My dearest brother,
Dear as these eyes to me, hath fame said true,
And art thou gone?

CHOR.　　　　　O Teucer ! he is dead.

TEU. Unhappy fate !

CHOR　　　　　　'Tis so indeed.

TEU.　　　　　　　　　　Alas !

Wretch that I am !

CHOR.　　　　　Oh ! thou hast cause to weep.

TEU. Dreadful calamity !

CHOR.　　　　　　It is indeed

Too much to bear.

TEU.　　　　　O wretched, wretched Teucer !

Where is the child ?　Is he at Troy ?

CHOR.　　　　　　　　　　Alone,

And in the tent.

TEU.　　　　　Will ye not bring him to me !

Lest he shall fall a victim to the foe,

Even as the hunters seize the lion's whelp

Left to its helpless dam ?　Quick ! fly ! assist me ;

For all are glad to triumph o'er the dead.

CHOR. To thee, O Teucer ! he bequeathed the care

Of his loved child, and thou obeyst him well.

TEU. O Ajax ! never did these eyes behold

A sight so dreadful.　Came I then for this

With luckless speed ?　O melancholy journey !

To seek thee long in vain, and thus at last

To find thee dead before me, O my brother !

Quick through the Grecian host, as if some god

Had brought the tidings, spread the dire report

Of thy untimely fate.　Far from thee then

I heard and wept, but now, alas ! I see

And am undone.　My best, my dearest Ajax !

Unveil the body ; let me view it well,

And count my miseries.　Horrid spectacle !

Oh ! rash advent'rous deed !　What weight of woe

Thy death has laid on me !　Alas ! to whom

Or whither shall I go ?　Oh, wherefore, Teucer,

Wert thou not here to stop a brother's hand ?

What will our poor unhappy father say,

The wretched Telamon ?　Will he receive me

With looks of love and pleasure, when I come

Without his Ajax ?　Oh ! he never will.

Even in the best of times he was not wont

To smile or joy in aught. What then will now
His anger vent? Will he not speak of me
As of a faithless, base, unworthy son,
The spurious offspring of a captive mother,
Who hath betrayed and slain his best-loved Ajax
To gain his fair possessions after death?
Thus will his wrath, sharpened by peevish age,
Upbraid me guiltless; and to slavery doomed,
A wretched exile from his native land,
Shall Teucer wander forth. Such dreadful ills
Must I expect at home. At Troy my foes
Are numerous, and my friends, alas! how few!
Thou art the cause of all: for, O my Ajax!
What shall I do? How can I save thee now
From this sad fate? Oh! who could have foreseen
That Hector, long since dead, at last should prove
The murderer of Ajax? By the gods
I do beseech you, mark the fate of both:
The belt, which Ajax did to Hector give,
Dragged the brave Trojan o'er the bloody field
Till he expired; and now, behold! the sword,
Which Hector gave to Ajax is the cause
Of Ajax' death. Erynnis' self did forge
The fatal steel, and Pluto made the belt.
Dreadful artificer! But this, and all
That happens to us, is the work of Heaven.
If there be those who doubt it, let them hold
Their diff'ring judgments—I shall keep my own.

CHOR. Teucer, no more; but rather now prepare
To bury Ajax, and defend thyself
Against thy foe, whom yonder I behold
This way advancing, with malignant smile
And looks of ill intent.

TEU.   Who can it be?
From the army, thinkst thou?

CHOR.   'Tis the man whose cause
We came to fight, e'en Menelaus.

TEU.   'Tis so.
As he approaches nigh, I know him well.

Scene V.

Menelaus, Teucer, Chorus.

Men. Stop there ! To thee I speak. Let go the body.
I will not have it touched.

Teu.　　　　　　　　　Why touch it not ?

Men. Because it is my will, and his who leads
The Grecian host.

Teu.　　　　　　　But wherefore is it so ?

Men. Greece fondly hoped that she had brought a
　　friend
And firm ally, but by experience found
That Troy herself was not so much our foe
As Ajax was, who nightly wandered forth
With deadliest rage to murder all our host,
And, but some god did frustrate his intent,
The fate himself hath met had been our own.
Then had he triumphed; but the gods ordained
It should not be, and 'gainst the flocks and herds
Turned all his fury; wherefore know, there lives not
A man of courage or of power sufficient
To bury Ajax. On the yellow shore
He shall be cast, to be the food of birds
That wander there. Thou mayst resent it too,
But 'twill be vain. At least we will command
When dead, whom living we could ne'er subdue,
Nor ask thy leave. He never would submit,
But now he must. Yield therefore, or we force thee.
'Tis the Plebeian's duty to obey
The voice of those who bear authority,
And he who doth not is the worst of men ;
For never can the state itself support
By wholesome laws, where there is no submission.
An army's best defence is modest fear
And reverence of its leaders ; without these
It cannot conquer. It becomes a man
How great soe'er his strength, still to remember
A little, very little, may destroy him.
He who is guarded by humility

And conscious shame alone in safety lies ;
But where licentious freedom and reproach
Injurious reign, each as his will directs
Still acting, know that city soon must fall
From all its bliss, and sink in deepest woe.
Remember, then, respect is due to me.
Let us not think when pleasure is enjoyed
We must not suffer too and taste of pain ;
For these to mortals still alternate rise.
There lived not one so proud and arrogant
As Ajax was.   I will be haughty now ;
It is my turn.   Take heed, then.   Touch him not,
Lest, while thou striv'st to bury him, thyself
Should drop into the tomb.

    CHOR.   O Menelaus !
Do not with maxims grave and wisdom's rules
Mix foul reproach and slander on the dead.

    TEU. It should not move our wonder, O my friend !
To see the vulgar err, of meaner souls
And birth obscure, when men so nobly born
Will talk thus basely.   Tell me, Menelaus—
For 'twas thy first assertion—didst thou bring
Our Ajax here to help the Grecian host ?
Or came he hither by himself alone
Conducted ?   Whence is thy command o'er him,
O'er these his followers ?   Who gave thee power ?
Who gave thee right ?   Thou mayst be Sparta's king,
But art not ours.   Ajax was bound by law
No more to thee than thou wert bound to Ajax :
Thyself no general, but to others here
Subjected ; therefore, lord it where thou mayst—
Command thy slaves ; go, threaten and chastise them.
But I will bury Ajax, spite of thee
And of thy brother, for I heed thee not.
He sailed not here to quarrel for the wife
Of Menelaus, like a hireling slave,
But to fulfil the strictly-binding oath
Which he had sworn ; he did not come for thee,
For he despised so poor a cause ; he came
With all his heralds and a numerous train,
And brought his captains too.   Remember, therefore,

Thy clamours ne'er shall turn me from my purpose
Whilst thou art what thou art.

MEN. A tongue like thine
But ill becomes thy state: 'tis most unseemly.

TEU. A keen reproach, with justice on its side,
Is always grating.

MEN. This proud archer here
Talks loudly.

TEU. 'Tis no mean illiberal art.

MEN. If thou couldst bear a shield, how insolent
And haughty wouldst thou be, when naked, thus,
Thou boast'st thy valour!

TEU. Naked as I am
I should not fly from thee with all thy arms.

MEN. Thy tongue but speaks thy pride.

TEU. I should be proud
When I am just.

MEN. Doth justice bid me love
Him who destroyed me?

TEU. Art thou then destroyed?
That's strange indeed, living and dead at once.

MEN. For him I had been so: the gods preserved me.

TEU. Do not dishonour then the powers divine
That saved thee.

MEN. Do I violate their laws?

TEU. If thou forbidst the burial of the dead
Thou dost offend the gods.

MEN. He was my foe,
And therefore I forbid it.

TEU. Art thou sure
That Ajax ever was thy foe?

MEN. I am;
Our hate was mutual, and thou knowst the cause.

TEU. Because thou wert corrupted, thy false voice
Condemned him.

MEN. 'Twas the judges' fault, not mine.

TEU. Thus mayst thou screen a thousand injuries.

MEN. Some one may suffer for this insolence.

TEU. Not more perhaps than others.

MEN. This alone
Remember, buried he shall never be.

Teu. Do thou remember too, I say he shall.

Men. So have I seen a bold imperious man
With froward tongue, before the storm began,
Urging the tardy mariner to sail,
But when the tempest rose no more was heard
The coward's voice, but wrapt beneath his cloak
Silent he laid, and suffered every foot
To trample on him. Thus it is with thee,
And thy foul tongue : forth from a little cloud
Soon as the storm shall burst, it will o'erwhelm thee,
And stop thy clamours.

Teu.   I too have beheld
A man with folly swollen reproach his friends
Oppressed with sore calamity, when straight
One came like me, with indignation fired,
Saw, and addressed him thus : " Cease, shameless wretch !
Nor thus oppress the dead ; for if thou dost,
Remember, thou shalt suffer for thy crime."
Thus spoke he to the weak insulting fool ;
Methinks I see him here—it must be he,
Even Menelaus. Have I guessed aright ?

Men. 'Tis well ; I'll leave thee. 'Tis a folly thus
To talk with those whom we have power to punish.

                                        [*Exit.*

Scene VI.

Teucer, Chorus.

Teu. Away ! This babbler is not to be borne.

Chor. The contest will grow warm. O Teucer ! haste,
Prepare some hollow fosse for the remains
Of Ajax. Raise him there a monument,
By after-ages ne'er to be forgotten.

Teu. And lo ! in happy hour this way advancing
The wife and son of our unhappy friend,
To pay due honours and adorn his tomb.

Scene VII.

Tecmessa, Eurysaces, Teucer, Chorus.

Teu. Come hither, boy, bend down and touch thy
    father;
There sit, and, holding in thy hands this hair
And hers and thine, the suppliant's humble treasure,
Offer thy pious prayers for thy dead father:
If from yon hostile camp the foe should come
To drive thee hence, far from his native land,
Whoe'er he be, unburied may he lie,
From his whole race uprooted, torn away,
E'en as this hair which here I cut before thee;
Oh! guard it well, my child; and you my friends,
Behave like men—assist, protect him now,
Till I return, and, spite of all our foes,
Perform the rites, and raise a tomb to Ajax.   [*Exit.*

Scene VIII.

Tecmessa, Eurysaces, Chorus.

Chorus.

Strophe 1.

When will the happy hour appear,
    That comes to calm our every fear,
From endless toil to bring us sweet repose,
    To bid our weary wanderings cease,
    To fold us in the arms of peace,
And put the wished-for period to our woes?
For since the day when first to Troy we came
Nought have we known but grief, reproach, and
    shame.

Antistrophe 1.

Oh! that the man, who erst inspired
    With horrid rage, our Grecians fired

To slaught'rous deeds, and taught them first to fight,
    Ere he had learned the dreadful trade,
    Himself had mingled with the dead,
Or scattered wide in air, or sunk in endless night !
For oh ! from war unnumbered evils flow,
The unexhausted source of every human woe.

Strophe 2.

By war disturbed, the genial board
No longer will its sweets afford ;
Their fragrant odours round my head
The verdant wreaths no longer spread ;
Nor music's charms my soul delight,
Nor love with rapture crowns the night;
No love, alas ! for me, but grief and care ;
For when I think of Troy I still despair,
And wet with many a tear my wild dishevelled hair.

Antistrophe 2.

Nor nightly fear nor hostile dart;
Whilst Ajax lived, appalled my heart,
But all our pleasures now are o'er,
The valiant Ajax is no more :
Oh ! could I climb the woody steep
That hangs incumbent o'er the deep,
From Sunium's cliff by waves for ever beat,
Then should my eye the lovely prospect greet,
And smile on sacred Athens rising at my feet.

ACT V.

Scene I.

Teucer, Agamemnon, Chorus.

Teucer. This way I bent my hasty steps to meet
The Grecian chief, who hither comes prepared
To vent his keen reproaches.

AGA.   I am told
That thou, e'en thou, the son of a vile slave,
Hast dared to utter foulest calumny
Against thy prince, and passed unpunished for it;
Mean as thy birth is, what had been thy pride
And high demeanour had thy mother sprung
From noble blood? Barbarian as thou art,
How couldst thou praise a wretch, who, like thyself,
Was nothing? We, it seems, for thou hast sworn it,
Are not the masters or of Greece or thee;
Ajax alone, thou sayst, was leader here.
Shall we be thus insulted by our slaves?
Who is this boaster? and what mighty deed
Hath he performed which I could not have done?
Is there no hero in the Grecian host
But Ajax? Vain indeed were our resolves
In the warm contest for Achilles' arms,
If Teucer yet shall question the decree
Against the general voice—resisting still,
And still reproachful, with delusive arts,
Though conquered, yet opposing. Wholesome laws
Will nought avail if those whom justice deems
Superior, to the vanquished must resign,
And first in virtue be the last in fame.
It must not be. Not always the huge size
Of weighty limbs ensures the victory;
They who excel in wisdom are alone
Invincible. Thou see'st the brawny ox,
How the small whip will drive him through the field;
What if the med'cine be applied to thee
For thy proud boasting and licentious tongue?
'Twill be thy portion soon, unless thou learnst
More wisdom; henceforth, mindful what thou art,
Bring with thee one of nobler blood to plead
Thy cause; for know, the language which thou talkst
Is barbarous, and I understand thee not.

CHOR. I can but wish that wisdom may attend
To guide you both.

TEU.   Alas! how very soon
Are all the merits of the dead forgotten!
O Ajax! is the memory of thee

Already lost, e'en by the man for whom
Thy life so oft was ventured in the field ?
But now 'tis past, and buried in oblivion.
Thou wordy slanderer!   Canst thou not remember
When, baffled and unequal to the foe,
Close pent within the walls our forces lay—
Canst thou not call to mind who came alone
To your deliverance, when devouring flames
Towered o'er our ships, when Hector leaped the fosse
And rushed amongst us ?   Then who fought for Greece?
Who drove him back, but Ajax, who, thou sayst,
Could never fight ? Did he not fight for you ?
He met the noble Hector hand to hand,
Unbidden dared the fortune of the field.
He scorned the coward's art to fix his lot
In the moist earth : forth from the crested helmet
It sprang the first.   Such were the deeds of Ajax,
And I was witness of them—I, the slave,
For so thou call'st me, sprung from a barbarian.
How dares a wretch like thee to talk of birth ?
Who was thy grandsire ?   Canst thou not remember
That old barbarian, Phrygian Pelops, tell me ?
Who was thy father—Atreus, was he not ?
That worst of men, who at a brother's table
Served up his children—horrible repast !
Thy mother, too, a Cretan and a slave—
A vile adultress, whom thy father caught
And headlong cast into the sea.   Shalt thou
Talk then to me of birth—to me, the son
Of valiant Telamon, renowned in war,
And wedded to a queen, the royal race
Of great Laomedon, and fairest gift
Of famed Alcides ?   Thus of noble blood
From either parent sprung, shall I disgrace
The man whom thou, inhuman, wouldst still keep
Unburied here ?   Dost thou not blush to think on't ?
But, mark me well ! If thou dost cast him forth,
Not he alone inglorious on the plain
Shall lie—together we will perish all :
To die with glory in a brother's cause
Is better far than fighting for the wife

Of Agamemnon or of Menelaus :
For thy own sake, and not for mine, remember,   /
If thou provoke me, thou'lt be sorry for it,
And wish thou'dst rather feared than angered Teucer.

Scene II.

Ulysses, Agamemnon, Menelaus, Teucer, Chorus.

Chor. Ulysses, if thou meanst not to inflame,
But to compose this dreadful strife, thou com'st
In happiest hour.
Uly.   Far off I heard the voice
Of the Atridæ o'er this wretched course ;
Whence rose the clamour, friends ?
· Men.   With bitterest words
This Teucer here, Ulysses, has reviled me.
Uly. What words ? For if he heard the same from
      thee,
I blame him not.
Aga.   He did provoke me to it.
Uly. What injury hath he done thee ?
Aga.   He declares
The body shall have sepulture, himself
Perforce will bury Ajax, spite of me
And of my power.
Uly.   Shall I be free, and speak
The truth to thee, without reproach or blame ?
Aga. Thou mayst ; for well thou knowst I hold
      Ulysses
Of all the Greeks my best and dearest friend.
Uly. Then hear me. By the gods I must entreat
      thee,
Do not, remorseless and inhuman, cast
The body forth unburied, nor permit
Authority to trample thus on justice.
E'er since our contest for Achilles' arms
Hath Ajax been my foe, and yet I scorn
To use him basely. E'en Ulysses owns,
Of all the Grecian chiefs who came from Troy

(Except Achilles), Ajax was the bravest.
Do not deny him, then, the honours due
To worth so great ; for know, it were a crime
Not against him alone, but 'gainst the gods—
A violation of the laws divine.
To hurt the brave and virtuous after death,
Even though he lived thy foe, is infamous.

AGA. Pleadst thou for Ajax ?

ULY.   Yes ; I was his foe
Whilst justice would permit me ; but he's dead ;
Therefore thou shouldst not triumph nor rejoice
With mirth unseemly o'er a vanquished man.

AGA. 'Tis not so easy for a king to act
By honour's strictest rules.

ULY.   'Tis always so
To hearken to the counsels of a friend,
When he advises well.

AGA.   But know, the good
And virtuous still submit to those who rule.

ULY. No more.   When thou art vanquished by thy
    friends,
Thou art thyself the conqueror.

AGA.   Still remember
For whom thou pleadst, Ulysses.

ULY.   For a foe,
But for a brave one.

AGA.   Dost thou thus revere
E'en after death thine enemy ?

ULY.   I do :
Virtue is dearer to me than revenge.

AGA. Such men are most unstable in their ways.

ULY. Our dearest friend may one day be our foe.

AGA. Dost thou desire such friends ?

ULY.   I cannot love
Or praise th' unfeeling heart.

AGA.   This day shall Greece
Mark us for cowards.

ULY.   Greece will call us just.

AGA. Wouldst thou persuade me then to grant him
    burial ?

ULY. I would, and for that purpose came I hither.

AGA. How every man consults his own advantage,
And acts but for himself !

ULY.   And who is he
Whom I should wish to serve before Ulysses?

AGA. 'Tis thy own work, remember, and not mine.

ULY. The deed will win thee praise, and every tongue
Shall call thee good.

AGA.   Thou knowst I'd not refuse
Ulysses more, much more than this ; but Ajax
Or buried or unburied is the same,
And must be hateful still to Agamemnon.
But do as it beseems thee best.

CHOR.   Ulysses,
The man who says thou art not wise and good
Is senseless and unjust.

ULY.   I tell thee, Teucer,
Henceforth I am as much the friend of Ajax
As once I was his foe : e'en now I mean
To join with thee, a fellow-labourer
In all the pious offices of love,
Nor would omit, what every man should pay,
The honours due to such exalted virtue !

TEU. O best of men ! thou hast my thanks and
      praise,
And well deserv'st them, for thou hast transcended
My utmost hopes. I little thought the worst
Of all his foes among the Grecian host
Would thus alone defend, alone protect
The dead from insult, when these thundering leaders
United came to cast his body forth
With infamy ; but may the god who rules
O'er high Olympus, and the vengeful Furies,
Daughters of Jove, the guilt-rewarding sisters,
With all-deciding justice soon repay
The haughty tyrants. For thy offered aid,
Son of Laertes, in the funeral rites,
Perhaps it might offend the honoured shade
Of our dead friend—it cannot be accepted.
For all beside we thank thee. If thou will'st
To send assistance from the Grecian camp,
'Twill be received ; the rest shall be my care.

Thou hast performed the duty of a friend,
And we acknowledge it.
    ULY.   I would have lent
My willing aid, but since it must not be,
I shall submit. Farewell!   [*Exit* ULYSSES.

SCENE III.

AGAMEMNON, MENELAUS, TEUCER, EURYSACES, CHORUS

    TEU.   Thus far is right.
The time already past doth chide our sloth:
My friends, be vigilant. Let some prepare
The hollow fosse, some o'er the sacred flame
Place the rich tripod for the funeral bath;
Forth from the camp a chosen band must bear
His glittering arms and trophies of the war.
Do thou, my child, if thou hast strength, uplift
                  [*To* EURYSACES.
Thy father's body. See, the veins, yet warm,
Spout forth with blood. Haste! Help, assist me, all
Who bear the name of friends, and pay with me
Your last sad duties to the noble Ajax;
For never was on earth a better man.
    CHOR. Whate'er of good or ill weak mortals know
Must from their best of guides, experience, flow.
Seek then no farther; for to man is given
The present state, the future left to Heaven.

ELECTRA.

DRAMATIS PERSONÆ.

ELECTRA, *Daughter of Agamemnon and Clytemnestra.*
ORESTES, *Brother of Electra.*
PYLADES, *Friend of Orestes.*
GOVERNOR OF ORESTES.
CLYTEMNESTRA, *Wife to Ægisthus.*

CHRYSOTHEMIS, *Sister of Electra.*
ÆGISTHUS, *King of Argos and Mycenæ.*
CHORUS, *composed of the principal Ladies of Mycenæ.*

SCENE.—MYCENÆ, *before the Palace of* ÆGISTHUS.

ACT I.

SCENE I.

ORESTES, PYLADES, GOVERNOR OF ORESTES.

GOVERNOR. O son of great Atrides ! he who led
Embattled Greece to Troy's devoted walls,
At length behold what thy desiring eyes
So long have sought. Behold thy native soil,
Thy much-loved Argos, and the hallowed grove
Of Io, frantic maid. On this side lies
The Lycian forum, on the left the fane
Of Juno, far renowned. Behold ! we come
To rich Mycenæ, and the slaughterous house
Of Pelops' hapless race, from whose sad walls
Long since I bore thee, at thy sister's hand

Gladly received, and with paternal care
To this blest day have fostered up thy youth,
Till riper years should give thee to return,
And pay with dire revenge thy father's murder.
Now, my Orestes, and thou dear companion.
Of all our sufferings, much-loved Pylades,
Let deepest counsel sway our just resolves;
For lo! resplendent Phœbus with his light
Calls up the cheerful birds to early song,
And gloomy night hath lost her starry train:
Come then, my friends, and ere th' awakened city
Pours forth her busy throngs, this instant here
Let us consult.   Believe me, 'tis no time
For dull delay; 'tis the decisive hour,
And this the very crisis of our fate.

   ORESTES. What proofs thou giv'st me of the noblest
    nature
And true benevolence, thou good old man!
Of servants sure the faithfullest and best
That ever bore the name: the generous steed,
Though worn with years, thus keeps his wonted courage,
And warns his master of approaching danger;
Like him thou stir'st me up to noble deeds,
And follow'st me undaunted: but attend
To what I have resolved, and if I err,
Let thy superior judgment set me right.
   When to the Delphic oracle I flew,
Eager to know how on my father's foes
I best might satiate my revenge, the god
Enjoined me not by force or open arms
To rush upon them, but with guileful arts
And silent well-conducted fraud betray them.
Such was his will.   Thou, therefore, soon as time
Shall lend thee opportunity, unknown
And unsuspected (as thy absence hence
For so long space and hoary age shall make thee)
Must steal upon them, learn their secret counsels,
As soon thou mayst, and quick inform us of them;
Say thou'rt of Phocis, from Phanoteus sent
By one who is their friend and firm ally;
Say, and confirm it with a solemn oath,

Orestes is no more—by a rude shock
Thrown from his chariot at the Pythian games.
Be this thy tale : meantime (for thus the god
His will divine expressed) my father's tomb
With due libations and devoted hair
Ourselves will crown ; and thence returning bring,
From the dark covert where thou knowst 'twas hid,
The brazen urn.   There, we shall tell the tyrant—
Thrice welcome news !—Orestes' ashes lie.
What should deter me from the pious fraud ?
Since my feigned death but gains me real fame,
And I shall wake to better life : the deed
Which brings success and honour, must be good.
Oft times the wisest and the best of men
From death like this have rose with added greatness ;
E'en so thy friend to his deluded foes
Shall soon return unlooked-for, and before them
Shine like a star with more distinguished lustre.
O my loved country ! and its guardian gods,
Receive Orestes, and with happy omen
Propitious smile !   And thou, paternal seat—
For lo ! by Heaven's command I come to purge thee
Of vile usurpers, and avenge thy wrongs—
Drive me not from thee an abandoned exile
With infamy, but grant me to possess
My father's throne, and fix his injured race.
Thus far 'tis well.   My faithful minister,
Thou to thy office, we to ours with speed ;
So time and opportunity require
On whom the fate of mortals must depend.
    ELECTRA [*from within*]. O misery !
    Gov.   Methought a mournful voice
Spake from within.
    ORES.   Perhaps the poor Electra :
Shall we not stay and hearken to it ?
    Gov.   No :
First be Apollo's great behests obeyed
Before thy father's tomb.   That pious deed
Performed shall fire our souls with nobler warmth,
And crown our bold attempt with fair success. [*Exeunt.*

Scene II.

Electra.

O sacred light! and O thou ambient air!
Oft have ye heard Electra's loud laments,
Her sighs and groans, and witnessed to her woes,
Which ever as each hateful morn appeared
I poured before you : what at eve retired
I felt of anguish my sad couch alone
Can tell, which watered nightly with my tears
Received me sorrowing—that best can tell
What pangs I suffered for a hapless father,
Whom not the god of war with ruthless hand
Struck nobly fighting in a distant soil,
But my fell mother, and the cursed Ægisthus,
The partner of her bed, remorseless slew.
Untimely didst thou fall, lamented shade,
And none but poor Electra mourns thy fate;
Nor shall she cease to mourn thee, while these eyes
View the fair heavens or behold the sun!
Never! oh, never! Like the nightingale,
Whose plaintive song bewails her ravished brood,
Here will I still lament my father's wrongs,
And teach the echo to repeat my moan.
O ye infernal deities! and thou
Terrestrial Hermes! and thou, Nemesis,
Replete with curses! and ye vengeful Furies,
Offspring of gods, the ministers of wrath
To vile adulterers, who with pity view
The slaughtered innocent—behold this deed!
Oh! come, assist, revenge my father's murder;
Quickly, oh, quickly bring me my Orestes;
For lo! I sink beneath oppressive woe,
And can no longer bear the weight alone.

Scene III.

Chorus, Electra.

Chor. O wretched daughter of an impious mother!
Wilt thou for ever mourn, for ever thus,
With unavailing tears and endless sorrow,
Lament the royal Agamemnon's fate,
By a vile woman's wicked arts betrayed?
Perish the hand (forgive the pious curse,
Ye heavenly powers!) that gave the deadly blow!

Elec. My noble friends and partners in affliction,
Who thus, to soothe my sorrows, kindly try
Each art which love and friendship can inspire;
Ye come to comfort me, I know ye do.
I know my tears are fruitless all and vain;
But, oh! permit me to indulge my griefs,
For I must weep.

Chor. Thy tears can ne'er recall him
From the dark mansions of the common grave—
No, nor thy prayers; they can but make thee wretched,
And sink thee deeper in calamity.
Why art thou then so fond of misery?

Elec. Devoid of sense and feeling is the heart
That can forget an injured parent's wrongs.
I love the airy messenger of Jove,
The mournful bird that weeps her Ity's fate,
And every night repeats the tender tale;
Thee, too, I reverence as a goddess—thee,
Unhappy Niobe! for still thou weepst,
And from the marble tears eternal flow.

Chor. But oh! reflect, that not to thee alone
Misfortune comes—that comes to all. Behold
Iphianassa, and Chrysothemis,
And him who hides his grief, illustrious youth,
The loved Orestes—these have suffered too.

Elec. Orestes! Yes, Mycenæ shall receive
In happy hour her great avenger; Jove,
With smiles auspicious, shall conduct him to me;
For him alone I wait—for him, a wretch

Despised, of children and of nuptial rites
Hopeless I wander.   He remembers not
What I have done for him, what suffered ; still
With airy promises he mocks my hopes,
And yet he comes not to me.

CHOR.   But he will.
Despair not, daughter; Jove is yet in heaven,
The god who sees, and knows, and governs all :
Patient to him submit, nor let thy rage
Too far transport thee, nor oblivion drown
The just remembrance of thy matchless woes ;
Time is a kind indulgent deity,
And he shall give thee succour ; he shall send
The god of Acheron, from Chrysa's shores
To bring Orestes and avenge thy wrongs.

ELEC. Oh ! but the while how much of life is gone !
And I a hapless wretched orphan still,
Without a friend to guard or to protect me—
Disgraced, dishonoured, like a stranger clad
In base attire, and fed with homeliest fare.

CHOR. Sad news indeed the hapless messenger
To Argos brought, that spoke the wished return
Of thy loved father to his native soil ;
Fatal the night when Agamemnon fell
Or by a mortal or immortal hand ;
The work of fraud and lust, a horrid deed !
Whoe'er performed it.

ELEC.   O detested feast !
O day, the bitt'rest sure that ever rose !
With him I perished then.   But may the gods
Repay the murderers ; never may they hear
The voice of joy, or taste of comfort more !

CHOR. Cease thy complaints ; already hast thou suffered
For thy loud discontents and threatened vengeance.
'Tis folly to contend with power superior.

ELEC. Folly indeed, and madness !   But my griefs
Will force their way, and whilst Electra breathes
She must lament ; for who will bring me comfort,
Or soothe my sorrows ?   Let me—let me go,
And weep for ever.

CHOR.   'Tis my love entreats ;

Trust me, I feel a mother's fondness for thee,
And fain would save thee from redoubled woes.

ELEC. And wouldst thou have me then neglect the
dead ?
Forget my father ! Can there be such guilt ?
When I do so, may infamy pursue me !
And if I wed, may all the joys of love
Be far removed ! If vengeance doth not fall
On crimes like these, for ever farewell, justice—
Shame, honour, truth, and piety, farewell !

CHOR. Pardon me, daughter; if my warmth offend,
Glad I submit. We'll follow, and obey thee.

ELEC. I am myself to blame, and blush to think
How much unfit I seem to bear the weight
Imposed upon me ; but indeed 'tis great.
Forgive me, friends, a woman born as I am,
Must she not grieve to see each added minute
Fraught with new mis'ries ? Thus to be a slave
E'en in my father's house, and from those hands
Which shed his blood to ask the means of life !
Think what my soul must suffer to behold
The cursed Ægisthus seated on the throne
Of Agamemnon, in the very robes
Which once were his—to see the tyrant pour
Libations forth e'en on the fatal spot
Where the sad deed was done. But, worst of all,
To see the murderer usurp his bed,
Embrace my mother (by that honoured name
If I may call a guilty wretch like her),
Who, pleased, returns his love, and, of her crimes
Unconscious, smiles, nor fears th' avenging Furies
But ever as the bloody day returns
Which gave the royal victim to her wiles,
Annual the dance and choral song proclaim
A solemn feast, nor impious sacrifice
Forgets she then to her protecting gods.
Shocked at the cruel banquet I retire,
And in some corner hide my griefs, denied
E'en the sad comfort to indulge my sorrows,
For Clytemnestra in opprobrious terms
Reviles me oft : "To thee alone," she cries,

" Is Agamemnon lost, detested maid !
Thinkst thou Electra only weeps his fate ?
Perdition on thee !   May th' infernal gods
Refuse thee succour, and protract thy pains ! "
Thus rails she bitter, and if chance she hear
Orestes is approaching, stung with rage
Wild she exclaims, " Thou art th' accursed cause ;
This is thy deed, who stole Orestes from me,
And hid him from my rage ; but be assured
Ere long my vengeance shall o'ertake thee for it
These threats her noble lord still urges on—
That vile adulterer, that abandoned coward,
Whose fearful soul called in a woman's aid
To execute his bloody purposes.
Meantime Electra sighs for her Orestes,
Her wished avenger ; his unkind delay
Destroys my hopes.   Alas ! my gentle friends,
Who can bear this, and keep an equal mind ?
To suffer ills like mine, and not to err
From wild distraction, would be strange indeed.
   CHOR. But say, Electra, is the tyrant near ?
Or may we speak our thoughts unblamed ?
   ELEC.   Thou mayst ;
I had not else beyond the palace dared
To wander hither.
   CHOR.   I would fain have asked thee——
   ELEC. Ask what thou wilt, Ægisthus is far off.
   CHOR. Touching thy brother then, inform me quick
If aught thou knowst that merits firm belief.
   ELEC. He promises, but comes not.
   CHOR.   Things of moment
Require deliberation and delay.
   ELEC. Oh ! but did I delay to save Orestes ?
   CHOR. He boasts a noble nature, and will ne'er
Forget his friends : be confident.
   ELEC.   I am,
Were I not so I had not lived till now.
   CHOR. But soft, behold the fair Chrysothemis
Advance this way, and in her hand she bears
Sepulchral offerings to the shades below.

Scene IV.

Chrysothemis, Electra, Chorus.

CHRY. Still, my Electra, pouring forth thy griefs?
Art thou not yet by sad experience taught
How little they avail? I too must feel
And could resent, as, were thy sister's power
But equal to her will, our foes should know.
Meantime with lowered sail to bear the storm
Befits us best, nor, helpless as we are,
With idle hopes to meditate revenge;
Yield then with me, and though impartial justice
Plead on thy side, remember, if we prize
Or life or liberty, we must obey.
ELEC. It ill becomes great Agamemnon's daughter
Thus to forget her noble father's worth,
And take a base unworthy mother's part;
For well I see from whom thy counsels flow;
Nought from thyself thou sayst but all from her?
Either thy reason's lost, or if thou hast it,
Thou hast forgot thy friends who should be dear
And precious to thee. Of thy boasted hate
Against our foes, and what thou vauntst to do
If thou hadst power I reck not, whilst with me
Thou wilt not join in great revenge, but still
Dissuadst me from it; is't not cowardly
To leave me thus? Tell me, I beg thee, tell me
What mighty gain awaits my tame submission,
Should I suppress my griefs. I can but live;
That I do now—a wretched life indeed!
But 'tis enough for me, and I am happy
Whilst I can torture them, and to the dead
Pay grateful honours—if to them such care
Aught grateful can bestow. Thy hate, I fear me,
Is but in word: thou dost befriend the murderers:
For me, not all the wealth they could bestow,
Not all the gifts which they have poured on thee,
Should bind me to 'em. Take thy costly banquets,
And let thy days with ease and pleasure flow;

Give me but food, and I am satisfied.
I wish not for thy honours, nor wouldst thou,
If thou wert wise, receive them at their hands.
Thou mightst be daughter to the best of fathers,
And art thy mother's only.   Take that name,
And henceforth all shall mark thee as a wretch
Who hath betrayed her father and her friends.

   CHOR. I do entreat you, let not anger come
Between you thus ; you both have reasoned well,
And much of mutual benefit may flow
If each to other lend a patient ear.

   CHRY. Custom, my noble friends, hath made re-
    proach
Familiar to me, and, so well I know
Her haughty mind, I had been silent still,
But that I saw the danger imminent,
And came to warn her of the fatal stroke
Which soon must end her and her griefs together.

   ELEC. Tell me this mighty danger; if aught more
It threaten than Electra long hath borne,
I yield me to thy counsels.

   CHRY.   Hear me then :
Know, thou art doomed, unless thou dost refrain
Thy clamorous griefs, far from the light of day
And this thy native soil, within a cell
Dismal and dark, to spend the poor remains
Of thy sad life, and there lament thy fate.

   ELEC. Is it decreed ?   Must it in truth be so ?
   CHRY. Soon as Ægisthus shall return, it must.
   ELEC. Quick let him come : I long to see him here.
   CHRY. Alas ! what dreadful imprecations these !
   ELEC. Would he were present, if for this he comes !
   CHRY. What ! to destroy thee ! Is thy mind dis-
    turbed ?
   ELEC. That I might fly for ever from thy sight.
   CHRY. Wilt thou not think how to preserve thy life ?
   ELEC. Mine is a blessed life indeed to think of.
   CHRY. It might be blest, if thou wouldst have it so.
   ELEC. Teach me not basely to betray my friends.
   CHRY. I do not ; all I ask thee is to yield
To powers superior.

Elec.   Fawn on them thyself;
Thou dost not know Electra.
  Chry.   Sure it better
Deserves the name of wisdom to avoid
Than hasten thy destruction.
  Elec.   No, to die
Were pleasure, could I but avenge my father.
  Chry. Our father, doubt it not, will pardon thee.
  Elec. 'Tis mean to think so.
  Chry.   Wilt thou not consent?
  Elec. Never, oh never, be my soul so weak!
  Chry. Then to my errand: fare thee well.
  Elec.   To whom,
Chrysothemis, and whither dost thou bear
Those sacred off'rings?
  Chry.   To our father's tomb,
From Clytemnestra.
  Elec.   To the man she hated?
The man, my sister——
  Chry.   Whom she killed, I know,
Thou would have said.
  Elec.   Why, what should move her to it?
  Chry. If I mistake not, horrors late impressed
From a sad vision.
  Elec.   O my country's gods!
Succour me now!
  Chry.   What hopes dost thou conceive
From this?
  Elec. The dream: and I will tell thee all.
  Chry. I know but little of it.
  Elec.   Tell me that:
Oftimes to words, how few soe'er they be,
Is given the power to save or to destroy.
  Chry. Once more to light returned (so fame reports)
Before her our loved father did appear,
The royal sceptre wielded in his hand
Which now Ægisthus bears, whence seemed to spring
A green and leafy branch, whose wide extent
O'er all Mycenæ spread its verdant shade:
This did I learn, and this alone, from one
Who listened long attentive while she told

Her vision to the sun; hence all her fears,
And hence my destined journey.

ELEC.   By the gods
Let me conjure thee, hear me. If thou dost not,
Too late shall thou repent, when for thy guilt
Evil o'ertake thee. O Chrysothemis!
Never, I beg thee, to our father's tomb
Bear thou those offerings; 'twere a horrid deed
From such a woman. Give 'em to the winds;
Let them be hid, deep buried in the sands,
And not the smallest grain escape to reach
That hallowed place; let 'em remain for her,
Safe in the earth till she shall meet 'em there.
None but this shameless, this abandoned woman,
Would e'er with impious off'rings thus adorn
The tomb of him she murdered. By the dead
Thinkst thou such gifts can be with joy received?
Gifts from that hand which from his mangled corse
Severed his lifeless limbs, and on the head
Of the poor victim wiped her bloody sword?
Madness to think that offerings and ablutions
Could purge such crimes, or wash her stains away;
Never, oh never! But of this no more.
Instant, my sister, thy devoted hair
With these dishevelled locks and this my zone,
Plain as it is and unadorned, shalt thou
Bear to our father. Wretched offerings these!
But, Oh! 'tis all Electra now can give.
Bear them, and suppliant on thy knees implore
      him
To smile propitious and assist his children;
Pray for Orestes, too, that soon with power
He may return, and trample on our foes;
So shall a fairer tribute one day grace
His honoured tomb, than now we can bestow.
Trust me, my sister, we are still his care—
I know we are. From him the vision came,
The horrid dream that shook her guilty soul:
Now then, I beg thee, be a friend to me,
Be to thyself a friend, a friend to him
Of all mankind the dearest, our dead father.

CHOR. Well doth the pious virgin speak, and thou
Must yield to her requests.
    CHRY.   And so I will.
Where reason dictates, strife should never come;
But quick, despatch! fulfil her just commands.
Yet, O my friends! remember, our attempt
Is full of danger, and let nought escape
That may betray me to my cruel mother;
For if it reach her ear, this daring act,
I fear me much, shall one day cost us dear.
                                 [*Exit* CHRYSOTHEMIS.

SCENE V.

CHORUS, ELECTRA.

CHORUS.

Strophe.

Or my prophetic mind is now no more
Attentive as of old to wisdom's lore,
Or justice comes, with speedy vengeance fraught;
   Behold! the goddess armed with power appears—
   It must be so, by Clytemnestra's fears,
And the dire dream that on her fancy wrought:
   Thy father, not unmindful of his fate,
   Shall hither come his wrongs to vindicate;
     And, in his gore imbrued,
   The fatal axe with him shall rise,
   Shall ask another sacrifice,
And drink with him the cruel tyrant's blood.

Antistrophe.

   Lo! with unnumbered hands and countless feet,
   The fury comes her destined prey to meet;
Deep in the covert hid she glides unseen,
   Hangs o'er the trembling murderer's head,
   Or steals to the adultrous bed,
An awful witness of the guilty scene;

                                 C

Doubtless the dream with all its terrors meant
For crimes like these some dreadful punishment,
If mortals aught from nightly visions know,
If truth from great Apollo's shrine
Appears in oracles divine,
Presaging bliss to come, or threat'ning future woe.

Epode.

O Pelops ! to thy country and to thee
The fatal course brought woe and misery ;
For since the time when, from his chariot thrown,
For thee the guilty wreath to gain,
The hapless Myrtilus was slain,
Nought has thy wretched race but grief and sorrow
known.

Act II.

Scene I.

CLYTEMNESTRA, ELECTRA, CHORUS

CLYTEMNESTRA. Ægisthus absent, who alone could curb
Thy haughty spirit and licentious tongue,
At large, it seems, thou rov'st, and unrestrained,
No deference paid to my authority,
But on thy mother ever pouring forth
Bitter invectives, while the listening crowd
Are taught to hold me proud and fierce of soul,
A lawless tyrant slandering thee and thine
I am no slanderer—I abhor the name ;
But oft reviled, of force I must reply,
And send thy foul reproaches back upon thee.
Thou sayst I slew thy father ; that alone
Is left to plead for all thy insolence.
I do confess the deed, and glory in it.
I slew thy father ; yet not I alone,
I had the hand of justice to assist me,

And should have had Electra's. Well thou knowst
That cruel father, for whom thus thy tears
Incessant flow, that father slew his child :
He, he alone of all the Grecian host
Gave up his daughter—horrid sacrifice—
To the offended gods : he never felt
A mother's pangs, and therefore thought not of them,
Or, if he did, why slay the innocent ?
For Greece, thou tellst me ! Greece could never claim
A right to what was mine. Or did she fall
For Menelaus ? He had children too :
Why might not they have died ? Their parent's guilt,
Source of the war, more justly had deserved it.
Or thinkst thou death with keener appetite
Could feast on mine, and Helen's not afford
As sweet a banquet ? Why was all the love,
To me and to my child so justly due,
With lavish hand bestowed on Menelaus ?
Was he not then a base inhuman father ?
He was ; and so, could Iphigenia speak,
Thy breathless sister, she too would declare.
Know then, I grieve not ; shame or penitence
I feel not for the deed ; and if to thee
It seems so heinous, weigh each circumstance,
Remember what he did, and lay the blame
On him who well deserved the fate he suffered.

    ELEC. Thou hast no plea for bitterness like this ;
Thou canst not say that I provoked thee to it.
I have been silent : had I leave to speak
I could defend an injured father's cause,
And tell thee wherefore Iphigenia fell.

    CLY. I do permit thee ; and if modest thus
Thou hadst addressed me always thy free speech
Had ne'er offended.

    ELEC.   Hast thou not confessed
That thou didst slay my father ? Whether justice
Approve or not, 'twas horrid to confess it :
But justice never could persuade thee—no !
I'll tell thee who it was, it was Ægisthus,
The wretch with whom thou liv'st. Go ask the goddess,
The immortal huntress, why the winds were stayed

So long at Aulis.   But thou must not ask
The chaste Diana!   Take it, then, from me.
My father once, as for the chase prepared,
Careless he wandered through her secret grove,
Forth from its covert roused a spotted hind
Of fairest form, with towering antlers graced,
Pursued and slew her.   Of the deity
Something with pride elate he uttered then
Disdainful.   Quick resenting the affront,
Latona's daughter stayed the Grecian fleet,
Nor would forgive, till for her slaughtered beast
Th' offending father sacrificed his child.
Thus Iphigenia fell; and but for her
Greece ne'er had seen or Ilion's lofty towers,
Or her own native soil.   The father strove
In vain to save, and not for Menelaus
He gave her up at last, but for his country.
Suppose a brother's fondness had prevailed,
And she was given for him, would that excuse
Thy horrid deed?   What law required it of thee?
That law alone by which thyself must fall;
If blood for blood be due, thy doom is fixed.
Plead not so poorly then, but tell me why
Thou liv'st adultrous thus with a vile ruffian,
Thy base assistant?   Why are those who sprung
From thy first nuptials cast unkindly forth
For his new race?   Was this thy piety?
Was this, too, to revenge thy daughter's death?
In pure revenge to wed her deadliest foe
Was noble, was it not?   But I forget:
You are my mother—so it seems you say—
And I must hold my peace.   But I deny it;
I say your are my mistress, not my mother—
A cruel mistress that afflicts my soul,
And makes this weary life a burthen to me.
Orestes too, the hapless fugitive,
Who once escaped thy fatal hand, now drags
A loathsome being.   Him, thou sayst, I looked for
To join in my revenge, and so I did;
I would have been revenged, I tell thee so.
Say, I am base, malicious, impudent,

Abusive, what thou wilt; for if I am
It speaks my birth, and I resemble thee.
    CHOR. Resentment deep hath fired the virgin's
      breast;
Whether with truth and justice on her side
She speak, I know not.
    CLY.   Can they plead for her?
What care, what love, or tenderness is due
To an abandoned child, who shameless thus
Reviles a parent? Is there, after this,
A crime in nature she would blush to act?
    ELEC. I am not base, nor shameless, as thou callst
      me,
For know, even now I blush for what is past—
Indecent warmth, and words that ill became
My tender years and virgin modesty;
But 'twas thy guilt, thy malice urged me to it:
From bad examples bad alone we learn—
I only erred because I followed thee.
    CLY. Impudent wretch! And am I then the cause
Of all thy clamorous insolence?
    ELEC.   Thou art:
Foul is thy speech, because thy deed was foul;
For words from actions flow.
    CLY.   By chaste Diana,
Soon as Ægisthus comes thy boldness meets
Its just reward.
    ELEC.   Is this thy promised leave,
So lately granted, freely to unfold
What, now incensed, thou dost refuse to hear?
    CLY. Have I not heard thee, and in base return
With luckless omen dost thou now retard
My pious sacrifice?
    ELEC.   Oh! far from me
Be guilt like that; perform it, I beseech thee.
In holy silence shall these lips be closed,
And not a word escape to thwart thy purpose.
    CLY. [*speaking to one of her attendants*]. Hither do thou
      the sacred offerings bring,
Of various fruits composed, that to the god
Whose altars we adorn my fervent prayer

May rise accepted, and dispel my fears.
Hear then, Apollo! great protector, hear
My secret vows, for with no friendly ear　　　　[*softly.*
My voice is heard: her malice would betray,
Should I unveil my heart, each word I uttered,
And scatter idle rumours through the crowd.
Thus then accept my prayers, Lycean Phœbus!　[*aloud.*
If in the doubtful visions of the night
Which broke my slumbers, aught presaging good
Thou seest, propitious, oh! confirm it all;
But if of dire portent, and fraught with ill
To me and mine they came, avert the omen,
And send the evil back upon my foes!
Oh! if there are whose fraudful arts conspire
To cast me forth from all my present bliss,
Let them not prosper, but protect me still!
Grant me to live and reign in quiet here,
To spend each happy hour with those I love—
With those my children who have ne'er offended
By malice, pride, and bitterness of soul—
Grant this, indulgent Phœbus!　What remains
Unasked thou seest; for nought escapes the eye
Of gods, such knowledge have the sons of Jove.

SCENE II.

GOVERNOR OF ORESTES, CLYTEMNESTRA, ELECTRA, CHORUS.

Gov. Is this the royal palace of Ægisthus?
Chor. Stranger, it is.
Gov.　　　　　　　　　And this—for such her form
And look majestic speak her—is his queen;
Is it not so?
Chor.　　　　It is.
Gov.　　　　　　　　Great sovereign, hail!
With joyful news I come, and from a friend,
To thee and to Ægisthus.
Cly.　　　　　　　　Stranger, welcome!
Say, first, from whom thy message?

Gov.   From Phanoteus ;
A Phocian sends thee things of utmost moment.
   CLY. Of moment sayst thou ? What ? Impart them
       quick !
Of friendly import, if from thence they come,
I know they must be.
   Gov.   Briefly then, 'tis this :
Orestes is no more.
   ELEC.   Undone Electra !
Now am I lost indeed.
   CLY.   What sayst thou ?   Speak !
Regard not her—go on !
   Gov.   I say again,
Orestes is no more.
   ELEC.   Then what am I ?
I too am nothing.
   CLY. [*to* ELECTRA]. Get thee hence—away !
Disturb us not—most welcome messenger !
                          [*to the* GOVERNOR.
Go on, I beg thee, let me hear it all !
Say how he died, tell every circumstance.
   Gov. For that I came, and I will tell thee all.
Know then, Orestes at the Pythian games,
Eager for glory, met assembled Greece.
Soon as the herald's far-resounding voice
Proclaimed the course, the graceful youth appeared,
And was by all admired.   Successful soon
He reached the goal, and bore his prize away.
Ne'er did these eyes behold such feats performed
By mortal strength ; in every course superior,
He rose victorious.   Theme of every tongue
Was the brave Argive, great Atrides' son,
Who led the Grecian host.   But oh ! in vain
Doth human valour strive when power divine
Pursues vindictive !   The succeeding morn
Uprose the sun, and with him all the train
Of youthful rivals in the chariot race :
One from Achaia, one from Sparta came,
Of Afric's sons advanced a noble pair,
And joined the throng.   With these Orestes drove
His swift Thessalian steeds ; Ætolia next,

For yellow coursers famed; and next Magnesia;
And Athens, built by hands divine, sent forth
Her skilful charioteer; an Ænian next
Drove his white horses through the field; and last
A brave Bæotian closed the warrior train.
And now in order ranged, as each by lot
Determined stood, forth at the trumpet's sound
They rushed together, shook their glittering reins,
And lashed their foaming coursers o'er the plain.
Loud was the din of rattling cars involved
In dusty clouds; close on each other pressed
The rival youths, together stopped, and turned
Together all, the hapless Ænian first:
His fiery steeds impatient of subjection,
Entangled on the Lybian chariot hung.
Confusion soon and terror through the crowd
Disastrous spread; the jarring axles rung;
Wheel within wheel now cracked, till Chrysa's field
Was with the scattered ruins quite o'erspread.
Th' Athenian cautious viewed the distant danger,
Drew in the rein, and turned his car aside,
Then passed them all. Orestes, who, secure
Of conquest, lagged behind, with eager pace
Now urged his rapid course, and swift pursued.
Sharp was the contest: now th' Athenian first,
And now Orestes o'er his coursers hung,
Now side by side they ran. When to the last
And fatal goal they came, Atrides' son,
As chance with slackened rein he turned the car,
Full on the pillar struck, tore from the wheel
Its brittle spokes, and from his seat down dropped
Precipitate. Entangled in the reins
His fiery coursers dragged him o'er the field,
Whilst shrieking crowds with pity viewed the
    youth,
Whose gallant deeds deserved a better fate.
Scarce could they stop the rapid car, or loose
His mangled corse, so drenched in blood, so changed,
That scarce a friend could say it was Orestes.
Straight on the pile they burnt his sad remains,
And, in an urn enclosed, a chosen few

From Phocis sent have brought his ashes home,
To reap due honours in his native land.

Thus have I told thee all, a dreadful tale!
But, oh! how far more dreadful to behold it,
And be like me a witness of the scene!

CHOR. Ah me! the royal race, the ancient house
Of my loved master is no more!

CLY.   Great Jove!
Th' event was happy, but 'tis mixed with woe.
For, oh! 'tis bitter to reflect that life
And safety must be purchased by misfortunes.

GOV. Why grieve you, madam?

CLY.   'Tis a bitter task
To bring forth children; though a mother's wronged,
A mother cannot hate the babe she bore.

GOV. Then with ungrateful news in vain I came.

CLY. Oh no! Most welcome is the man who brings
Such joyful tidings, that a thankless child
Is gone, who left a tender mother's arms
To live a voluntary exile from me;
Ne'er to these eyes returned, but absent raged,
And threatened vengeance for his murdered father.
Day had no rest for me, nor did the night
Bring needful slumbers—thoughts of instant death
Appalled me ever. But my fears are gone!
He cannot hurt me now, nor, worse than him,
This vile domestic plague, who haunts me still
To suck my vital blood; but henceforth safe,
Spite of her threats, shall Clytemnestra live.

ELEC. Now, my Orestes, I indeed must mourn
Thy cruel fate, embittered by reproach,
And from a mother's tongue. This is not well.

CLY. With him it is, and would it were with thee!

ELEC. Attend, O Nemesis! and hear the dead!

CLY. She heard that voice which best deserved her
     ear,
And her decrees are just.

ELEC.   Go on, proud woman;
Insult us now, whilst fortune smiles upon thee

CLY. Dost thou then hope that we shall fall here-
     after?

ELEC. No; we are fallen ourselves, and cannot hurt
  thee.

CLY. Thrice worthy is that messenger of joy
Whose gladsome news shall stop thy clamorous tongue.

GOV. My task performed, permit me to retire.

CLY. No, stranger, that were an affront to thee,
And to our friend who sent thee here.   Go in,
And leave that noisy wretch to bellow forth
Her sorrows, and bewail her lost Orestes.   [*Exeunt.*

SCENE III.

ELECTRA, CHORUS.

ELEC. Marked ye, my friends, did ye observe her
  tears?
Did she lament him? Did the mother weep
For her lost child?   Oh, no; she smiled and left me.
Wretched Electra!   O my dear Orestes!
Thou hast undone me; thou wert all my hope:
I thought thou wouldst have lived to aid my vengeance
For our loved father's death; deprived of both
Whither shall I betake me?   Left at last
A slave to those whom most on earth I hate,
The cruel murderers—must it then be so?
Never, oh never! Thus bereft of all,
Here will I lay me down, and on this spot
End my sad days.   If it offend the tyrants,
Let 'em destroy me—'twill be kindly done.
Life is a pain; I would not wish to keep it.

CHOR. Where is thy thunder, Jove? or where thy
  power,
O Phœbus! if thou dost behold this deed
And not avenge it?

ELEC.   Oh!

CHOR.   Why mournst thou thus?

ELEC. Alas!

CHOR.   Oh! do not groan thus.

ELEC.   Thou destroyst me.

CHOR. How have I hurt thee?

ELEC.   Why thus vainly try
To give me comfort, when I know he's dead?
You but insult my woes.
    CHOR.   Yet weep not thus.
Think on the golden bracelet that betrayed
Amphiaraus, who now——
    ELEC.   Oh me !
    CHOR.   In bliss
Immortal reigns among the shades below.
    ELEC. Alas !
    CHOR.   No more ; a woman was the cause,
Th' accursed cause.
    ELEC.   She suffered, did she not ?
    CHOR. She did ; she perished.
    ELEC.   Yes, I know it well;
He found a kind avenger of his wrongs,
But I have none, for he is ravished from me.
    CHOR. Thou art indeed unhappy.
    ELEC.   'Tis too true.
I am most wretched, it beats hard upon me ;
My sorrows never cease.
    CHOR.   We see thy woes.
    ELEC. Therefore no more attempt to bring me
      comfort ;
There is no hope.
    CHOR.   What sayst thou ?
    ELEC.   There is none,
None left for me—my noble brother slain !
    CHOR. Death is the lot of human race.
    ELEC.   But, oh !
Not death like his—entangled in the reins,
His mangled body dragged along the field.
    CHOR. A strange unthought-of chance.
    ELEC.   And then to fall
A wretched stranger in a foreign land !
    CHOR. Oh horrible !
    ELEC.   No sister there to close
His dying eyes, to grace him with a tomb,
Or pay the last sad tributary tear.

ACT III.

Scene I.

Chrysothemis, Electra, Chorus.

Chrysothemis. Forgive me, sister, if my hasty steps
Press unexpected on thee; but I come
With joyful tidings, to relieve thy toils,
And make thee happy.

Elec.   What canst thou have found
To soften ills that will admit no cure?

Chry. Orestes is arrived; as sure as here
I stand before thee, the dear youth is come.

Elec. Canst thou then make a mockery of my woes;
Or dost thou rave?

Chry.   No, by our father's gods,
I do not mean to scoff; but he is come.

Elec. Alas! who told thee so? What tongue deceived
Thy credulous ear?

Chry.   Know, from myself alone
I learned the truth, and confirmations strong
Oblige me to believe it.

Elec.   What firm proof
Canst thou produce? What hast thou seen or known
To raise such flattering hopes?

Chry.   Oh! by the gods,
I beg thee but to hear me, then approve
Or blame, impartial.

Elec.   If to tell thy tale
Can give thee pleasure, say it; I attend.

Chry. Know, then, that soon as to our father's tomb
Eager I came, my wondering eyes beheld
Down from its side a milky fountain flow,
As lately poured by some benignant hand;
With various flowers the sacred spot adorned
Increased my doubts: on every side I looked
And listened long impatient for the tread

Of human footsteps there; but all was peace.
Fearless approaching then the hallowed spot,
I saw it spread with fresh devoted hair;
Instant my soul recalled its dearest hope,
Nor doubted whence the pious offerings came;
I snatched them up and silent gazed, while joy
Sprang in my heart, and filled my eyes with tears —
They were, they must be his; ourselves alone
Excepted, who could bring them? 'twas not I,
And 'tis not given to thee to leave these walls
E'en for the gods : our mother scarce would do
So good an office; or e'en grant she might,
We must have known it soon.   Be confident,
It was Orestes then.   Rejoice, Electra,
Sister, rejoice!   The same destructive power
Doth not for ever rule.   Behold at last
A milder god, and happier days appear!

    ELEC. Madness and folly! How I pity thee!
    CHRY. Have I not brought most joyful tidings to
      thee?
    ELEC. Alas!   Thou knowst not where nor what thou
      art?
    CHRY. Not know it?   Not believe what I have seen?
    ELEC. I tell thee, wretched as thou art, he's dead;
He and thy hoped-for bliss are gone together.
Thou must not think of it.
    CHRY.   A wretch indeed
I am, if this be so; but oh! from whom,
Where didst thou learn the fatal news?
    ELEC.   From one
Who was a witness of his death.
    CHRY.   Where is he?
Amazement chills my soul.
    ELEC.   He is within;
And no unwelcome guest to Clytemnestra.
    CHRY. Alas! who then could bring those pious gifts?
    ELEC. Some friend of lost Orestes placed them there.
    CHRY. I flew with joy to tell thee better news,
And little thought to hear so sad a tale.
The griefs I came to cure are present still,
And a new weight of woes is come upon us.

ELEC. But know, my sister, all may yet be well,
If thou wilt hear me.
CHRY.   Can I raise the dead ?
ELEC. I am not mad that I should ask it of thee
CHRY. What wouldst thou have me do ?
ELEC.   I'd have thee act
As I shall dictate to thee.
CHRY.   If aught good
It may produce, I do consent.
ELEC.   Remember
That if we hope to prosper, we must bear ;
Success in all that's human must depend
On patience and on toil.
CHRY.   I know it well,
And stand resolved to bear my part in all.
ELEC. Hear then the solemn purport of my soul.
Thou knowst too well how friendless and forlorn
We both are left, by death bereaved of all
Who could support us.   Whilst Orestes lived,
I cherished flattering thoughts of sweet revenge ;
But he is gone, and thou art now my hope.
Yes, thou must join (for I will tell thee all)
With thy Electra to destroy Ægisthus—
To kill the murderer.   Why should we delay ?
Is aught of comfort left ?   Thou canst but weep
Thy ravished fortunes torn unjustly from thee ;
Thou canst but mourn thy loss of nuptial rites,
And each domestic bliss.   For, O my sister !
The tyrant cannot be so weak of soul
As e'er to suffer our detested race
To send new branches forth for his destruction.
Assist me then.   So shalt thou best deserve
A father's praises and a brother's love ;
So shalt thou still, as thou wert born, be free,
And gain a partner worthy of thy bed.
Dost thou not hear th' applauding voice of fame,
And every tongue conspire to praise the deed ?
Will they not mark us as we pass along,
And cry aloud, " Behold the noble pair !
The pious sisters who preserved their race,
Whose daring souls, unawed by danger, sought

The tyrant's life, regardless of their own.
What love to these, what reverence is due!
These shall th' assembled nation throng to praise,
And every feast with public honours crown,
The fit reward of more than female virtue."
Thus will they talk, my sister, whilst we live,
And after death our names shall be immortal.
Aid then a brother's, aid a sister's cause,
Think on thy father's wrongs, preserve Electra,
Preserve thyself; and, oh! remember well
That to the noble mind a life dishonoured
Is infamy and shame.

  CHOR.   Be prudence now
The guide of both.

  CHRY.   Her mind was sure disturbed,
My friends, or she would ne'er have talked so wildly.
Tell me, I beg thee tell me, my Electra,
How couldst thou think so rash an enterprise
Could e'er succeed, or how request my aid?
Hast thou considered what thou art? A woman,
Weak and defenceless, to thy foes unequal.
Fortune thou seest each hour flows in upon them,
Nor deigns to look on us. What hand shall deal
The fatal blow and pass unpunished for it?
Take heed, my sister, lest, thy counsel heard,
A heavier fate than what we now lament
Fall on us both. What will our boasted fame
Avail us then? It is not death alone
We have to fear—to die is not the worst
Of human ills; it is to wish for death
And be refused the boon. Consider well,
Ere we destroy ourselves and all our race.
Be patient, dear Electra; for thy words,
As they had ne'er been uttered, here they rest;
Learn to be wise at last, and when thou knowst
Resistance vain, submit to powers superior.

  CHOR. Submit, convinced that prudence is the
   first
Of human blessings.

  ELEC.   'Tis as I expected;
I knew full well thou wouldst reject my counsel.

But I can act alone; nor shall this arm
Shrink at the blow, or leave its work unfinished.

CHRY. Would thou hadst shown this so much vaunted
    prowess
When our loved father died!

ELEC.   I was the same
By nature then, but of a weaker mind.

CHRY. Be sure thy courage fail thee not hereafter.

ELEC. Thy aid will ne'er increase it.

CHRY.   'Twill be wanted;
For those who act thus rashly must expect
The fate they merit.

ELEC.   I admire thy prudence,
But I detest thy cowardice.

CHRY.   I hear thee
With patience; for the time must one day come
When thou shalt praise me.

ELEC.   Never.

CHRY.   Be that left
For time to judge; enough remains.

ELEC.   Away!
There's no dependence on thee.

CHRY.   But there is,
Hadst thou a mind disposed for its acceptance.

ELEC. Go, tell thy mother all.

CHRY.   I am not yet
So much thy enemy.

ELEC.   And yet would lead me
To infamy.

CHRY   To safety and to wisdom.

ELEC. Must I then judge as thy superior reason
May dictate to me?

CHRY.   When thy better mind
Shall come, I'll not refuse to follow thee.

ELEC. Pity who talks so well should act so poorly!

CHRY. That censure falls on thee.

ELEC.   What I have said
Is truth.

CHRY.   Truth, sister, may be dangerous.

ELEC. Rather than thus submit I will not live.

CHRY. Hereafter thou wilt praise me.

ELEC. shall act
As seems most fit, nor wait for thy direction.
CHRY. Art thou resolved then? Wilt thou not repent
And take my counsel?
ELEC. Counsel such as thine
Is of all ills the worst.
CHRY. Because, Electra,
Thou dost not seem to understand it.
ELEC. Know then,
That long ere this I had determined all.
CHRY. Then fare thee well! Thou canst not bear my
words,
Nor I thy actions.
ELEC. Go thy ways. Henceforth
I will not commune with thee. Nor thy prayers—
No, nor thy tears—should ever bend me to it;
Such idle commerce were the height of folly.
CHRY. If thou dost think this wisdom, think so still;
But when destruction comes, thou wilt approve
My better counsel, and be wise too late. [*Exeunt.*

SCENE II.

CHORUS.

Strophe 1.

Man's ungrateful wretched race
Shall the birds of heaven disgrace,
Whose ever-watchful, ever-pious young
Protect the feeble parent whence they sprung?
But if the blast of angry Jove
Hath power to strike, or justice reigns above,
Not long unpunished shall such crimes remain;
When thou, O Fame! the messenger of woe,
Shalt bear these tidings to the realms below,
Tidings to Grecia's chiefs of sorrow and of pain.

Antistrophe.

Bid the sad Atridæ mourn
Their house by cruel faction torn;
Tell 'em, no'longer, by affection joined,
The tender sisters bear a friendly mind;
The poor Electra now alone,
Making her fruitless solitary moan,
Like Philomela, weeps her father's fate;
Fearless of death and every human ill,
Resolved her steady vengeance to fulfil—
Was ever child so good, or piety so great!

Strophe 2.

Still are the virtuous and the good
By adverse fortune unsubdued,
Nor e'er will stoop to infamy and shame;
Thus Electra dauntless rose
The war to wage with virtue's foes,
To gain the meed of never-ending fame,

Antistrophe 2.

Far, far above thine enemies,
In power and splendour mayst thou rise,
And future bliss compensate present woe!
For thou hast shown thy pious love,
By all that's dear to heaven above,
Or sacred held by mortals here below.   [*Exeunt.*

ACT IV.

Scene I.

Orestes, Pylades (*with Attendants*), Electra, Chorus.

Orestes. Say, virgins, if by right instruction led
This way, I tend to——
        Chor.   Whither wouldst thou go?

Ores. The palace of Ægisthus.

Chor.   Stranger, well
Wert thou directed; thou art there already.

Ores. Who then amongst your train shall kindly
    speak
A friend's approach, who comes with joyful news
Of highest import?

Chor. [*pointing to* Electra]. Be that office hers
Whom bound by Nature's ties it best befits.

Ores. Go then, and say from Phocis are arrived
Who beg admittance to the king.

Elec.   Alas!
And com'st thou then to prove the dreadful tale
Already told?

Ores.   What you have heard I know not,
But of Orestes came I here to speak
By Strophius's command.

Elec.   What is it, say;
Oh, how I dread thy message!

Ores. [*showing the Urn*].   Here behold
His poor remains——

Elec.   O lost, undone Electra!
'Tis then too plain, and misery is complete.

Ores. If for Orestes thus thy sorrows flow,
Know that within this urn his ashes lie.

Elec. Do they indeed? Then let me, by the gods
I do entreat thee, let me snatch them from thee!
Let me embrace them—let me weep my fate,
And mourn our hapless race.

Ores.   Give her the urn,
Whoe'er she be; for not with hostile mind
She craves the boon; perhaps some friend, perhaps
By blood united.

Elec. [*taking the Urn*]. O ye dear remains
Of my Orestes, the most loved of men!
How do I see thee now! How much unlike
What my fond hopes presaged, when last we parted!
I sent thee forth with all the bloom of youth
Fresh on thy cheek, and now, O dismal change!
I bear thee in these hands an empty shade.
Would I had died ere I had sent thee hence,

Ere I had saved thee from the tyrant's hand!
Would thou hadst died thyself that dreadful day,
And joined thy murdered father in the tomb,
Rather than thus a wretched exile fallen,
Far from thy sister, in a foreign land!
I was not there with pious hands to wash
Thy breathless corpse, or from the greedy flame
To gather up thy ashes.   What have all
My pleasing toils, my fruitless cares availed,
E'en from thy infant years, that as a mother
I watched thee still, and as a mother loved?
I would not trust thee to a servant's hand,
But was myself the guardian of thy youth,
Thy dear companion.   All is gone with thee!
Alas! thy death, like the devouring storm,
Hath borne down all.   Thy father is no more,
And thou art gone, and I am going too.
Our foes rejoice.   Our mother, mad with joy,
Smiles at our miseries—that unnatural mother,
She whom thou oft hast promised to destroy.
But cruel fate hath blasted all my hopes,
And for my dear Orestes left me naught
But this poor shadow.   Oh! th' accursed place
Where I had sent thee!   Oh! my hapless brother,
Thou hast destroyed Electra.   Take me then—
Oh! take me to thee!   Let this urn enclose
My ashes too, and dust to dust be joined,
That we may dwell together once again:
In life united by one hapless fate,
I would not wish in death to be divided.
The dead are free from sorrows.

CHOR.   Fair Electra!
Do not indulge thy griefs; but, oh! remember,
Sprung from a mortal like thyself, Orestes
Was mortal too—that we are mortal all.

    ORES. [*aside*]. What shall I say?   I can refrain no
      longer.
    ELEC. Why this emotion?
    ORES. [*looking at* ELECTRA]. Can it be Electra,
That lovely form?
    ELEC.   It is indeed that wretch.

ORES. Oh, dreadful!

ELEC.   Stranger, dost thou weep for me?

ORES. By impious hands to perish thus!

ELEC.   For me
Doubtless thou weepst, for I am changed indeed.

ORES. Of nuptial rites, and each domestic joy
To live deprived!

ELEC.   Why dost thou gaze upon me?

ORES. Alas! I did not know I was so wretched.

ELEC. Why, what hath made thee so?

ORES.   I see thy woes.

ELEC. Not half of them.

ORES.   Can there be worse than these?

ELEC. To live with murderers!

ORES.   What murderers, whom?

ELEC. The murderers of my father; bound to serve
them.

ORES. Who binds thee?

ELEC.   One who calls herself a mother;
A name she little merits.

ORES.   But say, how?
Doth she withhold the means of life, or act
With brutal violence to thee?

ELEC.   Both, alas!
Are my hard lot; she tries a thousand means
To make me wretched.

ORES.   And will none assist,
Will none defend thee?

ELEC.   None. My only hope
Lies buried there.

ORES.   Oh! how I pity thee!

ELEC. 'Tis kindly done; for none will pity me—
None but thyself. Art thou indeed a stranger,
Or doth some nearer tie unite our sorrows?

ORES. I could unfold a tale. But—say, these
virgins,
May I depend on them?

ELEC.   They are our friends,
And faithful all.

ORES.   Then lay the urn aside,
And I will tell thee.

ELEC.   Do not take it from me;
Do not, dear stranger.
    ORES.   But I must indeed.
    ELEC. Do not, I beg thee.
    ORES.   Come, you'll not repent it.
    ELEC. O my poor brother! If thy dear remains
Are wrested from me, I am most unhappy.
    ORES. No more; thou must not grieve for him.
    ELEC.   Not grieve
For my Orestes?
    ORES.   No; you should not weep.
    ELEC. Am I unworthy of him then?
    ORES.   Oh, no!
But do not grieve.
    ELEC.   Not when I bear the ashes
Of my dear brother?
    ORES.   But they are not there
Unless by fiction and a well-wrought tale,
That hath deceived thee.
    ELEC.   Where then is his tomb?
    ORES. The living need none.
    ELEC.   Ha! what sayst thou?
    ORES.   Truth.
    ELEC. Does he then live?
    ORES.   If I have life, he lives.
    ELEC. And art thou he?
    ORES.   Look here, and be convinced;
This mark, 'tis from our father.
    ELEC.   O blest hour!
    ORES. Blessed indeed!
    ELEC.   Art thou then here?
    ORES.   I am.
    ELEC. Do I embrace thee?
    ORES.   Mayst thou do it long!
    ELEC. O my companions! O my dearest friends!
Do ye not see Orestes, once by art
And cruel fiction torn from life and me,
But now by better art to life restored?
    CHOR. Daughter, we do; and see 'midst all our
      woes
From every eye fast flow the tears of joy.

ELEC. Oh! ye are come, my friends, in happiest hour,
E'en to behold, to find again the man
Whom your souls wished for, ye are come.
  CHOR.   We are;
But oh! in silence hide thy joys, Electra.
  ELEC. Wherefore in silence?
  CHOR.   Lest our foes within
Should hear thee.
  ELEC.   Never, by the virgin power
Of chaste Diana, will I hide my joys,
Nor meanly stoop to fear an idle throng
Of helpless women.
  ORES.   Women have their power,
And that thou knowest.
  ELEC.   Alas! and so I do;
For oh! thou hast called back the sad remembrance
Of that misfortune which admits no cure,
And ne'er can be forgot.
  ORES.   A fitter time
May come when we must think of that.
  ELEC.   All times,
All hours are fit to talk of justice in,
And best the present, now when I am free.
  ORES. Thou art so, be so still.
  ELEC.   What's to be done?
  ORES. Talk not, when prudence should restrain thy
    tongue.
  ELEC. Who shall restrain it? Who shall bind Electra
To fearful silence, when Orestes comes?
When thus I see thee here, beyond my thoughts,
Beyond my hopes!
  ORES.   The gods have sent me to thee;
They bade me come.
  ELEC.   Indeed! More grateful still
Is thy return. If by the gods' command
Thou cam'st, the gods will sure protect thee here.
  ORES. I would not damp thy joys, and yet I fear
Lest they should carry thee too far.
  ELEC.   Oh, no!
But after so long absence, thus returned
To thy afflicted sister, sure thou wouldst not——

ORES. Do what?

ELEC. Thou wouldst not grudge me the dear pleasure
Of looking on thee.

ORES.   No; nor suffer any
To rob thee of it.

ELEC.   Shall I then!

ORES.   No doubt.

ELEC. I hear that voice, my friends, I never thought
To hear again. Ye know, when I received
The dreadful news, I kept my grief within,
Silent and sad; but now I have thee here,
Now I behold thee, now I fix my eyes
On that dear form, which never was forgotten.

ORES. Spend not thy time in fruitless words, nor tell
     me
How Clytemnestra lives, nor how Ægisthus
Hath lavished all our wealth. The present hour
Demands our strict attention. Tell me how,
Whether by fraud, or open force, our foes
May best be vanquished. Let no cheerful smile
Betray thee to thy mother. Seem to grieve
As thou wert wont. When we have done the deed,
Joy shall appear, and we will smile in safety.

ELEC. Thy will is mine. Not to myself I owe
My present bliss; I have it all from thee—
From thee, my brother; nor should aught persuade me
To give Orestes e'en a moment's pain.
That were ungrateful to th' indulgent power
Who thus hath smiled propitious. Know, Ægisthus
Has left the palace; Clytemnestra's there;
And for thy needless fears that I should smile,
Or wear a cheerful face, I never shall—
Hatred so strong is rooted in my soul,
The sight of them will make me sad enough.
The tears of joy perhaps may flow for thee,
And add to the deceit; for flow they must,
When I behold thee in one happy hour
Thus snatched from life, and thus to life restored.
I could not hope it. Oh! 'tis passing strange!
If from the tomb our father should arise
And say he lived, I think I should believe him;

And oh ! when thou art come so far, 'tis fit
I yield to thee in all.   Do thou direct
My every step; but know, had I been left
Alone, e'en I would not have failed in all,
But conquered bravely, or as bravely fell.

Ores. No more.   I hear the footsteps as of one
Coming this way.

Elec.   Strangers, go in, and bear
That which with joy they cannot but receive,
But which with joy they will not long possess.

Scene II.

GOVERNOR OF ORESTES, ELECTRA, ORESTES, CHORUS.

Gov. Madness and folly thus to linger here !
Have ye no thought ?   Is life not worth your care ?
Do ye not know the dangers that surround you ?
Had I not watched myself before the palace,
Ere ye had entered, all your secret plan
Had been discovered to our foes within.
Wherefore no more of this tumultuous joy,
And lengthened converse; 'tis not fitting now.
Go in ; away, delays are dangerous
At such an hour ; our fate depends upon it.

Ores. May I with safety ?   Is all well within ?

Gov. None can suspect you.

Ores.   Spake you of my death
As we determined ?

Gov.   Living as thou art,
They do account thee one among the dead.

Ores. And are they glad ?   What say they ?

Gov.   By-and-by
We'll talk of that ; let it suffice that all
Is right within ; and that which most they think so,
May prove most fatal to them.

Elec. [*pointing to the* GOVERNOR]. Who is this?

Ores. Do you not know ?

Elec.   I cannot recollect him.

Ores. Not know the man to whom you trusted me !
Under whose care——

ELEC.   When? how?

ORES.   To Phocis sent,
I 'scaped the tyrant.

ELEC.   Can it then be he,
Among the faithless only faithful found
When our dear father fell?

ORES.   It is the same.

ELEC. [*to the* GOVERNOR]. Dearest of men, great
    guardian of our race,
Art thou then here?   Thou, who hast saved us both
From countless woes!   Swift were thy feet to bring
Glad tidings to me, and thy hand stretched forth
Its welcome succour.   But, oh! why deceive me?
Why wouldst thou kill me with thy dreadful tale,
E'en when thou hadst such happiness in store?
Hail! father, hail!—for I must call thee so—
Know, thou hast been to me, in one short day,
Both the most hated and most loved of men.

Gov. No more of that.   We shall have time enough
To talk of it hereafter.   Let us go.
This is the hour; the queen is now alone,
And not a man within.   If ye delay,
Expect to meet more formidable foes,
In wisdom and in numbers far superior.

ORES. We will not talk, my Pylades, but act.
Let us go in.   But to the gods who guard
This place be first due adoration paid.

ELEC. Hear, then, Apollo, great Lycæan, hear
Their humble prayer!   Oh! hear Electra too,
Who with unsparing hand her choicest gifts
Hath never failed to lay before thy altars!
Accept the little all which now remains
For me to give, accept my humblest prayers,
My vows, my adorations; smile propitious
On all our counsels!   Oh! assist us now,
And show mankind what punishment remains
For guilty mortals from offended Heaven.   [*Exeunt.*

CHORUS.

Strophe.

Behold, he comes! the slaughter-bearing god
Mars, ever thirsting for the murderer's blood;
    And see! the dogs of war are close behind;
Naught can escape their all-devouring rage.
This did my conscious heart long since presage,
    And the fair dream that struck my raptured mind.

Antistrophe.

Th' avenger steals along with silent feet,
And sharpened sword, to his paternal seat,
    His injured father's wrongs to vindicate;
Concealed from all by Maia's fraudful son,
Who safe conducts him till the deed be done,
    Nor longer will delay the needful work of fate.

                                 [*Exeunt.*

ACT V.

SCENE I.

ELECTRA, CHORUS.

ELECTRA. O my dear friends! they are about it now.
The deed is doing. But be still.
    CHOR.   What deed?
How? where?
    ELEC.   She doth prepare the funeral banquet;
But they are not far from her.
    CHOR.   Why then leave them?
    ELEC. To watch Ægisthus, lest he steal upon us
And blast our purpose.
    CLY. [*behind the scenes*]. Oh! I am betrayed!
My palace full of murderers; not a friend
Left to protect me.

ELEC.   Some one cries within ;
Did you not hear ?
CHOR.   It is too horrible
For mortal ear ; I tremble at the sound.
CLY. [*within*]. Ægisthus, oh ! where art thou ?
ELEC.   Hark ! again
The voice, and louder.
CLY. [*within*].   O my child ! my child !
Pity thy mother, pity her who bore thee !
ELEC. Be thine the pity which thou showedst to him,
And to his father.
CHOR.   O unhappy kingdom !
O wretched race ! thy misery is full ;
This day will finish all.
CLY. [*within*].   Oh ! I am wounded !
ELEC. Another stroke—another, if thou canst !
CLY. Ah me ! again !
ELEC.   Oh ! that Ægisthus too
Groaned with thee now !
CHOR.   Then vengeance is complete.
The dead arise and shed their murderers' blood
In copious streams.

SCENE II.

ORESTES, PYLADES, GOVERNOR OF ORESTES, ELECTRA,
                CHORUS.

ELEC. Behold them here ! their hands
Dropping with gore, a pious sacrifice
To the great god of war.   How is 't, Orestes ?
ORES. 'Tis very well.   All 's well, if there be truth
In great Apollo's oracles.   She 's dead.
Thou needst not fear a cruel mother now.
CHOR. No more ! Ægisthus comes.
ELEC.   Instant go in ;
Do you not see him ?   Joyful he returns.
CHOR. Retire.   Thus far is right—go on, and prosper.
ORES. Fear not !   We'll do it.
CHOR.   . But immediately.
ORES. I'm gone.
                [*Exeunt* ORESTES, PYLADES, *and* GOVERNOR.

Elec.   For what remains here to be done,
Be it my care.   I'll whisper in his ear
A few soft flattering words, that he may rush
Unknowing down precipitate on ruin.

Scene III.

Ægisthus, Electra, Chorus.

Ægis. Which of you knows aught of these Phocian
      guests,
Who come to tell us of Orestes' death?
You first I ask, Electra, once so proud
And fierce of soul; it doth concern you most;
And therefore you, I think, can best inform me.
  Elec. Yes, I can tell thee.   Is it possible
I should not know it?   That were not to know
A circumstance of dearest import to me.
  Ægis. Where are they then?
  Elec.   Within.
  Ægis.   And spake they truth?
  Elec. They did; a truth not proved by words alone,
But facts undoubted.
  Ægis.   Shall we see him then?
  Elec. Aye, and a dreadful sight it is to see.
  Ægis. Thou art not wont to give me so much joy;
Now I am glad indeed.
  Elec.   Glad mayst thou be,
If aught there is in that can give thee joy.
  Ægis. Silence within! and let my palace gates
Be opened all—that Argos and Mycenæ
May send her millions forth to view the sight;
And if there are who nourish idle hopes
That still Orestes lives, behold him here,
And learn submission, nor inflame the crowd
Against their lawful sovereign, lest they feel
An angry monarch's heaviest vengeance on them.
  Elec. Already I have learned the task, and yield
To power superior.

Scene IV.

Opens and discovers the Body of Clytemnestra *extended on a bier, and covered with a veil.*

Orestes, Pylades, Governor of Orestes, Ægisthus, Electra, Chorus, *and a Crowd of Spectators from the city.*

Ægis.   What a sight is here!
O deity supreme! this could not be
But by thy will; and whether Nemesis
Shall still o'ertake me for my crime, I know not.
Take off the veil, that I may view him well;
He was by blood allied, and therefore claims
Our decent sorrows.
      Ores.   Take it off thyself!
'Tis not my office; thee it best befits
To see and to lament.
      Ægis.   And so it does;
And I will do it.   Send Clytemnestra hither.
                              [*Taking off the veil.*
      Ores. She is before thee.
      Ægis.   Ha! what do I see?
      Ores. Why, what's the matter?   What affrights thee
          so?
Do you not see him?
      Ægis.   In what dreadful snare
Am I then fallen?
      Ores.   Dost thou not now behold
That thou art talking with the dead?
      Ægis.   Alas!
Too well I see it, and thou art—Orestes.
      Ores. So great a prophet thou, and guess so ill!
      Ægis. I know that I am lost, undone for ever;
But let me speak to thee.
      Elec.   Do not, Orestes;
No, not a word.   What can a moment's space
Profit a wretch like him, to death devoted?
Quick let him die, and cast his carcase forth

To dogs and vultures ; they will best perform
Fit obsequies for him.   By this alone
We can be free and happy.

    ORES.   Get thee in !
This is no time for talk—thy life, thy life !

    ÆGIS. But why go in ?   If what thou meanst to do
Be just, what need of darkness to conceal it ?
Why not destroy me here ?

    ORES.   It is not thine
Now to command.   Hence to the fatal place
Where our dear father fell, and perish there.

    ÆGIS. This palace then is doomed to be the witness
Of all the present, all the future woes
Of Pelops' hapless race.

    ORES.   Of thine, at least
It shall be witness ; that 's my prophecy,
And a most true one.

    ÆGIS.   'Tis not from thy father.

    ORES. Thou talkst, and time is lost.   Away !

    ÆGIS.   I follow.

    ORES. Thou shalt go first.

    ÆGIS.   Thinkst thou I mean to fly ?

    ORES. No ; but I'd make thy end most bitter to thee
In every circumstance, nor let thee choose
The softest means.   Were all like thee to perish
Who violate the laws, 'twould lessen much
The guilt of mortals, and reform mankind.   *[Exeunt.*

    CHOR. O race of Atreus ! after all thy woes,
How art thou thus by one adventurous deed
To freedom and to happiness restored !

PHILOCTETES.

DRAMATIS PERSONÆ.

ULYSSES, *King of Ithaca.*
NEOPTOLEMUS, *Son of Achilles.*
PHILOCTETES, *Son of Pæan and Companion of Hercules.*
A SPY.

HERCULES.
CHORUS, *composed of the Companions of Ulysses and Neoptolemus.*

SCENE.—LEMNOS, *near a Grotto in a rock by the Seaside.*

ACT I.

SCENE I.

ULYSSES, NEOPTOLEMUS, ATTENDANT.

ULYSSES. At length, my noble friend, thou bravest son
Of a brave father—father of us all,
The great Achilles—we have reached the shore
Of sea-girt Lemnos, desert and forlorn,
Where never tread of human step is seen,
Or voice of mortal heard, save his alone,
Poor Philoctetes, Pæan's wretched son,
Whom here I left; for such were my commands
From Grecia's chiefs, when by his fatal wound
Oppressed, his groans and execrations dreadful
Alarmed our hosts, our sacred rites profaned,
And interrupted holy sacrifice.

D

But why should I repeat the tale? The time
Admits not of delay. We must not linger,
Lest he discover our arrival here,
And all our purposed fraud to draw him hence
Be ineffectual. Lend me then thy aid.
Surveying round thee, canst thou see a rock
With double entrance—to the sun's warm rays
In winter open, and in summer's heat
Giving free passage to the welcome breeze?
A little to the left there is a fountain
Of living water, where, if yet he breathes,
He slakes his thirst. If aught thou seest of this
Inform me; so shall each to each impart
Council most fit, and serve our common cause.

 Neo. [*leaving* Ulysses *a little behind him*]. If I
  mistake not, I behold a cave,
E'en such as thou describst.
 Uly.   Dost thou? which way?
 Neo. Yonder it is; but no path leading thither,
Or trace of human footstep.
 Uly.   In his cell
A chance but he hath lain him down to rest;
Look if he hath not.
 Neo. [*advancing to the cave*]. Not a creature there.
 Uly. Nor food, nor mark of household preparation?
 Neo. A rustic bed of scattered leaves.
 Uly.   What more?
 Neo. A wooden bowl, the work of some rude hand,
With a few sticks for fuel.
 Uly.   This is all
His little treasure here.
 Neo.   Unhappy man!
Some linen for his wounds.
 Uly.   This must be then
His place of habitation; far from hence
He cannot roam; distempered as he is,
It were impossible. He is but gone
A little way for needful food, or herb
Of power to 'suage and mitigate his pain.
Wherefore despatch this servant to some place
Of observation, whence he may espy

His every motion, lest he rush upon us.
There's not a Grecian whom his soul so much
Could wish to crush beneath him as Ulysses.
[*Makes a signal to the Attendant, who retires.*

Scene II.

Neoptolemus, Ulysses.

Neo. He's gone to guard each avenue; and now,
If thou hast aught of moment to impart
Touching our purpose, say it; I attend
Uly. Son of Achilles, mark me well! Remember,
What we are doing not on strength alone,
Or courage, but on conduct will depend;
Therefore if aught uncommon be proposed,
Strange to thy ears and adverse to thy nature,
Reflect that 'tis thy duty to comply,
And act conjunctive with me.
Neo. Well, what is it?
Uly. We must deceive this Philoctetes; that
Will be thy task. When he shall ask thee who
And what thou art, Achilles' son reply—
Thus far within the verge of truth, no more.
Add that resentment fired thee to forsake
The Grecian fleet, and seek thy native soil,
Unkindly used by those who long with vows
Had sought thy aid to humble haughty Troy,
And when thou cam'st, ungrateful as they were,
The arms of great Achilles, thy just right,
Gave to Ulysses. Here thy bitter taunts
And sharp invectives liberally bestow
On me. Say what thou wilt, I shall forgive,
And Greece will not forgive thee if thou dost not;
For against Troy thy efforts are all vain
Without his arrows. Safely thou mayst hold
Friendship and converse with him, but I cannot.
Thou wert not with us when the war began,
Nor bound by solemn oath to join our host,

D 2

As I was; me he knows, and if he find
That I am with thee, we are both undone.
They must be ours then, these all-conquering arms;
Remember that.   I know thy noble nature
Abhors the thought of treachery or fraud.
But what a glorious prize is victory!
Therefore be bold : we will be just hereafter.
Give to deceit and me a little portion
Of one short day, and for thy future life
Be called the holiest, worthiest, best of men.

    NEO. What but to hear alarms my conscious soul,
Son of Laertes, I shall never practise.
I was not born to flatter or betray;
Nor I, nor he—the voice of fame reports—
Who gave me birth.   What open arms can do .
Behold me prompt to act, but ne'er to fraud
Will I descend.   Sure we can more than match
In strength a foe thus lame and impotent.
I came to be a helpmate to thee, not
A base betrayer; and, O king! believe me,
Rather, much rather would I fall by virtue
Than rise by guilt to certain victory.

    ULY. O noble youth! and worthy of thy sire!
When I like thee was young, like thee of strength
And courage boastful, little did I deem
Of human policy; but long experience
Hath taught me, son, 'tis not the powerful arm,
But soft enchanting tongue that governs all.

    NEO. And thou wouldst have me tell an odious false-
       hood?

   ULY. He must be gained by fraud.

    NEO.   By fraud?   And why
Not by persuasion?

    ULY.   ·   He'll not listen to it;
And force were vainer still.

    NEO.   What mighty power
Hath he to boast?

    ULY.   His arrows winged with death
Inevitable.

    NEO.   Then it were not safe
E'en to approach him.

ULY.   No; unless by fraud
He be secured.

NEO.   And thinkst thou 'tis not base
To tell a lie then?

ULY.   Not if on that lie
Depends our safety.

NEO.   Who shall dare to tell it
Without a blush?

ULY.   We need not blush at aught
That may promote our interest and success.

NEO. But where 's the interest that should bias me?
Come he or not to Troy, imports it aught
To Neoptolemus?

ULY.   Troy cannot fall
Without his arrows.

NEO.   Saidst thou not that I
Was destined to destroy her?

ULY.   Without them
Naught canst thou do, and they without thee nothing.

NEO. Then I must have them.

ULY.   When thou hast, remember
A double prize awaits thee.

NEO.   What, Ulysses?

ULY. The glorious names of valiant and of wise.

NEO. Away! I'll do it.   Thoughts of guilt or shame
No more appal me.

ULY.   Wilt thou do it then?
Wilt thou remember what I told thee of?

NEO. Depend on 't; I have promised—that 's sufficient.

ULY. Here then remain thou; I must not be seen.
If thou stay long, I'll send a faithful spy,
Who in a sailor's habit well disguised
May pass unknown; of him, from time to time,
What best may suit our purpose thou shalt know.
I'll to the ship.   Farewell! and may the god
Who brought us here, the fraudful Mercury,
And great Minerva, guardian of our country,
And ever kind to me, protect us still!   [*Exeunt.*

SCENE III.

CHORUS, NEOPTOLEMUS.

CHOR. Master, instruct us, strangers as we are,
What we may utter, what we must conceal.
Doubtless the man we seek will entertain
Suspicion of us; how are we to act?
To those alone belongs the art to rule
Who bear the sceptre from the hand of Jove;
To thee of right devolves the power supreme,
From thy great ancestors delivered down;
Speak then, our royal lord, and we obey.

NEO. If you would penetrate yon deep recess
To seek the cave where Philoctetes lies,
Go forward; but remember to return
When the poor wanderer comes this way, prepared
To aid our purpose here if need require.

CHOR. O king! we ever meant to fix our eyes
On thee, and wait attentive to thy will;
But, tell us, in what part is he concealed?
'Tis fit we know the place, lest unobserved
He rush upon us. Which way doth it lie?
Seest thou his footsteps leading from the cave,
Or hither bent?

NEO. [*advancing towards the cave*]. Behold the double
    door
Of his poor dwelling, and the flinty bed.

CHOR. And whither is its wretched master gone?

NEO. Doubtless in search of food, and not far off,
For such his manner is; accustomed here,
So fame reports, to pierce with winged arrows
His savage prey for daily sustenance,
His wound still painful, and no hope of cure.

CHOR. Alas! I pity him. Without a friend,
Without a fellow-sufferer, left alone,
Deprived of all the mutual joys that flow
From sweet society—distempered too!
How can he bear it? O unhappy race
Of mortal man! doomed to an endless round

Of sorrows, and immeasurable woe !
Second to none in fair nobility
Was Philoctetes, of illustrious race ;
Yet here he lies, from every human aid
Far off removed, in dreadful solitude,
And mingles with the wild and savage herd ;
With them in famine and in misery
Consumes his days, and weeps their common fate,
Unheeded, save when babbling echo mourns
In bitterest notes responsive to his woe.

    NEO. And yet I wonder not ; for if aright
I judge, from angry heaven the sentence came,
And Chrysa was the cruel source of all ;
Nor doth this sad disease inflict him still
Incurable, without assenting gods ?
For so they have decreed, lest Troy should fall
Beneath his arrows ere th' appointed time
Of its destruction come.

    CHOR.   No more, my son !

    NEO. What sayst thou ?

    CHOR.   Sure I heard a dismal groan
Of some afflicted wretch.

    NEO.   Which way ?

    CHOR.   E'en now
I hear it, and the sound as of some step
Slow-moving this way. He is not far from us.
His plaints are louder now. Prepare, my son !

    NEO. For what ?

    CHOR.   New troubles; for behold he comes !
Not like the shepherd with his rural pipe
And cheerful song, but groaning heavily.
Either his wounded foot against some thorn
Hath struck, and pains him sorely, or perchance
He hath espied from far some ship attempting
To enter this inhospitable port,
And hence his cries to save it from destruction.

                                         [*Exeunt.*

ACT II.

Scene I.

Philoctetes, Neoptolemus, Chorus.

Philoctetes. Say, welcome strangers, what disastrous
    fate
Led you to this inhospitable shore,
Nor haven safe, nor habitation fit
Affording ever? Of what clime, what race?
Who are ye? Speak! If I may trust that garb,
Familiar once to me, ye are of Greece,
My much-loved country. Let me hear the sound
Of your long wished-for voices. Do not look
With horror on me, but in kind compassion
Pity a wretch deserted and forlorn
In this sad place. Oh! if ye come as friends,
Speak then, and answer—hold some converse with me,
For this at least from man to man is due.
    Neo. Know, stranger, first what most thou seemst to
    wish;
We are of Greece.
    Phil.   Oh! happiness to hear!
After so many years of dreadful silence,
How welcome was that sound! Oh! tell me, son,
What chance, what purpose, who conducted thee?
What brought thee thither, what propitious gale?
Who art thou? Tell me all—inform me quickly.
    Neo. Native of Scyros, hither I return;
My name is Neoptolemus, the son
Of brave Achilles. I have told thee all.
    Phil. Dear is thy country, and thy father dear
To me, thou darling of old Lycomede;
But tell me in what fleet, and whence thou cam'st.
    Neo. From Troy.
    Phil.   From Troy? I think thou wert not with us
When first our fleet sailed forth.

NEO.   Wert thou then there?
Or knowst thou aught of that great enterprise?
   PHIL. Know you not then the man whom you behold?
   NEO. How should I know whom I had never seen?
   PHIL. Have you ne'er heard of me, nor of my name?
Hath my sad story never reached your ear?
   NEO.   Never.
   PHIL. Alas! how hateful to the gods,
How very poor a wretch must I be then,
That Greece should never hear of woes like mine!
But they who sent me hither, they concealed them,
And smile triumphant, whilst my cruel wounds
Grow deeper still.   O, sprung from great Achilles!
Behold before thee Pæan's wretched son,
With whom, a chance but thou hast heard, remain
The dreadful arrows of renowned Alcides,
E'en the unhappy Philoctetes—him
Whom the Atridæ and the vile Ulysses
Inhuman left, distempered as I was
By the envenomed serpent's deep-felt wound.
Soon as they saw that, with long toil oppressed,
Sleep had o'ertaken me on the hollow rock,
There did they leave me when from Chrysa's shore
They bent their fatal course; a little food
And these few rags were all they would bestow.
Such one day be their fate!   Alas! my son,
How dreadful, thinkst thou, was that waking to me,
When from my sleep I rose and saw them not!
How did I weep! and mourn my wretched state!
When not a ship remained of all the fleet
That brought me here—no kind companion left
To minister or needful food or balm
To my sad wounds.   On every side I looked,
And nothing saw but woe; of that indeed
Measure too full.   For day succeeded day,
And still no comfort came; myself alone
Could to myself the means of life afford,
In this poor grotto.   On my bow I lived:
The winged dove, which my sharp arrow slew,
With pain I brought into my little hut,
And feasted there; then from the broken ice

I slaked my thirst, or crept into the wood
For useful fuel; from the stricken flint
I drew the latent spark, that warms me still
And still revives.   This with my humble roof
Preserve me, son.   But, oh! my wounds remain.
Thou seest an island desolate and waste;
No friendly port nor hopes of gain to tempt,
Nor host to welcome in the traveller;
Few seek the wild inhospitable shore.
By adverse winds, sometimes th' unwilling guests,
As well thou mayst suppose, were hither driven;
But when they came, they only pitied me,
Gave me a little food, or better garb
To shield me from the cold; in vain I prayed
That they would bear me to my native soil,
For none would listen.   Here for ten long years
Have I remained, whilst misery and famine
Keep fresh my wounds, and double my misfortune.
This have th' Atridæ and Ulysses done,
And may the gods with equal woes repay them!

   CHOR. O, son of Pæan! well might those, who came
And saw thee thus, in kind compassion weep;
I too must pity thee—I can no more.

   NEO. I can bear witness to thee, for I know
By sad experience what th' Atridæ are,
And what Ulysses.

   PHIL.   Hast thou suffered then?
And dost thou hate them too?

   NEO.   Oh! that these hands
Could vindicate my wrongs!   Mycenæ then
And Sparta should confess that Scyros boasts
Of sons as brave and valiant as their own.

   PHIL. O noble youth!   But wherefore cam'st thou
     hither?
Whence this resentment?

   NEO.   I will tell thee all,
If I can bear to tell it.   Know then, soon
As great Achilles died——

   PHIL.   Oh, stay, my son!
Is then Achilles dead?

   NEO.   He is, and not

By mortal hand, but by Apollo's shaft
Fell glorious.

PHIL.   Oh! most worthy of each other,
The slayer and the slain! Permit me, son,
To mourn his fate, ere I attend to thine.   [*He weeps.*

NEO. Alas! thou needst not weep for others' woes,
Thou hast enough already of thy own.

PHIL. 'Tis very true; and therefore to thy tale.

NEO. Thus then it was. Soon as Achilles died,
Phœnix, the guardian of his tender years,
Instant sailed forth, and sought me out at Scyros;
With him the wary chief Ulysses came.
They told me then (or true or false I know not),
My father dead, by me, and me alone
Proud Troy must fall. I yielded to their prayers;
I hoped to see at least the dear remains
Of him whom living I had long in vain
Wished to behold. Safe at Sigeum's port
Soon we arrived. In crowds the numerous host
Thronged to embrace me, called the gods to witness
In me once more they saw their loved Achilles
To life restored; but he, alas! was gone.
I shed the duteous tear, then sought my friends
Th' Atridæ—friends I thought 'em!—claimed the arms
Of my dead father, and what else remained
His late possession: when—O cruel words!
And wretched I to hear them—thus they answered:
"Son of Achilles, thou in vain demandst
Those arms already to Ulysses given;
The rest be thine." I wept. "And is it thus,"
Indignant I replied, "ye dare to give
My right away?" "Know, boy," Ulysses cried,
"That right was mine, and therefore they bestowed
The boon on me: me who preserved the arms,
And him who bore them too." With anger fired
At this proud speech, I threatened all that rage
Could dictate to me if he not returned them.
Stung with my words, yet calm, he answered me:
"Thou wert not with us; thou wert in a place,
Where thou shouldst not have been; and since thou
   meanst

To brave us thus, know, thou shalt never bear
Those arms with thee to Scyros; 'tis resolved."
Thus injured, thus deprived of all I held
Most precious, by the worst of men, I left
The hateful place, and seek my native soil.
Nor do I blame so much the proud Ulysses
As his base masters—army, city, all
Depend on those who rule.   When men grow vile
The guilt is theirs who taught them to be wicked.
I've told thee all, and him who hates the Atridæ
I hold a friend to me and to the gods.

CHORUS.

Strophe.

O Earth! thou mother of great Jove,
  Embracing all with universal love,
   Author benign of every good,
  Through whom Pactolus rolls his golden flood!
    To thee, whom in thy rapid car
    Fierce lions draw, I rose and made my prayer—
    To thee I made my sorrows known,
     When from Achilles' injured son
  Th' Atridæ gave the prize, that fatal day
  When proud Ulysses bore his arms away.

PHIL. I wonder not, my friend, to see you here,
And I believe the tale; for well I know
The man who wronged you, know the base Ulysses
Falsehood and fraud dwell on his lips, and nought
That's just or good can be expected from him.
But strange it is to me that, Ajax present,
He dare attempt it.
NEO.   Ajax is no more;
Had he been living, I had ne'er been spoiled
Thus of my right.
PHIL.   Is he then dead?
NEO.   He is.
PHIL. Alas! the son of Tydeus, and that slave,

Sold by his father Sisyphus, they live,
Unworthy as they are.
    NEO.   Alas! they do,
And flourish still.
    PHIL.   My old and worthy friend
The Pylian sage, how is he? He could see
Their arts, and would have given them better counsels.
    NEO. Weighed down with grief he lives, but most
       unhappy,
Weeps his lost son, his dear Antilochus.
    PHIL. O double woe! whom I could most have wished
To live and to be happy, those to perish!
Ulysses to survive! It should not be.
    NEO. Oh! tis a subtle foe; but deepest plans
May sometimes fail.
    PHIL.   Where was Patroclus then,
Thy father's dearest friend?
    NEO.   He too was dead.
In war, alas—so fate ordains it ever—
The coward 'scapes, the brave and virtuous fall.
    PHIL. It is too true; and now thou talkst of cowards,
Where is that worthless wretch, of readiest tongue,
Subtle and voluble?
    NEO.   Ulysses?
    PHIL.   No;
Thersites; ever talking, never heard.
    NEO. I have not seen him, but I hear he lives.
    PHIL. I did not doubt it: evil never dies;
The gods take care of that. If aught there be
Fraudful and vile, 'tis safe; the good and just
Perish unpitied by them. Wherefore is it?
When gods do ill, why should we worship them?
    NEO. Since thus it is, since virtue is oppressed,
And vice triumphant, who deserve to live
Are doomed to perish, and the guilty reign.
Henceforth, O son of Pæan! far from Troy
And the Atridæ will I live remote.
I would not see the man I cannot love.
My barren Scyros shall afford me refuge,
And home-felt joys delight my future days.
So, fare thee well, and may th' indulgent gods

Heal thy sad wound, and grant thee every wish
Thy soul can form! Once more, farewell! I go,
The first propitious gale.
    PHIL.   What! now, my son?
So soon?
    NEO.   Immediately; the time demands
We should be near, and ready to depart.
    PHIL. Now, by the memory of thy honoured sire,
By thy loved mother, by whate'er remains
On earth most dear to thee, oh! hear me now,
Thy suppliant! Do not, do not thus forsake me,
Alone, oppressed, deserted, as thou seest,
In this sad place. I shall, I know it must, be
A burthen to thee. But, oh! bear it kindly;
For ever doth the noble mind abhor
Th' ungenerous deed, and loves humanity;
Disgrace attends thee if thou dost forsake me,
If not, immortal fame rewards thy goodness.
Thou mayst convey me safe to Œta's shores
In one short day; I'll trouble you no longer.
Hide me in any part where I may least
Molest you. Hear me! By the guardian god
Of the poor suppliant, all-protecting Jove,
I beg. Behold me at thy feet, infirm,
And wretched as I am, I clasp thy knees.
Leave me not here then, where there is no mark
Of human footstep—take me to thy home!
Or to Eubœa's port, to Œta, thence
Short is the way to Trachin, or the banks
Of Sperchius' gentle stream, to meet my father,
If yet he lives; for, oh! I begged him oft
By those who hither came, to fetch me hence—
Or is he dead, or they neglectful bent
Their hasty course to their own native soil.
Be thou my better guide! Pity and save
The poor and wretched. Think, my son, how frail
And full of danger is the state of man—
Now prosperous, now adverse. Who feels no ills
Should therefore fear them; and when fortune smiles
Be doubly cautious, lest destruction come
Remorseless on him, and he fall unpitied.

CHOR. Oh, pity him, my lord, for bitterest woes
And trials most severe he hath recounted;
Far be such sad distress from those I love!
Oh! if thou hat'st the base Atridæ, now
Revenge thee on them, serve their deadliest foe;
Bear the poor suppliant to his native soil;
So shalt thou bless thy friend, and 'scape the wrath
Of the just gods, who still protect the wretched.

    NEO. Your proffered kindness, friends, may cost you
       dear;
When you shall feel his dreadful malady
Oppress you sore, you will repent it.

    CHOR.   Never
Shall that reproach be ours.

    NEO.   In generous pity
Of the afflicted thus to be o'ercome
Were most disgraceful to me; he shall go.
May the kind gods speed our departure hence,
And guide our vessels to the wished-for shore!

    PHIL. O happy hour! O kindest, best of men!
And you my dearest friends! how shall I thank you?
What shall I do to show my grateful heart?
Let us be gone! But, oh! permit me first
To take a last farewell of my poor hut,
Where I so long have lived. Perhaps you'll say
I must have had a noble mind to bear it.
The very sight to any eyes but mine
Were horrible, but sad necessity
At length prevailed, and made it pleasing to me

    CHOR. One from our ship, my lord, and with him
      comes
A stranger. Stop a moment till we hear
Their business with us.

             [*Enter a* SPY *in the habit of a Merchant,*
             with another Grecian.

SCENE II.

NEOPTOLEMUS, PHILOCTETES, CHORUS, SPY.

SPY.   Son of great Achilles,
Know, chance alone hath brought me hither, driven
By adverse winds to where thy vessels lay,
As home I sailed from Troy.   There did I meet
This my companion, who informed me where
Thou mightst be found.   Hence to pursue my course
And not to tell thee what concerns thee near
Had been ungenerous, thou perhaps meantime
Of Greece and of her counsels naught suspecting,
Counsels against thee not by threats alone
Or words enforced, but now in execution.
   NEO. Now by my virtue, stranger, for thy news
I am much bound to thee, and will repay
Thy service.   Tell me what the Greeks have done.
   SPY. A fleet already sails to fetch thee back,
Conducted by old Phœnix, and the sons
Of valiant Theseus.
   NEO.   Come they then to force me ?
Or am I to be won by their persuasion ?
   SPY. I know not that ; you have what I could learn.
   NEO. And did th' Atridæ send them ?
   SPY.   Sent they are,
And will be with you soon.
   NEO.   But wherefore then
Came not Ulysses ?   Did his courage fail ?
   SPY. He, ere I left the camp, with Diomede
On some important embassy sailed forth
In search—
   NEO.   Of whom ?
   SPY.   There was a man—but stay,
Who is thy friend here, tell me, but speak softly.
                  [*Whispering him.*
   NEO. The famous Philoctetes.
   SPY,   Ha ! begone then !
Ask me no more—away, immediately !

PHIL. What do these dark mysterious whispers mean?
Concern they me, my son?
NEO.　　　　　　　　I know not what
He means to say, but I would have him speak
Boldly before us all, whate'er it be.
SPY. Do not betray me to the Grecian host,
Nor make me speak what I would fain conceal.
I am but poor—they have befriended me.
NEO. In me thou seest an enemy confest
To the Atridæ.　This is my best friend
Because he hates them too; if thou art mine,
Hide nothing then.
SPY.　　　　　　Consider first.
NEO.　　　　　　　　　I have.
SPY. The blame will be on you.
NEO.　　　　　　　　Why, let it be:
But speak, I charge thee.
SPY.　　　　　　Since I must then, know,
In solemn league combined, the bold Ulysses
And gallant Diomede have sworn by force
Or by persuasion to bring back thy friend:
The Grecians heard Laertes' son declare
His purpose; far more resolute he seemed
Than Diomede, and surer of success.
NEO. But why th' Atridae, after so long time,
Again should wish to see this wretched exile?
Whence this desire?　Came it from th' angry gods
To punish thus their inhumanity?
SPY. I can inform you; for perhaps from Greece
Of late you have not heard.　There was a prophet,
Son of old Priam, Helenus by name,
Him, in his midnight walks, the wily chief
Ulysses, curse of every tongue, espied;
Took him, and led him captive, to the Greeks
A welcome spoil.　Much he foretold to all,
And added last that Troy should never fall
Till Philoctetes from this isle returned.
Ulysses heard, and instant promise gave
To fetch him hence; he hoped by gentle means
To gain him; those successless, force at last
Could but compel him.　He would go, he cried,

And if he failed his head should pay the forfeit.
I've told thee all, and warn thee to be gone,
Thou and thy friend, if thou wouldst wish to save him.

 PHIL. And does the traitor think he can persuade me?
As well might he persuade me to return
From death to life, as his base father did.

 SPY. Of that I know not : I must to my ship.
Farewell, and may the gods protect you both! [*Exit.*

 PHIL. Lead me—expose me to the Grecian host!
And could the insolent Ulysses hope
With his soft flatteries e'er to conquer me?
No! Sooner would I listen to the voice
Of that fell serpent, whose envenomed tongue
Hath lamed me thus. But what is there he dare not
Or say or do? I know he will be here
E'en now, depend on't. Therefore, let's away!
Quick let the sea divide us from Ulysses.
Let us be gone; for well-timed expedition,
The task performed, brings safety and repose.

 NEO. Soon as the wind permits us we embark,
But now 'tis adverse.

 PHIL.   Every wind is fair
When we are flying from misfortune.

 NEO.   True;
And 'tis against them too.

 PHIL.   Alas! no storms
Can drive back fraud and rapine from their prey.

 NEO. I'm ready. Take what may be necessary,
And follow me.

 PHIL.   I want not much.

 NEO.   Perhaps
My ship will furnish you.

 PHIL.   There is a plant
Which to my wound gives some relief; I must
Have that.

 NEO.   Is there aught else?

 PHIL.   Alas! my bow
I had forgot. I must not lose that treasure.
    [PHILOCTETES *steps towards his Grotto, and
     brings out his bow and arrows.*

 NEO. Are these the famous arrows then?

PHIL. They are.

NEO. And may I be permitted to behold,
To touch, to pay my adoration to them?

PHIL. In these, my son, in everything that 's mine
Thou hast a right.

NEO. But if it be a crime.
I would not; otherwise——

PHIL. Oh! thou art full
Of piety; in thee it is no crime;
In thee, my friend, by whom alone I look
Once more with pleasure on the radiant sun—
By whom I live—who giv'st me to return
To my dear father, to my friends, my country:
Sunk as I was beneath my foes, once more
I rise to triumph o'er them by thy aid:
Behold them, touch them, but return them to me,
And boast that virtue which on thee alone
Bestowed such honour. Virtue made them mine.
I can deny thee nothing: he, whose heart
Is grateful can alone deserve the name
Of friend, to every treasure far superior.

NEO. Go in.

PHIL. Come with me; for my painful wound
Requires thy friendly hand to help me onward.

(*Exeunt.*

CHORUS.

Strophe.

Since proud Ixion, doomed to feel
The tortures of th' eternal wheel,
   Bound by the hand of angry Jove,
Received the due rewards of impious love;
  Ne'er was distress so deep or woe so great
  As on the wretched Philoctetes wait;
   Who ever with the just and good,
   Guiltless of fraud and rapine, stood,
And the fair paths of virtue still pursued;
Alone on this inhospitable shore,
Where waves for ever beat and tempests roar,
   How could he e'er or hope or comfort know,
Or painful life support beneath such weight of woe?

Antistrophe.

Exposed to the inclement skies,
Deserted and forlorn he lies,
No friend or fellow-mourner there
To soothe his sorrows and divide his care,
Or seek the healing plant of power to 'suage
His aching wound and mitigate its rage;
 But if perchance, awhile released
 From torturing pain, he sinks to rest,
Awakened soon, and by sharp hunger prest,
Compelled to wander forth in search of food,
He crawls in anguish to the neighbouring wood;
Even as the tottering infant in despair
Who mourns an absent mother's kind supporting care.

Strophe 2.

The teeming earth, who mortals still supplies
With every good, to him her seed denies;
 A stranger to the joy that flows
From the kind aid which man on man bestows;
 Nor food, alas! to him was given,
Save when his arrows pierced the birds of heaven;
Nor e'er did Bacchus' heart-expanding bowl
 For ten long years relieve his cheerless soul;
 But glad was he his eager thirst to slake
In the unwholesome pool, or ever-stagnant lake.

Antistrophe 2.

But now, behold the joyful captive freed;
A fairer fate, and brighter days succeed:
 For he at last hath found a friend
Of noblest race, to save and to defend,
 To guide him with protecting hand,
And safe restore him to his native land;
On Sperchius' flowery banks to join the throng
Of Melian nymphs, and lead the choral song
On Œta's top, which saw Alcides rise,
And from the flaming pile ascend his native skies.

ACT III.

SCENE I.

NEOPTOLEMUS, PHILOCTETES, CHORUS.

NEO. Come, Philoctetes; why thus silent?   Wherefore
This sudden terror on thee?
   PHIL.   Oh!
   NEO.   Whence is it?
   PHIL. Nothing, my son; go on!
   NEO.   Is it thy wound
That pains thee thus?
   PHIL.   No; I am better now.
O gods!
   NEO.   Why dost thou call thus on the gods?
   PHIL. To smile propitious, and preserve us——   Oh!
   NEO. Thou art in misery.   Tell me—wilt thou not?
What is it?
   PHIL.   O my son! I can no longer
Conceal it from thee.   Oh! I die, I perish;
By the great gods let me implore thee, now
This moment, if thou hast a sword, oh! strike,
Cut off this painful limb, and end my being!
   NEO. What can this mean, that unexpected thus
It should torment thee?
   PHIL.   Know you not, my son?
   NEO. What is the cause?
   PHIL.   Can you not guess it?
   NEO.   No.
   PHIL. Nor I.
   NEO.   That's stranger still.
   PHIL.   My son, my son!
   NEO. This new attack is terrible indeed!
   PHIL. 'Tis inexpressible!   Have pity on me!
   NEO. What shall I do?
   PHIL.   Do not be terrified,
And leave me.   Its returns are regular,

And like the traveller, when its appetite
Is satisfied, it will depart.   Oh! oh!
   Neo. Thou art oppressed with ills on every side.
Give me thy hand.   Come, wilt thou lean upon me?
    Phil. No; but these arrows, take; preserve 'em   for
    me.
A little while, till I grow better.   Sleep
Is coming on me, and my pains will cease.
Let me be quiet.   If meantime our foes
Surprise thee, let nor force nor artifice
Deprive thee of the great, the precious trust
I have reposed in thee; that were ruin
To thee, and to thy friend.
    Neo.   Be not afraid—
No hands but mine shall touch them; give them to me.
    Phil. Receive them, son; and let it be thy prayer
They bring not woes on thee, as they have done
To me and to Alcides.
                     [Gives him the bow and arrows.
   Neo.   May the gods
Forbid it ever!   May they guide our course
And speed our prosperous sails!
    Phil.   Alas! my son,
I fear thy vows are vain.   Behold my blood
Flows from the wound?   Oh! how it pains me!   Now
It comes, it hastens!   Do not, do not leave me!
Oh! that Ulysses felt this racking torture,
E'en to his inmost soul!   Again it comes!
O Agamemnon! Menelaus! why
Should not you bear these pangs as I have done?
O death! where art thou, death? so often called,
Wilt thou not listen? wilt thou never come?
Take thou the Lemnian fire, my generous friend,
Do me the same kind office which I did
For my Alcides.   These are thy reward;
He gave them to me.   Thou alone deservest
The great inheritance.   What says my friend?
What says my dear preserver?   Oh! where art thou?
    Neo. I mourn thy hapless fate.
    Phil.   Be of good cheer,

Quick my disorder comes, and goes as soon ;
I only beg thee not to leave me here.
  Neo. Depend on 't, I will stay.
  Phil.   Wilt thou indeed ?
  Neo. Trust me, I will.
  Phil.   I need not bind thee to it
By oath.
  Neo. Oh, no ! 'twere impious to forsake thee.
  Phil. Give me thy hand, and pledge thy faith.
  Neo.   I do.
  Phil. Thither, oh, thither lead !
               [Pointing up to heaven.
  Neo.   What sayst thou ? where ?
  Phil, Above.
  Neo.   What, lost again ? Why lookst thou thus
On that bright circle ?
  Phil.   Let me, let me go !
  Neo. *[lays hold of him].*   Where wouldst thou go ?
  Phil.   Loose me.
  Neo.   I will not.
  Phil.   Oh !
You'll kill me, if you do not.
  Neo. *[lets him go].*   There, then ; now
Is thy mind better ?
  Phil.   Oh ! receive me, earth !
Receive a dying man. Here must I lie ;
For, oh ! my pain's so great I cannot rise.
      *[Philoctetes sinks down on the earth near
        the entrance of the cave.*

Scene II.

Neoptolemus; Chorus.

  Neo. Sleep hath o'ertaken him. See, his head is lain
On the cold earth ; the balmy sweat thick drops
From every limb, and from the broken vein
Flows the warm blood ; let us indulge his slumbers.

Chorus.

INVOCATION TO SLEEP.

Sleep, thou patron of mankind,
Great physician of the mind,
Who dost nor pain nor sorrow know,
Sweetest balm of every woe,
Mildest sovereign, hear us now;
Hear thy wretched suppliant's vow;
His eyes in gentle slumbers close,
And continue his repose;
Hear thy wretched suppliant's vow,
Great physician, hear us now.

And now, my son, what best may suit thy purpose
Consider well, and how we are to act.
What more can we expect? The time is come;
For better far is opportunity
Seized at the lucky hour than all the counsels
Which wisdom dictates or which craft inspires.
   Neo. He hears us not. But easy as it is
To gain the prize, it would avail us nothing
Were he not with us? Phœbus hath reserved
For him alone the crown of victory;
But thus to boast of what we could not do,
And break our word, were most disgraceful to us.
   Chor. The gods will guide us, fear it not, my son;
But what thou sayst speak soft, for well thou knowst
The sick man's sleep is short. He may awake
And hear us; therefore let us hide our purpose.
If then thou thinkst as he does—thou knowst whom—
This is the hour. At such a time, my son,
The wisest err. But mark me, the wind's fair,
And Philoctetes sleeps, void of all help—
Lame, impotent, unable to resist,
He is as one among the dead. E'en now
We'll take him with us. 'Twere an easy task.
Leave it to me, my son. There is no danger.
   Neo. No more! His eyes are open. See, he moves.

Scene III.

Philoctetes, Neoptolemus, Chorus.

Phil. [*awaking*]. O fair returning light! beyond
 my hope;
You too, my kind preservers! O my son!
I could not think thou wouldst have stayed so long
In kind compassion to thy friend. Alas!
The Atridæ never would have acted thus.
But noble is thy nature, and thy birth,
And therefore little did my wretchedness,
Nor from my wounds the noisome stench deter
Thy generous heart. I have a little respite;
Help me, my son! I'll try to rise; this weakness
Will leave me soon, and then we'll go together.
 Neo. I little thought to find thee thus restored.
Trust me, I joy to see thee free from pain,
And hear thee speak; the marks of death were on thee.
Raise thyself up; thy friends here, if thou wilt,
Shall carry thee, 'twill be no burthen to them
If we request it.
 Phil. No; thy hand alone;
I will not trouble them; 'twill be enough
If they can bear with me and my distemper
When we embark.
 Neo. Well, be it so; but rise.
 Phil. [*rising*]. Oh! never fear; I'll rise as well as ever.
 [*Exeunt.*

ACT IV.

Scene I.

Neoptolemus, Philoctetes, Chorus.

Neoptolemus. How shall I act?
Phil. What says my son?

NEO.   Alas!
I know not what to say; my doubtful mind——
   PHIL. Talked you of doubts? You did not surely.
   NEO.   Aye,
That's my misfortune.
   PHIL.   Is then my distress
The cause at last you will not take me with you?
   NEO. All is distress and misery when we act
Against our nature and consent to ill.
   PHIL. But sure to help a good man in misfortunes
Is not against thy nature.
   NEO.   Men will call me
A villain; that distracts me.
   PHIL.   Not for this;
For what thou meanst to do thou mayst deserve it.
   NEO. What shall I do? Direct me, Jove! To hide
What I should speak, and tell a base untruth
Were double guilt.
   PHIL.   He purposes at last,
I fear it much, to leave me.
   NEO.   Leave thee! No!
But how to make thee go with pleasure hence,
There I'm distressed.
   PHIL.   I understand thee not;
What means my son?
   NEO.   I can no longer hide
The dreadful secret from thee; thou art going
To Troy, e'en to the Greeks, to the Atridæ.
   PHIL. Alas! what sayest thou?
   NEO.   Do not weep, but hear me.
   PHIL. What must I hear? what wilt thou do with me?
   NEO. First set thee free; then carry thee, my friend,
To conquer Troy.
   PHIL.   Is this indeed thy purpose?
   NEO. This am I bound to do.
   PHIL.   Then am I lost,
Undone, betrayed. Canst thou, my friend, do this?
Give me my arms again.
   NEO.   It cannot be.
I must obey the powers who sent me hither;
Justice enjoins—the common cause demands it.

PHIL. Thou worst of men, thou vile artificer
Of fraud most infamous, what hast thou done?
How have I been deceived? Dost thou not blush
To look upon me, to behold me thus
Beneath thy feet imploring? Base betrayer!
To rob me of my bow, the means of life,
The only means—give 'em, restore 'em to me!
Do not take all! Alas! he hears me not,
Nor deigns to speak, but casts an angry look
That says I never shall be free again.
O mountains, rivers, rocks, and savage herds!
To you I speak—to you alone I now
Must breathe my sorrows; you are wont to hear.
My sad complaints, and I will tell you all
That I have suffered from Achilles' son,
Who, bound by solemn oath to bear me hence
To my dear native soil, now sails for Troy.
The perjured wretch first gave his plighted hand,
Then stole the sacred arrows of my friend,
The son of Jove, the great Alcides; those
He means to show the Greeks, to snatch me hence
And boast his prize, as if poor Philoctetes,
This empty shade, were worthy of his arm.
Had I been what I was, he ne'er had thus
Subdued me, and e'en now to fraud alone
He owes the conquest. I have been betrayed!
Give me my arms again, and be thyself
Once more. Oh, speak! Thou wilt not? Then I'm lost.
O my poor hut! again I come to thee
Naked and destitute of food; once more
Receive me, here to die; for now, no longer
Shall my swift arrow reach the flying prey,
Or on the mountains pierce the wandering herd;
I shall myself afford a banquet now
To those I used to feed on—they the hunters,
And I their easy prey; so shall the blood
Which I so oft have shed be paid by mine;
And all this too fron him whom once I deemed
Stranger to fraud nor capable of ill;
And yet I will not curse thee till I know
Whether thou still retainst thy horrid purpose,

Or dost repent thee of it; if thou dost not,
Destruction wait thee!

CHOR.   We attend your pleasure,
My royal lord, we must be gone; determine
To leave, or take him with us.

NEO.   His distress
Doth move me much.   Trust me, I long have felt
Compassion for him.

PHIL.   Oh! then by the gods
Pity me now, my son, nor let mankind
Reproach thee for a fraud so base.

NEO.   Alas!
What shall I do?   Would I were still at Scyros!
For I am most unhappy.

PHIL.   O my son!
Thou art not base by nature, but misguided
By those who are, to deeds unworthy of thee.
Turn then thy fraud on them who best deserve it;
Restore my arms, and leave me.

NEO.   Speak, my friends,
What's to be done?

SCENE II.

PHILOCTETES, NEOPTOLEMUS, CHORUS, ULYSSES.

ULY.   Ah! dost thou hesitate?
Traitor, be gone!   Give me the arms.

PHIL.   Ah me!
Ulysses here?

ULY.   Aye! 'tis Ulysses' self
That stands before thee.

PHIL.   Then I'm lost, betrayed!
This was the cruel spoiler.

ULY.   Doubt it not.
'Twas I; I do confess it.

PHIL. [*to* NEOPTOLEMUS].   O my son!
Give me them back.

ULY.   It must not be; with them
Thyself must go, or we shall drag thee hence.

PHIL. And will they force me? O thou daring villain!

ULY. They will, unless thou dost consent to go.

PHIL. Wilt thou, O Lemnos! wilt thou, mighty
    Vulcan!
With thy all-conquering fire, permit me thus
To be torn from thee?

ULY.   Know, great Jove himself
Doth here preside. He hath decreed thy fate;
I but perform his will.

PHIL.   Detested wretch,
Mak'st thou the gods a cover for thy crime?
Do they teach falsehood?

ULY.   No, they taught me truth,
And therefore, hence—that way thy journey lies.
                    [*Pointing to the sea.*

PHIL. It doth not.

ULY.   But I say it must be so.

PHIL. And Philoctetes then was born a slave!
I did not know it.

ULY.   No; I mean to place thee
E'en with the noblest, e'en with those by whom
Proud Troy must perish.

PHIL.   Never will I go,
Befall what may, whilst this deep cave is open
To bury all my sorrows.

ULY.   What wouldst do?

PHIL. Here throw me down, dash out my desperate
    brains
Against this rock, and sprinkle it with my blood.

ULY. [*to the* CHORUS]. Seize, and prevent him!
                    [*They seize him.*

PHIL.   Manacled! O hands!
How helpless are you now! those arms, which once
Protected, thus torn from you!   [*To* ULYSSES.
                Thou abandoned,
Thou shameless wretch! from whom nor truth nor
    justice,
Naught that becomes the generous mind, can flow,
How hast thou used me! how betrayed! Suborned
This stranger, this poor youth, who, worthier far
To be my friend than thine, was only here
Thy instrument; he knew not what he did,

And now, thou seest, repents him of the crime
Which brought such guilt on him, such woes on me.
But thy foul soul, which from its dark recess
Trembling looks forth, beheld him void of art,
Unwilling as he was, instructed him,
And made him soon a master in deceit.
I am thy prisoner now; e'en now thou meanst
To drag me hence, from this unhappy shore,
Where first thy malice left me, a poor exile,
Deserted, friendless, and though living, dead
To all mankind.   Perish the vile betrayer!
Oh! I have cursed thee often, but the gods
Will never hear the prayers of Philoctetes.
Life and its joys are thine, whilst I, unhappy,
Am but the scorn of thee, and the Atridæ,
Thy haughty masters.   Fraud and force compelled
     thee,
Or thou hadst never sailed with them to Troy.
I lent my willing aid; with seven brave ships
I ploughed the main to serve them.   In return
They cast me forth, disgraced me, left me here.
Thou sayst they did it; they impute the crime
To thee.   And what will you do with me now?
And whither must I go?   What end, what purpose
Could urge thee to it?   I am nothing, lost
And dead already.   Wherefore—tell me, wherefore?—
Am I not still the same detested burthen,
Loathsome and lame?   Again must Philoctetes
Disturb your holy rites?   If I am with you
How can you make libations?   That was once
Your vile pretence for inhumanity.
Oh! may you perish for the deed!   The gods
Will grant it sure, if justice be their care—
And that it is I know.   You had not left
Your native soil to seek a wretch like me
Had not some impulse from the powers above,
Spite of yourselves, ordained it.   O my country!
And you, O gods! who look upon this deed,
Punish, in pity to me, punish all
The guilty band!   Could I behold them perish,
My wounds were nothing; that would heal them all.

CHOR. [*to* ULYSSES]. Observe, my lord, what bitterness
    of soul
His words express; he bends not to misfortune,
But seems to brave it.
    ULY.   I could answer him,
Were this a time for words; but now, no more
Than this—I act as best befits our purpose.
Where virtue, truth, and justice are required
Ulysses yields to none; I was not born
To be o'ercome, and yet submit to thee.
Let him remain. Thy arrows shall suffice;
We want thee not; Teucer can draw thy bow
As well as thou; myself with equal strength
Can aim the deadly shaft, with equal skill.
What could thy presence do? Let Lemnos keep thee.
Farewell! perhaps the honours once designed
For thee may be reserved to grace Ulysses.
    PHIL. Alas! shall Greece then see my deadliest foe
Adorned with arms which I alone should bear?
    ULY. No more! I must be gone.
    PHIL. [*to* NEOPTOLEMUS].   Son of Achilles,
Thou wilt not leave me too? I must not lose
Thy converse, thy assistance.
    ULY. [*to* NEOPTOLEMUS.   Look not on him;
Away, I charge thee! 'Twould be fatal to us.
    PHIL. [*to the* CHORUS]. Will you forsake me, friends?
        Dwells no compassion
Within your breasts for me?
    CHOR. [*pointing to* NEOPTOLEMUS]. He is our master;
We speak and act but as his will directs.
    NEO. I know he will upbraid me for this weakness,
But 'tis my nature, and I must consent,
Since Philoctetes asks it. Stay you with him,
Till to the gods our pious prayers we offer,
And all things are prepared for our departure;
Perhaps, meantime, to better thoughts his mind
May turn relenting. We must go. Remember,
When we shall call you, follow instantly.
                    [*Exit with* ULYSSES

Scene III.

Philoctetes, Chorus.

PHIL. O my poor hut ! and is it then decreed
Again I come to thee to part no more,
To end my wretched days in this sad cave,
The scene of all my woes ? For whither now
Can I betake me ? Who will feed, support,
Or cherish Philoctetes ? Not a hope
Remains for me. Oh ! that th' impetuous storms
Would bear me with them to some distant clime !
For I must perish here. .
CHOR.   Unhappy man !
Thou hast provoked thy fate ; thyself alone
Art to thyself a foe, to scorn the good,
Which wisdom bids thee take, and choose misfortune.
PHIL. Wretch that I am, to perish here alone !
Oh ! I shall see the face of man no more,
Nor shall my arrows pierce their wingèd prey,
And bring me sustenance ! Such vile delusions
Used to betray me ! Oh ! that pains like those
I feel might reach the author of my woes !
CHOR. The gods decreed it ; we are not to blame.
Heap not thy curses therefore on the guiltless,
But take our friendship.
PHIL. [*pointing to the sea-shore.*] I behold him there ;
E'en now I see him laughing me to scorn
On yonder shore, and in his hands the darts
He waves triumphant, which no arms but these
Had ever borne. O my dear glorious treasure !
Hadst thou a mind to feel th' indignity,
How wouldst thou grieve to change thy noble master,
The friend of great Alcides, for a wretch
So vile, so base, so impious as Ulysses !
CHOR. Justice will ever rule the good man's tongue,
Nor from his lips reproach and bitterness
Invidious flow. Ulysses, by the voice
Of Greece appointed, only sought a friend   .
To join the common cause, and serve his country.

PHIL. Hear me, ye winged inhabitants of air,
And you, who on these mountains love to feed,
My savage prey, whom once I could pursue;
Fearful no more of Philoctetes, fly
This hollow rock—I cannot hurt you now;
You need not dread to enter here.   Alas!
You now may come, and in your turn regale
On these poor limbs, when I shall be no more.
Where can I hope for food? or who can breathe
This vital air, when life-preserving earth
No longer will assist him?
 CHOR.   By the gods!
Let me entreat thee, if thou dost regard
Our master, and thy friend, come to him now,
Whilst thou mayst 'scape this sad calamity;
Who but thyself would choose to be unhappy
That could prevent it?
 PHIL.   Oh! you have brought back
Once more the sad remembrance of my griefs;
Why, why, my friends, would you afflict me thus?
 CHOR. Afflict thee—how?
 PHIL.   Think you I'll e'er return
To hateful Troy?
 CHOR.   We would advise thee to it.
 PHIL. I'll hear no more.   Go, leave me!
 CHOR.   That we shall
Most gladly.   To the ships, my friends; away! [*Going.*
Obey your orders.
 PHIL. [*stops them*]. By protecting Jove,
Who hears the suppliant's prayer, do not forsake me!
 CHOR. [*returning*]. Be calm then.
 PHIL.   O my friends! will you then stay?
Do, by the gods I beg you.
 CHOR.   Why that groan?
 PHIL. Alas! I die. My wound, my wound! Hereafter
What can I do?   You will not leave me!   Hear——
 CHOR. What canst thou say we do not know already?
 PHIL. O'erwhelmed by such a storm of griefs as I am,
You should not thus resent a madman's frenzy.
 CHOR. Comply then and be happy.
 PHIL.   Never, never!
              F.

Be sure of that.   Tho' thunder-bearing Jove
Should with his lightnings blast me, would I go?
No!   Let Troy perish, perish all the host
Who sent me here to die ; but, O my friends!
Grant me this last request.
    CHOR.   What is it?   Speak.
    PHIL. A sword, a dart, some instrument of death.
    CHOR. What wouldst thou do?
    PHIL.   I'd hack off every limb.
Death, my soul longs for death.
    CHOR.   But wherefore is it ?
    PHIL. I'll seek my father.
    CHOR.   Whither?
    PHIL.   In the tomb;
There he must be.   O Scyros! O my country !
How could I bear to see thee as I am—
I who had left thy sacred shores to aid
The hateful sons of Greece?   O misery !
                              [*Goes into the cave.   Exeunt.*

ACT V.

SCENE I.

ULYSSES, NEOPTOLEMUS, CHORUS.

    CHORUS. Ere now we should have taken thee to our
      ships,
But that advancing this way I behold
Ulysses, and with him Achilles' son.
    ULY. Why this return ?   Wherefore this haste?
    NEO.   I come
To purge me of my crimes.
    ULY.   Indeed!   What crimes?
    NEO. My blind obedience to the Grecian host
And to thy counsels.

ULY.   Hast thou practised aught
Base or unworthy of thee?
    NEO.   Yes; by art
And vile deceit betrayed th' unhappy.
    ULY.   Whom?
Alas! what mean you?
    NEO.   Nothing.   But the son
Of Pæan——
    ULY.   Ha! what wouldst thou do?   My heart
Misgives me.   [*Aside.*
    NEO.   I have ta'en his arms, and now——
    ULY. Thou wouldst restore them!   Speak!   Is that
        thy purpose?
Almighty Jove!
    NEO.   Unjustly should I keep
Another's right?
    ULY.   Now, by the gods, thou meanst
To mock me!   Dost thou not?
    NEO.   If to speak truth
Be mockery.
    ULY.   And does Achilles' son
Say this to me?
    NEO.   Why force me to repeat
My words so often to thee?
    ULY.   Once to hear them
Is once indeed too much.
    NEO.   Doubt then no more,
For I have told thee all.
    ULY.   There are, remember,
There are who may prevent thee.
    NEO.   Who shall dare
To thwart my purpose?
    ULY.   All the Grecian host,
And with them, I.
    NEO.   Wise as thou art, Ulysses,
Thou talkst most idly.
    ULY.   Wisdom is not thine
Either in word or deed.
    NEO.   Know, to be just
Is better far than to be wise.
    ULY.   But where,

Where is the justice, thus unauthorized,
To give a treasure back thou ow'st to me,
And to my counsels?
  NEO.   I have done a wrong,
And I will try to make atonement for it.
  ULY. Dost thou not fear the power of Greece?
  NEO.   I fear
Nor Greece nor thee, when I am doing right.
  ULY. 'Tis not with Troy then we contend, but thee.
  NEO. I know not that.
  ULY.   Seest thou this hand? behold,
It grasps my sword.
  NEO.   Mine is alike prepared,
Nor seeks delay.
  ULY.   But I will let thee go;
Greece shall know all thy guilt, and shall revenge it.
            [Exit ULYSSES.

SCENE II.

NEOPTOLEMUS, CHORUS.

NEO. 'Twas well determined; always be as wise
As now thou art, and thou mayst live in safety.
       [Approaching towards the cave.
Ho! son of Pæan! Philoctetes, leave
Thy rocky habitation, and come forth.
  PHIL. [*from the cave*]. What noise was that? Who
  calls on Philoctetes?   *[He comes out.*

SCENE III.

PHILOCTETES, NEOPTOLEMUS, CHORUS.

  PHIL. Alas! what would you, strangers? Are you
  come
To heap fresh miseries on me?
  NEO.   Be of comfort,
And hear the tidings which I bring.

PHIL. I dare not;
Thy flattering tongue already hath betrayed me.

NEO. And is there then no room for penitence?

PHIL. Such were thy words, when, seemingly sincere,
Yet meaning ill, thou stolst my arms away.

NEO. But now it is not so. I only came
To know if thou art resolute to stay,
Or sail with us.

PHIL. No more of that; 'tis vain
And useless all.

NEO. Art thou then fixed?

PHIL. I am;
It is impossible to say how firmly.

NEO. I thought I could have moved thee, but I've
done.

PHIL. 'Tis well thou hast; thy labour had been vain;
For never could my soul esteem the man
Who robbed me of my dearest, best possession,
And now would have me listen to his counsels—
Unworthy offspring of the best of men!
Perish th' Atridæ! perish first Ulysses!
Perish thyself!

NEO. Withhold thy imprecations,
And take thy arrows back.

PHIL. A second time
Wouldst thou deceive me?

NEO. By th' almighty power
Of sacred Jove I swear.

PHIL. O joyful sound!
If thou sayst truly.

NEO. Let my actions speak.
Stretch forth thy hand, and take thy arms again.

[*Gives him the arrows.*

SCENE IV.

ULYSSES, PHILOCTETES, NEOPTOLEMUS, CHORUS.

ULY. Witness ye gods! Here, in the name of Greece
And the Atridæ, I forbid it.

PHIL. Ha!
What voice is that? Ulysses'?
ULY. Aye, 'tis I—
I who perforce will carry thee to Troy
Spite of Achilles' son.
PHIL. [*raising his arm as intending to throw an
arrow at* ULYSSES]. Not if I aim
This shaft aright.
NEO. Now, by the gods, I beg thee
Stop thy rash hand! [*Laying hold of him.*
PHIL. Let go my arm.
NEO. I will not.
PHIL. Shall I not slay my enemy?
NEO. Oh, no!
'Twould cast dishonour on us both.
PHIL. Thou knowst,
These Grecian chiefs are loud pretending boasters,
Brave but in tongue, and cowards in the field.
NEO. I know it; but remember, I restored
Thy arrows to thee, and thou hast no cause
For rage or for complaint against thy friend.
PHIL. I own thy goodness. Thou hast shown thyself
Worthy thy birth; no son of Sisyphus,
But of Achilles, who on earth preserved
A fame unspotted, and amongst the dead
Still shines superior, an illustrious shade.
NEO. Joyful I thank thee for a father's praise,
And for my own; but listen to my words,
And mark me well. Misfortunes, which the gods
Inflict on mortals, they perforce must bear:
But when, oppressed by voluntary woes,
They make themselves unhappy, they deserve not
Our pity or our pardon. Such art thou.
Thy savage soul, impatient of advice,
Rejects the wholesome counsel of thy friend,
And treats him like a foe; but I will speak,
Jove be my witness! Therefore hear my words,
And grave them in thy heart. The dire disease
Thou long hast suffered is from angry heaven,
Which thus afflicts thee for thy rash approach
To the fell serpent, which on Chrysa's shore

Watched o'er the sacred treasures. Know beside,
That whilst the sun in yonder east shall rise,
Or in the west decline, distempered still
Thou ever shalt remain, unless to Troy
Thy willing mind transport thee. There the sons
Of Æsculapius shall restore thee—there
By my assistance shalt thou conquer Troy.
I know it well; for that prophetic sage,
The Trojan captive Helenus, foretold
It should be so. "Proud Troy (he added then)
This very year must fall; if not, my life
Shall answer for the falsehood." Therefore yield.
Thus to be deemed the first of Grecians, thus
By Pæan's favourite sons to be restored,
And thus marked out the conqueror of Troy,
Is sure distinguished happiness.
   PHIL.   O life!
Detested, why wilt thou still keep me here?
Why not dismiss me to the tomb! Alas!
What can I do? How can I disbelieve
My generous friend? I must consent, and yet
Can I do this, and look upon the sun?
Can I behold my friends—will they forgive,
Will they associate with me after this?
And you, ye heavenly orbs that roll around me,
How will ye bear to see me linked with those
Who have destroyed me, e'en the sons of Atreus,
E'en with Ulysses, source of all my woes?
My sufferings past I could forget; but oh!
I dread the woes to come; for well I know
When once the mind's corrupted it brings forth
Unnumbered crimes, and ills to ills succeed.
It moves my wonder much that thou, my friend,
Shouldst thus advise me, whom it ill becomes
To think of Troy. I rather had believed
Thou wouldst have sent me far, far off from those
Who have defrauded thee of thy just right,
And gave thy arms away. Are these the men
Whom thou wouldst serve? whom thou wouldst thus compel me
    To save and to defend? It must not be.

Remember, O my son! the solemn oath
Thou gav'st to bear me to my native soil.
Do this, my friend, remain thyself at Scyros,
And leave these wretches to be wretched still.
Thus shalt thou merit double thanks, from me
And from thy father; nor by succour given
To vile betrayers prove thyself as vile.

NEO. Thou sayst most truly.   Yet confide in heaven,
Trust to thy friend, and leave this hated place.

PHIL. Leave it! For whom? For Troy and the
    Atridæ?
These wounds forbid it.

NEO.   They shall all be healed,
Where I will carry thee.

PHIL.   An idle tale
Thou tellst me, surely; dost thou not?

NEO.   I speak
What best may serve us both.

PHIL.   But, speaking thus,
Dost thou not fear th' offended gods?

NEO.   Why fear them?
Can I offend the gods by doing good?

PHIL. What good? To whom? To me or to th'
    Atridæ?

NEO. I am thy friend, and therefore would persuade
    thee.

PHIL. And therefore give me to my foes.

NEO.   Alas!
Let not misfortunes thus transport thy soul
To rage and bitterness.

PHIL.   Thou wouldst destroy me.

NEO. Thou knowst me not.

PHIL. I know th' Atridæ well,
Who left me here.

NEO.   They did; yet they perhaps,
E'en they, O Philoctetes! may preserve thee.

PHIL. I never will to Troy.

NEO.   What's to be done?
Since I can ne'er persuade thee, I submit;
Live on in misery.

PHIL.　　　　　　　　Then let me suffer ;
Suffer I must ; but, oh ! perform thy promise ;
Think on thy plighted faith, and guard me home
Instant, my friend, nor ever call back Troy
To my remembrance ; I have felt enough
From Troy already.
　　NEO.　　　　　　　Let us go ; prepare !
　　PHIL. O glorious sound !
　　NEO.　　　　　　　　　Bear thyself up.
　　PHIL.　　　　　　　　　　　　　　I will,
If possible.
　　NEO.　　　But how shall I escape
The wrath of Greece ?
　　PHIL　　　　　Oh ! think not of it.
　　NEO..　　　　　　　　　　　What
If they should waste my kingdom ?
　　PHIL.　　　　　　　　　I'll be there.
　　NEO. Alas ! what canst thou do ?
　　PHIL.　　　　　　　　And with these arrows
Of my Alcides——
　　NEO.　　　　　Ha ! What sayst thou ?
　　PHIL.　　　　　　　　　　　　Drive
Thy foes before me. Not a Greek shall dare
Approach thy borders.
　　NEO.　　　　　　If thou wilt do this,
Salute the earth, and instant hence. Away !

SCENE IV.

HERCULES, ULYSSES, NEOPTOLEMUS, PHILOCTETES,
CHORUS.

　　HER. [*descends and speaks*]. Stay, son of Pæan ! Lo
　　　to thee 'tis given
Once more to see and hear thy loved Alcides,
Who for thy sake hath left yon heavenly mansions,
And comes to tell thee the decrees of Jove ;
To turn thee from the paths thou meanst to tread,

And guide thy footsteps right.   Therefore attend.
Thou knowst what toils, what labours I endured,
Ere I by virtue gained immortal fame ;
Thou too like me by toils must rise to glory—
Thou too must suffer, ere thou canst be happy;
Hence with thy friend to Troy, where honour calls,
Where health awaits thee—where, by virtue raised
To highest rank, and leader of the war,
Paris, its hateful author, shalt thou slay,
Lay waste proud Troy, and send thy trophies home,
Thy valour's due reward, to glad thy sire
On Œta's top.   The gifts which Greece bestows
Must thou reserve to grace my funeral pile,
And be a monument to after-ages
Of these all-conquering arms.   Son of Achilles
                              [*turning to* NEOPTOLEMUS
(For now to thee I speak), remember this,
Without his aid thou canst not conquer Troy,
Nor Philoctetes without thee succeed ;
Go then, and, like two lions in the field
Roaming for prey, guard ye each other well ;
My Æsculapius will I send e'en now
To heal thy wounds.   Then go, and conquer Troy ;
But when you lay the vanquished city waste,
Be careful that you venerate the gods ;
For far above all other gifts doth Jove,
Th' almighty father, hold true piety ;
Whether we live or die, that still survives
Beyond the reach of fate, and is immortal.
    NEO. Once more to let me hear that wished-for voice,
To see thee after so long time, was bliss
I could not hope for.   Oh! I will obey
Thy great commands most willingly.
    PHIL.   And I.
    HER. Delay not then.   For lo ! a prosperous wind
Swells in thy sail.   The time invites.   Adieu !
                              [HERCULES *reascends.*

SCENE V.

PHILOCTETES, ULYSSES, NEOPTOLEMUS, CHORUS.

PHIL. I will but pay my salutations here,
And instantly depart. To thee, my cave,
Where I so long have dwelt, I bid farewell!
And you, ye nymphs, who on the watery plains
Deign to reside, farewell! Farewell the noise
Of beating waves, which I so oft have heard
From the rough sea, which by the black winds driven
O'erwhelmed me, shivering. Oft th' Hermæan mount
Echoed my plaintive voice, by wintry storms
Afflicted, and returned me groan for groan.
Now, ye fresh fountains, each Lycæan spring,
I leave you now. Alas! I little thought
To leave you ever. And thou sea-girt isle,
Lemnos, farewell! Permit me to depart
By thee unblamed, and with a prosperous gale
To go where fate demands, where kindest friends
By counsel urge me, where all-powerful Jove
In his unerring wisdom hath decreed.

CHOR. Let us be gone, and to the ocean nymphs
Our humble prayers prefer, that they would all
Propitious smile, and grant us safe return.

ANTIGONE.

DRAMATIS PERSONÆ.

CREON, *King of Thebes.*
EURYDICE, *Wife of Creon.*
HÆMON, *Son of Creon.*
ANTIGONE, *Daughter of Œdipus.*
ISMENE, *Sister of Antigone.*

TIRESIAS, *a Prophet.*
A MESSENGER, GUARD, SER-
  VANT, *and* ATTENDANTS.
CHORUS, *composed of Ancient
  Men of Thebes.*

ACT I.

SCENE I.

ANTIGONE, ISMENE.

ANTIGONE. O my dear sister, my best-beloved Ismene!
Is there an evil, by the wrath of Jove
Reserved for Œdipus' unhappy race,
We have not felt already ? Sorrow and shame,
And bitterness and anguish, all that's sad,
All that's distressful, hath been ours, and now
This dreadful edict from the tyrant comes
To double our misfortunes. Hast thou heard
What harsh commands he hath imposed on all,
Or art thou still to know what future ills
Our foes have yet in store to make us wretched ?

Ism. Since that unhappy day, Antigone,
When by each other's hand our brothers fell,
And Greece dismissed her armies, I have heard
Naught that could give or joy or grief to me.

Ant. I thought thou wert a stranger to the tidings,
And therefore called thee forth, that here alone
I might impart them to thee.

Ism.   Oh! what are they?
For something dreadful labours in thy breast.

Ant. Know then, from Creon, our indulgent lord,
Our hapless brothers met a different fate:
To honour one, and one to infamy
He hath consigned.   With funeral rites he graced
The body of our dear Eteocles,
Whilst Polynices' wretched carcase lies
Unburied, unlamented, left exposed
A feast for hungry vultures on the plain.
No·pitying friend will dare to violate
The tyrant's harsh command, for public death
Awaits th' offender.   Creon comes himself
To tell us of it—such is our condition.
This is the crisis, this the hour, Ismene,
That must declare thee worthy of thy birth,
Or show thee mean, base, and degenerate.

Ism. What wouldst thou have me do?—defy his
     power?
Contemn the laws?

Ant.   To act with me, or not:
Consider and resolve.

Ism.   What daring deed
Wouldst thou attempt?   What is it?   Speak!

Ant.   To join
And take the body, my Ismene.

Ism.   Ha!
And wouldst thou dare to bury it, when thus
We are forbidden?

Ant.   Aye, to bury *him!*
He is my brother, and thine too, Ismene;
Therefore, consent or not, I have determined
I'll not disgrace my birth.

Ism.   Hath not the king
Pronounced it death to all?

ANT.   He hath no right,
No power to keep me from my own.
   ISM.   Alas!
Remember our unhappy father's fate:
His eyes torn out by his own fatal hand,
Oppressed with shame and infamy he died;
Fruit of his crimes! a mother, and a wife—
Dreadful alliance!—self-devoted, fell;
And last, in one sad day, Eteocles
And Polynices by each other slain.
Left as we are, deserted and forlorn,
What from our disobedience can we hope
But misery and ruin? Poor weak women,
Helpless, nor formed by nature to contend
With powerful man. We are his subjects too.
Therefore to this, and worse than this, my sister,
We must submit. For me, in humblest prayer
Will I address me to th' infernal powers
For pardon of that crime which well they know
Sprang from necessity, and then obey;
Since to attempt what we can never hope
To execute, is folly all and madness.
   ANT. Wert thou to proffer what I do not ask—
Thy poor assistance—I would scorn it now.
Act as thou wilt; I'll bury him myself;
Let me perform but that, and death is welcome:
I'll do the pious deed, and lay me down
By my dear brother. Loving and beloved
We'l rest together; to the powers below
'Tis sp. we pay obedience; longer there
We must remain than we can breathe on earth.
There I shall dwell for ever; thou, meantime,
What the gods hold most precious mayst despise.
   ISM. I reverence the gods; but, in defiance
Of laws, and unassisted to do this,
It were most dangerous.
   ANT.   That be thy excuse,
Whilst I prepare the funeral pile.
   ISM.   Alas!
I tremble for thee.
   ANT.   Tremble for thyself,
And not for me.

Ism.   Oh! do not tell thy purpose,
I beg thee, do not. I shall ne'er betray thee.
   Ant. I'd have it known; and I shall hate thee
      more
For thy concealment, than, if loud to all,
Thou wouldst proclaim the deed.
   Ism.   Thou hast a heart
Too daring, and ill-suited to thy fate.
   Ant. I know my duty, and I'll pay it there
Where 'twill be best accepted.
   Ism.   Couldst thou do it!
But 'tis not in thy power.
   Ant.   When I know that
It will be time enough to quit my purpose.
   Ism. It cannot be; 'tis folly to attempt it.
   Ant. Go on, and I shall hate thee! Our dead brother,
He too shall hate thee as his bitterest foe;
Go, leave me here to suffer for my rashness;
Whate'er befalls, it cannot be so dreadful
As not to die with honour.
   Ism.   Then farewell,
Since thou wilt have it so; and know, Ismene
Pities thy weakness, but admires thy virtue.   [*Exeunt.*

Scene II.

Chorus.

Strophe 1.

By Dirce's sweetly-flowing stream,
   Ne'er did the golden eye of day
On Thebes with fairer lustre beam,
   Or shine with more auspicious ray.
See the proud Argive, with his silver shield
   And glittering armour, quits the hostile plain;
No longer dares maintain the luckless field,
   But vanquished flies, nor checks the loosened rein.
With dreadful clangour, like the bird of Jove,
On snowy wings descending from above,

His vaunted powers to this devoted land,
  In bitterest wrath did Polynices lead,
With crested helmets, and a numerous band
  He came, and fondly hoped that Thebes should
    bleed.

Antistrophe 1.

High on the lofty tower he stood,
  And viewed th' encircled gates below,
With spears that thirsted for our blood,
  And seemed to scorn th' unequal foe;
But, fraught with vengeance, ere the rising flame
  Could waste our bulwarks, or our walls surround,
Mars to assist the fiery serpent came,
  And brought the towering eagle to the ground.
That god who hates the boastings of the proud
Saw the rude violence of th' exulting crowd;
  Already now the triumph was prepared,
    The wreath of victory and the festal song,
  When Jove the clash of golden armour heard,
    And hurled his thunder on the guilty throng.

Strophe 2.

Then Capaneus, elate with pride,
  Fierce as the rapid whirlwind came,
Eager he seemed on every side
  To spread the all-devouring flame;
But soon he felt the wingèd lightning's blast,
  By angry heaven with speedy vengeance sent—
Down from the lofty turrets headlong cast,
  For his foul crimes he met the punishment.
Each at his gate, long time the leaders strove,
Then fled, and left their arms to conquering Jove;
  Save the unhappy death-devoted pair,
    The wretched brethren, who unconquered stood,
  With rancorous hate inspired, and fell despair,
    They reeked their vengeance in each other's blood.

Antistrophe 2.

And lo! with smiles propitious see
   To Thebes, for numerous cars renowned,
The goddess comes, fair Victory,
   With fame and endless glory crowned!
Henceforth, no longer vexed by war's alarms,
   Let all our sorrows, all our labours cease;
Come, let us quit the din of rattling arms,
   And fill our temples with the songs of peace.
The god of Thebes shall guide our steps aright,
And crown with many a lay the festive night.
   But see, still anxious for his native land,
      Our king, Menæceus' valiant son, appear;
   With some fair omen by the gods' command
      He comes to met his aged council here.   [*Exeunt.*

ACT II.

SCENE I.

CREON, CHORUS

CREON. At length our empire, shook by civil broils,
The gods to peace and safety have restored;
Wherefore, my friends, you had our late request
That you should meet us here; for well I know
Your firm allegiance to great Laius, next
To Œdipus, and his unhappy sons;
These by each other's hand untimely slain,
To me the sceptre doth of right descend,
As next in blood. Never can man be know,
His mind, his will, his passions ne'er appear
Till power and office call them forth; for me,
'Tis my firm thought, and I have held it ever,
That he who rules and doth not follow that

Which wisdom counsels, but, restrained by fear,
Shuts up his lips, must be the worst of men;
Nor do I deem him worthy who prefers
A friend, how dear soever, to his country.
Should I behold—witness all-seeing Jove!—
This city wronged, I never would be silent,
Never would make the foe of Thebes my friend,
For on her safety must depend our own;
And if she flourish we can never want
Assistance or support.   Thus would I act,
And therefore have I sent my edict forth
Touching the sons of Œdipus, commanding
That they should bury him who nobly fought
And died for Thebes, the good Eteocles,
Gracing his memory with each honour due
To the illustrious dead.   For Polynices,
Abandoned exile, for a brother's blood
Thirsting insatiate—he who would in flames
Have wasted all, his country and his gods,
And made you slaves—I have decreed he lie
Unburied, his vile carcase to the birds
And hungry dogs a prey.   There let him rot
Inglorious—'tis my will; for ne'er from me
Shall vice inherit virtue's due reward,
But him alone who is a friend to Thebes,
Living or dead shall Creon reverence still.

 Chor. Son of Menæceus, 'twas thy great behest
Thus to reward them both; thine is the power
O'er all supreme, the living and the dead.
 Creon. Be careful then my orders are obeyed.
 Chor. O sir! to younger hands commit the task.
 Creon. I have appointed some to watch the body.
 Chor. What then remains for us?
 Creon.   To see that none
By your connivance violate the law.
 Chor. Scarce will the man be found so fond of death
As to attempt it.
 Creon.   Death is the reward
Of him who dares it; but oftimes by hope
Of sordid gain are men betrayed to ruin.

SCENE II.

MESSENGER, CREON, CHORUS.

MES. O king! I cannot boast that hither sent
I came with speed, for oft my troubled thoughts
Have driven me back; oft to myself I said,
Why dost thou seek destruction? Yet again
If thou report it not, from other tongues
Creon must hear the tale, and thou wilt suffer.
With doubts like these oppressed, slowly I came,
And the short way seemed like a tedious journey;
At length I come, resolved to tell thee all:
Whate'er the event, I must submit to fato.

CREON. Whence are thy fears, and why this hesita-
tion?

MES. First for myself; I merit not thy wrath;
It was not I, nor have I seen the man
Who did the guilty deed.

CREON.   Something of weight
Thou hast t'impart, by this unusual care
To guard thee from our anger.

MES.   Fear will come
Where danger is.

CREON.   Speak, and thou hast thy pardon.

MES. The body of Polynices some rash hand
Hath buried, scattered o'er his corpse the dust,
And funeral rites performed.

CREON.   Who dared do this?

MES. 'Tis yet unknown; no mark of instrument
Is left behind: the earth still level all,
Nor worn by track of chariot wheel. The guard,
Who watched that day, call it a miracle;
No tomb was raised; light lay the scattered earth,
As only meant to avoid the imputed curse;
Nor could we trace the steps of dog or beast
Passing that way. Instant a tumult rose;
The guards accused each other; nought was proved,
But each suspected each, and all denied,
Offering, in proof of innocence, to grasp

The burning steel, to walk through fire, and take
Their solemn oath they knew not of the deed ;
At length, one mightier than the rest, proposed—
Nor could we think of better means—that all
Should be to thee discovered ; 'twas my lot
To bring th' unwelcome tidings, and I come
To pour my news unwilling into ears
Unwilling to receive it, for I know
None ever loved the messenger of ill.

CHOR. To me it seems as if the hand of heaven
Were in this deed.

CREON. Be silent, ere my rage,
Thou rash old man, pronounce thee fool and dotard ;
Horrid suggestion ! Think'st thou, then, the gods
Take care of men like these? Would they preserve
Or honour him who came to burn their altars,
Profane their rites, and trample on their laws?
Will they reward the bad? It cannot be.
But well I know the murmuring citizens
Brooked not our mandate, shook their heads in
    secret,
And, ill-affected to me, would not stoop
Their haughty crests, or bend beneath my yoke.
By hire corrupted, some of these have dared
The venturous deed. Gold is the worst of ills
That ever plagued mankind : this wastes our cities,
Drives forth their natives to a foreign soil,
Taints the pure heart, and turns the virtuous mind
To basest deeds ; artificer of fraud
Supreme, and source of every wickedness.
The wretch corrupted for this hateful purpose
Must one day suffer ; for, observe me well,
As I revere that power by whom I swear,
Almighty Jove, if you conceal him from me,
If to my eyes you do not bring the traitor,
Know, death alone shall not suffice to glut
My vengeance ; living shall you hang in torments
Till you confess, till you have learned from me
There is a profit not to be desired,
And own dishonest gains have ruined more
Than they have saved.

MES.   O king! may I depart,
Or wait thy further orders?
    CREON.   Knowst thou not
Thy speech is hateful?   Hence!
    MES.   Wherefore, my lord?
    CREON. Know you not why?
    MES.   I but offend your ear,
They who have done the deed afflict your soul.
    CREON. Away!   Thy talk but makes thy guilt appear.
    MES. My lord, I did not do it.
    CREON.   Thou hast sold
Thy life for gain.
    MES.   'Tis cruel to suspect me.
    CREON. Thou talkst it bravely; but remember all,
Unless you do produce him, you shall find
The miseries which on ill-got wealth await.   [*Exit.*
    MES. Would he were found.   That we must leave to
        fate;
Be it as it may, I never will return:
Thus safe beyond my hopes, 'tis fit I pay
My thanks to the kind gods who have preserved me.
                            [*Exit.*

SCENE III.

CHORUS.

Strophe 1.

Since first this active world began,
Nature is busy all in every part;
But passing all in wisdom and in art,
    Superior shines inventive man:
Fearless of wintry winds and circling waves,
He rides the ocean and the tempest braves;
    On him unwearied earth with lavish hand,
    Immortal goddess, all her bounty pours,
Patient beneath the rigid plough's command,
    Year after year she yields her plenteous stores.

Antistrophe 1.

To drive the natives of the wood
From their rude haunts, or in the cruel snare,
To catch the winged inhabitants of air,
    Or trap the scaly brood;
To tame the fiery courser yet unbroke
With the hard rein, or to the untried yoke
To bend the mountain bull, who wildly free
    O'er the steep rocks had wandered unconfined—
These are the arts of mortal industry,
    And such the subtle power of humankind.

Strophe 2.

By learning, and fair science crowned,
Behold him now full-fraught with wisdom's lore,
The laws of nature anxious to explore,
    With depth of thought profound.
But naught, alas! can human wisdom see
In the dark bosom of futurity.
The power of wisdom may awhile prevail,
    Awhile suspend a mortal's fleeting breath,
But never can her fruitless arts avail
    To conquer fate, or stop the hand of death.

Antistrophe. 2.

Man's ever-active changeful will
Sometimes to good shall bend his virtuous mind,
Sometimes behold him to foul deeds inclined,
    And prone to every ill.
Who guiltless keeps the laws is still approved
By every tongue, and by his country loved;
    But he who doth not, from his native land
    A wretched exile, far, oh! far from me
May he be driven, by angry Heaven's command,
    And live devote to shame and infamy!

CHOR. Amazement! Can it be Antigone?
Or do my eyes deceive me? No, she comes.
O! wretched daughter of a wretched father!
Hast thou transgressed the laws, and art thou ta'en
In this adventurous deed, unhappy maid?

Scene IV.

Antigone, Guard, Chorus.

Guard. Behold the woman who hath done the deed!
I' th' very act of burial we surprised her.
Where is the king?
    Chor.   Returned, as we could wish;
E'en now he comes this way.

Scene V.

Creon, Antigone, Guard, Chorus.

    Creon.   Whom have we here?
Doth justice smile upon us?
    Guard.   O my lord!
Never should man too confident assert,
Much less by oath should bind himself to aught,
For soon our judgments change, and one opinion
Destroys another. By thy threats alarmed
But now, I vowed I never would return;
Yet thus preserved beyond my hopes, I come,
Bound by that duty which I owe to thee
And to my country, to bring here this virgin,
Whom, as she sprinkled o'er her brother's dust
The varied wreath, we seized. The willing task
Was mine, nor as of late by lot determined.
Receive her then, O king! Judge and condemn
The guilty as it best becomes thy wisdom;
Henceforth I stand acquitted.
    Creon.   But say how,
Where didst thou find her?
    Guard.   To say all, 'twas she
Who buried Polynices.
    Creon.   Art thou sure?
    Guard. These eyes beheld her.
    Creon.   But say, how discovered?
    Guard. Thus then it was. No sooner had I left thee

Than, mindful of thy wrath, with careful hands
From off the putrid carcase we removed
The scattered dust; then, to avoid the stench,
Exhaling noisome, to a hill retired;
There watched at distance, till the mid-day sun
Scorched o'er our heads. Sudden a storm arose,
Shook every leaf, and rattled through the grove,
Filling the troubled element. We closed
Our eyes, and patient bore the wrath of heaven.
At length the tempest ceased, when we beheld
This virgin issuing forth, and heard her cries
Distressful, like the plaintive bird who views
The plundered nest, and mourns her ravished young.
E'en thus the maid, when on the naked corse
She cast her eyes, loud shrieked, and cursed the hand
That did the impious deed, then sprinkled o'er
The crumbled earth, and from a brazen urn,
Of richest work, to the loved relics thrice
Her due libations poured. We saw, and straight
Pursued her. Unappalled she seemed, and still
As we did question her, confessed it all.
It pleased, and yet methought it grieved me too.
To find ourselves released from woe is bliss
Supreme, but thus to see our friends unhappy
Embitters all. I must be thankful still
For my own safety, which I hold most dear.

    CREON. Speak thou, who bendst to earth thy drooping
      head;
Dost thou deny the fact?
    ANT.   Deny it? No!
'Twas I.
    CREON. [*to the* GUARD]. Retire, for thou art free; and
      now   [*turning to* ANTIGONE
Be brief, and tell me; heardst thou our decree?
    ANT. I did; 'twas public. How could I avoid it?
    CREON. And dar'st thou then to disobey the law?
    ANT. I had it not from Jove, nor the just gods
Who rule below; nor could I ever think
A mortal's law of power or strength sufficient
To abrogate th' unwritten law divine,
Immutable, eternal, not like these

Of yesterday, but made ere time began.
Shall man persuade me then to violate
Heaven's great commands, and make the gods my foes?
Without thy mandate, death had one day come;
For who shall 'scape it? and if now I fall
A little sooner, 'tis the thing I wish.
To those who live in misery like me,
Believe me, king, 'tis happiness to die;
Without remorse I shall embrace my fate;
But to my brother had I left the rites
Of sepulture unpaid, I then indeed
Had been most wretched.   This to thee may seem
Madness and folly.   If it be, 'tis fit
I should act thus—it but resembles thee.

   CREON.   Sprung from a sire perverse and obstinate,
Like him she cannot bend beneath misfortune;
But know, the proudest hearts may be subdued;
Hast thou not marked the hardest steel by fire
Made soft and flexible?   Myself have seen
By a slight rein the fiery courser held.
'Tis not for slaves to be so haughty; yet
This proud offender, not content, it seems,
To violate my laws, adds crime to crime,
Smiles at my threats, and glories in her guilt;
If I should suffer her to 'scape my vengeance,
She were the man, not I; but though she sprang
E'en from my sister, were I bound to her
By ties more dear than is Hercæan Jove,
She should not 'scape.   Her sister too I find
Accomplice in the deed—go, call her forth!

                               [*to one of the Attendants*
She is within, I saw her raving there,
Her senses lost, the common fate of those
Who practise dark and deadly wickedness.

                               [*Turning to* ANTIGONE.
I cannot bear to see the guilty stand
Convicted of their crimes, and yet pretend
To gloss them o'er with specious names of virtue.

   ANT.   I am thy captive; thou wouldst have my life;
Will that content thee?

   CREON.   Yes; tis all I wish.

ANT. Why this delay then, when thou knowst my
To thee as hateful are as thine to me ?   [words
Therefore dispatch ; I cannot live to do
A deed more glorious ; and so these would all
                              [*pointing to the* CHORUS
Confess, were not their tongues restrained by fear ;
It is the tyrant's privilege, we know,
To speak and act whate'er he please, uncensured.
    CREON. Lives there another in the land of Thebes
Who thinks as thou dost ?
    ANT.   Yes, a thousand ; these—
These think so too, but dare not utter it.
    CREON. Dost thou not blush ?
    ANT.   For what ?   Why blush to pay
A sister's duty ?
    CREON.   But, Eteocles !
Say, was not he thy brother too ?
    ANT.   He was.
    CREON. Why then thus reverence him who least de-
        served it ?
    ANT. Perhaps that brother thinks not so.
    CREON.   He must,
If thou payst equal honour to them both.
    ANT. He was a brother, not a slave.
    CREON.   One fought
Against that country which the other saved.
    ANT. But equal death the rites of sepulture
Decrees to both.
    CREON.   What !   Reverence alike
The guilty and the innocent !
    ANT.   Perhaps
The gods below esteem it just.
    CREON.   A foe,
Though dead, should as a foe be treated still.
    ANT. My love shall go with thine, but not my hate.
    CREON. Go then, and love them in the tomb !   But know,
No woman rules in Thebes whilst Creon lives.
    CHOR. Lo !   At the portal stands the fair Ismene,
Tears in her lovely eyes, a cloud of grief
Sits on her brow, wetting her beauteous cheek
With pious sorrow for a sister's fate.

Scene VI.

Ismene, Antigone, Creon, Chorus.

Creon. Come forth, thou serpent! Little did I think
That I had nourished two such deadly foes
To suck my blood, and cast me from my throne.
What sayst thou? Wert thou accomplice in the deed,
Or wilt thou swear that thou art innocent?

Ism. I do acknowledge it, if she permit me;
I was accomplice, and the crime was mine.

Ant. 'Tis false; thou didst refuse, nor would I hold
Communion with thee.

Ism. But in thy misfortunes
Let me partake, my sister; let me be
A fellow-suffer with thee.

Ant. Witness, death,
And ye infernal gods, to which belongs
The great, the glorious deed! I do not love
These friends in word alone.

Ism. Antigone,
Do not despise me; I but ask to die
With thee, and pay due honours to the dead.

Ant. Pretend not to a merit which thou hast not.
Live thou; it is enough for me to perish.

Ism. But what is life without thee?

Ant. Ask thy friend
And patron there. [*Pointing to* Creon.

Ism. Why that unkind reproach,
When thou shouldst rather comfort me?

Ant. Alas!
It gives me pain when I am forced to speak
So bitterly against thee.

Ism. Is there aught
That I can do to save thee?

Ant. Save thyself,
I shall not envy thee.

Ism. And will you not
Permit me then to share your fate?

ANT.   Thy choice
Was life.   'Tis mine to die.

ISM.   I told thee oft
It would be so.

ANT.   Thou didst, and was 't not well
Thus to fulfil thy prophecy?

ISM.   The crime
Was mutual; mutual be the punishment.

ANT. Fear not. Thy life is safe, but mine long
    since
Devoted to the dead.

CREON.   Both seem deprived
Of reason. One indeed was ever thus.

ISM. O king! The mind doth seldom keep her
    seat
When sunk beneath misfortunes.

CREON.   Sunk indeed
Thou wert in wretchedness to join wi   er.

ISM. But what is life without Antigone?

CREON. Then think not of it. For she is no more.

ISM. Wouldst thou destroy thy son's long-destined
    wife?

CREON. Oh! we shall find a fitter bride.

ISM.   Alas!
He will not think so.

CREON.   I'll not wed my son
To a base woman.

ANT.   O my dearest Hæmon!
And is it thus thy father doth disgrace thee?

CREON. Such an alliance were as hateful to me
As is thyself.

ISM.   Wilt thou then take her from him?

CREON. Their nuptials shall be finished by death.

ISM. She then must perish?

CREON.   So must you and I;
Therefore no more delay. Go, take them hence;
Confine them both. Henceforth they shall not stir;
When death is near at hand the bravest fly.

Chorus.

Strophe 1.

Thrice happy they, whose days in pleasure flow,
Who never taste the bitter cup of woe;
   For when the wrath of heaven descends
On some devoted house, there foul disgrace,
    With grief and all her train attends,
And shame and sorrow o'erwhelm the wretched race,
   E'en as the Thracian sea, when vexed with storms,
Whilst darkness hangs incumbent o'er the deep,
   When the black north the troubled scene deforms,
And the black sands in rapid whirlwinds sweep,
   The groaning waves beat on the trembling shore,
   And echoing hills rebellow to the roar.

Antistrophe 1.

O Labdacus! thy house must perish all—
E'en now I see the stately ruin fall;
   Shame heaped on shame, and ill on ill,
    Disgrace and never-ending woes;
   Some angry god pursues thee still,
    Nor grants or safety or repose.
One fair and lovely branch unwithered stood
    And braved th' inclement skies;
But Pluto comes, inexorable god—
    She sinks, she raves, she dies.

Strophe 2.

Shall man below control the gods above,
   Whose eyes by all-subduing sleep
Are never closed as feeble mortals' are,
   But still their watchful vigils keep
Through the large circle of th' eternal year!
   Great lord of all, whom neither time nor age
With envious stroke can weaken or decay;
   He who alone the future can presage,
Who knows alike to-morrow as to-day;
   Whilst wretched man is doomed, by Heaven's decree,
   To toil and pain, to sin and misery.

Antistrophe 2.

Oftimes the flatterer Hope, that joy inspires,
Fills the proud heart of man with fond desires ;
   He, careless traveller, wanders still
     Through life, unmindful of deceit,
   Nor dreads the danger, till he feel
     The burning sands beneath his feet.
When heaven impels to guilt the maddening mind,
     Then good like ill appears,
And vice, for universal hate designed,
     The face of virtue wears.   *[Exeunt.*

ACT III.

SCENE I.

CREON, HÆMON, CHORUS.

CHORUS. Behold, O king ! thy youngest hope appear—
The noble Hæmon.   Lost in grief he seems,
Weeping the fate of poor Antigone.
    CREON. He comes, and better than a prophet, soon
Shall we divine his inmost thoughts.   My son,
Com'st thou, well knowing our decree, to mourn
Thy promised bride, and angry to dispute
A father's will ; or, whatsoe'er we do
Still to hold best, and pay obedience to us ?
    HÆ. My father, I am thine.   Do thou command,
And I in all things shall obey.   'Tis fit
My promised nuptial rites give place to thee.
    CREON. It will become thee with obedience thus
To bear thee ever, and in every act
To yield submissive to a father's will :
'Tis therefore, O my son ! that men do pray

For children who with kind officious duty
May guard their helpless age, resist their foes,
And like their parents love their parents' friend;
But he who gets a disobedient child,
What doth he get but misery and woe?
His enemies will laugh the wretch to scorn.
Take heed, my son, thou yield not up thy reason,
In hopes of pleasure from a worthless woman;
For cold is the embrace of impious love,
And deep the wounds of false dissembled friendship.
Hate then thy bitterest foe, despise her arts,
And leave her to be wedded to the tomb.
Of all the city her alone I found
Rebellious; but I have her, nor shall Thebes
Say I'm a liar: I pronounced her fate,
And she must perish.   Let her call on Jove,
Who guards the rights of kindred and the ties
Of nature; for if those by blood united
Transgress the laws, I hold myself more near
E'en to a stranger.   Who in private life
Is just and good, will to his country too
Be faithful ever; but the man who, proud
And fierce of soul, contemns authority,
Despiseth justice, and o'er those who rule
Would have dominion, such shall never gain
Th' applauding voice of Creon.   He alone,
Whom the consenting citizens approve
Th' acknowledged sovereign, should in all command,
Just or unjust his laws, in things of great
Or little import, whatsoe'er he bids:
A subject is not to dispute his will;
He knows alike to rule and to obey;
And in the day of battle will maintain
The foremost rank, his country's best defence.
Rebellion is the worst of human ills;
This ruins kingdoms, this destroys the peace
Of noblest families, this wages war,
And puts the brave to flight; whilst fair obedience
Keeps all in safety.   To preserve it ever
Should be a king's first care.   We will not yield
To a weak woman; if we must submit,

ANTIGONE. 161

At least we will be conquered by a man,
Nor by a female arm thus fall inglorious.
   HÆ. Wisdom, my father, is the noblest gift
The gods bestow on man, and better far
Than all his treasures. Why thy judgment deems
Most fit, I cannot, would not reprehend.
Others perhaps might call it wrong. For me,
My duty only bids me to inform you
If aught be done or said that casts reproach
Or blame on you. Such terror would thy looks
Strike on the low plebeian, that he dare not
Say aught unpleasing to thee; be it mine
To tell thee then what I of late have heard
In secret whispered. Your afflicted people
United mourn th' unhappy virgin's fate
Unmerited, most wretched of her sex,
To die for deeds of such distinguished virtue,
For that she would not let a brother lie
Unburied, to the dogs and birds a prey;
Was it not rather, say the murmuring crowd,
Worthy of golden honours and fair praise?
Such are their dark and secret discontents.
Thy welfare and thy happiness alone
Are all my wish; what can a child desire
More than a father's honour, or a father
More than his child's? Oh! do not then retain
Thy will, and still believe no sense but thine
Can judge aright! The man who proudly thinks
None but himself or eloquent, or wise,
By time betrayed, is branded for an idiot;
True wisdom will be ever glad to learn,
And not too fond of power. Observe the trees
That bend to wintry torrents, how their boughs
Unhurt remain, whilst those that brave the storm,
Uprooted torn, shall wither and decay;
The pilot, whose unslackened sail defies
Contending winds, with shattered bark pursues
His dangerous course. Then mitigate thy wrath
My father, and give way to sweet repentance.
If to my youth be aught of judgment given,
He, who by knowledge and true wisdom's rules

F

Guides every action, is the first of men ;
But since to few that happiness is given,
The next is he, who, not too proud to learn,
Follows the counsels of the wise and good,
    CHOR. O king ! if right the youth advise, 'tis fit
That thou shouldst listen to him ; so to thee
Should he attend, as best may profit both.
    CREON. And have we lived so long then to be taught
At last our duty by a boy like thee ?
    HÆ. Young though I am, I still may judge aright ;
Wisdom in action lies, and not in years,
    CREON. Call you it wisdom then to honour those
Who disobey the laws ?
    HÆ.   I would not have thee
Protect the wicked.
    CREON.   Is she not most guilty
 HÆ. Thebes doth not think her so.
    CREON.   Shall Thebes prescribe
To Creon's will ?
    HÆ.   How weakly dost thou talk !
    CREON. Am I king here, or shall another reign ?
    HÆ. 'Tis not a city where but one man rules.
    CREON. The city is the king's.
    HÆ.   Go by thyself then,
And rule henceforth o'er a deserted land.
    CREON. [*to the* CHORUS]. He pleads the woman's
    cause.
    HÆ.   If thou art she,
I do ; for, oh ! I speak but for thy sake—
My care is all for thee.
    CREON.   Abandoned wretch !
Dispute a father's will !
    HÆ.   I see thee err,
And therefore do it.
    CREON.   Is it then a crime
To guard my throne and rights from violation ?
    HÆ. He cannot guard them who contemns the gods
And violates their laws.
    CREON.   Oh ! thou are worse,
More impious e'en than her thou hast defended.
    HÆ. Naught have I done to merit this reproof.

CREON. Hast thou not pleaded for her?

HÆ.   No, for thee,
And for myself—for the infernal gods.

CREON. But know, she shall not live to be thy wife.

HÆ. Then she must die ; another too may fall.

CREON. Ha ! dost thou threaten me, audacious traitor ?

HÆ. What are my threats ? Alas !   thou heedst them
    not.

CREON. That thou shalt see ; thy insolent instruction
Shall cost thee dear.

HÆ.   But for thou art my father
Now would I say thy senses were impaired.

CREON. Think not to make me thus thy scorn and
    laughter,
Thou woman's slave.

HÆ.   Still wouldst thou speak thyself,
And never listen to the voice of truth ;
Such is thy will.

CREON.   Now, by Olympus here !
I swear thy vile reproaches shall not pass
Unpunished.   Call her forth!

                         [*To one of the Attendants.*
                         Before her bridegroom
She shall be brought, and perish in his sight.

HÆ. These eyes shall never see it.   Let the slaves
Who fear thy rage submit to it ; but know,
'Tis the last time thou shalt behold thy son.

                                   [*Exit* HÆMON.

SCENE II.

CREON, CHORUS.

CHOR. Sudden in anger fled the youth.   O king !
A mind oppressed like his is desperate.

CREON. Why, let him go ! and henceforth better
    learn
Than to oppose me.   Be it as it may,
Death is their portion, and he shall not save them.

CHOR. Must they both die then ?

                                   F 2

CREON.   No ; 'tis well advised,
Ismene lives ; but for Antigone——
   CHOR. O king ! what death is she decreed to suffer?
   CREON. Far from the haunts of men I'll have her led,
And in a rocky cave, beneath the earth,
Buried alive ; with her a little food,
Enough to save the city from pollution.
There let her pray the only god she worships
To save her from this death : perhaps he will,
Or, if he doth not, let her learn how vain
It is to reverence the powers below.   [*Exit* CREON.

SCENE III.

CHORUS.

Strophe 1.

Mighty power, all powers above,
Great unconquerable love !
Thou, who liest in dimple sleek
On the tender virgin's cheek,
Thee the rich and great obey,
Every creature owns thy sway.
O'er the wide earth and o'er the main
Extends thy universal reign ;
All thy maddening influence know,
Gods above and men below ;
All thy powers resistless prove,
Great unconquerable love !

Antistrophe 1.

Thou canst lead the just astray
From wisdom and from virtue's way ;
The ties of nature cease to bind,
When thou disturbst the captive mind
Behold, enslaved by fond desire,
The youth condemns his aged sire
Enamoured of his beauteous maid,
Nor laws nor parents are obeyed ;

Thus Venus wills it from above,
And great unconquerable love.

CHOR. E'en I beyond the common bounds of grief
Indulge my sorrows, and from these sad eyes
Fountains of tears will flow, when I behold
Antigone, unhappy maid, approach
The bed of death, and hasten to the tomb.

SCENE IV.

ANTIGONE, CHORUS.

ANT. Farewell, my friends, my countrymen, farewell!
Here on her last sad journey you behold
The poor Antigone; for never more
Shall I return, or view the light of day:
The hand of death conducts me to the shore
Of dreary Acheron; no nuptial song
Reserved for me—the wretched bride alone
Of Pluto now, and wedded to the tomb.
CHOR. Be it thy glory still, that by the sword
Thou fallst not, nor the slow-consuming hand
Of foul distemperature, but far distinguished
Above thy sex, and to thyself a law,
Doomst thy own death: so shall thy honour live,
And future ages venerate thy name.
ANT. Thus Tantalus' unhappy daughter fell,
The Phrygian Niobe. High on the top
Of towering Sipylus the rock enfolds her,
E'en as the ivy twines her tendrils round
The lofty oak; there still (as fame reports)
To melting showers and everlasting snow
Obvious she stands, her beauteous bosom wet
With tears, that from her ever-streaming eyes
Incessant flow. Her fate resembles mine.
CHOR. A goddess she, and from a goddess sprung;
We are but mortal, and of mortals born:
To meet the fate of gods thus in thy life,
And in thy death, oh! 'tis a glorious doom!

ANT. Alas! thou mockst me! Why, whilst yet I live,
Wouldst thou afflict me with reproach like this?
O my dear country! and my dearer friends
Its blest inhabitants, renowned Thebes!
And ye Dircæan fountains! you I call
To witness that I die by laws unjust,
To my deep prison unlamented go,
To my sad tomb—no fellow-sufferer there
To soothe my woes, the living, or the dead.

CHOR. Rashness like thine must meet with such
reward;
A father's crimes, I fear, lie heavy on thee.

ANT. Oh! thou hast touched my worst of miseries,
My father's fate, the woes of all our house,
The wretched race of Labdacus, renowned
For its misfortunes! Oh! the guilty bed
Of those from whom I sprang—unhappy offspring
Of parents most unhappy! Lo! to them
I go accursed—a virgin and a slave.
O my poor brother! most unfortunate
Were thy sad nuptials—they have slain thy sister.

CHOR. Thy piety demands our praise; but know,
Authority is not to be despised;
'Twas thy own rashness brought destruction on thee.

ANT. Thus friendless, unlamented, must I tread
The destined path, no longer to behold
Yon sacred light, and none shall mourn my fate.

SCENE V.

CREON, ANTIGONE, CHORUS,

CREON. Know ye not, slaves like her, to death
devoted,
Would never cease their wailings? Wherefore is it
You thus delay to execute my orders?
Let her be carried instant to the cave,
And leave her there alone, to live, or die;
Her blood rests not on us; but she no longer
Shall breathe on earth.   [*Exit* CREON.

SCENE VI.

ANTIGONE, CHORUS.

ANT.   O dreadful marriage bed!
O my deep dungeon!   My eternal home,
Whither I go to join my kindred dead!
For not a few hath fell Persephone
Already ta'en; to her I go, the last
And most unhappy, ere my time was come;
But still I have sweet hope I shall not go
Unwelcome to my father, nor to thee,
My mother.   Dear to thee, Eteocles,
Still shall I ever be.   These pious hands
Washed your pale bodies, and adorned you both
With rites sepulchral, and libations due!
And thus, my Polynices, for my care
Of thee am I rewarded, and the good
Alone shall praise me.   For a husband dead,
Nor, had I been a mother, for my children
Would I have dared to violate the laws:
Another husband and another child
Might soothe affliction.   But, my parents dead,
A brother's loss could never be repaired,
And therefore did I dare the venturous deed,
And therefore die by Creon's dread command.
Ne'er shall I taste of Hymen's joys, or know
A mother's pleasures in her infant race;
But, friendless and forlorn, alive descend
Into the dreary mansions of the dead.
And how have I offended the just gods!
But wherefore call on them?   Will they protect me,
When thus I meet with the reward of ill
For doing good?   If this be just, ye gods,
If I am guilty, let me suffer for it.
But if the crime be theirs, oh! let them feel
That weight of misery they have laid on me!
   CHOR. The storm continues, and her angry soul
Still pours its sorrows forth.

Scene VII.

Creon, Antigone, Chorus.

Creon.   The slaves shall suffer
For this delay.
      Ant.   Alas! death cannot be
Far from that voice.
      Creon.   I would not have thee hope
A moment's respite.
      Ant.   O my country's gods!
And thou, my native Thebes! I leave you now.
Look on me, princes—see the last of all
My royal race—see what I suffer, see
From whom I bear it, from the worst of men,
Only because I did delight in virtue.   [*Exit* Creon.

Scene VIII.

Antigone, Chorus.

Chorus.

Strophe 1.

Remember what fair Danae endured,
      Condemned to change heaven's cheerful light
      For scenes of horror and of night,
Within a brazen tower long time immured;
      Yet was the maid of noblest race,
      And honoured e'en with Jove's embrace;
But, oh! when fate decrees a mortal's woe
Naught can reverse the doom or stop the blow—
Nor heaven above, nor earth and seas below.

Antistrophe 1.

The Thracian monarch, Dryas' hapless son,
      Chained to a rock in torment lay,
      And breathed his angry soul away,
By wrath misguided, and by pride undone;

Taught by the offended god to know
From foul reproach what evils flow;
For he the rites profaned with slanderous tongue,
The holy flame he quenched, disturbed the song,
And waked to wrath the Muses' tuneful throng.

Strophe 2.

His turbid waves where Salmydessus rolled,
  And proud Cyanea's rocks divide the flood,
There from thy temple, Mars, didst thou behold
    The sons of Phineus weltering in their blood;
      A mother did the cruel deed,
      A mother bade her children bleed;
Both by her impious hand, deprived of light,
In vain lamented long their ravished sight,
And closed their eyes in never-ending night.

Antistrophe 2.

Long time they wept a better mother's fate,
  Unhappy offspring of a luckless bed?
Yet nobly born, and eminently great
    Was she, and midst sequestered caverns bred—
      Her father's angry storms among,
      Daughter of gods, from Boreas sprung—
Equal in swiftness to the bounding steed,
She skimmed the mountains with a courser's speed,
Yet was the nymph to death and misery decreed.
                       [*Exeunt.*

ACT IV.

SCENE I.

TIRESIAS, GUIDE, CREON, CHORUS.

TIR. Princes of Thebes, behold, conducted hither
By my kind guide—such is the blind man's fate—
Tiresias comes !
    CREON.   O venerable prophet !
What hast thou to impart ?
    TIR.   I will inform thee ;
Observe, and be obedient.
    CREON.   Have I not
been ever so ?
    TIR.   Thou hast ; and therefore Thebes
Hath flourished still——
    CREON.   By thy protecting hand.
    TIR. Therefore be wise.   For know, this very hour
Is the important crisis of thy fate.
        CREON. Speak then !   What is it ?   How I dread thy
          words !
        TIR. When thou hast heard the portents which my
          art
But now discovered, thou wilt see it all.
Know then that, sitting on my ancient throne
Augurial, whence each divination comes,
Sudden a strange unusual noise was heard
Of birds, whose loud and barbarous dissonance
I knew not how to interpret.   By the sound
Of clashing wings I could discover well
That with their bloody claws they tore each other ;
Amazed and fearful, instantly I tried
On burning altars holy sacrifice—
When, from the victim, lo ! the sullen flame
Aspired not.   Smothered in the ashes still
Laid the moist flesh, and, rolled in smoke, repelled
The rising fire, whilst from their fat the thighs
Were separate.   All these signs of deadly omen,

Boding dark vengeance, did I learn from him ;
> [*Pointing to the* GUIDE.

He is my leader, king, and I am thine.
Then mark me well. From thee these evils flow,
From thy unjust decree. Our altars all
Have been polluted by th' unhallowed food
Of birds and dogs, that preyed upon the corse
Of wretched Œdipus' unhappy son ;
Nor will the gods accept our offered prayers,
Or from our hands receive the sacrifice ;
No longer will the birds send forth their sounds
Auspicious, fattened thus with human blood.
Consider this, my son. And, oh ! remember,
To err is human—'tis the common lot
Of frail mortality ; and he alone
Is wise and happy, who, when ills are done,
Persists not, but would heal the wound he made ;
But self-sufficient obstinacy ever
Is folly's utmost height. Where is the glory
To slay the slain or persecute the dead ?
I wish thee well, and therefore have spoke thus ;
When those who love advise 'tis sweet to learn.

   CREON. I know, old man, I am the general mark,
The butt of all, and you all aim at me.
For me I know your prophecies were made,
And I am sold to this detested race—
Betrayed to them. But make your gains ! Go, purchase
Your Sardian amber, and your Indian gold ;
They shall not buy a tomb for Polynices.
No, should the eagle seek him for his food,
And towering bear him to the throne of Jove,
I would not bury him. For well I know
The gods by mortals cannot be polluted ;
But the best men, by sordid gain corrupt,
Say all that's ill, and fall beneath the lowest.

   TIR. Who knows this, or who dare accuse us of it ?
   CREON. What meanst thou by that question ? Askst
    thou who ?
   TIR. How far is wisdom beyond every good !
   CREON. As far as folly beyond every ill.
   TIR. That's a distemper thou 'rt afflicted with.

CREON. I'll not revile a prophet.

TIR. But thou dost;
Thou 'lt not believe me.

CREON. Your prophetic race
Are lovers all of gold.

TIR. Tyrants are so,
Howe'er ill-gotten.

CREON. Knowst thou 'tis a king
Thou 'rt talking thus to?

TIR. Yes, I know it well;
A king who owes to me his country's safety.

CREON. Thou 'rt a wise prophet, but thou art unjust.

TIR. Thou wilt oblige me then to utter that
Which I had purposed to conceal.

CREON. Speak out,
Say what thou wilt, but say it not for hire.

TIR. Thus may it seem to thee.

CREON. But know, old man,
I am not to be sold.

TIR. Remember this:
Not many days shall the bright sun perform
His stated course, ere, sprung from thy own loins,
Thyself shall yield a victim. In thy turn
Thou too shalt weep, for that thy cruel sentence
Decreed a guiltless virgin to the tomb,
And kept on earth, unmindful of the gods,
Ungraced, unburied, an unhallowed corse,
Which not to thee, nor to the gods above
Of right belonged. 'Twas arbitrary power:
But the avenging furies lie concealed,
The ministers of death have spread the snare,
And with like woes await to punish thee.
Do I say this from hopes of promised gold?
Pass but a little time, and thou shalt hear
The shrieks of men, the women's loud laments
O'er all thy palace; see th' offended people
Together rage; thy cities all by dogs
And beasts and birds polluted, and the stench
Of filth obscene on every altar laid.
Thus from my angry soul have I sent forth
Its keenest arrows—for thou hast provoked me—

Nor shall they fly in vain, or thou escape
The destined blow. Now, boy, conduct mo home.
On younger heads the tempest of his rage
Shall fall ; but, henceforth let him learn to speak
In humbler terms, and bear a better mind.

[Exit TIRESIAS.

SCENE II.

CREON, CHORUS.

CHOR. He's gone, and dreadful were his prophecies;
Since these grey hairs were o'er my temples spread
Nought from those lips hath flowed but sacred truth.
  CREON. I know there hath not, and am troubled
      much
For the event ; 'tis grating to submit,
And yet the mind spite of itself must yield
In such distress.
  CHOR.   Son of Menæceus, now
Thou needst most counsel.
  CREON.   What wouldst thou advise?
I will obey thee.
  CHOR.   Set the virgin free,
And let a tomb be raised for Polynices.
  CREON. And dost thou counsel thus?—and must I
      yield?
  CHOR. Immediately, O king ! for vengeance falls
With hasty footsteps on the guilty head.
  CREON. I cannot—yet I must reverse the sentence;
There is no struggling with necessity.
  CHOR. Do it thyself, nor trust another hand.
  CREON. I will ; and you my servants, be prepared ;
Each with his axe quick hasten to the place ;
Myself—for thus I have resolved—will go,
And the same hand that bound shall set her free ;
For, oh ! I fear 'tis wisest still through life
To keep our ancient laws, and follow virtue.

Scene III.

Chorus.

Strophe 1.

Bacchus, by various names to mortals known,
 Fair Semele's illustrious son,
  Offspring of thunder-bearing Jove,
Who honourst famed Italia with thy love!
Who dwellst where erst the dragon's teeth were
 strewed,
Or where Ismenus pours his gentle flood;
Who dost o'er Ceres' hallowed rites preside,
And at thy native Thebes propitious still reside.

Antistrophe 1.

Where famed Parnassus' forked hills uprise,
 To thee ascends the sacrifice;
  Corycia's nymphs attend below,
Whilst from Castalia's fount fresh waters flow:
O'er Nysa's mountains wreaths of ivy twine,
And mix their tendrils with the clustering vine:
Around their master crowd the virgin throng,
And praise the god of Thebes in never-dying song.

Strophe 2.

Happiest of cities, Thebes! above the rest
 By Semele and Bacchus blest!
Oh! visit now thy once beloved abode,
Oh! heal our woes, thou kind protecting god!
From steep Parnassus, or th' Eubœan sea,
With smiles auspicious come, and bring with thee
Health, joy, and peace, and fair prosperity.

Antistrophe 2.

Immortal leader of the maddening choir,
Whose torches blaze with unextinguished fire,
Great son of Jove, who guidst the tuneful throng,
Thou, who presidest o'er the nightly song,

Come with thy Naxian maids, a festive train,
Who, wild with joy, and raging o'er the plain,
For thee the dance prepare, to thee devote the strain.

       [Exeunt.

ACT V.

SCÈNE I.

MESSENGER, CHORUS.

MESSENGER. Ye race of Cadmus, sons of ancient
  Thebes,
Henceforth no state of human life by me
Shall be or valued or despised : for all
Depends on fortune ; she exalts the low,
And casts the mighty down. The fate of men
Can never be foretold. There was a time
When Creon lived in envied happiness,
Ruled o'er renowned Thebes, which from her foes
He had delivered, with successful power ;
Blest in his kingdom, in his children blest,
He stretched o'er all his universal sway.
Now all is gone : when pleasure is no more,
Man is but an animated corse,
Nor can be said to live ; he may be rich,
Or decked with regal honours, but if joy
Be absent from him, if he tastes them not,
'Tis useless grandeur all, and empty shade.
 CHOR. Touching our royal master, bringst thou news
Of sorrow to us?
 MES.   They are dead ; and those
Who live the dreadful cause.
 CHOR.   Quick, tell us who—
The slayer and the slain !
 MES.   Hæmon is dead.
 CHOR. Dead ! by what hand, his father's or his own ?

MES. Enraged and grieving for his murdered love,
He slew himself.

    CHOR.   O prophet ! thy predictions
Were but too true !

    MES.   Since thus it be, 'tis fit
We should consult ; our present state demands it,

    CHOR. But see ! Eurydice, the wretched wife
Of Creon, comes this way ; or chance hath brought her,
Or Hæmon's hapless fate hath reached her ear.

SCENE II.

EURYDICE, MESSENGER, CHORUS.

    EUR. O citizens ! as to Minerva's fane
E'en now I went to pay my vows, the doors
I burst, and heard imperfectly the sound
Of most disastrous news which touched me near.
Breathless I fell amidst the virgin throng ;
And now I come to know the dreadful truth :
Whate'er it be, I'll hear it now ; for, oh !
I am no stranger to calamity.

    MES. Then mark, my mistress, I will tell thee all,
Nor will I pass a circumstance unmentioned.
Should I deceive thee with an idle tale
'Twere soon discovered.   Truth is always best.
Know then, I followed Creon to the field,
Where, torn by dogs, the wretched carcase lay
Of Polynices.   First to Proserpine
And angry Pluto, to appease their wrath,
Our humble prayers addressing, there we laved
In the pure stream the body ; then, with leaves
Fresh gathered covering, burnt his poor remains,
And on the neighbouring turf a tomb upraised.
Then, towards the virgin's rocky cave advanced,
When from the dreadful chamber a sad cry
As from afar was heard, a servant ran
To tell the king, and still as we approached
The sound of sorrow from a voice unknown
And undistinguished issued forth.   Alas !

Said Creon: "Am I then a faithful prophet?
And do I tread a more unhappy path
Than e'er I went before? It is my son—
I know his voice! But get ye to the door,
My servants, close, look through the stony heap;
Mark if it be so. Is it Hæmon's voice?"
Again he cried: "Or have the gods deceived me?"
Thus spoke the king. We, to our mournful lord
Obedient, looked, and saw Antigone
Down in the deepest hollow of the cave,
By her own vestments hung. Close by her side
The wretched youth, embracing in his arms
Her lifeless corse, weeping his father's crime,
His ravished bride, and horrid nuptial bed,
Creon beheld, and loud reproaching cried:
"What art thou doing? What's thy dreadful purpose?
What means my son? Come forth, my Hæmon, come!
Thy father begs thee." With indignant eye
The youth looked up, nor scornful deigned an answer,
But silent drew his sword, and with fell rage
Struck at his father, who by flight escaped
The blow; then on himself bent all his wrath,
Full in his side the weapon fixed; but still,
Whilst life remained, on the soft bosom hung
Of the dear maid, and his lost spirit breathed
O'er her pale cheek discoloured with his blood.
Thus lay the wretched pair in death united,
And celebrate their nuptials in the tomb—
To future times a terrible example
Of the sad woes which rashness ever brings.

[*Exit* EURYDICE.

SCENE III.

MESSENGER, CHORUS.

CHOR. What can this mean? She's gone, without a
    word.
MES. 'Tis strange, and yet I trust she will not loud
Proclaim her griefs to all, but—for I know
She's ever prudent—with her virgin train
In secret weep her murdered Hæmon's fate.

CHOR. Clamour indeed were vain; but such deep
    silence
Doth ever threaten horrid consequence.
    MES. Within we soon shall know if aught she hide
Of deadly purport in her angry soul;
For well thou sayst her silence is most dreadful.
                          [*Exit* MESSENGER.
    CHOR. But lo! the king himself: and in his arms
See his dead son, the monument accursed
Of his sad fate, which, may we say unblamed,
Sprang not from others' guilt, but from his own.

SCENE IV.

CREON, MESSENGER, CHORUS.

CREON *enters, bearing the body of* HÆMON.

    CREON. Ah me! What deadly woes from the bad mind
Perpetual flow. Thus in one wretched house
Have you beheld the slayer and the slain!
O fatal counsels! O unhappy son!
Thus with thy youthful bride to sink in death;
Thou diest, my child, and I alone have killed thee!
    CHOR. O king! thy justice comes too late.
    CREON.   It doth,
I know it well, unhappy as I am;
For oh! the god this heavy weight of woe
Hath cast upon me, and his fiercest wrath
Torments me now, changing my joyful state
To keenest anguish. Oh! the fruitless toils
Of wretched mortals!

SCENE V.

MESSENGER, CREON, CHORUS.

    MES.   Thus oppressed, my lord,
With bitterest misfortune, more affliction
Awaits thee still, which thou wilt find within.

CREON. And can there be more woes? Is aught to come
More horrible than this?
   MES.   The queen is dead;
Her wounds yet fresh. Eager, alas! to show
A mother's love, she followed her lost child.
   CREON. O death insatiate! how dost thou afflict me!
What cruel news, thou messenger of ill,
Hast thou brought now?
   CHOR.   A wretch, already dead
With grief, thy horrid tale once more hath slain.
   CREON. Didst thou not say a fresh calamity
Had fallen upon me? · Didst thou not say my wife
Was dead, alas! for grief of Hæmon's fate?
      [*Scene opens and discovers the body of* EURYDICE.
   MES. Behold her there!
   CREON.   O me! another blow!
What now remains? What can I suffer more,
Thus bearing in these arms my breathless son?
My wife too dead! O most unhappy mother!
And oh! thou wretched child!
   MES.   Close by the altar
She drew the sword, and closed her eyes in death,
Lamenting first her lost Megareus' fate
And Hæmon's death, with imprecations dire
Still poured on thee, the murderer of thy son.
   CREON. I shudder at it? Will no friendly hand
Destroy me quickly? For oh! I am most wretched—
Beset with miseries!
   MES.   She accused thee oft,
And said the guilt of both their deaths was thine.
   CREON. Alas! I only am to blame. 'Twas I
Who killed thee, Hæmon; I confess my crime.
Bear me, my servants, bear me far from hence,
For I am—nothing.
   CHOR.   If in ills like these
Aught can be well, thou hast determined right:
When least we see our woes, we feel them least.
   CREON. Quick let my last, my happiest hour appear!
Would it were come, the period of my woes!
Oh! that I might not see another day!

CHOR. Time must determine that : the present hour
Demands our care ; the rest be left to heaven.
    CREON. But I have wished and prayed for 't.
    CHOR.   Pray for nothing ;
There's no reversing the decrees of fate.
    CREON. Take hence this useless load, this guilty
        wretch
Who slew his child, who slew e'en thee, my wife ;
I know not whither to betake me, where
To turn my eyes, for all is dreadful round me,
And fate hath weighed me down on every side.
    CHOR. Wisdom alone is man's true happiness ;
We are not to dispute the will of heaven ;
For ever are the boastings of the proud
By the just gods repaid, and man at last
Is taught to fear their anger, and be wise.

TRACHINIÆ.

DRAMATIS PERSONÆ.

HERCULES.	NURSE.
HYLLUS, *Son of Hercules.*	OLD MAN.
DEIANIRA, *Wife of Hercules.*	MESSENGER.
LICHAS, *a Herald.*	CHORUS, *composed of Virgins*
ATTENDANT *on Deianira.*	*of Trachis.*

SCENE.—*Before the Palace of* CEYX *in* TRACHIS.

ACT I.

SCENE I.

DEIANIRA, ATTENDANT.

DEIANIRA. Of ancient fame, and long for truth received,
Hath been the maxim, that nor good nor ill
Can mortal life be called before we die.
Alas! it is not so; for, oh! my friends,
Ere to the shades of Orcus I descend,
Too well I know that Deianira's life
Hath ever been, and ever must be, wretched.
Whilst in my native Pleuron Æneus watched
My tender years with kind paternal care,
If ever woman suffered from the dread
Of hated nuptials, I endured the worst

And bitterest woes, when Achelous came,
The river-god, to ask a father's voice,
And snatched me to his arms.   With triple form
He came affrighting—now to sight appeared
A bull, and now with motley scales adorned
A wreathèd serpent, now with human shape
And bestial head united ; from his beard,
Shadowed with hair, as from a fountain, dripped
The ever-flowing water.   Horrid form !
This to escape my prayers incessant rose
That I might rather die than e'er approach
His hated bed.   When lo! the welcome hour,
Though late, arrived, that brought the son of Jove
And fair Alcmena to my aid.   He came,
He fought, he freed me.   How the battle passed
Who unconcerned beheld it best can tell.
Alas ! I saw it not, oppressed with fear
Lest from my fatal beauty should arise
Some sad event.   At length, deciding Jove
Gave to the doubtful fight a happy end,
If I may call it so ; for, since the hour
That gave me to Alcides' wished-for bed
Fears rise on fears ; still is my anxious heart
Solicitous for him ; oftimes the night,
Which brings him to me, bears him from my arms
To other labours and a second toil.
Our children too, alas ! he sees them not,
But as the husbandman who ne'er beholds
His distant lands, save at the needful time
Of seed or harvest.   Wandering thus, and thus
Returning ever, is he sent to serve
I know not whom.   When crowned with victory,
Then most my fears prevail ; for since he slew
The valiant Iphitus, at Trachis here
We live in exile with our generous friend,
The hospitable Ceyx ; he meantime
Is gone, and none can tell me where.   He went
And left me most unhappy.   Oh ! some ill
Hath sure befallen him ! for no little time
Hath he been absent ; 'tis full fifteen moons
Since I beheld him, and no messenger

Is come to Deianira.   Some misfortune
Doubtless hath happened, for he left behind
A dreadful scroll.   Oh ! I have prayed the gods
A thousand times it may contain no ill.
   ATTEN. My royal mistress, long have I beheld
Thy tears and sorrows for thy lost Alcides ;
But if the counsels of a slave might claim
Attention, I would speak—would ask thee wherefore
Amongst thy sons, a numerous progeny,
None hath been sent in search of him, and chief
Thy Hyllus, if he holds a father's health
And safety dear : but, e'en as we could wish,
Behold him here !   If what I have advised
Seem fitting, he is come in happiest hour
To execute our purpose.

SCENE II.

HYLLUS, DEIANIRA, ATTENDANT.

   DEI.   O my son !
Oft from the meanest tongue the words of truth
And safety flow.   This woman, though a slave,
Hath spoke what would have well become the mouth
Of freedom's self to utter.
   HYL.   May I know
What she hath said ?
   DEI.   She says it doth reflect
Disgrace on thee, thy father so long absent,
Not to have gained some knowledge of his fate.
   HYL. I have already, if I may rely
On what report hath said of him.
   DEI.   Oh, where—
Where is he then, my son ?
   HYL.   These twelve months past,
If fame say true, a Lydian woman held him
In shameful servitude.
   DEI.   If it be so,
May every tongue reproach him !
   HYL.   But I hear
He now is free.

DEI.   And where doth rumour say
He is? alive or dead.

HYL.   'Tis said, he leads,
Or means to lead, his forces towards Eubœa,
The land of Eurytus.

DEI.   Alas! my son,
Dost thou not know the oracles he left
Touching that kingdom?

HYL.   No, I know not of them;
What were they?

DEI.   There, he said, or he should die,
Or if he should survive, his life to come
Would all be happy.   Wilt thou not, my son,
In this important crisis strive to aid
Thy father?   If he lives, we too shall live
In safety.   If he dies, we perish with him.

HYL. Mother, I go.   Long since I had been there
But that the oracle did never reach
Mine ears before.   Meantime that happy fate,
Which on my father ever wont to smile
Propitious, should not suffer us to fear;
Thus far informed, I will not let the means
Of truth escape me, but will know it all.

DEI. Haste then away, my son; and know, good deeds,
Though late performed, are crowned with sure success.

SCENE III.

CHORUS, DEIANIRA, ATTENDANT.

Strophe 1.

On thee we call, great god of day,
  To whom the night, with all her starry train,
      Yields her solitary reign,
    To send us some propitious ray:
    Say thou, whose all-beholding eye
    Doth nature's every part descry,
What dangerous ocean, or what land unknown
From Deianira keeps Alcmena's valiant son.

Antistrophe 1.

For she nor joy nor comfort knows,
But weeps her absent lord, and vainly tries
To close her ever-streaming eyes,
  Or soothe her sorrows to repose :
Like the sad bird of night, alone
She makes her solitary moan ;
And still, as on her widowed bed reclined
She lies, unnumbered fears perplex her anxious mind.

Strophe 2.

E'en as the troubled billows roar,
When angry Boreas rules th' inclement skies,
And waves on waves tumultuous rise
  To lash the Cretan shore :
Thus sorrows still on sorrows prest
Fill the great Alcides' breast ;
Unfading yet shall his fair virtues bloom,
And some protecting god preserve him from the tomb.

Antistrophe 2.

Wherefore, to better thoughts inclined,
Let us with hope's fair prospect fill thy breast,
Calm thy anxious thoughts to rest,
  And ease thy troubled mind :
No bliss on man, unmixed with woe,
Doth Jove, great lord of all, bestow ;
But good with ill, and pleasure still with pain,
Like heaven's revolving signs, alternate reign.

Epode.

Not always do the shades of night remain,
  Nor ever with hard fate is man oppressed ;
The wealth that leaves us may return again,
  Sorrow and joy successive fill the breast ;
    Fearless then of every ill,
    Let cheerful hope support thee still :
Remember, queen, there is a power above ;
And when did the great father, careful Jove,
Forget his children dear, and kind paternal love ?

DEI. The fame, it seems, of Deianira's woes
Hath reached thine ears, but oh ! thou little knowst
What I have suffered ! Thou hast never felt
Sorrows like mine. And long may be the time
Ere sad experience shall afflict thy soul
With equal woes ! Alas ! the youthful maid
In flowery pastures still exulting feeds,
Nor feels the scorching sun, the wintry storm,
Or blast of angry winds. Secure she leads
A life of pleasure, void of every care,
Till to the virgin's happy state succeeds
The name of wife. Then shall her portion come
Of pain and anguish, then her terrors rise
For husband and for children. Then perchance
You too may know what 'tis to be unhappy,
And judge of my misfortunes by your own.
Long since oppressed by many a bitter woe
Oft have I wept, but this transcends them all ;
For I will tell thee, when Alcides last
Forth on his journey went, he left behind
An ancient scroll. Alas ! before that time
In all his labours he did never use
To speak as one who thought of death—secure
Always he seemed of victory ; but now
This writing marks, as if he were to die,
The portion out reserved for me, and wills
His children to divide th' inheritance ;
Fixes the time, in fifteen moons, it says,
He should return. That past or he must perish,
Or, if he 'scape the fatal hour, thenceforth
Should lead a life of happiness and joy :
Thus had the gods, it said, decreed his life
And toils should end : so from their ancient beach
Dodona's doves foretold. Th' appointed hour
Approaches that must bring th' event, e'en now,
My friends, and therefore nightly do I start
From my sweet slumbers, struck with deadly fear,
Lest I should lose the dearest, best of men.

CHOR. Of better omen be thy words. Behold
A messenger, who bears (for on his brow
I see the laurel crown) some joyful news.

Scene IV.

Messenger, Deianira, Attendant, Chorus.

Mes. I come, my royal mistress, to remove
Thy fears, and bring the first glad tidings to thee,
To tell thee that Alcmena's son returns
With life and victory ; e'en now he comes
To lay before his country's gods the spoils
Of glorious war.
  Dei.   What dost thou say, old man ?
What dost thou tell me ?
  Mes.   That thy dear Alcides,
Thy valiant lord, with his victorious bands,
Will soon attend thee.
  Dei.   From our citizens
Didst thou learn this, or from a stranger's tongue ?
  Mes. The herald Lichas, in yon flowery vale,
But now reported, and I fled impatient
Soon as I heard it, that I first might tell thee
And be rewarded for the welcome tale.   .
  Dei. But wherefore tarries Lichas if he bring
Glad tidings to me ?
  Mes.   'Tis impossible
To reach thee, for the Melian people throng
Around him—not a man but longs to know
Some news of thy Alcides, stops his journey,
Nor will release him till he hear it all.
Spite of himself he waits to satisfy
Their eager doubts ; but thou wilt see him soon.
  Dei. O thou who dwellst on Œta's sacred top,
Immortal Jove ! At length, though late, thou giv'st
The wished-for boon. Let every female now—
You that within the palace do reside,
And you, my followers here—with shouts proclaim
The blest event ! For, lo ! a beam of joy,
I little hoped, breaks forth, and we are happy.

Strophe.

Quick let sounds of mirth and joy
Every cheerful hour employ ;
Haste, and join the festive song,
You, who lead the youthful throng,
On whom the smiles of prosperous fate,
And Hymen's promised pleasures wait,
Now all your Io Pæans sing
To Phœbus, your protector and your king.

Antistrophe.

And you, ye virgin train, attend,
Not unmindful of your friend,
His sister huntress of the groves,
Who still her native Delos loves—
Prepare the dance, and choral lays,
To hymn the chaste Diana's praise ;
To her, and her attendant choir
Of mountain-nymphs, attune the votive lyre.

Epode.

Already hath the god possessed
My soul, and rules the sovereign of my breast ;
Evoë, Bacchus ! Io ! I come to join
Thy throng. Around me doth the thyrsus twine,
And I am filled with rage divine ;
See ! the glad messenger appears
To calm thy doubts, and to remove thy fears
Let us our Io Pæans sing
To Phœbus, our protector and our king.

ACT II.

Scene I.

Deianira, Chorus.

Deianira. These eyes deceive me, friends, or I behold
A crowd approach this way, and with them comes
The herald Lichas. Let me welcome him,
If he bring joyful news.

Scene II.

Lichas, Iole, Slaves, Deianira, Chorus.

Lic.   My royal mistress,
We greet thee with fair tidings of success,
And therefore shall our words deserve thy praise.
  Dei. O thou dear messenger! Inform me first
What first I wish to know, my loved Alcides,
Doth he yet live—shall I again behold him?
  Lic. I left him well. In health and manly strength
Exulting.
  Dei.   Where? In his own native land,
Or 'midst barbarians?
  Lic.   On Eubœa's shore
He waits, with various fruits to crown the altar,
And pay due honours to Cenæan Jove.
  Dei. Commanded by some oracle divine
Performs he this, or means but to fulfil
A vow of gratitude for conquest gained?
  Lic. For victory o'er the land, whence we have
     brought   .
These captive women, whom thou seest before thee.
  Dei. Whence come the wretched slaves? for if I
     judge
Their state aright, they must indeed be wretched.
  Lic. Know, when Alcides had laid waste the city

Of Eurytus, to him and to the gods
Were these devoted.
    Dei.   In Œchalia then
Hath my Alcides been this long, long time ?
    Lic. Not so: in Lydia (as himself reports)
Was he detained a slave. So Jove ordained ;
And who shall blame the high decrees of Jove ?
Sold to barbarian Omphale, he served
Twelve tedious months ; ill brooked he the foul shame.
Then in his wrath he made a solemn vow
He would revenge the wrong on the base author,
And bind in chains his wife and all his race :
Nor fruitless the resolve, for when the year
Of slavery past had expiated the crime
Imputed, soon with gathered force he marched
'Gainst the devoted Eurytus, the cause
(For so he deemed him) of those hateful bonds.
Within his palace he had erst received
Alcides, but with bitterest taunts reviled him,
Boasting, in spite of his all-conquering arrows,
His son's superior skill, and said a slave
Like him should bend beneath a freeman's power ;
Then, midst the banquet's mirth, inflamed with wine,
Cast forth his ancient guest. This to revenge
When Iphitus to search his pastured steeds
Came to Tyrinthia, Hercules surprised,
And, as he turned his wandering eyes aside,
Hurled headlong from the mountain's top. Great Jove,
Father of men, from high Olympus saw
And disapproved the deed, unworthy him
Who ne'er before by fraud destroyed his foes ;
With open force had he revenged the wrong
Jove had forgiven, but violence concealed
The gods abhor, and therefore was he sold
To slavery. Eurytus' unhappy sons
Were punished too, and dwell in Erebus ;
Their city is destroyed, and they, whom here
Thou seest, from freedom and prosperity,
Reduced to wretchedness. To thee they come,
Such was Alcides' will ; which I, his slave,
Have faithfully performed. Himself ere long

Thou shalt behold, when to paternal Jove
He hath fulfilled his vows.   Thus my long tale
Ends with the welcomest news which thou couldst
    hear :
Alcides comes !.
    CHOR.   O queen ! thy happiness
Is great indeed, to see these slaves before thee,
And know thy lord approaches.
    DEI.   I am happy—
To see my Hercules with victory crowned
'Tis fit I should rejoice ; and yet, my friends,
If we consider well, we still should fear
For the successful, lest they fall from bliss.
It moves my pity much when I behold
These wretched captives in a foreign land,
Without a parent and without a home,
Thus doomed to slavery here, who once perhaps
Enjoyed fair freedom's best inheritance :
O Jove ! averter of each mortal ill,
Let not my children ever feel thy arm
Thus raised against them ? or, if 'tis decreed,
Let it not be whilst Deianira lives :
The sight of these alarms my fears.   But tell me
Thou poor afflicted captive, who thou art.   [*To* IOLE.
Art thou a mother ? or, as by thy years
Thou seemst, a virgin, and of noble birth ?
Canst not thou tell me, Lichas, whence she sprang ?
Inform me, for of all these slaves she most
Hath won my pity, and in her alone
Have I observed a firm and generous mind.
    LIC. Why ask of me ?   I know not who she is;
Perhaps of no mean rank.
    DEI.   The royal race
Of Eurytus?
    LIC.   l know not, nor did e'er
Inquire.
    DEI.   And didst thou never hear her name
From her companions ?
    LIC.   Never.   I performed
My work is silence.
    DEI.   Tell me then thyself,

Thou wretched maid, for I am most unhappy
Till I know who thou art.
    Lic.   She will not speak;
I know she will not.   Not a word hath passed
Her lips e'er since she left her native land,
But still in tears the hapless virgin mourns
The burthen of her sad calamity.
Her fate is hard: she merits your forgiveness.
    Dei. Let her go in: I'll not disturb her peace,
Nor would I heap fresh sorrows on her head,
She hath enough already.   We'll retire.
Go where thou wilt; my cares within await me. [*To* Iole.
                [*Exeunt* Lichas, Iole, *and* Slaves.

Scene III.

Messenger, Deianira, Chorus.

    Mes. Stay thee awhile.   I have a tale to tell
Touching these captives, which imports thee nearly,
And I alone am able to inform thee.
    Dei. What dost thou know? and why wouldst thou
      detain me?
    Mes. Return, and hear me; when I spake before
I did not speak in vain, nor shall I now.
    Dei. Wouldst thou I call them back, or meanst to
      tell
Thy secret purpose here to me alone?
    Mes. To thee, and these thy friends—no more.
    Dei.   They're gone.
Now speak in safety.
    Mes.   Lichas is dishonest,
And either now, or when I saw him last,
Hath uttered falsehood.
    Dei.   Ha! what dost thou say?
I understand thee not—explain it quickly!
    Mes. I heard him say, before attendant crowds,
It was this virgin, this fair slave destroyed
Œchalia's lofty towers: 'twas love alone
That waged the war—no Lydian servitude,
Nor Omphale, nor the pretended fall

Of Iphytus—for so the tale he brings
Would fain persuade thee.   Know, thy own Alcides,
For that he could not gain th' assenting voice
Of Eurytus to his unlawful love,
Laid waste the city where her father reigned,
And slew him.   Now the daughter, as a slave,
Is sent to thee.   The reason is too plain :
Nor think he meant her for a slave alone—
The maid he loves, that would be strange indeed!
My royal mistress, most unwillingly
Do I report th' unwelcome news, but thought
It was my duty : I have told the truth,
And the Trachinians bear me witness of it.

    DEI. Wretch that I am !   To what am I reserved ?
What hidden pestilence within my roof
Have I received unknowing !   Hapless woman !
She seemed of beauteous form and noble birth ;
Have you not heard her name ? for Lichas said
He knew it not.

    MES.   Daughter of Eurytus,
Her name Iole ; he had not inquired
Touching her race.

    CHOR.   Perdition on the man,
Of all most wicked, who hath thus deceived thee !

    DEI. What's to be done, my friend ?   This dreadful
    news
Afflicts me sorely.

    CHOR.   Go, and learn the whole
From his own lips ; compel him to declare
The truth.

    DEI.   I will ; thou counselst me aright.

    CHOR. Shall we attend you ?

    DEI.   No ; for see he comes,
Uncalled.

SCENE IV.

LICHAS, DEIANIRA, ATTENDANT, MESSENGER, CHORUS.

    LIC. O queen ! what are thy last commands
To thy Alcides? for e'en now I go
To meet him.

                     O

DEI.   Hast thou ta'en so long a journey
To Trachis, and wouldst now so soon return,
Ere I can hold some further converse with thee?
    LIC. If thou wouldst question me of aught, behold
    me
Ready to tell thee.
    DEI.   Wilt thou tell me truth?
    LIC. In all I know; so bear me witness, Jove!
    DEI. Who is that woman thou has brought?
    LIC.   I hear
She's of Euboea; for her race and name
I know them not.
    DEI.   Look on me; who am I?
    LIC. Why ask me this?
    DEI.   Be bold, and answer me.
    LIC. Daughter of Œneus, wife of Hercules,
If I am not deceived 'tis Deianira,
My queen, my mistress?
    DEI.   Am I so indeed?
Am I thy mistress?
    LIC.   Doubtless.
    DEI.   Why, 'tis well
Thou dost confess it: then what punishment
Wouldst thou deserve if thou wert faithless to her?
    LIC. How faithless? meanst thou to betray me?
    DEI.   No;
The fraud is thine.
    LIC.   'Twas folly thus to stay
And hear thee. I must hence.
    DEI.   Thou shalt not go
Till I have asked thee one short question.
    LIC.   Ask it,
For so it seems thou art resolved.
    DEI.   Inform me;
This captive—dost thou know her?
    LIC.   I have told thee;
What wouldst thou more?
    DEI.   Didst thou not say, this slave—
Though now, it seems, thou knowst her not—was
    daughter
Of Eurytus, her name Iole!

Lic.　　　　　　　　　　Where?
To whom did I say this?　What witness have you?

Dei. Assembled multitudes.　The citizens
Of Trachis heard thee.

Lic.　　　　　　　They might say they heard
Reports like these.　But must it therefore seem
A truth undoubted?

Dei.　　　　　　Seem?　Didst thou not swear
That thou hadst brought this woman to partake
The bed of my Alcides?

Lic.　　　　　　　　Did I say so?
But tell me who this stranger is.

Dei.　　　　　　　　　The man
Who heard thee say, Alcides' love for her,
And not the Lydian, laid the city waste.

Lic. Let him come forth and prove it.　'Tis no mark
Of wisdom thus to trifle with th' unhappy.

Dei. Oh! do not, I beseech thee by that power
Whose thunders roll o'er Œta's lofty grove,
Do not conceal the truth.　Thou speakst to one
Not unexperienced in the ways of men—
To one who knows we cannot always joy
In the same object.　'Tis an idle task
To take up arms against all-powerful love:
Love which commands the gods.　Love conquered me,
And wherefore should it not subdue another,
Whose nature and whose passions are the same?
If my Alcides is indeed oppressed
With this sad malady, I blame him not;
That were a folly.　Nor this hapless maid,
Who meant no ill, no injury to me.
'Tis not for this I speak.　But, mark me well;
If thou wert taught by him to utter falsehood,
A vile and shameful lesson didst thou learn;
And if thou art thy own instructor, know
Thou shalt seem wicked e'en when most sincere,
And never be believed.　Speak then the truth;
For to be branded with the name of liar
Is ignominy fit for slaves alone,
And not for thee.　Nor think thou canst conceal it;
Those who have heard the tale will tell it me.

If fear deters thee, thou hast little cause;
For to suspect his falsehood is my grief—
To know it, none. Already have I seen
Alcides' heart estranged to other loves,
Yet did no rival ever hear from me
One bitter word, nor will I now reproach
This wretched slave, e'en though she pines for him
With strongest love. Alas! I pity her,
Whose beauty thus hath been the fatal cause
Of all her misery, laid her country waste,
And brought her here, far from her native land,
A helpless captive. But no more of this;
Only remember, if thou must be false,
Be false to others, but be true to me.

   CHOR. She speaks most kindly to thee. Be persuaded.
Hereafter thou shalt find her not ungrateful;
We too will thank thee.

   LIC.   O my dearest mistress!
Not unexperienced thou in human life,
Nor ignorant. And therefore naught from thee
Will I conceal, but tell thee all the truth:
'Tis as he said, and Hercules indeed
Doth love Iole. For her sake alone
Œchalia, her unhappy country, fell;
This—for 'tis fit I tell thee—he confessed,
Nor willed me to conceal it. But I feared
'Twould pierce thy heart to hear th' unwelcome tale,
And therefore own I would have kept it from thee;
That crime, if such it was, 1 have committed.
But since thou knowst it all, let me entreat thee,
For her sake and thy own, oh! do not hate
This wretched captive, but remember well,
What thou hast promised faithfully perform.
He, whose victorious arm hath conquered all,
Now yields to her, and is a slave to love.

   DEI. 'Tis my resolve to act as thou advisest.
I'll not resist the gods, nor add fresh weight
To my calamity. Let us go in,
That thou mayst bear my orders to Alcides,
And with them gifts in kind return for those
We have received from him. Thou must not hence

With empty hand, who hither broughtst to me
Such noble presents and so fair a train.　　　[*Exeunt.*

SCENE V.

CHORUS.

Strophe.

Thee, Venus, gods and men obey,
　And universal is thy sway;
Need I recount the powers subdued by love?
　Neptune, who shakes the solid ground,
　The king of Erebus profound,
Or, the great lord of all, Saturnian Jove?
　To mortals let the song descend,
　To pity our afflicted friend,
And soothe the injurd Deianira's woes:
　For her the angry rivals came,
　For her they felt an equal flame,
For her, behold! the doubtful battle glows.

Antistrophe.

In dreadful majesty arrayed,
　Affrighting sore the fearful maid,
Uprose the horned monarch of the flood;
　He who through fair Ætolia's plain
　Pours his rich tribute to the main:
A bull's tremendous form belied the god;
　From his own Thebes, to win her love,
　With him the happier son of Jove,
The great Alcides came, and in his hand
　The club, the bow, and glittering spear;
　Whilst Venus, to her votaries near,
Waved o'er their heads her all-deciding wand.

Epode.

Warm and more warm the conflict grows,
Dire was the noise of rattling bows,

Of front to front opposed, and hand to hand;
　　Deep was the animated strife
　　For love, for conquest, and for life ;
Alternate groans re-echoed thro' the land :
　　Whilst pensive on the distant shore
　　She heard the doubtful battle roar,
Many a sad tear the hapless virgin shed ;
　　Far from her tender mother's arms,
　　She knows not yet for whom her charms
She keeps, or who shall share her bridal bed.   [*Exeunt.*

ACT III.

Scene I.

Deianira, Chorus.

Deianira. My guest, in pity to the captive train,
Laments their woes, and takes his kind farewell;
Meantime, my friends, in secret came I here
To pour forth all my miseries, and impart
To you my inmost thoughts—my last resolve.
Alas ! within these walls I have received,
Like the poor sailor, an unhappy freight
To sink me down : no virgin, but a wife—
The wife of my Alcides; his loved arms
Now must embrace us both.   My faithful lord—
Faithful and good I thought him—thus rewards
My tender cares, and all the tedious toils
I suffered for him ; but I will be calm,
For 'tis an evil I have felt before.
And yet to live with her! with her to share
My husband's bed !   What woman can support it ?
Her youth is stealing onward to its prime,
Whilst mine is withered ; and the eye which longs
To pluck the opening flower from the dry leaf
Will turn aside.   Her younger charms, I fear,
Have conquered, and henceforth in name alone

Shall Deianira be Alcides' wife.
But ill do rage and violence become
The prudent matron; therefore, mark me well,
And hear what I have purposed to relieve
My troubled heart. Within a brazen urn,
Concealed from every eye, I long have kept
That ancient gift which Nessus did bequeath me—
The hoary centaur, who was wont for hire
To bear the traveller o'er the rapid flood
Of deep Evenus. Not with oars or sail
He stemmed the torrent, but with nervous arm
Opposed and passed it. Me, when first a bride
I left my father's hospitable roof
With my Alcides, in his arms he bore
Athwart the current; half way o'er, he dared
To offer violence. I shrieked aloud,
When lo! the son of Jove, his bow swift bent,
Sent forth a shaft and pierced the monster's breast,
Who with his dying voice did thus address me:
"Daughter of Œneus, listen to my words,
So shalt thou profit by the last sad journey
Which I shall ever go. If in thy hand
Thou take the drops outflowing from the wound
This arrow made, dipped in the envenomed blood
Of the Lernæan hydra, with that charm
Mayst thou subdue the heart of thy Alcides,
Nor shall another ever gain his love."
Mindful of this, my friends—for from that hour
In secret have I kept the precious gift—
Behold a garment, dipped i' th' very blood,
He gave me; nor did I forget to add
What he enjoined, but have prepared it all.
I know no evil arts, nor would I learn them,
For they who practise such are hateful to me.
I only wish the charm may be of power
To win Alcides from this virgin's love,
And bring him back to Deianira's arms,
If he shall deem it lawful, but if not
I'll go no farther.
    CHOR.   Could we be assured
Such is indeed th' effect, 'tis well determined.

DEI. I cannot but believe it, though as yet
Experience never hath confirmed it to me.
   CHOR. Thou shouldst be certain; thou but seemst to
      know
If thou hast never tried.
   DEI.   I'll try it soon.
For see e'en now he comes out at the portal:
Let him not know our purpose. If the deed
Be wrong, concealment may prevent reproach;
Therefore be silent.

SCENE II.

LICHAS, DEIANIRA, CHORUS.

   LIC.   Speak thy last commands,
Daughter of Œneus, for already long
Have we delayed our journey.
   DEI.   Know then, Lichas,
That whilst thou commun'dst with thy friends, myself
Have hither brought a garment which I wove
For my Alcides; thou must bear it to him.
Tell him, no mortal must with touch profane
Pollute the sacred gift, nor sun behold it,
Nor holy temple, nor domestic hearth,
Ere at the altar of paternal Jove
Himself shall wear it. 'Twas my solemn vow
Whene'er he should return, that, clothed in this,
He to the gods should offer sacrifice.
Bear too this token: he will know it well.
Away! Remember to perform thy office,
But go no farther, so shall double praise
And favour from us both reward thy duty.
   LIC. If I have aught of skill, by Hermes right
Instructed in his art, I will not fail
To bear thy gift, and faithful to report
What thou hast said.
   DEI.   Begone! What here hath passed
Thou knowst.
   LIC.   I do, and shall bear back the news
That all is well.

DEI.   Thou art thyself a witness
How kindly I received the guest he sent me.
  LIC. It filled my heart with pleasure to behold it.
  DEI. What canst thou tell him more? Alas! I fear
He'll know too well the love I bear to him.
Would I could be as certain he'd return it!   [*Exeunt.*

SCENE III.

CHORUS.

Strophe 1.

You who on Œta's craggy summit dwell,
    Or from the rock, whence gushing riv'lets flow,
    Bathe in the warmer springs below.
    You who near the Melian bay
    To golden-shafted Diana hymn the lay,
Now haste to string the lyre, and tune the vocal shell.

Antistrophe 1.

No mournful theme demands your pensive strain,
    But such as, kindled by the sacred fire,
    The Muses might themselves admire—
    A loud and cheerful song. For see,
    The son of Jove returns with victory,
And richest spoils reward a life of toil and pain.

Strophe 2.

Far from his native land he took his way:
    For twelve long moons, uncertain of his fate,
    Did we lament his exiled state.
    What time his anxious wife deplored,
    With never-ceasing tears her absent lord;
But Mars at last hath closed his long laborious day.

Antistrophe 2.

Let him from fair Eubœa's isle appear.
    Let winds and raging seas oppose no more,
    But waft him to the wished-for shore.
    Th' anointed vest's persuasive charms
    Shall bring him soon to Deianira's arms.
Soon shall we see the great the loved Alcides here.

ACT IV.

SCENE I.

DEIANIRA, CHORUS.

DEIANIRA. Alas! my friends, I fear I've gone too far.
CHOR. Great queen, in what?
DEI.   I know not what, but dread
Something to come; lest where I had most hope
Of happiness, I meet with bitterest woe.
CHOR. Meanst thou thy gift to Hercules?
DEI.   I do.
Nor would I henceforth counsel those I loved
To do a dark and desperate deed like this,
Uncertain of th' event.
CHOR.   How was it?   Speak,
If thou canst tell us.
DEI.   Oh! 'twas wonderful!
For you shall hear it.   Know then, the white wool
Wherein I wrapped th' anointed vest, untouched
By any hand, dropped self-consumed away,
And down the stone, e'en like a liquid, flowed
Dissolving—but 'tis fit I tell you all—
Whate'er the wounded centaur did enjoin me
Mindful to practise, sacred as the laws
On brazen tablets graved, I have performed:
Far from the fire, and from the sun's warm beams
He bade me keep the charm; from every eye
In secret hid, till time should call on me
To anoint and use it.   This was done: and now,
The fleece in secret plucked, the charm prepared,
Long from the sun within a chest concealed;
At length I brought it forth, and sent the gift
To my Alcides, when behold a wonder,
Most strange for tongue to tell, or heart of man
E'en to conceive!   Perchance the wool I cast
Into the sunshine; soon as it grew warm
It fell to dust, consuming all away
In most strange manner, then from th' earth uprose

In frothy bubbles, e'en as from the grape
In yellow autumn flows the purple wine.
I know not what to think; but much I fear
I've done a horrid deed. For, why, my friends,
Why should the dying savage wish to serve
His murderer? That could never be. Oh no!
He only meant by flattery to destroy
Me, his destroyer. Truth is come too late,
And I alone have slain my dear Alcides;
I know that by his arrows Chiron fell,
I know whate'er they touched they still were fatal,
That very poison mingled with the blood
Of dying Nessus, will not that too kill
My Hercules? It must: but if he dies,
My resolution is to perish with him;
Those, who their honour and their virtue prize,
Can never live with infamy and shame.

CHOR. 'Tis fit we tremble at a deed of horror;
But 'tis not fitting, ere we know th' event,
To give up hope, and yield us to despair.

DEI. There is no hope where evil counsel's ta'en.

CHOR. But when we err from ignorance alone,
Small is the crime and slight the punishment;
Such is thy fault.

DEI. The guiltless may talk thus,
Who know no ill; not those who are unhappy.

CHOR. No more; unless thou meanst thy son should
hear thee,
Who now returns in search of thy Alcides;
Behold him here.

SCENE II.

HYLLUS, DEIANIRA, CHORUS.

HYL. Oh! would that thou wert dead!
Would I were not thy son! or, being so,
Would I could change thy wicked heart!

DEI. My son,
What means this passion?

HYL. Thou hast slain thy husband;
This very day my father hast thou slain.

DEI. Alas! my child, what sayst thou?

HYL. What is past,
And therefore must be; who can e'er undo
The deed that's done?

DEI. But who could say I did it?

HYL. I saw it with these eyes; I heard it all
From his own lips.

DEI. Where didst thou see him then?
Tell me, oh! quickly tell me.

HYL. If I must,
Observe me well: when Hercules, returned
From conquest, had laid waste the noble city
Of Eurytus, with fair triumphal spoils
He to Eubœa came, where o'er the sea,
Which beats on every side, Cenæum's top
Hangs dreadful, thither to paternal Jove
His new raised altars in the leafy wood
He came to visit: there did my glad eyes
Behold Alcides first. As he prepared
The frequent victim, from the palace came
Lichas thy messenger, and with him brought
The fatal gift: wrapped in the deadly garment
(For such was thy command) twelve oxen then
Without a blemish, firstlings of the spoil,
He slew; together next a hundred fell,
The mingled flock. Pleased with his gaudy vest,
And happy in it, he awhile remained,
Offering with joy his grateful sacrifice;
But, lo! when from the holy victim rose
The bloody flame, and from the pitchy wood
Exhaled its moisture, sudden a cold sweat
Bedewed his limbs, and to his body stuck
As by the hand of some artificer
Close joined to every part, the fatal vest;
Convulsion racked his bones, and through his veins,
Like the fell serpent's deadly venom, raged;
Then questioned he the wretched guiltless Lichas
By what detested arts he had procured
The poisoned garb; he, ignorant of all,
Could only say it was the gift he brought
From Deianira. When Alcides heard it,

Tortured with pain, he took him by the foot,
And hurled him headlong on a pointed rock
That o'er the ocean hung; his brains dashed forth
With mingled blood flowed through his clotted hair
In horrid streams; the multitude with shrieks
Lamented loud the fury of Alcides,
And Lichas' hapless fate; none durst oppose
His raging frenzy; prostrate on the earth
Now would he lay and groan; and now uprising
Would bellow forth his griefs; the mountain-tops
Of Locris, and Eubœa's rocks returned
His dreadful cries; then on the ground outstretched,
In bitterest wrath he cursed the nuptial bed
Of Œneus, and his execrations poured
On thee his worst of foes: at length his eyes,
Distorted forth from the surrounding smoke,
He cast on me, who midst attending crowds
Wept his sad fate; "Approach," he cried, " my son,
Do not forsake thy father; rather come
And share his fate than leave me here. oh! haste,
And take me hence; bear me where never eye
Of mortal shall behold me. O my child,
Let me not perish here." Thus spake my father,
And I obeyed: distracted with his pains
A vessel brings him to this place, and soon
Living or dead you will behold him here.
This have thy horrid machinations done
For thy Alcides: Oh! may justice doom thee
To righteous punishment, if it be lawful
For me to call down vengeance on a mother,
As sure it is on one who hath disclaimed
All piety like thee; the earth sustains not
A better man than him whom thou has murdered,
Nor shalt thou e'er behold his like again.

[*Exit* DEIANIRA.

CHOR. Whence this abrupt departure? Knowst thou
  not
To go in silence thus confirms thy guilt?
  HYL. Let her be gone; and may some prosperous
  gale
Waft her far off, that these abhorring eyes

May never see her more! What boots the name
Of mother, when no longer she performs
A mother's duty? Let her go in peace,
And for her kindness to my father soon
May she enjoy the blessing she bestowed!

CHORUS.

Strophe 1.

True was the oracle divine,
Long since delivered from Dodona's shrine,
　　Which said, Alcides' woes should last
　　Till twelve revolving years were past;
Then should his labours end in sweet repose:
　　Behold, my friends, 'tis come to pass,
　　'Tis all fulfilled; for who, alas!
In peaceful death, or toil or slavery knows?

Antistrophe 1.

If deep within his tortured veins
The centaur's cruel poison reigns,
　　That from the Hydra's baleful breath
　　Destructive flowed, replete with death,
On him another sun shall never rise;
　　The venom runs through every part,
　　And, lo! to Nessus' direful art
Alcides falls a helpless sacrifice.

Strophe 2.

Poor Deianira long deplored
Her waning charms, and ever faithless lord;
　　At length by evil counsel swayed
　　Her passion's dictates she obeyed,
Resolved Alcides' doubtful truth to prove;
　　But now, alas! laments his fate
　　In ceaseless woe, and finds too late
A dying husband, and a foreign love.

Antistrophe 2.

Another death must soon succeed,
Another victim soon shall bleed,
Fatal, Alcides, was the dart
That pierced the rival monarch's heart,
And brought Iole from her native land ;
From Venus did our sorrows flow.
The secret spring of all our woe,
For nought was done but by her dread command.

                            [*Exeunt.*

ACT V.

Scene I.

[*A noise within the Palace.*]

Chorus.

Or I'm deceived, or I did hear loud shrieks
Within the palace; 'twas the voice of one
In anguish; doubtless some calamity
Hath fallen upon us now.   What can it be ?
But see, yon matron, with contracted brow
And unaccustomed sadness, comes to tell
The dreadful news.

Scene II.

Nurse, Chorus.

Nurse.   What woes, my hapless daughters,
Alcides' fatal gift hath brought upon us !
   Chor. What dost thou tell us ?
   Nurse.   Deianira treads
The last sad path of mortals.
   Chor.   Is she gone ?

NURSE. 'Tis so indeed.

CHOR. What! dead?

NURSE. Again I say
She is no more.

CHOR. Alas! how did she perish?

NURSE. Most fearfully: 'twas dreadful to behold.

CHOR. How fell she then?

NURSE. By her own hand.

CHOR. But wherefore?
What madness, what disorder, what could move her
To perpetrate so terrible a deed?
Thus adding death to death.

NURSE. The fatal steel
Destroyed her.

CHOR. Didst thou see it?

NURSE. I was by,
Close by her side.

CHOR. How was it?

NURSE. Her own arm
Struck the sad blow.

CHOR. Indeed!

NURSE. Most veritably.

CHOR. In evil hour this rival virgin came
To bring destruction here.

NURSE. And so she did;
Hadst thou like me been witness to the deed,
Thou wouldst much more have pitied her.

CHOR. Alas!
How could a woman do it?

NURSE. 'Twas most dreadful,
As thou shalt hear, for I will tell thee all:
Soon as she entered at the palace gate
And saw her son prepare the funeral bed,
To th' inmost chamber silent she retired
From every eye, there, at the altar's feet
Falling, lamented loud her widowed state;
And ever as she lit on aught her hands
Had used in happier days, the tears would flow;
From room to room she wandered, and if chance
A loved domestic crossed her she would weep
And mourn her fate, for ever now deprived

Of converse sweet, and hymeneal joys;
Then would she strew her garments on the bed
Of her Alcides (for, concealed, I watched
Her every motion), throw herself upon it,
And as the tears in a warm flood burst forth,
" Farewell! " she cried, " for ever farewell now,
My nuptial couch! for never shalt thou more
Receive this wretched burthen." Thus she spake,
And with quick hand the golden button loosed,
Then cast her robe aside, her bosom bared
And seemed prepared to strike. I ran and told
The dreadful purpose to her son; too late
We came, and saw her wounded to the heart.
The pious son beheld his bleeding mother,
And wept; for well he knew, by anger fired,
And the fell centaur's cruel fraud betrayed,
Unweeting she had done the dreadful deed.
Close to her side he laid him down, and joined
His lips to hers, lamenting sore that thus
He had accused her guiltless; then deplored
His own sad fate, thus suddenly bereaved
Of both his parents. You have heard my tale.
Who to himself shall promise length of life?
None but the fool. For, oh! to-day alone
Is ours. We are not certain of to-morrow.
    CHOR. Which shall I weep? which most our hearts
        should fill
With grief, the present or the future ill?
The dying or the dead? 'Tis equal woe
To feel the stroke, or fear th' impending blow.

Strophe.

Oh! for a breeze to waft us o'er
Propitious to some distant shore!
To shield our souls from sore affright,
And save us from the dreadful sight:
That sight the hardest heart would move
In his last pangs the son of Jove;
To see the poison run through every vein,
And limbs convulsed with agonising pain.

Antistrophe.

Behold th' attendant train is nigh,
I hear the voice of misery;
E'en as the plaintive nightingale,
That warbles sweet her mournful tale;
Silent and slow they lead him on;
Hark! I hear Alcides groan!
Again 'tis silence all! This way they tread;
Or sleeps he now, or rests he with the dead?

Scene III.

Hercules, Hyllus, Nurse, Chorus, Attendants.

Hyl. Alas! my father; whither shall I go?
Wretch that I am. Oh! where shall I betake me?
What will become of thy afflicted son?
Atten. Speak softly, youth, do not awake his pains;
Refrain thy grief, for yet Alcides lives,
Though verging to the tomb; be calm.
Hyl.   What sayst thou?
Doth he yet live?
Atten.   He doth; disturb not thus
His slumbers, nor provoke the dire disease.
Hyl. Alas! I cannot bear to see him thus.
Her. [*awakes*]. O Jove! where am I, and with
        whom? What land
Contains the wretched Hercules, oppressed
With never-ending woes? Ah me! again
The deadly poison racks me.
Atten. [*to* Hyllus].   Seest thou not
'Twere better far to have remained in silence,
And not awaked him.
Hyl.   'Twas impossible
Unmoved to look on such calamity;
I could not do it.
Her.   O Cenæan rocks!
Where smoke the sacred altars, is it thus,
O Jove! thou dost reward my piety?

What dreadful punishment is this thy hand
Hath laid on me, who never could deserve
Such bitter wrath? What incantations now,
What power of medicine can assuage my pain,
Unless great Jove assisted? Health to me
Without him were a miracle indeed.
Let me, oh! let me rest; refuse me not
A little slumber; why will ye torment me?
Why bend me forward? Oh! 'tis worse than death;
Had you not waked me, I had been at peace.
Again it rages with redoubled force;
Where are you now, ye thankless Grecians, where,
Whom I have toiled to serve on the rough main,
And through the pathless wood? Where are you now
To help a dying wretch? Will no kind hand
Stretch forth the friendly sword, or in the flame
Consume me? None, alas! will cut me off
From hated life.

ATTEN.   O youth! assist thy father;
It is beyond my strength; thy quicker sight
May be more useful.

HYL.   My poor aid is ready;
But wheresoe'er I am, 'tis not in me
To expel the subtle poison that destroys him;
Such is the will of Jove.

HER.   My son, my son!
Where art thou? Bear me up, assist me. Oh!
Again it comes, th' unconquerable ill,
The dire disease. O Pallas! aid me now,
Draw forth thy sword, my son; strike, strike thy father,
And heal the wound thy impious mother made.
Oh! could I see her like myself destroyed,
I should be happy! Brother of great Jove,
Sweet Pluto, hear me! Oh! with speedy death
Lay me to rest, and bury all my woes.

CHOR. The anguish of th' unhappy man, my friends,
Is terrible; I tremble but to hear him.

HER. What hath this body suffered? Oh! the toils,
The labours I endured, the pangs I felt,
Unutterable woes! but never aught
So dreadful as this sore calamity.

Oppressed Alcides! Not the wife of Jove,
Nor vile Eurystheus, could torment me thus,
As, Œneus, thy deceitful daughter hath.
Oh! 1 am tangled in a cruel net,
Woven by the Furies: it devours my flesh,
Dries up my veins, and drinks the vital blood;
My body's withered, and I cannot break
Th' indissoluble chain. Nor hostile spear,
Nor earth-born giants, nor the savage herd,
The wild Barbarian, or the Grecian host,
Not all the nations I have journeyed o'er
Could do a deed like this. At last I fall,
Like a poor coward, by a woman's hand,
Unarmed and unassisted. O my son!
Now prove thyself the offspring of Alcides;
Nor let thy reverence of a mother's name
Surpass thy duty to an injured father.
Go, bring her hither, give her to my wrath,
That I may see whom thou wilt most lament
When thou beholdst my vengeance fall on her.
Fear not, my son, but go. Have pity on me,
Pity thy father: all must pity me,
Whilst they behold, e'en as the tender maid,
Alcides weep, who never wept before.
I bore my sorrows all without a groan,
But now thou seest I am a very woman.
Come near, my child. Oh! think what I endure,
For I will show thee. Look on this poor body—
Let all behold it: what a sight is here!
O me! again the cruel poison tears
My entrails, nor affords a moment's ease.
Oh! take me, Pluto, to thy gloomy reign;
Father of lightning, mighty Jove, send down
Thy bolt, and strike me now! Again it racks,
It tortures me! O hands! that once had strength,
And you, my sinewy arms, was it by you
The terrible Nemæan lion fell,
The dreadful hydra, and the lawless race
Of centaurs? Did this withered hand subdue
The Erymanthian boar—wide-wasting plague!
And from the shades of Orcus drag to light

The triple-headed monster? By this arm
Did the fierce guardian of the golden fruit
In Libya's deserts fall? Unnumbered toils
Have I endured of old, and never yet
Did mortal bear a trophy from Alcides.
But nerveless now this arm—see, from the bone
Darts the loose flesh. I waste beneath the power
Of this dark pestilence. O Hercules!
Why boast thy mother sprung of nobler race,
And vainly call thyself the son of Jove?
But, mark me well: this creeping shadow still,
Poor as it is, shall yet revenge itself
On her who did the execrable deed.
Would she were here to feel my wrath, to know
And teach mankind that Hercules, though dead,
As whilst he lived, can scourge the guilty still!

CHOR. Unhappy Greece! How wilt thou mourn the
Of such a man?   [loss

HYL.   Permit me but to speak,
Distempered as thou art, my father, hear me;
Nought shall I ask unfit for thee to grant;
Be calm and listen to me; yet thou knowst not
How groundless thy complaints, and what new joy
Awaits thee still.

HER.   Be brief then, and inform me;
My pains afflict me so I cannot guess
Thy subtle purpose.

HYL.   'Twas to speak of her,
My mother; 'twas to tell thee of her state
And how unweeting she offended thee.

HER. Thou worst of children! Wouldst thou then
    defend
The murderer of thy father? Dar'st thou thus
Recall the sad remembrance of her crime?

HYL. It must not be concealed; I know too well
I can no longer hide it.

HER.   What! Her guilt?
'Tis known already.

HYL.   Thou 'lt not always think so.

HER. Speak then, but take good heed thou show
    thyself

Worthy thy father.

HYL. Know then, she is dead.

HER. Oh! dreadful, murdered? By what hand?

HYL. Her own.

HER. Would she had fallen by mine!

HYL. Alas! my father,
Didst thou know all, thy anger would be changed
To pity for her.

HER. That were strange indeed;
Why dost thou think so?

HYL. She did mean thee well,
But erred unknowing.

HER. Meant she well to slay
Thy father?

HYL. Thy new marriage was the cause:
She had prepared a philtre for thy love,
And knew not 'twas a poison.

HER. But say, who
So skilled in magic arts at Trachis here
Could give her this?

HYL. The savage centaur Nessus,
Who did persuade her it would restore thy love
Given to another wife.

HER. Undone, Alcides!
I die, my child; there is no life for me.
Alas! I see it now; I see my woes;
Hyllus, away, thy father is no more;
Begone, and call thy brothers, call Alcmena,
The wife, alas! in vain, the wife of Jove;
Go, bring them here, that with my latest breath
I may declare my fate long since foretold
By oracles divine.

HYL. Alcmena's gone
To Tyrinth. With her many of thy sons
Remain. Some dwell at Thebes, the rest are here,
And wait with me to hear and to obey thee.

HER. Then listen to me, for the time is come
When thou must prove thyself indeed my son.
Know, Jove, my heavenly sire, long since foretold
I was not born to perish by the hand
Of living man, but from some habitant

Of Pluto's dark abode should meet my fate.
The centaur Nessus—so was it fulfilled—
Though dead destroyed me.   But I'll tell thee more,
New oracles confirmed the old, for know
When to the Selli's sacred grove I came—
The wandering priests who o'er the mountains roam,
And rest their wearied limbs on the cold ground—
An ancient oak prophetic did declare
That if I lived to this decisive hour,
Here all my labours, all my toils should end.
I thought it told me I should live in peace.
Alas! it only meant that I must die,
For death will put an end to every care.
Since thus it is, my son, thou too must join
To ease Alcides.   Let me not reproach thee,
But yield thy willing aid, nor e'er forget
The best of laws, obedience to a father.

HYL. Thy words affright me; but declare thy
    purpose—   .
Behold me ready to perform thy orders
Whate'er they be.
    HER.   First give me then thy hand.
    HYL. But why this pledge, and wherefore anxious
    thus
Dost thou require it?
    HER.   Wilt thou give it me
Or dost refuse?
    HYL.   There, take it; I obey.
    HER. First swear then by the head of Jove my sire.
    HYL. I will; but what?
    HER.   Swear that thou wilt perform
All I enjoin thee.
    HYL.   Bear me witness, Jove!
I swear.
    HER.   And imprecate the wrath divine
If thou performst it not.
    HYL.   I shall not fail;
But if I do, may vengeance swift o'ertake me!
    HER. Thou knowst the top of Œta's sacred hill.
    HYL. I know it well, and many a sacrifice
Have offered there.

HER.   That is the destined place,
Where thou, assisted by thy chosen friends,
My son, must bear the body of Alcides;
There shalt thou cut thee many a leafy branch
From the wild olive and deep-rooted oak,
Then cast me on it, take thy torch, and light
My funeral pile; without one tear or groan
Unmanly do it, if thou art my son;
For if thou failst, remember, after death
A father's curses will sit heavy on thee.

    HYL. Alas! my father, what hast thou commanded?
What hast thou bade me do?

HER.   What must be done,
Or thou art not the son of Hercules.

    HYL. A dreadful deed!   And must I then become
A parricide, and murder thee?

HER.   Oh, no!
My kind physician, balm of all my woes.

    HYL. Myself to cast thee in the flames!   Is that
An office fit for me?

Her.   If that alone
Seem dreadful to thee, yet perform the rest.

    HYL. I'll bear thee thither.

HER.   Wilt thou raise the pile?

    HYL. I will do anything but be myself
Thy executioner.

HER.   'Tis well, my son;
But one thing more, and I am satisfied;
'Tis but a little.

HYL.   Be it e'er so great,
I shall obey.

HER.   Thou knowst the virgin daughter
Of Eurytus.

HYL.   Iole?

HER.   Her, my son;
Remember, 'tis a father's last command,
And thou hast sworn obedience.   That Iole
I do bequeath thee; take her to thy arms
When I am dead, and let her be thy wife:
It is not fitting she who lay by th' side
Of Hercules to any but the son

Of Hercules should e'er descend; to thee
Alone I yield her. Speak not, but obey me;
After thy kind compliance, to refuse
So slight a favour were to cancel all.

HYL. [*aside*]. Alas! distempered as he is, to chide him
Were most unkind; and yet, what madness this!

HER. Thou wilt not do it then?

HYL.   What! marry her
Who slew my mother! her, who hath brought thee
To this sad state! It were an act of frenzy:
Death be my portion rather than to live
With those I hate.

HER. [*turning to the* CHORUS]. He will not pay me then
The duty which he owes a dying father!
But if thou dost not, curses from the gods
Await thee.

HYL.   Oh! thou rav'st; it is the rage
Of thy distemper makes thee talk so wildly.

HER. Thou hast awakened all my woes; again
They torture now.

HYL.   Alas! what doubts arise,
What fears perplex me!

HER.   Meanst thou to dispute
A father's will?

HYL.   Must I then learn of thee
To do a wicked deed?

HER.   It is not wicked
If I request it of thee.

HYL.   Is it just?

HER. It is; the gods are witnesses 'tis just.

HYL. Then by those gods I swear I will perform
What thou commandst: I never can be deemed
Or base, or impious, for obeying thee.

HER. 'Tis well, my son; one added kindness more,
And I am satisfied: before the racks
Of dire convulsion, and the pangs of madness
Again attack me, throw me on the pile.
Haste then, and bear me to it, there at last
I shall have peace and rest from all my sorrows

Hyl. Since 'tis thy will, my father, we submit.
Her. Now, ere the dreadful malady return,
Be firm, my soul, e'en as the hardened steel;
Suspend thy cries, and meet the fatal blow
With joy and pleasure; bear me hence, my friends,
For you have shown yourselves my friends indeed,
And prove the base ingratitude of those
From whom I sprang, the cruel gods, who saw
Unmoved the woes of their unhappy son.
'Tis not in mortal to foresee his fate;
Mine is to them disgraceful, and to me
Most terrible—to me of all mankind
The most distressed, the poor, the lost Alcides.
Chor. Iole, come not forth, unhappy virgin,
Already hast thou seen enough of woe,
And yet fresh sorrows wait thee; but remember,
All is decreed, and all the work of Jove.

ŒDIPUS TYRANNUS.

DRAMATIS PERSONÆ.

ŒDIPUS, *King of Thebes.*
JOCASTA, *Wife of Œdipus.*
CREON, *Brother to Jocasta.*
TIRESIAS, *a Blind Prophet of Thebes.*
A SHEPHERD, *from Corinth.*
A MESSENGER.

AN OLD SHEPHERD, *formerly belonging to Laius.*
HIGH PRIEST OF JUPITER.
CHORUS, *composed of the Priests and Ancient Men of Thebes, Theban Youths, Children of Œdipus, Attendants, &c.*

SCENE.—THEBES, *before the Palace of* ŒDIPUS.

ACT I.

SCENE I.

ŒDIPUS, HIGH PRIEST OF JUPITER.

ŒDIPUS. O my loved sons! the youthful progeny
Of ancient Cadmus, wherefore sit you here
And suppliant thus, with sacred boughs adorned,
Crowd to our altars? Frequent sacrifice
And prayers and sighs and sorrows fill the land.
I could have sent to learn the fatal cause;
But see, your anxious sovereign comes himself
To know it all from you; behold your king,
Renowned Œdipus; do thou, old man,

For best that office suits thy years, inform me,
Why you are come; is it the present ill
That calls you here, or dread of future woe?
Hard were indeed the heart that did not feel
For grief like yours, and pity such distress:
If there be aught that Œdipus can do
To serve his people, know me for your friend.

   PRIEST. O king! thou seest what numbers throng thy
     altars;
Here, bending sad beneath the weight of years,
The hoary priests, here crowd the chosen youth
Of Thebes, with these a weak and suppliant train
Of helpless infants, last in me behold
The minister of Jove : far off thou seest
Assembled multitudes, with laurel crowned,
To where Minerva's hallowed temples rise
Frequent repair, or where Ismenus laves
Apollo's sacred shrine: too well thou knowst
Thy wretched Thebes, with dreadful storms oppressed,
Scarce lifts her head above the whelming flood;
The teeming earth her blasted harvest mourns,
And on the barren plain the flocks and herds
Unnumbered perish; dire abortion thwarts
The mother's hopes, and painful she brings forth
The half-formed infant; baleful pestilence
Hath laid our city waste, the fiery god
Stalks o'er deserted Thebes; whilst with our groans
Enriched, the gloomy god of Erebus
Triumphant smiles. O Œdipus! to thee
We bend; behold these youths, with me they kneel,
And suppliant at thy altars sue for aid,
To thee the first of men, and only less
Than them whose favour thou alone canst gain,
The gods above; thy wisdom yet may heal
The deep-felt wounds, and make the powers divine
Propitious to us. Thebes long since to thee
Her safety owed, when from the Sphynx delivered
Thy grateful people saw thee, not by man
But by the gods instructed, save the land :
Now then, thou best of kings, assist us now.
Oh! by some mortal or immortal aid

Now succour the distress! ∤ On wisdom oft,
And prudent counsels in the hour of ill,
Success awaits. O dearest prince! support,
Relieve thy Thebes; on thee, its saviour once,
Again its calls. Now, if thou wouldst not see
The mem'ry perish of thy former deeds,
Let it not call in vain, but rise, and save!
With happiest omens once and fair success
We saw thee crowned: oh! be thyself again,
And may thy will and fortune be the same!
If thou art yet to reign, O king! remember
A sovereign's riches is a peopled realm;
For what will ships or lofty towers avail
Unarmed with men to guard and to defend them?

   ŒDI. O my unhappy sons! too well I know
Your sad estate. I know the woes of Thebes;
And yet amongst you lives not such a wretch
As Œdipus; for oh! on me, my children,
Your sorrows press. Alas! I feel for you
My people, for myself, for Thebes, for all!
Think not I slept regardless of your ills;
Oh no! with many a tear I wept your fate,
And oft in meditation deep revolved
How best your peace and safety to restore:
The only medicine that my thoughts could find
I have administered: Menæceus' son,
The noble Creon, went by my command
To Delphos from Apollo's shrine, to know
What must be done to save this wretched land:
'Tis time he were returned: I wonder much
At his delay. If, when he comes, your king
Perform not all the god enjoins, then say
He is the worst of men.

   PRIEST.   O king! thy words
Are gracious, and if right these youths inform
    me,
Creon is here.

   ŒDI.   O Phœbus! grant he come
With tidings cheerful as the smile he wears!

   PRIEST. He is the messenger of good; for see,
His brows are crowned with laurel.

ŒDI.   We shall soon
Be satisfied : he comes.

Scene II.

Creon, Œdipus, Priest, Chorus.

ŒDI.   My dearest Creon,
Oh ! say, what answer bearst thou from the god :
Or good, or ill ?
     Creon.   Good, very good ; for know,
The worst of ills, if rightly used, may prove
The means of happiness.
     ŒDI.   What says my friend ?
This answer gives me nought to hope or fear.
    Creon. Shall we retire, or would you that I speak
In public here ?
     ŒDI.   Before them all declare it ;
Their woes sit heavier on me than my own.
     Creon. Then mark what I have heard : the god
        commands
That instant we drive forth the fatal cause
Of this dire pestilence, nor nourish here
The accursed monster.
     ŒDI.   Who ? What monster ? How
Remove it ?
     Creon.   Or by banishment, or death.
Life must be given for life ; for yet his blood
Rests on the city.
     ŒDI.   Whose ? What means the god ?
     Creon. O king ! before thee Laius ruled o'er Thebes.
     ŒDI. I know he did, though I did ne'er behold him.
     Creon. Laius was slain, and on his murderers,
So Phœbus says, we must have vengeance.
     ŒDI.   Where,
Where are the murderers ? Who shall trace the guilt
Buried so long in silence ?
     Creon.   Here, he said,
E'en in this land, what's sought for may be found,
But truth unsearched for seldom comes to light.

ŒDI. How did he fall, and where?—at home,
   abroad?
Died he at Thebes, or in a foreign land?
   CREON. He left his palace, fame reports, to seek
Some oracle; since that, we ne'er beheld him.
   ŒDI. But did no messenger return? Not one
Of all his train, of whom we might inquire
Touching this murder?
   CREON.   One, and one alone,
Came back, who, flying, 'scaped the general slaughter.
But nothing save one little circumstance
Or knew, or e'er related.
   ŒDI.   What was that?
Much may be learned from that. A little dawn
Of light appearing may discover all.
   CREON. Laius, attacked by robbers, and oppressed
By numbers, fell. Such is his tale.
   ŒDI.   Would they—
Would robbers do so desperate a deed,
Unbribed and unassisted?
   CREON.   So, indeed,
Suspicion whispered then. But—Laius dead—
No friend was found to vindicate the wrong.
   ŒDI. But what strange cause could stop inquiry
   thus
Into the murder of a king?
   CREON.   The Sphynx.
Her dire enigma kept our thoughts intent
On present ills, nor gave us time to search
The past mysterious deed.
   ŒDI.   Myself will try
Soon to unveil it. Thou, Apollo, well,
And well hast thou, my Creon, lent thy aid.
Your Œdipus shall now perform his part.
Yes, I will fight for Phœbus and my country.
And so I ought. For not to friends alone,
Or kindred, owe I this, but to myself.
Who murdered him, perchance would murder me!
His cause is mine. Wherefore, my children, rise;
Take hence your suppliant boughs, and summon here
The race of Cadmus—my assembled people.

Nought shall be left untried. Apollo leads,
And we shall rise to joy, or sink for ever.
   PRIEST. Haste, then, my sons, for this we hither
      came :
About it quick, and may the god who sent
This oracle, protect, defend, and save us!   [*Exeunt.*

CHORUS.

Strophe 1.

O thou great oracle divine !
Who didst to happy Thebes remove
   From Delphi's golden shrine,
And in sweet sounds declare the will of Jove.
   Daughter of hope, oh ! soothe my soul to rest,
   And calm the rising tumult in my breast.
Look down, O Phœbus ! on thy loved abode.
   Speak, for thou knowst the dark decrees of fate,
   Our present and our future state.
O Delian ! be thou still our healing god ?

Antistrophe 1.

Minerva, first on thee I call,
Daughter of Jove, immortal maid,
   Low beneath thy feet we fall :
Oh ! bring thy sister Dian to our aid.
   Goddess of Thebes, from thy imperial throne
   Look with an eye of gentle pity down ;
And thou, far-shooting Phœbus, once the friend
   Of this unhappy, this devoted land,
   Oh ! now, if ever, let thy hand
Once more be stretched to save and to defend !

Strophe 2.

Great Thebes, my sons, is now no more ;
She falls and ne'er again shall rise,
   Nought can her health or strength restore,
The mighty nation sinks, she droops, she dies.

Stripped of her fruits, behold the barren earth—
The half-formed infant struggles for a birth.
The mother sinks unequal to her pain :
   Whilst quick as birds in airy circles fly,
   Or lightnings from an angry sky,
Crowds press on crowds to Pluto's dark domain.

Antistrophe 2.

Behold what heaps of wretches slain,
Unburied, unlamented lie,
   Nor parents now nor friends remain
To grace their deaths with pious obsequy.
   The aged matron and the blooming wife,
   Cling to the altars—sue for added life.
With sighs and groans united Pæans rise ;
   Re-echoed, still doth great Apollo's name
   Their sorrows and their wants proclaim.
Frequent to him ascends the sacrifice.

Strophe 3.

Haste then, Minerva, beauteous maid,
Descend in this afflictive hour,
   Haste to thy dying people's aid,
Drive hence this baneful, this destructive power !
   Who comes not armed with hostile sword or shield,
   Yet strews with many a corse th' ensanguined field ;
To Amphitrite's wide extending bed
   Oh ! drive him, goddess, from thy favourite land,
   Or let him, by thy dread command,
Bury in Thracian waves his ignominious head.

Antistrophe 3.

Father of all, immortal Jove !
Oh ! now thy fiery terrors send ;
   From thy dreadful stores above
Let lightnings blast him and let thunders rend
   And thou, O Lydian king ! thy aid impart ;
   Send from thy golden bow, th' unerring dart ;

H

Smile, chaste Diana, on this loved abode,
   Whilst Theban Bacchus joins the maddening throng,
   O god of wine and mirth and song!
Now with thy torch destroy the base inglorious god.
                                [*Exeunt.*

ACT II.

SCENE I.

ŒDIPUS, CHORUS.   *The People assembled.*

ŒDI. Your prayers are heard: and if you will obey
Your king, and hearken to his words, you soon
Shall find relief; myself will heal your woes.
I was a stranger to the dreadful deed,
A stranger e'en to the report till now;
And yet without some traces of the crime
I should not urge this matter; therefore hear me.
I speak to all the citizens of Thebes,
Myself a citizen—observe me well:
If any know the murderer of Laius,
Let him reveal it; I command you all.
But if restrained by dread of punishment
He hide the secret, let him fear no more;
For nought but exile shall attend the crime
Whene'er confessed; if by a foreign hand
The horrid deed was done, who points him out
Commands our thanks, and meets a sure reward;
But if there be who knows the murderer,
And yet conceals him from us, mark his fate,
Which here I do pronounce: Let none receive
Throughout my kingdom, none hold converse with him,
Nor offer prayer, nor sprinkle o'er his head
The sacred cup; let him be driven from all,
By all abandoned, and by all accursed,
For so the Delphic oracle declared;

And therefore to the gods I pay this duty
And to the dead.   Oh! may the guilty wretch,
Whether alone, or by his impious friends
Assisted, he performed the horrid deed,
Denied the common benefits of nature,
Wear out a painful life!   And oh! if here,
Within my palace, I conceal the traitor,
On me and mine alight the vengeful curse!
To you, my people, I commit the care
Of this important business; 'tis my cause,
The cause of Heaven, and your expiring country.
E'en if the god had nought declared, to leave
This crime unexpiated were most ungrateful.
He was the best of kings, the best of men;
That sceptre now is mine which Laius bore;
His wife is mine; so would his children be
Did any live; and therefore am I bound,
E'en as he were my father, to revenge him.
Yes, I will try to find this murderer,
I owe it to the son of Labdacus,
To Polydorus, Cadmus, and the race
If great Agenor.   Oh! if yet there are,
Who will not join me in the pious deed,
From such may earth withhold her annual store,
And barren be their bed, their life most wretched,
And their death cruel as the pestilence
That wastes our city!   But on you, my Thebans,
Who wish us fair success, may justice smile
Propitious, and the gods for ever bless!

CHOR. O king! thy imprecations unappalled
I hear, and join thee, guiltless of the crime,
Nor knowing who committed it.   The god
Alone, who gave the oracle, must clear
Its doubtful sense, and point out the offender.

ŒDI. 'Tis true.   But who shall force the powers
    divine
To speak their hidden purpose?
CHOR.   One thing more,
If I might speak.
ŒDI.   Say on, whate'er thy mind
Shall dictate to thee.

CHOR.　　　　　　As amongst the gods
All-knowing Phœbus, so to mortal men
Doth sage Tiresias in foreknowledge sure
Shine forth pre-eminent.　Perchance his aid
Might much avail us.
　　　ŒDI.　　　　　　Creon did suggest
The same expedient, and by his advice
Twice have I sent for this Tiresias ; much
I wonder that he comes not.
　　　CHOR.　　　　　　'Tis most fitting
We do consult him ; for the idle tales
Which rumour spreads are not to be regarded.
　　　ŒDI. What are those tales? for nought should we
　　　　　despise.
　　　CHOR. 'Tis said some travellers did attack the king
　　　ŒDI. It is ; but still no proof appears.
　　　CHOR.　　　　　　And yet,
If it be so, thy dreadful execration
Will force the guilty to confess.
　　　ŒDI.　　　　　　Oh no!
Who fears not to commit the crime will ne'er
Be frightened at the curse that follows it.
　　　CHOR. Behold he comes, who will discover all,
The holy prophet.　See! they lead him hither ;
He knows the truth and will reveal it to us.

SCENE II.

TIRESIAS, ŒDIPUS, CHORUS.

　　　ŒDI. O sage Tiresias, thou who knowest all
That can be known, the things of heaven above
And earth below, whose mental eye beholds,
Blind as thou art, the state of dying Thebes,
And weeps her fate, to thee we look for aid,
On thee alone for safety we depend.
This answer, which perchance thou hast not heard,
Apollo gave : the plague, he said, should cease
When those who murdered Laius were discovered
And paid the forfeit of their crime by death

Or banishment.   Oh ! do not then conceal
Aught that thy art prophetic from the flight
Of birds or other omens may disclose.
Oh ! save thyself, save this afflicted city,
Save Œdipus, avenge the guiltless dead
From this pollution !   Thou art all our hope ;
Remember, 'tis the privilege of man,
His noblest function, to assist the wretched.

TIR.   Alas ! what misery it is to know
When knowledge is thus fatal !   O Tiresias !
Thou art undone !   Would I had never come !

ŒDI.   What sayst thou ?   Whence this strange
     dejection ?   Speak.

TIR.   Let me be gone ; 'twere better for us both
That I retire in silence : be advised.

ŒDI.   It is ingratitude to Thebes, who bore
And cherished thee—it is unjust to all,
To hide the will of heaven.

TIR.   'Tis rash in thee
To ask, and rash I fear will prove my answer.

CHOR.   Oh ! do not, by the gods, conceal it from us,
Suppliant we all request, we all conjure thee.

TIR.   You know not what you ask ; I'll not unveil
Your miseries to you.

ŒDI.   Knowst thou then our fate,
And wilt not tell it ?   Meanst thou to betray
Thy country and thy king ?

TIR.   I would not make
Myself and thee unhappy ; why thus blame
My tender care, nor listen to my caution ?

ŒDI.   Wretch as thou art, thou wouldst provoke a
     stone—
Inflexible and cruel—still implored
And still refusing.

TIR.   Thou condemn'st my warmth,
Forgetful of thy own.

ŒDI.   Who would not rage
To see an injured people treated thus
With vile contempt ?

TIR.   What is decreed by heaven
Must come to pass, though I reveal it not.

ŒDI. Still, 'tis thy duty to inform us of it.

TIR. I'll speak no more, not though thine anger
    swell
E'en to its utmost.

ŒDI.   Nor will I be silent.
I tell thee once for all thou wert thyself
Accomplice in this deed. Nay, more, I think,
But for thy blindness, wouldst with thy own hand
Have done it too.

TIR.   'Tis well. Now hear, Tiresias.
The sentence, which thou didst thyself proclaim,
Falls on thyself. Henceforth shall never man
Hold converse with thee, for thou art accursed—
The guilty cause of all this city's woes.

ŒDI. Audacious traitor! thinkst thou to escape
The hand of vengeance?

TIR.   -Yes, I fear thee not;
For truth is stronger than a tyrant's arm.

ŒDI. Whence didst thou learn this? Was it from
    thy art?

TIR. I learned it from thyself. Thou didst compel
    me
To speak, unwilling as I was.

ŒDI.   Once more
Repeat it then, that I may know my fate
More plainly still.

TIR.   Is it not plain already?
Or meanst thou but to tempt me?

ŒDI.   No, but say,
Speak it again.

TIR.   Again then I declare
Thou art thyself the murderer whom thou seekst.

ŒDI. A second time thou shalt not pass unpunished.

TIR. What wouldst thou say, if I should tell thee all?

ŒDI. Say what thou wilt. For all is false.

TIR.   Know then,
That Œdipus, in shameful bonds united
With those he loves, unconscious of his guilt,
Is yet most guilty.

ŒDI.   Dar'st thou utter more,
And hope for pardon?

TIR.   Yes, if there be strength
In sacred truth.
ŒDI.   But truth dwells not in thee :
Thy body and thy mind are dark alike,
For both are blind.   Thy ev'ry sense is lost.
   TIR. Thou dost upbraid me with the loss of that
For which thyself ere long shall meet reproach
From every tongue.
   ŒDI.   Thou blind and impious traitor !
Thy darkness is thy safeguard, or this hour
Had been thy last.
   TIR.   It is not in my fate
To fall by thee.   Apollo guards his priest.
   ŒDI. Was this the tale of Creon, or thy own ?
   TIR. Creon is guiltless, and the crime is thine.
   ŒDI. O riches, power, dominion ! and thou far
Above them all, the best of human blessings,
Excelling wisdom, how doth envy love
To follow and oppress you !   This fair kingdom,
Which by the nation's choice, and not my own,
I here possess, Creon, my faithful friend,
For such I thought him once, would now wrest from me,
And hath suborned this vile impostor here,
This wandering hypocrite, of sharpest sight
When interest prompts, but ignorant and blind
When fools consult him.   Tell me, prophet, where
Was all thy art when the abhorred Sphynx
Alarmed our city?   Wherefore did not then
Thy wisdom save us?   Then the man divine
Was wanting.   But thy birds refused their omens,
Thy god was silent.   Then came Œdipus,
This poor, unlearned, uninstructed sage ;
Who not from birds uncertain omens drew,
But by his own sagacious mind explored
The hidden mystery.   And now thou com'st
To cast me from the throne my wisdom gained,
And share with Creon my divided empire.
But you should both lament your ill-got power,
You and your bold compeer.   For thee, this moment,
But that I bear respect unto thy age,
I'd make thee rue thy execrable purpose.

CHOR. You both are angry, therefore both to blame;
Much rather should you join, with friendly zeal
And mutual ardour, to explore the will
Of all-deciding Heaven.

TIR.   What though thou rul'st
O'er Thebes despotic, we are equal here:
I am Apollo's subject, and not thine,
Nor want I Creon to protect me. No;
I tell thee, king, this blind Tiresias tells thee,
Seeing thou seest not, knowst not where thou art,
What, or with whom. Canst thou inform me who
Thy parents are, and what thy horrid crimes
'Gainst thy own race, the living and the dead?
A father's and a mother's curse attend thee;
Soon shall their furies drive thee from the land,
And leave thee dark like me. What mountain then,
Or conscious shore, shall not return the groans
Of Œdipus, and echo to his woes?
When thou shalt look on the detested bed,
And in that haven where thou hop'st to rest,
Shalt meet with storm and tempest, then what ills
Shall fall on thee and thine! Now vent thy rage
On old Tiresias and the guiltless Creon;
We shall be soon avenged, for ne'er did Heaven
Cut off a wretch so base, so vile as thou art.

ŒDI. Must I bear this from thee? Away, begone!
Home, villain, home!

TIR.   I did not come to thee
Unsent for.

ŒDI. Had I thought thou wouldst have thus
Insulted me, I had not called thee hither.

TIR. Perhaps thou holdst Tiresias as a fool
And madman; but thy parents thought me wise.

ŒDI. My parents, saidst thou? Speak, who were my
        parents?

TIR. This day, that gives thee life, shall give thee
        death.

ŒDI. Still dark, and still perplexing are the words
Thou utter'st.

TIR. 'Tis thy business to unriddle,
And therefore thou canst best interpret them.

ŒDI. Thou dost reproach me for my virtues.
TIR.   They,
And thy good fortune, have undone thee.
ŒDI.   Since
I saved the city, I'm content.
TIR.   Farewell.
Boy, lead me hence.
ŒDI. Away with him, for here
His presence but disturbs us ; being gone,
We shall be happier.
TIR.   Œdipus, I go,
But first inform me, for I fear thee not,
Wherefore I came.   Know then, I came to tell thee,
The man thou seekst, the man on whom thou pouredst
Thy execrations, e'en the murderer
Of Laius, now is here—a seeming stranger
And yet a Theban.   He shall suffer soon
For all his crimes : from light and affluence driven
To penury and darkness, poor and blind,
Propped on his staff, and from his native land
Expelled, I see him in a foreign clime
A helpless wanderer ; to his sons at once
A father and a brother ; child and husband
Of her from whom he sprang.   Adulterous,
Incestuous parricide, now fare thee well !
Go, learn the truth, and if it be not so,
Say I have ne'er deserved the name of prophet.

CHORUS.

Strophe 1.

When will the guilty wretch appear,
    Whom Delphi's sacred oracle demands ;
    Author of crimes too black for mortal ear,
    Dipping in royal blood his sacrilegious hands ?
Swift as the storm by rapid whirlwinds driven ;
Quick let him fly th' impending wrath of Heaven ;
    For lo ! the angry son of Jove,
    Armed with red lightnings from above,
Pursues the murderer with immortal hate,
And round him spreads the snares of unrelenting fate.

Antistrophe 1.

From steep Parnassus' rocky cave,
  Covered with snow, came forth the dread command;
    Apollo thence his sacred mandate gave,
  To search the man of blood through every land:
Silent and sad, the weary wanderer roves
O'er pathless rocks and solitary groves,
    Hoping to 'scape the wrath divine,
    Denounced from great Apollo's shrine;
Vain hopes to 'scape the fate by Heaven decreed,
For vengeance hovers still o'er his devoted head.

Strophe 2.

Tiresias, famed for wisdom's lore,
  Hath dreadful ills to Œdipus divined;
    And as his words mysterious I explore,
  Unnumbered doubts perplex my anxious mind.
Now raised by hope, and now with fears oppressed,
Sorrow and joy alternate fill my breast:
    How should these hapless kings be foes,
    When never strife between them rose?
Or why should Laius, slain by hands unknown,
Bring foul disgrace on Polybus' unhappy son?

Antistrophe 2.

From Phœbus and all-seeing Jove
  Nought can be hid of actions here below;
    But earthly prophets may deceitful prove,
  And little more than other mortals know:
Though much in wisdom man doth man excel,
In all that's human error still must dwell:
    Could he commit the bloody deed,
    Who from the Sphinx our city freed?
Oh, no! he never shed the guiltless blood;
The Sphynx declares him wise, and innocent, and good.

                                  [Exeunt.

ACT III.

SCENE I.

CREON, CHORUS

CREON. O citizens! with grief I hear your king
Hath blasted the fair fame of guiltless Creon!
And most unjustly brands me with a crime
My soul abhors: whilst desolation spreads
On every side, and universal ruin
Hangs o'er the land, if I in word or deed
Could join to swell the woes of hapless Thebes,
I were unworthy—nay, I would not wish—
To live another day: alas! my friends,
Thus to be deemed a traitor to my country,
To you my fellow-citizens, to all
That hear me, 'tis infamy and shame;
I cannot, will not bear it.
 CHOR.   'Twas th' effect
Of sudden anger only—what he said
But could not think.
 CREON.   Who told him I suborned
The prophet to speak falsely? What could raise
This vile suspicion?
 CHOR.   Such he had, but whence
I know not.
 CREON.   Talked he thus with firm composure
And confidence of mind?
 CHOR.   I cannot say;
'Tis not for me to know the thoughts of kings,
Or judge their actions! But behold! he comes.

SCENE II.

ŒDIPUS, CREON, CHORUS.

ŒDI. Ha! Creon here? And dar'st thou thus
 approach
My palace, thou who wouldst have murdered me,

And ta'en my kingdom?   By the gods I ask thee;
Answer me, traitor, didst thou think me fool,
Or coward, that I could not see thy arts,
Or had not strength to vanquish them?   What madness,
What strange infatuation led thee on,
Without or force or friends, to grasp at empire,
Which only their united force can give?
What wert thou doing?

CREON.   Hear what I shall answer,
Then judge impartial.

ŒDI.   Thou canst talk it well,
But I shall ne'er attend to thee; thy guilt
Is plain; thou art my deadliest foe.

  CREON.   But hear
What I shall urge.

ŒDI.   Say not thou art innocent.

CREON. If self-opinion void of reason seem
Conviction to thee, know, thou err'st most grossly

ŒDI. And thou more grossly, if thou thinkst to pass
Unpunished for this injury to thy friend.

CREON. I should not, were I guilty; but what crime
Have I committed?   Tell me.

ŒDI.   Wert not thou
The man who urged me to require the aid
Of your all-knowing prophet?

CREON.   True, I was;
I did persuade you; so I would again.

ŒDI. How long is it since Laius——

CREON.   Laius!   What?

ŒDI. Since Laius fell by hands unknown?

CREON.   A long,
Long tract of years.

ŒDI.   Was this Tiresias then
A prophet?

CREON.   Ay; in wisdom and in fame
As now excelling.

ŒDI.   Did he then say aught
Concerning me?

CREON.   I never heard he did.

ŒDI. Touching this murder, did you ne'er inquire
Who were the authors?

CREON.   Doubtless; but in vain.

ŒDI. Why did not this same prophet then inform you

CREON. I know not that, and when I'm ignorant
I'm always silent.

ŒDI.   What concerns thyself
At least thou knowst, and therefore shouldst declare it.

CREON. What is it?   Speak; and if 'tis in my power,
I'll answer thee.

ŒDI.   Thou knowst, if this Tiresias
Had not combined with thee, he would not thus
Accuse me as the murderer of Laius.

CREON. What he declares, thou best canst tell: of me,
What thou requirest, myself am yet to learn.

ŒDI. Go, learn it then; but ne'er shalt thou discover,
That Œdipus is guilty.

CREON.   Art not thou
My sister's husband?

ŒDI.   Granted.

CREON.   Joined with her,
Thou rul'st o'er Thebes.

ŒDI.   'Tis true, and all she asks
Most freely do I give her.

CREON.   Is not Creon
In honour next to you?

ŒDI.   Thou art; and therefore
The more ungrateful.

CREON.   Hear what I shall plead
And thou wilt never think so.   Tell me, prince,
Is there a man who would prefer a throne,
With all its dangers, to an equal rank
In peace and safety?   I am not of those
Who choose the name of king before the power;
Fools only make such wishes: I have all
From thee, and fearless I enjoy it all:
Had I the sceptre, often must I act
Against my will.   Know then, I am not yet
So void of sense and reason as to quit
A real 'vantage for a seeming good.
Am I not happy, am I not revered,
Embraced, and loved by all?   To me they come
Who want thy favour, and by me acquire it:

What then should Creon wish for; shall he leave
All this for empire? Bad desires corrupt
The fairest mind. I never entertained
A thought so vile, nor would I lend my aid
To forward such base purposes. But go
To Delphos, ask the sacred oracle
If I have spoke the truth; if there you find
That with the prophet I conspired, destroy
The guilty Creon; not thy voice alone
Shall then condemn me, for myself will join
In the just sentence. But accuse me not
On weak suspicion's most uncertain test.
Justice would never call the wicked good,
Or brand fair virtue with the name of vice,
Unmerited: to cast away a friend,
Faithful and just, is to deprive ourselves
Of life and being, which we hold most dear:
But time and time alone revealeth all;
That only shows the good man's excellence:
A day sufficeth to unmask the wicked.

 CHOR. O king! his caution merits your regard;
Who judge in haste do seldom judge aright.

 ŒDI. When they are quick who plot against my life,
'Tis fit I should be quick in my defence;
If I am tame and silent, all they wish
Will soon be done, and Œdipus must fall.

 CREON. What wouldst thou have? my banishment?

 ŒDI.   Thy death,

 CREON. But first inform me wherefore I should die.

 ŒDI. Dost thou rebel then? Wilt thou not submit?

 CREON. Not when I see thee thus deceived.

 ŒDI.   'Tis fit
I should defend my own.

 CREON.   And so should I.

 ŒDI. Thou art a traitor.

 CREON.   What if it should prove
I am not so.

 ŒDI.   A king must be obeyed.

 CREON. Not if his orders are unjust.

 ŒDI.   O Thebes!
O citizens!

CREON.   I too can call on Thebes;
She is my country.

CHOR.   Oh! no more, my lords;
For see, Jocasta comes in happiest hour
To end your contest.

SCENE III.

JOCASTA, CREON, ŒDIPUS, CHORUS.

JOC.   Whence this sudden tumult?
O princes! Is this well, at such a time
With idle broils to multiply the woes
Of wretched Thebes? Home, home, for shame! nor
      thus
With private quarrels swell the public ruin.

CREON. Sister, thy husband hath most basely used
      me;
He threatens me with banishment or death.

ŒDI. I do confess it; for he did conspire
With vile and wicked arts against my life.

CREON. Oh! may I never prosper, but accursed,
Unpitied, perish if I ever did.

JOC. Believe him, Œdipus; revere the gods
Whom he contests, if thou dost love Jocasta;
Thy subjects beg it of thee.

CHOR.   Hear, O king!
Consider, we entreat thee.

ŒDI.   What wouldst have?
Think you I'll e'er submit to him?

CHOR.   Revere
His character, his oath, both pleading for him.

ŒDI. But know you what you ask?

CHOR.   We do.

ŒDI.   What is it?

CHOR. We ask thee to believe a guiltless friend,
Nor cast him forth dishonoured thus, on slight
Suspicion's weak surmise.

ŒDI.   Requesting this,
You do request my banishment, or death.

CHOR. No; by yon leader of the heavenly host,

Th' immortal sun, I had not such a thought;
I only felt for Thebes' distressful state,
And would not have it by domestic strife
Embittered thus.
  ŒDI.   Why, let him then depart:
If Œdipus must die, or leave his country
For shameful exile, be it so; I yield
To thy request, not his; for hateful still
Shall Creon ever be.
  CREON.   Thy stubborn soul
Bends with reluctance, and when anger fires it
Is terrible; but natures formed like thine
Are their own punishment.
  ŒDI.   Wilt thou not hence?
Wilt not begone?
  CREON.   I go; thou knowst me not;
But these will do me justice.   [*Exit* CREON.

SCENE IV.

JOCASTA, ŒDIPUS, CHORUS.

  CHOR.   Princess, now
Persuade him to retire.
  JOC.   First, let me know
The cause of this dissension.
  CHOR.   From reports
Uncertain, and suspicions most injurious,
The quarrel rose.
  JOC.   Was th' accusation mutual?
  CHOR. It was.
  JOC.   What followed then?
  CHOR.   Ask me no more;
Enough 's already known; we 'll not repeat
The woes of hapless Thebes.
  ŒDI.   You are all blind,
Insensible, unjust; you love me not,
Yet boast your piety.
  CHOR.   I said before,
Again I say, that not to love my king

E'en as myself, would mark me for the worst
Of men. For thou didst save expiring Thebes.
Oh! rise once more, protect, preserve thy country!

Joc. O king! inform me, whence this strange dissension?

ŒDI. I'll tell thee, my Jocasta, for thou knowst
The love I bear thee, what this wicked Creon
Did artfully devise against me.

Joc.   Speak it,
If he indeed be guilty.

ŒDI.   Creon says
That I did murder Laius.

Joc.   Spake he this
As knowing it himself, or from another?

ŒDI. He had suborned that evil-working priest,
And sharpens every tongue against his king.

Joc. Let not a fear perplex thee, Œdipus;
Mortals know nothing of futurity,
And these prophetic seers are all impostors;
I'll prove it to thee. Know then, Laius once,
Not from Apollo, but his priests, received
An oracle, which said it was decreed
He should be slain by his own son, the offspring
Of Laius and Jocasta. Yet he fell
By strangers, murdered, for so fame reports,
By robbers, in the place where three ways meet.
A son was born, but ere three days had passed
The infant's feet were bored. A servant took
And left him on the pathless mountain's top,
To perish there. Thus Phœbus ne'er decreed
That he should kill his father, or that Laius,
Which much he feared, should by his son be slain.
Such is the truth of oracles. Henceforth
Regard them not. What heaven would have us know,
It can with ease unfold, and will reveal it.

ŒDI. What thou hast said, Jocasta, much disturbs
me;
I tremble at it.

Joc.   Wherefore shouldst thou fear?

ŒDI. Methought I heard thee say, Laius was slain
Where three ways meet.

Joc.   'Twas so reported then,
And is so still.

Œdi.   Where happened the misfortune?

Joc. In Phocis, where the roads unite that lead
To Delphi and to Daulia.

Œdi.   How long since?

Joc. A little time ere you began to reign
O'er Thebes, we heard it.

Œdi.   O almighty Jove!
What wilt thou do with me?

Joc.   Why talkst thou thus?

Œdi. Ask me no more; but tell me of this Laius:
What was his age and stature?

Joc.   He was tall;
His hairs just turning to the silver hue;
His form not much unlike thy own.

Œdi.   O me!
Sure I have called down curses on myself
Unknowing.

Joc.   Ha! what sayst thou, Œdipus?
I tremble whilst I look on thee.

Œdi.   Oh! much
I fear the prophet saw too well; but say,
One thing will make it clear.

Joc.   I dread to hear it;
Yet speak, and I will tell thee.

Œdi.   Went he forth
With few attendants, or a numerous train,
In kingly pomp?

Joc.   They were but five in all,
The herald with them; but one chariot there,
Which carried Laius.

Œdi.   Oh! 'tis but too plain.
Who brought the news?

Joc.   A servant, who alone
Escaped with life.

Œdi.   That servant, is he here?

Joc. Oh no! His master slain, when he returned
And saw thee on the throne of Thebes, with prayer
Most earnest he beseeched me to dismiss him,
That he might leave this city, where he wished

No longer to be seen, but to retire,
And feed my flocks ; I granted his request,
For that and more his honest services
Had merited.

    ŒDI.   I beg he may be sent for
Immediately.

    Joc.   He shall ; but wherefore is it ?

    ŒDI. I fear thou 'st said too much, and therefore wish
To see him.

    Joc.   He shall come ; but, O my lord !
Am I not worthy to be told the cause
Of this distress ?

    ŒDI.   Thou art, and I will tell thee ;
Thou art my hope—to whom should I impart
My sorrows, but to thee ? Know then, Jocasta,
I am the son of Polybus, who reigns
At Corinth, and the Dorian Merope
His queen ; there long I held the foremost rank,
Honoured and happy, when a strange event
(For strange it was, though little meriting
The deep concern I felt) alarmed me much :
A drunken reveller at a feast proclaimed,
That I was only the supposed son
Of Corinth's king. Scarce could I bear that day
The vile reproach. The next, I sought my parents
And asked of them the truth ; they too, enraged,
Resented much the base indignity.
I liked their tender warmth, but still I felt
A secret anguish, and, unknown to them,
Sought out the Pythian oracle. In vain.
Touching my parents nothing could I learn ;
But dreadful were the miseries it denounced
Against me. 'Twas my fate, Apollo said,
To wed my mother, to produce a race
Accursed and abhorred ; and last, to slay
My father who begat me. Sad decree !
Lest I should e'er fulfil the dire prediction,
Instant I fled from Corinth, by the stars
Guiding my hapless journey to the place
Where thou report'st this wretched king was slain.
But I will tell thee the whole truth. At length

I came to where the three ways meet, when, lo!
A herald, with another man like him
Whom thou describst, and in a chariot, met me.
Both strove with violence to drive me back ;
Enraged, I struck the charioteer, when straight,
As I advanced, the old man saw, and twice
Smote me o' th' head, but dearly soon repaid
The insult on me ; from his chariot rolled
Prone on the earth, beneath my staff he fell,
And instantly expired ! Th' attendant train
All shared his fate. If this unhappy stranger
And Laius be the same, lives there a wretch
So cursed, so hateful to the gods as I am ?
Nor citizen nor alien must receive,   ·
Or converse, or communion hold with me,
But drive me forth with infamy and shame.
The dreadful curse pronounced with my own lips
Shall soon o'ertake me. I have stained the bed
Of him whom I had murdered ; am I then
Aught but pollution ? If I fly from hence,
The bed of incest meets me, and I go
To slay my father Polybus, the best,
The tenderest parent. This must be the work
Of some malignant power. Ye righteous gods !
Let me not see that day, but rest in death,
Rather than suffer such calamity.

    CHOR. O king ! we pity thy distress; but wait
With patience his arrival, and despair not.

    ŒDI. That shepherd is my only hope : Jocasta,
Would he were here !

    JOC.   Suppose he were ; what then !
What wouldst thou do ?

    ŒDI.   I'll tell thee : if he says
The same as thou dost, I am safe and guiltless.

    JOC. What said I, then ?

    ŒDI.   Thou saidst he did report
Laius was slain by robbers ; if 'tis true
He fell by numbers, I am innocent,
For I was unattended ; if but one
Attacked and slew him, doubtless I am he.

Joc. Be satisfièd it must be as he first
Reported it ; he cannot change the tale :
Not I alone, but the whole city heard it.
Or grant he should, the oracle was ne'er
Fulfilled ; for Phœbus said, Jocasta's son
Should slay his father.   That could never be ;
For, oh ! Jocasta's son long since is dead.
He could not murder Laius ; therefore never
Will I attend to prophecies again.
   ŒDI. Right, my Jocasta ; but, I beg thee, send
And fetch this shepherd ; do not fail.
   Joc.   I will
This moment ; come, my lord, let us go in :
I will do nothing but what pleases thee.   [*Exeunt.*

SCENE V.

CHORUS.

Strophe 1.

Grant me henceforth, ye powers divine,
   In virtue's purest paths to tread !
   In every word, in every deed,
May sanctity of manners ever shine !
   Obedient to the laws of Jove,
   The laws descended from above,
Which, not like those by feeble mortals given,
   Buried in dark oblivion lie,
   Or worn by time decay, and die,
But bloom eternal like their native heaven !

Antistrophe 1.

Pride first gave birth to tyranny :
   That hateful vice, insulting pride,
   When, every human power defied,
She lifts to glory's height her votary ;
   Soon stumbling, from her tottering throne
   She throws the wretched victim down.

But may the god indulgent hear my prayer,
   That god whom humbly I adore,
   Oh! may he smile on Thebes once more,
And take its wretched monarch to his care!

Strophe 2.

Perish the impious and profane,
   Who, void of reverential fear,
   Nor justice nor the laws revere,
Who leave their god for pleasure or for gain!
   Who swell by fraud their ill-got store,
   Who rob the wretched and the poor!
If vice unpunished virtue's meed obtain,
   Who shall refrain the impetuous soul,
   The rebel passions who control,
Or wherefore do I lead this choral train?

Antistrophe 2.

No more to Delphi's sacred shrine
   Need we with incense now repair,
   No more shall Phocis hear our prayer;
Nor fair Olympia see her rites divine;
   If oracles no longer prove
   The power of Phœbus and of Jove.
Great lord of all, from thy eternal throne
   Behold, how impious men defame
   Thy loved Apollo's honoured name;
Oh! guard his rights, and vindicate thy own.   [*Exeunt.*

ACT IV.

SCENE I.

JOCASTA, CHORUS.

JOCASTA. Sages and rulers of the land, I come
To seek the altars of the gods, and there
With incense and oblations to appease

Offended Heaven.   My Œdipus, alas!
No longer wise and prudent, as you all
Remember once he was, with present things
Compares the past, nor judges like himself;
Unnumbered cares perplex his anxious mind,
And every tale awakes new terrors in him;
Vain is my counsel, for he hears me not.
First, then, to thee, O Phœbus! for thou still
Art near to help the wretched, we appeal,
And suppliant beg thee now to grant thy aid
Propitious; deep is our distress; for, oh!
We see our pilot sinking at the helm,
And much already fear the vessel lost.

Scene II.

Shepherd from Corinth, Jocasta, Chorus.

SHEP. Can you instruct me, strangers, which way
    lies
The palace of king Œdipus; himself
I would most gladly see.   Can you inform me?
CHOR. This is the palace; he is now within;
Thou seest his queen before thee.
SHEP.   Ever blest
And happy with the happy mayst thou live!
JOC. Stranger, the same good wish to thee, for well
Thy words deserve it; but say, wherefore com'st thou,
And what's thy news?
SHEP.   To thee, and to thy husband,
Pleasure and joy.
JOC.   What pleasure?   And whence art thou?
SHEP. From Corinth.   To be brief, I bring thee
    tidings
Of good and evil.
JOC.   Ha! what mean thy words
Ambiguous?
SHEP.   Know then, if report say true,
The Isthmian people will choose Œdipus
Their sovereign.

Joc.   Is not Polybus their king ?

Shep. No ;   Polybus is dead.

Joc.   What sayst thou ?   Dead ?

Shep. If I speak falsely, may death seize on me !

Joc. [*to one of her* Attendants]. Why fliest thou not
      to tell thy master ?   Hence !
What are you now, you oracles divine ?
Where is your truth ?   The fearful Œdipus
From Corinth fled, lest he should slay the king,
This Polybus, who perished, not by him,
But by the hand of Heaven.

Scene III.

Œdipus, Jocasta, Shepherd, Chorus.

Œdi.   My dear Jocasta,
Why hast thou called me hither ?

Joc.   Hear this man,
And when thou hearst him, mark what faith is due
To your revered oracles.

Œdi.   Who is he ?
And what doth he report ?

Joc.   He comes from Corinth,
And says thy father Polybus is dead.

Œdi. What sayst thou, stranger ?   Speak to me—oh !
      speak !

Shep. If touching this thou first desir'st my answer ;
Know, he is dead.

Œdi.   How died he ?   Say, by treason,
Or some disease ?

Shep.   Alas ! a little force
Will lay to rest the weary limbs of age.

Œdi. Distemper then did kill him ?

Shep.   That in part,
And part a length of years that wore him down.

Œdi. Now, my Jocasta, who shall henceforth trust
To prophecies, and seers, and clamorous birds
With their vain omens—they who had decreed
That I should kill my father.   He thou seest

Beneath the earth lies buried, whilst I live
In safety here and guiltless of his blood :
Unless perhaps sorrow for loss of me
Shortened his days, thus only could I kill
My father.   But he's gone, and to the shades
Hath carried with him those vain oracles
Of fancied ills, no longer worth my care.
   Joc. Did I not say it would be thus?
   Œdi.   Thou didst ;
But I was full of fears.
   Joc.   Henceforth, no more
Indulge them.
   Œdi.   But my mother's bed—that still
Must be avoided.   I must fly from that.
   Joc. Why should man fear, whom chance, and chance
     alone,
Doth ever rule?   Foreknowledge, all is vain,
And can determine nothing.   Therefore best
It is to live as fancy leads, at large,
Uncurbed, and only subject to our will.
Fear not thy mother's bed.   Oftimes in dreams
Have men committed incest.   But his life
Will ever be most happy who contemns
Such idle phantoms.
   Œdi.   Thou wert right, Jocasta,
Did not my mother live.   But as it is,
Spite of thy words, I must be anxious still.
   Joc. Think on thy father's death ; it is a light
To guide thee here.
   Œdi.   It is so.   Yet I fear
Whilst she survives him.
   Shep.   Who is it you mean ?
What woman fear you?
   Œdi.   Merope, the wife
Of Polybus.
   Shep.   And wherefore fear you her ?
   Œdi. Know, stranger, a most dreadful oracle
Concerning her affrights me.
   Shep.   May I know it,
Or must it be revealed to none but thee?
   Œdi. Oh no ! I'll tell thee.   Phœbus hath declared

That Œdipus should stain his mother's bed,
And dip his hands in his own father's blood;
Wherefore I fled from Corinth, and lived here,
In happiness indeed.   But still thou knowst
It is a blessing to behold our parents,
And that I had not.

SHEP.   Was it for this cause
Thou wert an exile then?

ŒDI.   It was.   I feared
That I might one day prove my father's murderer.

SHEP. What if I come, O king! to banish hence
Thy terrors, and restore thy peace?

ŒDI.   Oh stranger!
Couldst thou do this, I would reward thee nobly.

SHEP. Know then, for this I came.   I came to serve,
And make thee happy.

ŒDI.   But I will not go
Back to my parents.

SHEP.   Son, I see thou knowst not
What thou art doing.

ŒDI.   Wherefore thinkst thou so?
By heaven I beg thee then do thou instruct me.

SHEP. If thou didst fly from Corinth for this cause——
ŒDI. Apollo's dire predictions still affright me.
SHEP. Fearst thou pollution from thy parents?
ŒDI.   That,
And that alone I dread.

SHEP.   Thy fears are vain.
ŒDI. Not if they are my parents.
SHEP.   Polybus
Was not akin to thee.

ŒDI.   What sayst thou?   Speak
Say, was not Polybus my father?

SHEP.   No;
No more than he is mine.

ŒDI.   Why call me then
His son?

SHEP.   Because long since I gave thee to him—
He did receive thee from these hands.

ŒDI.   Indeed!
And could he love another's child so well?

SHEP. He had no children ; that persuaded him
To take and keep thee.

ŒDI.   Didst thou buy me, then,
Or am I thine, and must I call thee father ?

SHEP. I found thee in Cithæron's woody vale.

ŒDI. What brought thee there ?

SHEP.   I came to feed my flocks
On the green mountain's side.

ŒDI.   It seems thou wert
A wandering shepherd.

SHEP.   Thy deliverer ;
I saved thee from destruction.

ŒDI.   How ?   What then
Had happened to me ?

SHEP.   Thy own feet will best
Inform thee of that circumstance.

ŒDI.   Alas !
Why callst thou to remembrance a misfortune
Of so long date ?

SHEP.   'Twas I who loosed the tendons
Of thy bored feet.

ŒDI.   It seems in infancy
I suffered much, then.

SHEP.   To this incident
Thou ow'st thy name.

ŒDI.   My father, or my mother,
Who did it ?   Knowst thou ?

SHEP.   He who gave thee to me
Must tell thee that.

ŒDI.   Then from another's hand
Thou didst receive me.

SHEP.   Ay ; another shepherd.

ŒDI. Who was he ?   Canst thou recollect ?

SHEP.   'Twas one,
At least so called, of Laius' family.

ŒDI. Laius, who ruled at Thebes ?

SHEP.   The same ; this man
Was shepherd to King Laius.

ŒDI.   Lives he still ?
And could I see him ?

SHEP. [*pointing to the* CHORUS]. Some of these perhaps,
His countrymen, may give you information.

ŒDI. [*to the* CHORUS]. Oh! speak, my friends, if any of
    you know
This shepherd; whether still he lives at Thebes,
Or in some neighbouring country. Tell me quick,
For it concerns us near.
CHOR.   It must be he
Whom thou didst lately send for; but the queen
Can best inform thee.
ŒDI.   Knowst thou, my Jocasta,
Whether the man whom thou didst order hither,
And whom the shepherd speaks of, be the same ?
Joc Whom meant he ? for I know not. Œdipus,
Think not so deeply of this thing.
ŒDI.   Good heaven!
Forbid, Jocasta, I should now neglect
To clear my birth, when thus the path is marked
And open to me.
Joc.   Do not, by the gods
I beg thee, do not, if thy life be dear,
Make further search, for I have felt enough
Already from it.
ŒDI.   Rest thou satisfied;
Were I descended from a race of slaves,
'Twould not dishonour thee.
Joc.   Yet hear me; do not,
Once more I beg thee, do not search this matter.
ŒDI. I will not be persuaded. I must search
And find it too.
Joc.   I know it best, and best
Advise thee.
ŒDI.   That advice perplexes more.
Joc. Oh! would to heaven that thou mayst never know
Or who, or whence thou art!
ŒDI. [*to the* ATTENDANTS]. Let some one fetch
That shepherd quick, and leave this woman here
To glory in her high descent.
Joc.   Alas!
Unhappy Œdipus! that word alone
I now can speak: remember 'tis my last.

                           [*Exit* JOCASTA.

Scene IV.

ŒDIPUS, CHORUS.

CHOR. Why fled the queen in such disorder hence ?
Sorely distressed she seemed, and much I fear
Her silence bodes some sad event.
    ŒDI.   Whate'er
May come of that, I am resolved to know
The secret of my birth, how mean soever
It chance to prove. Perhaps her sex's pride
May make her blush to find I was not born
Of noble parents ; but I call myself
The son of fortune, my indulgent mother,
Whom I shall never be ashamed to own.
The kindred months that are like me, her children,
The years that roll obedient to her will,
Have raised me from the lowest state to power
And splendour. Wherefore, being what I am,
I need not fear the knowledge of my birth.

Scene V.

CHORUS.

Strophe.

If my prophetic soul doth well divine,
Ere on thy brow to-morrow's sun shall shine,
   Cithæron, thou the mystery shalt unfold ;
The doubtful Œdipus, no longer blind,
Shall soon his country and his father find,
   And all the story of his birth be told.
      Then shall we in grateful lays
      Celebrate our monarch's praise,
And in the sprightly dance our songs triumphant raise.

Antistrophe.

What heavenly power gave birth to thee, O king !
From Pan, the god of mountains, didst thou spring,
    With some fair daughter of Apollo joined ;
Art thou from him who o'er Cyllene reigns,
Swift Hermes, sporting in Arcadia's plains?
    Some nymph of Helicon did Bacchus find—
        Bacchus, who delights to rove
        Through the forest, hill and grove—
And art thou, prince, the offspring of their love ?

Scene VI.

ŒDIPUS, CHORUS, SHEPHERD FROM CORINTH.

ŒDI. If I may judge of one whom yet I ne'er
Had converse with, yon old man, whom I see
This way advancing, must be that same shepherd
We lately sent for, by his age and mien,
E'en as this stranger did describe him to us ;
My servants too are with him.   But you best
Can say, for you must know him well.
    CHOR.   'Tis he,
My lord ; the faithful shepherd of King Laius.
    ŒDI. [*to the* SHEPHERD *from Corinth*]. What sayst
        thou, stranger ?— is it he ?
    SHEP.   It is.

Scene VII.

OLD SHEPHERD, ŒDIPUS, SHEPHERD FROM CORINTH, CHORUS.

ŒDI. Now answer me, old man ; look this way—
        speak :
Didst thou belong to Laius?
    OLD SHEP.   Sir, I did ;
No hireling slave, but in his palace bred,
I served him long.

ŒDI.   What was thy business there?

OLD SHEP. For my life's better part I tended sheep.

ŒDI. And whither didst thou lead them?

OLD SHEP.   To Cithæron,
And to the neighbouring plains.

ŒDI.   Behold this man :
          [*pointing to the* SHEPHERD *of Corinth*
Dost thou remember to have seen him?

OLD SHEP.   Whom?
What hath he done?

ŒDI.   Him, who now stands before thee,
Callst thou to mind, or converse or connection
Between you in times past?

OLD SHEP.   I cannot say
I recollect it now.

SHEP. *of Corinth.* I do not wonder
He should forget me, but I will recall
Some facts of ancient date.   He must remember
When on Cithæron we together fed
Our several flocks, in daily converse joined
From spring to autumn, and when winter bleak
Approached, retired.   I to my little cot
Conveyed my sheep; he to the palace led
His fleecy care.   Canst thou remember this?

   OLD SHEP. I do ; but that is long, long since

   SHEP. *of Corinth.* It is ;
But say, good shepherd, canst thou call to mind
An infant whom thou didst deliver to me,
Requesting me to breed him as my own?

   OLD SHEP. Ha ! wherefore askst thou this?

   SHEP. *of Corinth* [*pointing to* ŒDIPUS]. Behold him
      here,
That very child.

   OLD SHEP.   Oh ! say it not : away !
Perdition on thee !

   ŒDI.   Why reprove him thus?
Thou art thyself to blame, old man.

   OLD SHEP.   In what
Am I to blame, my lord?

   ŒDI.   Thou wilt not speak
Touching this boy.

OLD SHEP. Alas ! poor man, he knows not
What he hath said.

ŒDI.   If not by softer means
To be persuaded, force shall wring it from thee.

OLD SHEP. Treat not an old man harshly.

ŒDI. [*to the* ATTENDANTS].   Bind his hands.

OLD SHEP. Wherefore, my lord ?   What wouldst thou
  have me do ?

ŒDI. That child he talks of, didst thou give it to
  him ?

OLD SHEP. I did ; and would to heaven I then had
  died !

ŒDI. Die soon thou shalt, unless thou tellst it all.

OLD SHEP. Say, rather if I do.

ŒDI.   This fellow means
To trifle with us, by his dull delay.

OLD SHEP. I do not ; said I not I gave the child ?

ŒDI. Whence came the boy ?   Was he thy own, or who
Did give him to thee ?

OLD SHEP.   From another hand
I had received him.

ŒDI.   Say, what hand ?   From whom ?
Whence came he ?

OLD SHEP.   Do not—by the gods I beg thee,
Do not inquire.

ŒDI.   Force me to ask again,
And thou shalt die.

OLD SHEP.   In Laius' palace born——

ŒDI. Son of a slave, or of the king ?

OLD SHEP.   Alas !
'Tis death for me to speak.

ŒDI.   And me to hear ;   .
Yet say it.

OLD SHEP. He was called the son of Laius ;
But ask the queen, for she can best inform thee.

ŒDI. Did she then give the child to thee ?

OLD SHEP.   She did.

ŒDI. For what ?

OLD SHEP.   To kill him.

ŒDI.   Kill her child !   Inhuman
And barbarous mother !

OLD SHEP.   A dire oracle
Affrighted, and constrained her to it.
    ŒDI.   Ha!
What oracle?
    OLD SHEP.   Which said, her son should slay
His parents.
    ŒDI.   Wherefore gav'st thou then the infant
To this old shepherd?
    OLD SHEP.   Pity moved me to it:
I hoped he would have soon conveyed his charge
To some far distant country; he, alas!
Preserved him but for misery and woe;
For, O my lord! if thou indeed art he,
Thou art of all mankind the most unhappy.
    ŒDI. O me! at length the mystery's unravelled;
'Tis plain, 'tis clear; my fate is all determined.
Those are my parents who should not have been
Allied to me; she is my wife, e'en she
Whom Nature had forbidden me to wed;
I have slain him who gave me life; and now
Of thee, O light! I take my last farewell,
For Œdipus shall ne'er behold thee more.   [*Exeunt.*

SCENE VIII.

CHORUS.

Strophe 1.

O hapless state of human race!
How quick the fleeting shadows pass
Of transitory bliss below,
Where all is vanity and woe!
By thy example taught, O prince! we see
Man was not made for true felicity.

Antistrophe 1.

Thou, Œdipus, beyond the rest
Of mortals wert supremely blest;
Whom every hand conspired to raise,
Whom every tongue rejoiced to praise,

I

When from the Sphinx thy all-preserving hand
Stretched forth its aid to save a sinking land.

Strophe 2.

Thy virtues raised thee to a throne,
And grateful Thebes was all thy own;
Alas! how changed that glorious name!
Lost are thy virtues and thy fame;
How couldst thou thus pollute thy father's bed?
How couldst thou thus thy hapless mother wed?

Antistrophe 2.

How could that bed unconscious bear
So long the vile incestuous pair?
But time, of quick and piercing sight,
Hath brought the horrid deed to light;
At length Jocasta owns her guilty flame,
And finds a husband and a child the same.

Epode.

Wretched son of Laius, thee
Henceforth may I never see,
But absent shed the pious tear,
And weep thy fate with grief sincere!
For thou didst raise our eyes to life and light,
To close them now in everlasting night.

ACT V.

Scene I.

Messenger, Chorus.

Messenger. Sages of Thebes, most honoured and
        revered,
If e'er the house of Labdacus was dear
And precious to you, what will be your grief

When I shall tell the most disastrous tale
You ever heard, and to your eyes present
A spectacle more dreadful than they yet
Did e'er behold : not the wide Danube's waves
Nor Phasis' streams can wash away the stains
Of this polluted palace; the dire crimes
Long time concealed at length are brought to light;
But those which spring from voluntary guilt
Are still more dreadful.
    CHOR.   Nothing can be worse
Than that we know already; bringst thou more
Misfortunes to us?
    MES.   To be brief, the queen,
Divine Jocasta's dead.
    CHOR. Jocasta dead! Say, by what hand?
    MES.   Her own;
And what's more dreadful, no one saw the deed.
What I myself beheld you all shall hear.
Inflamed with rage, soon as she reached the palace,
Instant retiring to the nuptial bed,
She shut the door, then raved and tore her hair,
Called out on Laius dead, and bade him think
On that unhappy son who murdered him
And stained his bed; then turning her sad eyes
Upon the guilty couch, she cursed the place
Where she had borne a husband from her husband,
And children from her child; what followed then
I know not, by the cries of Œdipus
Prevented, for on him our eyes were fixed
Attentive; forth he came, beseeching us
To lend him some sharp weapon, and inform him
Where he might find his mother and his wife,
His children's wretched mother and his own.
Some ill-designing power did then direct him
(For we were silent) to the queen's apartment;
Forcing the bolt, he rushed into the bed,
And found Jocasta, where we all beheld her,
Entangled in the fata noose, which soon
As he perceived, loosing the pendant rope,
Deeply he groaned, and casting on the ground
His wretched body, showed a piteous sight

To the beholders; on a sudden, thence
Starting, he plucked from off the robe she wore
A golden buckle that adorned her side,
And buried in his eyes the sharpened point,
Crying, he ne'er again would look on her,
Never would see his crimes or miseries more,
Or those whom guiltless he could ne'er behold,
Or those to whom he now must sue for aid.
His lifted eyelids then, repeating still
These dreadful plaints, he tore ; whilst down his cheek
Fell showers of blood !   Such fate the wretched pair
Sustained, partakers in calamity,
Fallen from a state of happiness (for none
Were happier once than they) to groans and death,
Reproach and shame, and every human woe.
   Chor. And where is now the poor unhappy man ?
   Mes. Open the doors, he cries, and let all Thebes
Behold his parents' murderer, adding words
Not to be uttered ; banished now, he says,
He must be, nor, devoted as he is
By his own curse, remain in this sad place.
He wants a kind conductor and a friend
To help him now, for 'tis too much to bear.
But you will see him soon, for lo ! the doors
Are opened, and you will behold a sight
That would to pity move his deadliest foe.

SCENE II.

ŒDIPUS, MESSENGER, CHORUS.

   Chor. Oh ! horrid sight ! more dreadful spectacle
Than e'er these eyes beheld ! what madness urged thee
To this sad deed ?   What power malignant heaped
On thy poor head such complicated woe ?
Unhappy man, alas ! I would have held
Some converse with thee, but thy looks affright me ;
I cannot bear to speak to thee.
   Œdi.   O me !
Where am I ? and whence comes the voice I hear ?
Where art thou, fortune ?

CHOR.   Changed to misery,
Dreadful to hear, and dreadful to behold.
  ŒDI. O cruel darkness ! endless, hopeless night,
Shame, terrors, and unutterable woe !
More painful is the memory of my crimes
Than all the wounds my wild distraction made.
  CHOR. Thus doubly cursed, O prince ! I wonder not
At thy affliction.
  ŒDI.   Art thou here, my friend ?
I know thy voice ; thou wouldst not leave the wretched ;
Thou art my faithful, kind assistant still.
  CHOR. How couldst thou thus deprive thyself of sight ?
What madness drove thee to the desperate deed ?
What god inspired ?
  ŒDI.   Apollo was the cause ;
He was, my friends, the cause of all my woes ;
But for these eyes—myself did quench their light—
I want not them ; what use were they to me,
But to discover scenes of endless woe ;
  CHOR. 'Tis but too true.
  ŒDI.   What pleasure now remains
For Œdipus ? He cannot joy in aught
To sight or ear delightful. Curse on him,
Whoe'er he was, that loosened my bound feet,
And saved me, in Cithæron's vale, from death !
I owe him nothing : had I perished then,
Much happier had it been for you, my friends,
And for myself.
  CHOR. I too could wish thou hadst.
  ŒDI. I should not then have murdered Laius ; then
I had not ta'en Jocasta to my bed ;
But now I am a guilty wretch, the son
Of a polluted mother, father now
To my own brothers, all that 's horrible
To nature is the lot of Œdipus.
  CHOR. Yet must I blame this cruel act, for sure
The loss of sight is worse than death itself.
  ŒDI. I care not for thy counsel or thy praise ;
For with what eyes could I have e'er beheld
My honoured father in the shades below,
Or my unhappy mother, both destroyed

By me? This punishment is worse than death,
And so it should be. Sweet had been the sight
Of my dear children—them I could have wished
To gaze upon ; but I must never see
Or them, or this fair city, or the palace
Where I was born. Deprived of every bliss
By my own lips, which doomed to banishment
The murderer of Laius, and expelled
The impious wretch, by gods and men accursed :
Could I behold them after this? Oh no!
Would I could now with equal ease remove
My hearing too, be deaf as well as blind,
And from another entrance shut out woe!
To want our senses, in the hour of ill,
Is comfort to the wretched. O Cithæron!
Why didst thou e'er receive me, or received,
Why not destroy, that men might never know
Who gave me birth? O Polybus! O Corinth!
And thou, long time believed my father's palace,
Oh! what a foul disgrace to human nature
Didst thou receive beneath a prince's form!
Impious myself, and from an impious race.
Where is my splendour now? O Daulian path!
The shady forest, and the narrow pass
Where three ways meet, who drank a father's blood
Shed by these hands, do you not still remember
The horrid deed, and what, when here I came,
Followed more dreadful? Fatal nuptials, you
Produced me, you returned me to the womb
That bare me ; thence relations horrible
Of fathers, sons, and brothers came ; of wives,
Sisters, and mothers, sad alliance! all
That man holds impious and detestable.
But what in act is vile the modest tongue
Should never name. Bury me, hide me, friends,
From every eye; destroy me, cast me forth
To the wide ocean—let me perish there :
Do anything to shake off hated life.
Seize me ; approach, my friends—you need not fear,
Polluted though I am, to touch me ; none
Shall suffer for my crimes but I alone,

CHOR. In most fit time, my lord, the noble Creon
This way advances ; he can best determine
And best advise ; sole guardian now of Thebes,
To him thy power devolves.
  ŒDI.   What shall I say ?
Can I apply to him for aid whom late
I deeply injured by unjust suspicion ?

SCENE III.

CREON, ŒDIPUS, CHORUS.

CREON, I come not, prince, to triumph o'er thy woes
With vile reproach ; I pity thy misfortunes.
But, O my Thebans ! if you do not fear
The censure of your fellow-citizens,
At least respect the all-creating eye
Of Phœbus, who beholds you thus exposing
To public view a wretch accursed, polluted,
Whom neither earth can bear, nor sun behold,
Nor holy shower besprinkle. Take him hence
Within the palace ; those who are by blood
United should alone be witnesses
Of such calamity.
  ŒDI.   O Creon ! thou,
The best of men, and I the worst, how kind
Thou art to visit me ! Oh ! by the gods
, Let me entreat thee, since beyond my hopes
Thou art so good, now hear me ; what I ask,
Concerns thee most.
  CREON.   What is it thou desirest
Thus ardently ?
  ŒDI.   I beg thee, banish me
From Thebes this moment, to some land remote,
Where I may ne'er converse with man again.
  CREON. Myself long since had done it, but the gods
Must be consulted first.
  ŒDI.   Their will is known
Already, and their oracle declared
The guilty parricide should die.

CREON.   It hath;
But, as it is, 'twere better to inquire
What must be done.
     ŒDI.   For such a wretch as me
Wouldst thou again explore the will of Heaven?
    CREON. Thy hapless fate should teach us to believe,
And reverence the gods.
     ŒDI.   Now, Creon, list;
I beg thee, I conjure thee, let a tomb
Be raised, and all due honours paid to her
Who lies within : she was thy sister, Creon;
It is a duty which thou ow'st : for me,
I cannot hope this city now will deign
To keep me here.   O Creon! let me go,
And seek the solitary mountain's top,
My own Cithæron, by my parents doomed
Long since to be the grave of Œdipus;
Where would I die, as they decreed I should.
Alas! I cannot, must not perish yet,
Till I have suffered evils worse than death,
For I was only saved to be unhappy;
But I must meet my fate, whate'er it be.
My sons are men, and wheresoever fortune
May place them, cannot want the means of life;
They shall not burthen thee; but, O my friend!
What will become of my unhappy daughters,
With tenderest love, beneath a father's hand,
Cherished so long?   Oh! take them to thy care,
Thou best of men!   Oh! might I but embrace them,
But shed a tear o'er their disastrous fate,
Might I be suffered but to touch them here,
I should rejoice, and think I saw them still.
But hark! methinks e'en now I hear the voice
Of my dear daughters; hath the gracious Creon,
In pity to my woes, already brought
My children to me?—is it so?
    CREON.   It is :
Thy wishes are prevented; they are here.

Scene IV.

Daughters of Œdipus, Œdipus, Creon, Chorus.

Œdi. May Heaven reward thee for this goodness to
    me,
And give thee much more bliss than I have known!
Now, my dear children, come towards me, come
Towards your father and your—brother; see
These sightless eyes, pierced by my own mad hands;
Behold that wretched father who begat you
Unknowingly on her who gave me birth;
I cannot see you now—I can but weep
Your fate, to think what hours of wretchedness
You have to know hereafter. Whither now
Must my poor children fly? From every feast
Joyless with grief and shame, shall you return;
And when the time shall come when riper years
Should give you to the nuptial bed, who then,
Careless of fame, will let his child partake
The infamy of my abhorred race,
Sprnng from a wretch accursed, who killed his father,
And from the womb that bare him did beget
You my unhappy daughters? Such reproach
Must still be yours, to virgin solitude
Devoted ever, and a barren bed.
Son of Menæceus, thou alone art left
Their father now, for, oh! Jocasta's dead,
And I am—nothing. Do not then forsake
Thy kindred; nor, deserted and forlorn,
Suffer them still in penury and woe
To wander helpless, in their tender age:
Remember they have no support but thee.
O generous prince! have pity on them; give me
Thy friendly hand in promise of thy aid.
To you, my daughters, had your early years
Permitted, I had given my last advice:
Too young for counsel, all I ask of you
Is but to pray the gods that my sad life

May not be long ; but yours, my children, crowned
With many days, and happier far than mine.

    CREON. It is enough; go in—thy grief transports thee
Beyond all bounds.

      ŒDI.   'Tis hard ; but I submit.

      CREON. The time demands it ; therefore go.

      ŒDI.   O Creon !
Knowst thou what now I wish ?

      CREON.   .What is it ?   Speak.

      ŒDI. That I may quit this fatal place.

      CREON.   Thou ask'st
What Heaven alone can grant.

      ŒDI.   Alas ! to Heaven
I am most hateful.

      CREON.   Yet shalt thou obtain
What thou desirest.

      ŒDI.   Shall I indeed ?

      CREON.   Thou shalt ;
I never say aught that I do not mean.

      ŒDI. Then let me go : may I depart ?

      CREON.   Thou mayst ·
But leave thy children.

      ŒDI.   Do not take them from me.

    CREON. Thou must not always have thy will.   Already
Thou 'st suffered for it.

      CHOR.   Thebans, now behold
The great, the mighty Œdipus, who once
The Sphinx's dark enigma could unfold,
Who less to fortune than to wisdom owed,
In virtue as in rank to all superior,
Yet fallen at last to deepest misery.
Let mortals hence be taught to look beyond
The present time, nor dare to say, a man
Is happy till the last decisive hour
Shall close his life without the taste of woe.

ŒDIPUS COLONEUS.

DRAMATIS PERSONÆ.

ŒDIPUS.
CREON.
ANTIGONE, } Daughters of
ISMENE, } Œdipus.
POLYNICES, Son of Œdipus.
THESEUS, King of Athens.

AN ATHENIAN.
MESSENGER.
ATTENDANTS on Creon, Theseus,
and Ismene.
CHORUS, composed of Ancient
Men of Thebes.

SCENE.—A Grove at the entrance to the Temple of the FURIES.

ACT I.

SCENE I.

ŒDIPUS, ANTIGONE.

ŒDIPUS. Where are we now, my dear Antigone ?
Knowst thou the place ?   Will any here afford
Their scanty alms to a poor wanderer,
The banished Œdipus ?   I ask not much,
Yet less receive ; but I am satisfied :
Long time hath made my woes familiar to me,
And I have learned to bear calamity.
But tell me, daughter, if thou seest a place,
Or sacred, or profane, where I may rest,
There set me down, from some inhabitant
A chance but we may learn where now we are,
And act, so strangers ought, as he directs us.

ANT. O Œdipus! my poor, unhappy father,
Far as my eyes can reach I see a city,
With lofty turrets crowned, and, if I err not,
This place is sacred, by the laurel shade
Olive and vine thick-planted, and the songs
Of nightingales sweet warbling through the grove;
Here sit thee down, and rest thy wearied limbs
On this rude stone; 'tis a long way for age
Like thine to travel.

ŒDI.   Place me here, and guard
A sightless wretch.

ANT.   Alas! at such a time
Thou needst not tell Antigone her duty.

ŒDI. Knowst thou not where we are?

ANT.   As I have learned
From passing travellers, not far from Athens;
The place I know not; would you that I go
And straight inquire? But now I need not leave thee,
For, lo! a stranger comes this way, e'en now
He stands before you, he will soon inform us.

SCENE II.

AN ATHENIAN, ŒDIPUS, ANTIGONE.

ŒDI. Stranger, thou com'st in happy hour to tell us
What much we wish to know; let me then ask thee——

ATHE. Ask nothing; speak not till thou art removed
From off that hallowed spot where now thou standst,
By human footsteps not to be profaned.

ŒDI. To whom then is it sacred?

ATHE.   'Tis a place
Where but to tread is impious, and to dwell
Forbidden; where the dreadful goddesses,
Daughters of Earth and Night, alone inhabit.

ŒDI. Ha! let me hear their venerable names.

ATHE. By other names in other climes adored,
The natives here call them Eumenides,
Th' all-seeing powers.

ŒDI.   Oh! that they would but smile

Propitious, and receive a suppliant's prayer,
That I might never leave this blest abode!
   ATHE. What dost thou mean?
   ŒDI.   It suits my sorrows well.
   ATHE. I must inform the citizens; till then
Remain.
   ŒDI.   Oh! do not scorn a wretched exile,
But tell me, stranger——
   ATHE.   Speak; I scorn thee not.
   ŒDI. What place is this?
   ATHE.   I'll tell thee what I know.
This place is sacred all: great Neptune here
Presides, and he who bears the living fire,
Titan Prometheus; where thou treadst is called
The Brazen Way, the bulwark of our State:
From this equestrian hill, their safest guard,
The neighbouring villagers their general name
Derive, thence called Colonians all.
   ŒDI.   But say,
Are there who dwell here, then?
   ATHE.   There are, and called
From him they worship.
   ŒDI.   Is the power supreme
Lodged in the people's voice, or in the king?
   ATHE. 'Tis in the king.
   ŒDI.   Who is he?
   ATHE.   Theseus, son
Of Ægeus, their last sovereign.
   ŒDI.   Who will go
And tell him——
   ATHE.   What! to come and meet thee here?
   ŒDI. To tell him that a little help bestowed
Would amply be repaid.
   ATHE.   Why, what couldst thou do,
Dark as thou art?
   ŒDI.   My words will not be so.
   ATHE. Then mark me, that thou err not; for to me
Thy fortunes seem ill-suited to thy nature,
Which is most noble; therefore stay thou here
Till I return; I will not go to Athens,
But ask these villagers, who sojourn here,
Ifthou mayst stay.   [*Exit* ATHENIAN.

Scene III.

Œdipus, Antigone.

Œdi.   My daughter, is he gone?
Ant. He is, and thou mayst safely speak, for I
Alone am with thee.
Œdi.   Goddesses revered!
Since in your seats my wearied steps have found
Their first repose, not inauspicious smile
On Phœbus and on me! For know, the god
Who 'gainst unhappy Œdipus denounced
Unnumbered woes, foretold that here at last
I should have rest, within this hallowed grove
These hospitable shades, and finish here
A life of misery: happy those, he said,
Who should receive me, glorious their reward,
And woe to them who strove to drive me hence
Inhuman. This he promised to confirm
By signs undoubted; thunder, or the sound
Of dreadful earthquake, or the lightning's blast
Launched from the arm of Jove. I doubt it not,
From you some happy omen hither led
My prosperous steps, that first to you I came
Pure to the pure; and here on this rude seat
Reposed me, could not be the work of chance;
Wherefore, ye powers! as Phœbus hath decreed,
Here let me find a period of my woes,
Here end my wretched life! unless the man,
Who long hath groaned beneath the bitterest ills
That mortals feel, still seem to merit more.
Daughters of Ancient Night! oh, hear me now!
And thou, from great Minerva called, the best
And noblest city, Athens! pity me,
Pity the shadow of poor Œdipus;
For, oh! I am not what I was.
     Ant.   No more:
Behold a venerable band approach
Of ancient natives, come perchance to seek thee.
     Œdi. I've done; Antigone, remove me hence,

And hide me in the grove till by their words,
Listening, I learn their purpose; such foreknowledge
Will best direct us how to act hereafter.   [*Exeunt.*

Scene IV.

Chor. Where is he? Look, examine, search around
For this abandoned exile, of mankind
The most profane; doubtless some wretched stranger.
Who else had dared on this forbidden soil
To tread, where dwell the dreadful deities
We tremble e'en to name, and as we pass
Dare not behold, but silently revere,
Or soft with words of fairest omen greet?
Of these regardless, here we come to find
An impious wretch. I look around the grove,
But still he lurks unseen.

Scene V.

ŒDIPUS, ANTIGONE, CHORUS.

Œdi.   Behold me here;
For by your words I find you look for me.
   Chor. [*looking steadfastly at him*]. Dreadful his voice
     and terrible his aspect!
   Œdi. I am no outlaw; do not look thus on me.
   Chor. Jove the defender! who is this old man?
   Œdi. One on whom fortune little hath bestowed
To call for reverence from you; that, alas!
Is but too plain; thus by another's eyes
Conducted here, and on her aid depending,
Old as I am.
   Chor.   Alas! and wert thou born
Thus sightless? Full of sorrow and of years
Indeed thou seemst; but do not let on us
Thy curse devolve. Thou hast transgressed the bounds
Prescribed to mortals; shun this hallowed grove,

Where on the grassy surface to the powers
A welcome offering flows with honey mixed
The limpid stream; unhappy stranger, hence,
Away, begone! Thou seest 'tis a long space
Divides us: dost thou hear me, wretched exile?
This instant, if thou dost, depart, then speak,
But not before.

ŒDI.   Antigone, my daughter,
What's to be done?

ANT.   Obey the citizens;
Give me thy hand.

ŒDI.   I will; and now, my friends,
Confiding thus in you, and thus removing
As you directed, let me not be injured.

CHOR. Thou shalt not; be assured that thou art safe;
None shall offend or drive thee hence.

ŒDI.   Yet more
Must I approach?

CHOR.   A little farther still.

ŒDI. Will this suffice?

CHOR.   Remove him this way, virgin;
Thou hearst us.

ANT.   Thou must follow me, my father,
Weak as thou art; we are unhappy strangers,
And must submit; whate'er the city hates
Content to hate, and what she loves to love.

ŒDI. Lead me, my daughter, to some hallowed spot
For mutual converse fit, nor let us strive
With dire necessity.

CHOR.   Stop there, nor move
Beyond that stone.

DI.   Thus, then?

CHOR.   It is enough.

ŒDI. Where should I sit?

CHOR.   A little forward lean,
And rest thee there.

ANT. [*taking hold of him*]. Alas! 'tis my sad office—
Let me perform it—to direct thy steps;
To this loved hand commit thy aged limbs;
I will be careful.   [*She seats him on the stone.*

ŒDI.   O unhappy State!

CHOR. Now, wretched stranger, tell us who thou art,
Thy country, and thy name.

ŒDI.   Alas ! my lords,
A poor abandoned exile ; but, oh ! do not——

CHOR. What sayst thou ?

ŒDI.   Do not ask me who I am ;
Inquire no farther.

CHOR.   Wherefore ?

ŒDI.   My sad race——

CHOR. Speak on.

ŒDI. [*turning to* ANTIGONE]. My daughter, how shall
    I proceed ?

CHOR. Thy race, thy father——

ŒDI.   O Antigone !
What do I suffer ?

ANT.   Speak ; thou canst not be
More wretched than thou art.

ŒDI.   I will ; for, oh !
It cannot be concealed.

CHOR.   You do delay ;
Inform us straight.

ŒDI.   Know you the son of Laius ?

CHOR. Alas !

ŒDI.   The race of Labdacus.

CHOR.   O Jove !

ŒDI. Th' unhappy Œdipus.

CHOR.   And art thou he ?

ŒDI. Be not affrighted at my words.

CHOR.   O Heaven !

ŒDI. Wretch that I am ! what will become of me ?

CHOR. Away, begone, fly from this place !

ŒDI.   Then where
Are all your promises ? are they forgotten ?

CHOR. Justice divine will never punish those
Who but repay the injury they receive ;
And fraud doth merit fraud for its reward.
Wherefore, begone, and leave us, lest once more
Our city be compelled to force thee hence.

ANT. O my kind friends ! as you revere the name
Of virtue, though you will not hear the prayers
Of my unhappy father, worn with age

And laden with involuntary crimes;
Yet hear the daughter pleading for her sire,
And pity her who with no evil eye
Beholds you, but, as one of the same race,
Born of one common father, here entreats
Your mercy to th' unhappy, for on you,
As on some god alone, we must rely;
Then grant this wished-for boon—oh! grant it now,
By all that's dear to thee, thy sacred word,
Thy interest, thy children, and thy god;
'Tis not in mortals to avoid the crime
Which Heaven hath pre-ordained.

    CHOR.   We pity thee,
Daughter of Œdipus; we pity him,
And his misfortunes; but of wrath divine
Still fearful, dare not alter our decree.

    ŒDI. Now who shall trust to glory and fair fame?
What shall it profit that your pious city
Was once for hospitable rites renowned,
That she alone would pity and relieve
The afflicted stranger? Is she so to me
Who drives me hence, and trembles at a name?
Me you can never fear, and for my crimes
I am the sufferer, not the offender. What
Touching my father I have spoke, alas!
If 'tis for that you do abhor me thus,
Was I to blame? The injury received
I but repaid, and therefore had I known
The crime I acted, I were guiltless still.
Whither I came, I came unknowingly;
Not so they acted who have banished me.
By your commands already here removed,
Oh! by the gods, preserve, assist me now;
If you revere them, do not thus despise
What they decree; their eyes behold the good
And view the evil man, nor shall the wicked
Escape their wrath; use not their sacred names
To cover crimes and stain the fame of Athens.
As you received the suppliant, oh! remember
Your plighted faith—preserve me, save me now!
Look not contemptuous on this wretched form,

Or cast reproach unmerited; I come
Nor impious, nor profane, and with me bring
To Athens much of profit and renown,
As when your king arrives, you all shall know:
Meantime despise me not.

CHOR.   Old man, thy words
Are full of weight, and merit our observance;
If those who here preside but know thy purpose,
It doth suffice.

ŒDI.   But say, where is the king?

CHOR. Within his palace, but a messenger
Is gone to fetch him hither.

ŒDI.   O my friends!
Think you a sightless wretch like me will move
His pity or his care, that he will come?

CHOR. Most readily, when he shall hear the name
Of Œdipus.

ŒDI.   And who shall tell it him?

CHOR. The journey's long, but passing travellers
Will catch the tale, and he must hear it soon;
Fear not, thy story is already known
On every side; 'twill quicken his slow steps,
And bring him instant hither.

ŒDI.   May he come
In happy hour to Athens and to me!
He will; what good man doth not love his country?

ANT. O Jove! what shall I say or think? My
        father——

ŒDI. What says my daughter?

ANT.   This way bent, behold
On a Sicilian steed, a woman comes,
Her face concealed by a Thessalian veil,
To shield her from the sun: am I deceived,
Or is it she? I know not what to think.
It is my sister, now she smiles upon me;
It must, it can be none but my Ismene.

ŒDI. Who, my Antigone?.

ANT.   It is thy daughter,
My sister, but her voice will soon convince you.

Scene VI.

ISMENE AND ATTENDANT, ŒDIPUS, ANTIGONE, CHORUS.

ISM. O the sweet sounds! a father and a sister!
What pains have I not suffered in the search!
And now for grief can scarce behold you.
ŒDI.   Oh!
My daughter, art thou here?
ISM.   Alas! my father,
How terribly thou lookst!
ŒDI.   From the same blood
The father and the daughter.
ISM.   Wretched race!
ŒDI. And art thou come, my daughter?
ISM.   I have reached thee
With toil and labour.
ŒDI.   Touch me, O my child!
ISM. Let me embrace you both.
ŒDI.   Both miserable!
ISM. Join then a third as wretched as yourselves.
                          [They all embrace.
ŒDI. Ismene, wherefore art thou come?
ISM.   My care
For thee, my father, brought me here.
ŒDI.   For me?
ISM. That I might speak to thee; this faithful slave
Alone conducted me.   [Pointing to her ATTENDANT.
ŒDI.   Thy brothers, say,
What are they doing?
ISM.   They are—what they are;
For, oh! between them deadliest discord reigns.
ŒDI. How like th' unmanly sons of Egypt's clime,
Where the men sit inglorious at the loom,
And to their wives leave each domestic care!
E'en thus my sons, who should have laboured for me,
Like women idly sit at home, whilst you
Perform their office, and with filial care
Attend a wretched father. This kind maid,
                          [pointing to ANTIGONE
E'en from her infant days, hath wandered long

An exile with me, and supported still
My feeble age; oft through the savage woods,
Naked and hungry, by the wintry storms
Or scorching heats afflicted, led me on,
And gave me food, unmindful of her own.
Thou too, Ismene, wert my faithful guard
When I was driven forth; and now art come
To tell thy father what the gods declare;
A stranger now to Thebes, I know not what
Hath passed between them; thou hast some sad news,
I know thou hast, to tell thy wretched father.

 Ism. What I have suffered in the search of thee
I pass in silence o'er, since to repeat
Were but, alas! to double my misfortunes;
I only came to tell thee the sad fate
Of thy unhappy sons. Awhile they seemed
As if they meant to yield the throne to Creon,
Nor stain their guilty hands with Theban blood,
Mindful of that pollution which remained
On thy devoted race; but now some god
Or their own wicked minds have raised a flame
Of dire contention, which shall gain the power
Supreme, and reign in Thebes. Eteocles
Hath drove his elder Polynices forth,
Who, now an exile, seeks (as fame reports)
The Argians, and in solemn contract joined
With these his new allies would raise their fame
Above the stars, and sink our Thebes in ruin.
These are not words alone—'tis now in act,
Alas! e'en now I fear, nor know I when
The gods will take compassion on thy woes.

 Œdi. Hast thou no hope they'll pity me? .
 Ism.   I have;
Their oracles have said it.

 Œdi.   Ha! said what?
My daughter, tell me, what have they declared?

 Ism. The time would come, they said, when Thebes
  once more
Must seek thee, dead or living, for her safety.

 Œdi. Why, what could such a wretch as I do for
  them?

IsM. Their only hope, they say, is placed in thee.

ŒDI. I, that am nothing, grown so powerful ! Whence
Can it proceed?

IsM. The gods, who once depressed thee,
Now raise thee up again.

ŒDI. It cannot be;
Who falls in youth will never rise in age.

IsM. Know, for this very purpose Creon comes;
Ere long thou mayst expect him.

ŒDI. What to do,
My daughter?

IsM. To remove thee hence, and place thee
Nearer to Thebes, but not within her borders.

ŒDI. If not within, what profit can it be
To them?

IsM. Thy tomb, raised in a foreign land,
They fear would prove most fatal.

ŒDI. But how know they
It must be so, unless some god declared it?

IsM. For this alone they wish to have thee near
The borders, in their power, and not thy own.

ŒDI. To bury me at Thebes?

IsM. That cannot be;
Thy crime forbids it.

ŒDI. Then I'll never go. [ance.

IsM. A time will come when they shall feel thy venge-

ŒDI. What strange vicissitude can e'er produce
This wished event?

IsM. Thy wrath, when at thy tomb
They shall be forced to meet.

ŒDI. Who told thee this?
Ismene, say.

IsM. The sacred ministers
Of Delphos.

ŒDI. Came it from Apollo's shrine?

IsM. On their return to Thebes they did report it.

ŒDI. My sons, did they hear aught of this?

IsM. Both heard,
And know it well.

ŒDI. Yet, impious as they are,
Preferred a kingdom to their father's love.

Ism. With grief I tell thee what with grief I heard.

Œdi. Oh! may the gods doom them to endless strife;
Ne'er may the battle cease till Œdipus
Himself shall end it; then, nor he who bears
The sceptre now, should long maintain the throne,
Nor Polynices e'er to Thebes return;
They should not live who drove a parent forth
To misery and exile, left by those
Who should have loved, supported, and revered him;
I know they say the city but complied
With my request—I asked for banishment;
Not then I asked it. In my desperate mind,
When first I raged, I wished indeed for death;
It had been grateful then, but no kind friend
Would minister the boon. At length my grief
Gave way, and when they saw my troubled soul
Had taken ample vengeance on itself,
After long stay, the city drove me forth;
And those who could have saved me, my base sons,
Deaf to a father's prayers, permit me still
To roam abroad in poverty and exile.
From these alone, far as their tender sex
Can help me, I receive the means of life,
All the sweet comfort, food, or needful rest
Earth can afford me now, whilst to my sons
A throne was dearer than a father's love;
But they shall never gain me for their friend,
Ne'er reign in Thebes—these oracles declare
They never shall. I do remember too
Another prophecy which Phœbus erst
Delivered to me: let 'em send their Creon,
Or any other powerful citizen,
To drag me hence; my hospitable friends,
If to those all-protecting deities
Who here preside you too will lend your aid,
Athens shall find in me its best defence,
And vengeance strike the foes of Œdipus.

Chor. Thou and thy daughters well deserve our pity
And, for thy words are full of promised good
To our loved city, I will tell thee all
'Tis meet thou shouldst perform.

ŒDI.   My best of friends,
Instruct me ; I am ready to obey.

CHOR. An expiation instant must thou make
To the offended powers whose sacred seat
Thou has profaned.

ŒDI.   But how must it be done?

CHOR. First, with pure hands, from th' ever-flowing
     spring,
Thy due libations pour.

ŒDI.   What follows then?

CHOR. Take thou a cup wrought by some skilful hand,
Bind it with wreaths around.

ŒDI.   Of leaves or threads
Composed ?

CHOR.   Of wool, fresh from the new-shorn lamb.

ŒDI. Is there aught else ?

 CHOR.   Then, turning to the sun,
Make thy libations.

ŒDI.   From the cup, thou sayst,

CHOR. The water from three fountains drawn ; and
     last
Remember, none be left.

ŒDI.   With that alone
Must it be filled ?

CHOR.   Water with honey mixed—
No wine ; this pour on th' earth——

ŒDI.   What then remains?

CHOR. Take in thy hand of olive-boughs thrice nine,
And offering these, begin thy humble prayer.

ŒDI. But how address them ? That concerns me near.

CHOR. Their name thou knowst implies benevolent :
Intreat them therefore kindly now to prove
Benevolent to thee ; but, remember,
Low be the voice and short the supplication.
That done, return—be careful to perform it ;
I may assist thee then with confidence,
But if thou dost it not, must tremble for thee.

ŒDI. My daughters, heard you this?

ANT.   We did ; command
What's to be done.

ŒDI.   What I can never do,

Powerless and blind as I am; one of you,
My daughters, must perform it.
    ANT.   One alone
May do the task of many when the mind
Is active in it.
    ŒDI.   Hence then, quick, away!
But do not leave me here alone. These limbs
Without a guide will never find their way.
    ISM. Father, I go; but how to find the place
I know not.
    CHOR.   Stranger, t' other side of the grove;
There, some inhabitant will soon inform thee.
If thou shouldst want assistance or instruction.
    ISM. Meantime, Antigone, remain thou here,
And guard our father well: cares are not cares
When we endure them for a parent's sake.
                          [*Exit* ISMENE.

SCENE VII.

ŒDIPUS, ANTIGONE, CHORUS.

    CHOR. Stranger, albeit we know 'tis most ungrateful
To raise the sad remembrance of past woes,
Yet would we gladly hear——
    ŒDI.   What wouldst thou know?
    CHOR. The cause of thy unhappy state.
    ŒDI.   Alas!
By all the sacred hospitable rites,
I beg thee do not ask me to reveal it;
My crimes are horrible.
    CHOR.   Already fame
Hath spread them wide, and still talks loudly of them;
Tell us the truth.
    ŒDI.   Alas!
    CHOR.   Let me beseech thee!
    ŒDI. O me
    CHOR.   Comply: ask what thou wilt of me,
And thou shalt have it.
    ŒDI.   I have suffered much;

The gods can witness 'twas against my will;
I knew not of it.

    CHOR.   Knew not what?

    ŒDI.   The city,
Unknowing too, bound me in horrid nuptials.

    CHOR. And didst thou then pollute, as fame reports,
Thy mother's bed?

    ŒDI.   Oh! death to hear: I did.
Here, here they are.

    CHOR.   Who's there?

    ŒDI.   My crimes! my daughters!

    CHOR. Daughters and sisters of their father? Oh!
'Tis horrible indeed!

    ŒDI.   'Tis woe on woe.

    CHOR. Great Jove! both daughters of one hapless
      mother!
What hast thou suffered?

    ŒDI.   Ills not to be borne.

    CHOR. Didst thou then perpetrate the horrid deed?

    ŒDI. Oh no!

    CHOR.   Not do it?

    ŒDI.   I received from Thebes
A fatal gift; would I had never ta'en it!

    CHOR. And art thou not a murderer too?

    ŒDI.   What's that
Thou sayst?

    CHOR.   Thy father——

    ŒDI.   Thou add'st grief to grief.

    CHOR. Didst thou not murder him?

    ŒDI.   I did; but hear——

    CHOR. Hear what?

    ŒDI.   The cause.

    CHOR.   What cause?

    ŒDI.   I'll tell thee. Know then,
I murdered others too, yet by the laws
I stand absolved; 'twas done in ignorance.

    CHOR. [*seeing* THESEUS, *who enters*]. But lo! the king,
      Ægean Theseus, comes;
The fame of thee hath brought him here already.

Scene VIII.

Theseus, Œdipus, Antigone, Chorus.

The. O son of Laius! long ere this the tale
Of thy disastrous fate, by many a tongue
Related, I had heard: thy eyes torn forth
By thy own desperate hand: and now I see
It was too true. Thy garb and dreadful aspect
Speak who thou art. Unhappy Œdipus,
I come to ask, in pity to thy woes,
What's thy request to Athens or to me—
Thine, or this hapless virgin on thy steps
Attendant. Speak; for large must be the boon
I would refuse thee. I have known too well,
Myself a wretched wanderer, the woes
Of cruel exile, not to pity thine:
Of toils and dangers in a foreign land
Much have I suffered; therefore not to me
Shall the poor stranger ever sue in vain
For aid and safety. Mortals as we are,
Uncertain ever is to-morrow's fate,
Alike unknown to Theseus and to thee.

Œdi. Theseus, thy words declare thy noble nature,
And leave me little to reply. Thou knowst
My story—who and whence I am; no more
Remains, but that I tell thee my request,
And we have done.

The. Proceed then, and inform me

Œdi. I come to give this wretched body to thee,
To sight ungracious, but of worth more dear
To thee than fairest forms could boast.

The. What worhth?

Œdi. Hereafter thou shalt know—not now

The. But when
Shall we receive it?

Œdi. When I am no more
When thou shalt bury me.

THE.   Death is, it seems,
Thy chief concern, and life not worth thy care.
ŒDI. That will procure me all the means of life.
THE. And is this all thou ask'st, this little boon ?
ŒDI. Not little is the strife which shall ensue.
THE. What strife ? With whom—thy children, or my
own ?
ŒDI. Mine, Theseus; they would have me back to
Thebes.
THE. And wouldst thou rather be an exile here ?
ŒDI. Once they refused me.
THE.   Anger suits but ill
With low estate and miseries like thine.
ŒDI. Hear first, and then condemn me.
THE.   Not unheard
All thou canst urge, would I reprove thee. Speak.
ŒDI. O Theseus ! I have borne the worst of ills.
THE. The curses on thy race ?
ŒDI.   Oh no ! all Greece
Hath heard of them.
THE.   What more than mortal woe
Afflicts thee then ?
ŒDI.   E'en this : my cruel sons
Have driven me from my country ; nevermore
Must Thebes receive a parricide.
THE.   Why then
Recall thee now, if thou must ne'er return ?
ŒDI. Commanded by an oracle divine.
THE. Why, what doth it declare ?
ŒDI.   That Thebes shall yield
To thee, and to thy arms.
THE.   But whence should spring
Such dire contention ?
ŒDI.   Dearest son of Ægeus,
From age and death exempt, the gods alone
Immortal and unchangeable remain,
Whilst all things else fall by the hand of Time,
The universal conqueror. Earth laments
Her fertile powers exhausted. Human strength
Is withered soon. E'en faith and truth decay,

And from their ashes fraud and falsehood rise.
Nor friendship long from man to man endures,
Or realm to realm.   To each successive rise
Bitter and sweet, and happiness and woe.
Athens and Thebes thou seest united now,
And all is well; but passing time shall bring
The fatal day (and slight will be the cause)
That soon shall change the bonds of amity
And holy faith, for feuds and deadliest hate.
Then, buried long in earth, shall this cold corse
Drink their warm blood, which from the mutual wound
Frequent shall flow.   It must be as I tell thee,
If Jove be Jove, and great Apollo true.
But why should I reveal the fixed decree
Of all-deciding Heaven?   Permit me now
To end where I began.   Thy plighted faith
Once more confirm, and never shalt thou say
The wretched Œdipus to Theseus came
An useless and unprofitable guest,
If the immortal gods have not deceived me.

   CHOR. O king! already hath this man declared
The same goodwill to thee and to our country.

   THES. Can I reject benevolence and love
Like this, my friends?   Oh no! the common rites
Of hospitality, this altar here,
The witness of our mutual vows, forbid it;
He comes a suppliant to the goddesses,
And pays no little tribute both to me
And to my kingdom; he shall find a seat
Within my realms, for I revere his virtues.
If here it pleaseth him to stay, remember [*to the* CHORUS
'Tis my command you guard this stranger well;
If thou wouldst rather go with me, thou mayst;
I leave it to thy choice.   [*To* ŒDIPUS.

   ŒDI. Reward them, Jove.

   THE. What sayst thou? wilt thou follow me?

   ŒDI.   I would,
If it were lawful, but it must be here—
This is the place——

      THE.   For what?   I'll not deny thee——

ŒDI. Where I must conquer those who banished me.

. THE. That would be glory and renown to this
Thy place of refuge.

ŒDI.   If I may depend
On thy fair promise.

THE.   .Fear not, I shall ne'er
Betray my friend.

ŒDI.   I will not bind thee to it
By oath, like those whom we suspect of ill.

THE. Thou needst not, Œdipus; my word's my oath.

ŒDI. How must I act then?

THE.   Fear'st thou aught?

ŒDI.   I do.
A force will come against me.

THE. [*pointing to the* CHORUS]. Here's thy guard;
These shall protect thee.

ŒDI.   If thou goest, remember
And save me, Theseus.

THE.   Teach not me my duty.

ŒDI. Still am I fearful.

THE.   Theseus is not so.

ŒDI. Knowest thou not what they threatened?

THE.   This I know,
No power on earth shall wrest thee from this place.
Oftimes the angry soul will vent its wrath
In idle threats, with high and empty words,
Which ever, as the mind is to itself
Restored, are—nothing. They may boast their strength,
And say they'll tear thee from me; but I tell thee
The journey would be long and tedious to them;
They will not hazard it—they dare not : therefore
Be comforted, for if by Phœbus sent
Thou hither cam'st, thou'rt safe without my aid,
E'en if I leave thee safe ; for know, the name
Of Theseus here sufficeth to protect thee.

                              [*Exit* THESEUS.

Scene IX.

ŒDIPUS, ANTIGONE, CHORUS

Chorus.

Strophe 1.

Thou art come in happy time,
Stranger, to this blissful clime,
Long for swiftest steeds renowned,
Fertilest of the regions round;
Where, beneath the ivy shade,
In the dew-sprinkled glade,
Many a love-lorn nightingale
Warbles sweet her plaintive tale;
Where the vine in clusters pours
Her sweets, secured from wintry showers
Nor scorching suns, nor raging storm
The beauties of the year deform.

Antistrophe 1.

Where the sweet narcissus growing,
Where the yellow crocus blowing,
Round the sacred altars twine,
Offering to the powers divine;
Where the pure springs perpetual flow,
Watering the verdant meads below,
Which with its earth-enriching waves
The fair Cephisus ever laves;
Where, with his ever-sporting train,
Bacchus wantons on the plain,
Pleased with the Muses still to rove,
And golden Venus, queen of love.

Strophe 2.

Alone within this happy land,
Planted here by Nature's hand,
Which, nor Asia's fertile plains,
Nor Pelops' spacious isle contains,

Pallas, thy sacred olive grows,
Striking terror on our foes;
Ever free from hostile rage,
From wanton youth or greedy age;
Happy in sage Minerva's love,
And guarded still by Morian Jove.

Antistrophe 2.

But nobler gifts and fairer fame,
Athens, yet adorn thy name;
Such wondrous gifts hath poured on thee,
Thy great protecting deity.
Here first obedient to command,
Formed by Neptune's skilful hand,
The steed was taught to know the rein,
And bear the chariot o'er the plain;
Here first along the rapid tide
The stately vessels learned to ride,
And swifter down the currents flow
Than Nereids cut the waves below.　　　*[Exeunt.*

ACT II.

Scene I.

Antigone, Œdipus, Chorus.

Antigone. Great are thy praises, Attica, and now　*720*
The time is come to show thou dost deserve them.
　Œdi. What means my daughter? Speak; what new
　　event
Alarms thee?
　Ant.　　　　　Creon, with a numerous band
Of followers, comes this way.
　Œdi.　　　　　　　　　Oh! now, my friends,
If ever, help me.
　Chor.　　　　　Fear not; we'll protect thee.
Though I am old, the strength of Attica
Is not decayed.

SCENE II.

CREON (*with Attendants*), ŒDIPUS, ANTIGONE,
CHORUS.

CREON. Most honoured citizens,   *728*
I see you look with eyes of fear upon me,
Without a cause; for know, I came not here
Intending aught of violence or ill
Against a city so renowned in Greece
As yours hath ever been; I only came,
Commissioned by the State of Thebes, to fetch
This old man back, if by persuasion mild
I could induce him to return; not sent
By one alone, but the united voice
Of a whole people, who assigned the task
To me because, by blood united to him,
I felt for his misfortunes as my own.
Come therefore, Œdipus, attend me home;
Thebes calls thee back, thy kingdom now demands thee—
By me she calls thee; listen to thy friend,
For surely Creon were the worst of men,
If he could look on woes like thine unmoved
When I behold thee, in a foreign land
A wretched wanderer, forced to beg thy bread
From place to place, with this unhappy maid,
Whom little did I think to see exposed
To misery and shame, of nuptial rites
Hopeless, and thus bereft of every aid,—
Oh! 'tis reproach and infamy to us
And to our race; but 'tis already known,
And cannot be concealed. O Œdipus!
I here beseech thee, by our country's gods,
Return to Thebes; bid thou a kind farewell—
For she deserves it—to this noble city,
But still remember thy own dearer country.

    ŒDI. Thou daring hypocrite, whose specious wiles   *761*
Beneath fair semblance mean but to betray,
Why wouldst thou tempt me thus? Why thus once more

Ensnare me in thy toils, and make me still
More wretched than I am? Long time oppressed
By heaviest woes, I pined within my palace,
And longed for exile; but you then refused
To let me go, till, satiated with grief,
My soul at length was calm, and much I wished
To spend my few remaining years at home:
Then thou—for little did the kindred blood
Thou talkst of then avail—didst banish me;
And now again thou com'st to make me wretched.
Because thou seest this kind benignant city
Embrace and cherish, thou wouldst drag me hence,
With sweetest words covering thy bitter mind,
Professing love to those who choose it not.
He who denies his charitable aid
To the poor beggar in his utmost need,
And if abundance comes, should offer that
Which is not wanted, little merits thanks.
Such is thy bounty now—in word alone,
And not in deed, the friend of Œdipus.
But I will tell them what thou art. Thou cam'st not
To take me hence, but leave me in the borders
Of Thebes, that so thy kingdom may escape
The impending ills which this avenging city
Shall pour upon it; but 'twill come to pass
As I foretold: my evil genius still
Shall haunt yon, and my sons no more of Thebes
Inherit than shall serve them for a grave.
Thy country's fate is better known to me
Than to thyself, for my instruction comes
From surer guides—from Phœbus and from Jove.
Thy artful speech shall little serve thy purpose,
'Twill only hurt thy cause: therefore begone!
I'm not to be persuaded. Let me live
In quiet here, for, wretched as I am,
'Twill be some comfort to be far from thee.
    CREON. Thinkst thou I heed thy words? Who'll
       suffer most
For this perverseness—thou, or I?
    ŒDI. Thy little arts will nought avail with me,
Or with my friends.

CREON.   Poor wretch! no time can cure
Thy follies; thy old age is grown delirious.

ŒDI. Thou hast a hateful tongue; but few, how just
Soe'er they be, can always speak aright.

CREON. But to say much, and to say well, are things
Which differ widely.

ŒDI.   What thou sayst no doubt
Is brief, and proper too.

CREON.   'Twill hardly seem so
To those who think like thee.

ŒDI.   Away; nor dare
Direct my steps, as if thou-hadst the power
To place me where thou wilt.

CREON.   Remember all
To witness this, for he shall answer it
When he is mine.

ŒDI.   But who shall force me hence
Against the will of these my friends?

CRE.   Their aid
Is vain, already I have done what much
Will hurt thee.

ŒDI.   Ha! what threats are these?

CREON.   Thy daughters
Must go with me; one is secured, and now
This moment will I wrest the other from thee.

ŒDI. O me!

CREON.   I'll give thee much more cause for grief.

ŒDI. Hast thou my daughter?

CREON.   Ay, and will have this.

ŒDI. [*to the* CHORUS]. What will you do, my friends?
    Will you forsake me?
Will you not drive this vile, abandoned man
Forth from your city?

CHOR.   Stranger, hence, away!
Thy actions are most shameful and unjust.

CREON. Slaves, do your office; bear her off by force,
If she consents not.

ANT.   Whither shall I fly
For aid? What god or man shall I implore
To succour me?

CHOR.   Alas! what wouldst thou do?   .

CREON. I touch not him, but I must have my own.

ANT. O princes! aid me now.

CHOR.   'Tis most unjust.

CREON. I say 'tis just.

CHOR.   Then prove it.

CREON.   They are mine.

CHOR. O citizens!

ANT.   Oh! loose me : if you do not,
You shall repent this violence.

CREON.   Go on,
I will defend you.

ŒDI.   He, who injures me,
Offends the city.

CHOR.   Said I not before
It would be thus?

CREON. [*to the* CHORUS]. Let go the maid this instant.

CHOR. Command where thou hast power.

CREON.   Let her go.

CHOR. Begone thyself. What, ho! my countrymen,
The city is in danger; haste and save us.

                    [CREON'S *followers seize on* ANTIGONE.

ANT. I'm seized, my friends. Oh, help!

ŒDI.   Where is my daughter?

ANT. Torn from thee.

ŒDI   Oh! stretch forth thy hand.

ANT.   I cannot.

CREON. Away with her

ŒDI.   O wretched Œdipus!

CREON. No longer shall these tender props support
Thy feeble age; since thou art still resolved
Against thyself, thy country, and thy friends,
By whose command I come, remain perverse
And obstinate, old man; but know, hereafter
Time will convince thee thou hast ever been
Thy own worst foe; thy fiery temper still
Must make thee wretched.

CHOR.   Stranger, stir not hence.

CREON. I charge you, touch me not.

CHOR.   Thou shalt not go
Till thou restor'st the virgins.

CREON.   I must have

A nobler ransom from your city; these
Shall not suffice.

CHOR.   What meanst thou?

CREON.   He shall go,
This Œdipus.

CHOR.   Thy threats are terrible.

CREON. I'll do 't; and only he who governs here
Shall hinder me.

ŒDI.   O insolence! thou wilt not,
Thou dar'st not force me.

CREON.   Hold thy peace.

ŒDI.   Not e'en
The dreadful goddesses, who here preside,
Should bind my tongue from heaviest curses on thee,
For thou hast robbed me of the only light
These eyes could boast; but may th' all-seeing sun
Behold and punish thee and all thy race,
And load thy age with miseries like mine!

CREON. Inhabitants of Athens, hear ye this?

ŒDI. They do, and see that but with fruitless words
I can repay the injuries I receive;
For I am weak with age, and here alone.

CREON. No longer will I curb my just resentment,
But force thee hence.

ŒDI.   O me!

CHOR.   What boldness, stranger,
Could make thee hope to do a deed like this
Unpunished?

CREON.   'Tis resolved.

CHOR.   Our Athens then
Is fallen indeed, and is no more a city.

CREON. In a just cause the weak may foil the mighty.

ŒDI. Hear how he threatens——

CHOR.   What he'll ne'er perform.

CREON. That Jove alone can tell.

CHOR.   Shall injuries
Like these be suffered?

CREON.   Call it injury
Thou mayst, 'tis such as thou perforce must bear.

CHOR. This is too much; ye rulers of the land
My fellow-citizens, come forth and save us.

Scene III.

Theseus, Creon, Œdipus, Antigone, Chorus.

The. Whence is this clamour? Wherefore am I called
From sacred rites at Neptune's altar paid,
Our guardian god? Say, what's the cause that thus
In haste I'm summoned hither?
Œdi.   O my friend!—
For well I know thy voice—most cruelly
Have I been treated by this man.
The.   Who did it?
Œdi. This Creon, whom thou seest, hath ravished
   from me
My only help, my daughters.
The.   Ha! what sayst thou?
Œdi. 'Tis as I tell thee.
The. [*to his Attendants*]. Quick, dispatch my servants,
Fly to the altar, summon all my people,
Horsemen and foot; give o'er the sacrifice,
And instant to the double gate repair,
Lest with the virgins the base ravishers
Escape unpunished, and my guest thus injured
Laugh me to scorn for cowardice. Away!
Were I to punish this oppressor here [*turning to* Creon
As my resentment bids and he deserves,
He should this instant fall beneath my rage;
But the same justice he to others deals,
Himself shall meet from us; thou shalt not go
Till those whom thou didst basely ravish hence
Are brought before me. 'Twas unlike thyself,
Unworthy of thy country and thy race,
To enter thus a cultivated city,
Where law and justice reign, with violence
And rapine, snatching what thy fancy pleased.
Or didst thou think I ruled a desert land,
Or that my people were a race of slaves,
And Theseus but the shadow of a king?
Thebes never taught thee such destructive lessons,

For she abhors injustice : when she hears
That Creon, thus despising sacred laws,
Hath ta'en with brutal violence my right,
And would have stolen a wretched suppliant from me,
She'll not approve thy conduct; say I went
To Thebes, how just soever were the cause,
I should not seize on aught without the leave
Of him who governed there ; but, as becomes
A stranger, bear myself unblamed by all.
Thou hast disgraced thy country and thy friends,
And weight of years hath ta'en thy senses from thee.
Again I say, restore the virgins to me,
Or stay with me thyself, for so thou shalt,
Howe'er unwilling; what I've said, remember,
Is what I have resolved—therefore determine.
    CHOR. [*to* CREON]. Stranger, thy actions, noble as
      thou art,
But ill become thy family and name,
Because unjust ; but thou beholdst thy fate.
    CREON. Theseus, it was not that I thought this city
Without or guards to save, or laws to rule,
Which brought me here, nor unadvised I came ;
But that I hoped you never would receive
My kindred here against my will, nor e'er
Embrace a vile incestuous parricide,
Or cherish and protect him in a land
Whose court, renowned for justice, suffers not
Such poor abandoned exiles to reside
Within its borders ; therefore did I this,
Which yet I had not done but for the curses
Which he hath poured on me and all my race ;
Revenge inspired me ; anger, well thou knowst,
Can never be extinguished but by death,
Which closeth every wound.   At present, Theseus,
It must be as thou wilt ; my want of power,
How just soe'er my cause, demands submission ;
Yet, old and weak, I shall not tamely yield.
    ŒDI. Audacious man ! thinkst thou the vile reproach
Thou utter'st falls on me, or on thyself ?
Thou who upbraidst me thus for all my woes,
Murder and incest, which against my will

I had committed, so it pleased the gods,
Offended at my race for former crimes ;
But I am guiltless ; canst thou name a fault
Deserving this ?　For, tell me, was it mine,
When to my father Phœbus did declare
That he should one day perish by the hand
Of his own child?　Was Œdipus to blame,
Who had no being then ?　If, born at length
To wretchedness, he met his sire unknown,
And slew him, that involuntary deed
Canst thou condemn ?　And for my fatal marriage,
Dost thou not blush to name it ?　Was not she
Thy sister, she who bore me, ignorant
And guiltless woman, afterwards my wife,
And mother to my children ?　What she did,
She did unknowing ; not like thee, who thus
Dost purposely upbraid us both.　Heaven knows
Unwillingly I wedded her, and now
Unwillingly repeat the dreadful tale ;
But, nor for that, nor for my murdered father,
Have I deserved thy bitter taunts ; for tell me,
Thy life attacked, wouldst thou have stayed to ask
Th' assassin if he were thy father?　No ;
Self-love would urge thee to revenge the insult.
Thus was I drove to ill by th' angry gods ;
This, should my father's soul revisit earth,
Himself would own, and pity Œdipus.
Thy bold and impious tongue still utters all ;
Just or unjust, thou pourst thy foul reproach
On me, pretending to revere the name
Of Theseus and his country.　But remember,
The city, whom thou hast praised, is famed
For piety and reverence to the gods ;
Yet wouldst thou drive a needy suppliant thence,
And lead him captive.　Thou hast stolen my daughter ;
But I implore the dreadful goddesses
To grant me aid, that thou mayst feel the power
Which thou contemn'st, and know the force of Athens.
　　Chor. [*to* Theseus]. O king ! this stranger merits thy
　　　regard ;
His woes are great, his cause should be defended.

THE. No more the ravishers are fled with speed,
Whilst we, who suffer, stand inactive here.
   CREON. Speak thy commands, for I must yield to
     thee.
   THE. Go thou before me, I shall follow close ;
If here thou hast concealed the virgins, now
Discover them ; if hence, to others' hands
Committed, they are fled, they shall not 'scape ;
My servants soon will fetch them back. Meantime,
Remember thy condition, for thy fate
Hath caught thee in the net which thou hadst spread
For others ; but what evil means acquire
Is seldom kept : thou cam'st not naked here,
Or unattended, thus to do an act
Of violence. Ere long I'll know on what
Thou didst rely, nor by a single arm
Shall Athens fall inglorious. Hearst thou this,
Or are my words unheeded ?
   CREON.   'Tis not now
A time to answer ; we shall know at home
What must be done.
   THE.   Thou threatenest ; but go on.
Stay thou in quiet here, for if I live,
                  [*turning to* ŒDIPUS
I will not rest till I restore thy daughters.
         [*Exeunt* THESEUS *and* CREON.

SCENE IV.

ŒDIPUS, CHORUS.

CHORUS.

Strophe 1.

Now the combatants prepare,
  And hasten to the field of war,
  Theseus, their great and god-like friend,
  The hapless virgins shall defend.
Oh ! could I hear the dreadful battle roar,
  Or near Apollo's sacred shrine,

Or on the torch-enlightened shore,
Or Ceres, where thy priests their rights divine
Perform, with lips in solemn silence sealed,
And mysteries ne'er by mortal tongue revealed.

Antistrophe 1.

At yon snowy mountain's feet
Westward perchance the warriors meet ;
Chariot and horse with mutual rage
On Œta's flowery plains engage ;
Around their Theseus now, a valiant band,
    See Athens' martial sons unite
    To save their native land ;
All shake their glittering spears, and urge the fight ;
All who thy power, Equestrian Pallas, own,
Or bow to Neptune, Rhea's honoured son.

Strophe 2.

The bloody scene shall soon be o'er
Creon the virgin shall restore ;
My soul prophetic sees the maid
For pious duty thus repaid ;
For ever active is the power of Jove,
    From whom perpetual blessings flow :
    Oh ! that I now could, like the dove,
Soar through the skies, and mark the field below,
The wished-for conquest joyful to behold,
And triumph in the victory I foretold !

Antistrophe 2.

Thou power supreme, all powers above,
All-seeing, all-performing Jove,
Grant that the rulers of this land
May soon subdue the hostile band !
Thee, too, O Pallas ! hunter Phœbus, thee
    Do we invoke, with thee be joined
    Thy virgin sister deity,
Who loves o'er lawns to chase the spotted hind ;
On you we call, your aid propitious bring,
Oh ! haste, protect our country and our king.   *[Exeunt.*

ACT III.

SCENE I.

ŒDIPUS, THESEUS, ANTIGONE, ISMENE,
CHORUS.

CHOR. I'm no false prophet, stranger, for behold
Thy daughters.
    ŒDI.   Ha! what sayst thou? Where, oh! where?
    ANT. My father! O my father! what kind god
Raised up this friend who hath restored us to thee?
    ŒDI. Are then my daughters with me?
    ANT.   Theseus' arm
Hath brought us here: to him and to his friends
We owe our safety.
    ŒDI.   Oh! come nigh, my children;
Let me embrace you. Never did I think
Again to fold you in these arms.
    ANT.   We come
With joy, my father.
    ŒDI.   Oh! where are you?
    ANT.   Here.
    ŒDI. My dearest children!
    ANT.   To our father still
May every pleasure come!
    ŒDI. [*leaning on* ANTIGONE]. My best support!
    ANT. The wretched bear the wretched.
    ŒDI. [*embracing them*].   I have all
That's precious to me: were I now to die
Whilst you are here, I should not be unhappy.
Support me, daughters, to your father's side
Close pressed. Oh! soothe to peace a wretched exile,
Long time deserted. Tell me what hath happened;
But let the tale be short, as best becomes
Thy tender age.
    ANT. [*pointing to* THESEUS]. Here is our great pro-
      tector,

He will inform you; so shall what I speak
Be brief, as thou wouldst have it.
    ŒDI.   Noble Theseus,
My children thus beyond my hopes restored,
If I should talk too long on such a theme,
Thou wilt not wonder. 'Tis to thee alone
I owe my joys; thou didst protect and save
My much-loved daughters : may the gods repay
Thee and thy kingdom for this goodness to me !
Here only have I found or faith, or truth,
Or justice; you alone possess them all.
I will attest it, for I know it well.
I feel your virtues; what I have is all
From you. O king! permit me but to touch
Thy hand. Oh! stretch it forth; or let me kiss
Thy honoured lips. But, oh! what do I say?
Can such a wretch as Œdipus e'er hope
With guilty hands to touch a man like thee,
So pure, so spotless? Yet I must embrace thee;
They only who have known misfortune feel
For others' griefs with sympathizing woe.
Hail, best of men ! and mayst thou ever be,
As thou hast been, my guardian and my friend !
    THE. Thus happy as thou must be in thy children,
Hadst thou said more, much more, and talked to them
Rather than me, it had not moved my wonder;
Nor think I should resent it. Not by words
Would Theseus be distinguished, but by deeds
Illustrious. This thou knowst, for what I swore
I have performed—restored thy daughters to thee,
Safe from the tyrant's threats. How passed the conflict
Why should I boast? They at their leisure best
May tell you all. Meantime to what I heard
As hither coming, Œdipus, attend.
Of little import seemed the circumstance,
And yet 'twas strange; but nought should mortal man
Deem or beneath his notice or his care.
    ŒDI. What is it, son of Ægeus? Oh! inform me,
For nothing have I heard.
    THE.   A man, they say,
Who boasts himself by blood allied to thee,

At Neptune's altar, whilst I sacrificed,
In humblest posture stood.

ŒDI.   What could it mean ?
Whence came he ?

THE.   That I know not ; this alone
They told me : suppliant he requested much
To talk a while with thee.

ŒDI.   With me ?   'Tis strange,
And yet methinks important.

THE.   He desired
But to converse with thee, and then depart.

ŒDI. Who can it be ?

THE.   Hast thou no friend at Argos,
None of thy kindred there who wished to see thee ?

ŒDI. No more, my friend.

THE.   What sayst thou ?

ŒDI.   Do not ask me.

THE. Ask what——

ŒDI.   I know him now ; I know too well
Who 's at the altar.

THE.   Who is it ?

ŒDI.   My son—
That hateful son, whose voice I loathe to hear.

THE. But why not hear him ?   Still thou mayst refuse
What he shall ask.

ŒDI.   I cannot, cannot bear it :
Do not oblige me.

THE.   But the sacred place
Where now he stands, and reverence to the gods,
Demand it of thee.

ANT.   Let me, O my father !
Young as I am, admonish thee.   Oh ! grant
Thy friend his just request ; obey the gods,
And let our brother come : whate'er he says
It need not draw thee from thy first resolve.
What harm to hear him ?   Words have oft produced
The noblest works.   Remember, 'tis thy child—
Thou didst beget him ; though he were the worst
Of sons to thee, yet would it ill become
A father to return it.   Let him come.
Others like thee have base, unworthy children,

And yet their minds are softened to forgiveness
By friends' advice, and all their wrath subdued.
Think on thy own unhappy parent's fate,
Thence mayst thou learn what dreadful ills have flowed
From anger's bitter fountain; thou, alas!
Art a sad proof; those sightless eyes too well
Bear witness to it. Those who only ask
What justice warrants, should not ask in vain;
Nor who receives a benefit, forget
The hand that gave, but study to repay it.

ŒDI. You have o'ercome me: with reluctant pleasure
I yield. My children, be it as you please;
But if he comes, O Theseus! guard my life.

THE. I've said enough; no more. I will not boast,
But thou art safe if Heaven forsake not me.

SCENE II.

CHORUS.

Strophe.

In sacred wisdom's path is seldom seen
    The wretch, whom sordid love of wealth inspires;
Neglectful of the happy golden mean,
    His soul nor truth nor heavenly knowledge fires;
No length of days to him can pleasure bring,
        In death alone he finds repose,
        End of his wishes and his woes;
        In that uncomfortable night
    Where never music's charms delight,
Nor virgin choirs their hymeneals sing.

Antistrophe.

The happiest fate of man is not to be;
    And next in bliss is he who soon as born,
From the vain world and all its sorrows free,
    Shall whence he came with speediest foot return;

For youth is full of folly, toils, and woes,
 Of war, sedition, pain, and strife,
 With all the busy ills of life,
 Till helpless age come creeping on,
 Deserted, friendless, and alone,
Which neither power nor joy nor pleasure knows.

Epode.

The hapless Œdipus, like me,
Is doomed to age and misery;
E'en as around the northern shore
The bleak winds howl and tempests roar,
Contending storms in terror meet,
And dashing waves for ever beat;
Thus is the wretched king with grief oppressed,
And woes on woes afflict his long-distempered breast.
         [Exeunt.

ACT IV.

SCENE I.

ŒDIPUS, ANTIGONE, ISMENE, CHORUS.

ANT. This way, my father. Lo! the wretched man
Approaches, unattended, and in tears.
 ŒDI. Who comes, my child?
 ANT.   E'en he I told thee of—
Poor Polynices.

SCENE II.

POLYNICES, ŒDIPUS, ANTIGONE, ISMENE, CHORUS.

POL.   O my sisters! see
Of all mankind the most unhappy. Where
Shall I begin? shall I lament my own,
Or shall I weep an aged parent's fate?
For, oh! 'tis horrible to find him thus

A wandering exile in a foreign land;
In this mean garb, with wild dishevelled hair,
Bereft of sight, and destitute, perhaps,
Of needful food and nourishment.   Alas!
Too late I know it; worthless as I am,
I flew to succour him, to plead my cause,
That not from others he might hear the tale
Of my misfortunes.   Sacred pity sits
Fast by the throne of Jove, o'er all his works
Presiding gracious.   Oh! let her inspire
Thy breast, my father.   Crimes already done,
Which cannot be recalled, may still be healed
By kind forgiveness: why, then, art thou silent?
Oh! speak, my father; do not turn aside.
Wilt thou not answer?   Wilt thou let me go
Without one word; nor tell me whence thy wrath
Contemptuous springs?   My sisters, you at least
Will try to move his unrelenting heart,
And loosen his closed lips, that not thus spurned
And thus unanswered, though a suppliant here
At Neptune's altar, I return with shame
And foul disgrace.

ANT.   Say, wherefore didst thou come,
My hapless brother?   Tell thy mournful tale;
Such is the power of words, that whether sweet
They move soft pity, or when bitter urge
To violence and wrath, at least they ope
Th' unwilling lips, and make the silent speak.

POLY. 'Tis well advised, and I will tell thee all.
Oh! may that deity propitious smile
Whose altar late I left, whence Theseus raised
This wretched suppliant, and in converse free
Mixed gracious with me!   May I hope from you
The like benevolence?   And now, my father,
I'll tell thee wherefore Polynices came.
Thou seest me banished from my native land—
Unjustly banished, for no other crime
But that I strove to keep the throne of Thebes,
By birthright mine, from him who drove me thence,
The young Eteocles: not his the claim
By justice, nor to me his fame in arms

Superior ; but by soft persuasive arts
He won the rebel city to his love.
Thy curse, my father, was the cause of all—
I know it was ; for so the priests declared
In oracles divine.   To Argos then
I came, and, to Adrastus' daughter joined
In marriage, gained the Argive chiefs, renowned
For martial deeds; seven valiant leaders march
To Thebes, resolved to conquer or to die.
Therefore to thee, my father, came I here,
To beg thy aid for me and these my friends,
Companions of the war, who threaten Thebes
With their united powers, in order thus :
The wise and brave Amphiaraus, or skilled
To cast the spear, or with prophetic tongue
Disclose the will of Heaven ; with Œneus' son
Ætolian Tydeus, and Eteocles,
At Argos born ; to these Hippomedon,
Sent by Talaus, his renowned sire ;
Bold Capaneus, who threatens soon to raze
The walls of mighty Thebes ; to close the train,
Parthenopæan Arcas comes, the son
Of Atalantis, from her virgin name
So called.   With these thy hapless son (the child
Of dire misfortune rather) leads his force
From Argos to rebellious Thebes.   For these,
And for their children, for the lives of all,
Suppliant to thee we come—in humble prayer
To deprecate thy wrath against a wretch
Who, injured much, but seeks the vengeance due
To a base brother, whose oppressive hand
Hath drove me from my country and my throne.
If there be truth in what the gods declare,
On him shall victory smile for whom thy vows
Shall rise propitious ; therefore, by our gods
And native fountains, oh ! remit thy anger,
And smile upon me, on a banished man,
A beggar like thyself, who lives, like thee,
By others' bounty—in one common fate
We are united, whilst the tyrant sits
In ease at home, and laughs our woes to scorn.

Yet if thou wouldst but listen to my vows,
Soon might I cast him forth, restore thee soon
To thy dear native land, and seat myself
In my own kingdom. Thy assent, my father,
Is all I ask; but, oh! without thy aid
I have no hope of safety or revenge.
   CHOR. For Theseus' sake, oh! give him answer now,
And let him go.
   ŒDI.   But that the noble Theseus,
Who hither brought him did request it of me,
He ne'er had heard the voice ef Œdipus;
And little pleasure will it now bestow.
Ungrateful wretch! who, when the throne of Thebes,
                      [*turning to* POLYNICES
Where now thy brother sits, was thine, didst drive
Thy father hence, to penury and woe,
Now, when thou seest me in this mean attire,
Thou weepst my fate because 'tis like thy own; .
But I'll not weep, for I can bear it all,
Still, wicked parricide, remembering thee,
The cruel cause of all; thou mad'st me thus
On others' bounty to rely for food
And nourishment; for thee, I might have perished,
But these my pious daughters, these alone,
Beyond their sex's power, with manly aid
Have cherished and protected me. For you,
Who call yourselves my sons, ye are not mine—
I know you not; though Heaven hath spared you long,
Death will o'ertake you. When thy forces come
To Thebes, which shall not fall before thy arms,
There soon shalt thou, and thy vile brother, die.
Long since my curses did declare thy fate,
Which here I do repeat, that you may learn
The reverence due to parents, and no more
Reproach a sightless father. Look on these,
My duteous daughters: did they act like you?
They never did; and therefore to the throne
Which you have forfeited shall they succeed,
If justice still, as she is ever wont,
Sits at the hand of Jove. Meantime thou worst,
Thou most abandoned of the race of men,

Begone—away ! and with thee bear this curse
Which here I do pronounce : To Argos ne'er
Mayst thou return ! never may Thebes be thine !
Soon mayst thou perish by a brother's hand,
Slaying the slayer ! may dark Erebus
Receive them both !   And now on you I call,
Ye goddesses revered, and thou, O Mars !
Thou who hast raised the bitter strife between
My impious sons, bear witness to my words !
Farewell !   Now go, and tell the Thebans, tell
Thy faithful friends, how fair an heritage
Your Œdipus hath here bequeathed his children.

    Chor. O Polynices ! little is the joy
Which we can give thee of this fatal journey ;
Therefore away and leave us.

    Poly.   A sad path
These steps have trod indeed, of woe to me
And to my friends.   Was it for this, alas !
I came from Argos ?   I can never tell
My mournful story there, never return ;
Oh ! I must bury it in silence all.
My sisters, ye have heard the dreadful curse
Which he pronounced.   Oh ! if it be fulfilled,
And some kind hand restore you back to Thebes,
At least remember me ; at least perform
The funeral rights, and hide me in the tomb ;
So shall your names, for pious tenderness
To an unhappy father long revered,
With added praises crowned, exalted shine,
For this kind office to a brother's shade.

    Ant. O Polynices ! let me beg thee, hear
Thy sister now.

    Poly.   My dear Antigone,
What sayst thou ?

    Ant.   Lead thy armies back to Argos,
Nor thus destroy thy country and thyself.

    Poly. It cannot be ; my forces once dismissed
Through fear, what power shall e'er reunite them ?

    Ant. But wherefore all this rage?   What canst thou
       hope
Of fame or profit by the fall of Thebes?

POLY. 'Tis base to fly, and, eldest born as I am,
To be the laughter of a younger brother.

ANT. Dost thou not dread the oracles pronounced
Against you both—death by each other's hand?

POLY. I know the sentence; but we must go on.

ANT. Alas! and who shall dare to follow thee
After this dire prediction?

POLY.   None shall know it.
The prudent general tells the good alone,
And keeps the threatened ill unknown to all.

ANT. Art thou determined then, and wilt thou go?

POLY. Do not dissuade me, for the task is mine;
And though a father's fatal curse attend me,
Though vengeful furies shall await my steps,
Yet I must go.   May Jove indulgent smile
On you, my sisters, if when I am dead,
As soon I shall be, to my breathless corpse
You pay due honours! Now, farewell for ever,
For living ye shall ne'er again behold me.

ANT. Alas! my brother!

POLY.   Do not weep for me.

ANT. Who would not weep to see thee rushing thus
On certain death?

POLY.   If I must die, I must.

ANT. Yet be persuaded.

POLY.   Ask me not to do
A deed unworthy of me.

ANT.   Losing thee,
I shall be most unhappy.

POLY.   To the gods
Alone belong the fate of mortals; some
Are born to happiness and some to woe:
You may they guard from every ill, for sure
Ye merit all the good they can bestow.

                              [*Exit* POLYNICES

Scene III.

ŒDIPUS, ANTIGONE, ISMENE, CHORUS.

CHOR. Fresh sorrows hath this hapless stranger
    brought
On me and all; but so hath Heaven decreed,
Which nothing doth in vain; whilst time beholds
And orders all, inflicting woe on woe.
But, hark! the thunder roars: almighty Jove!
    ŒDI. My daughters! O my daughters! who will
    bring
The noble Theseus here, that best of men?
    ANT. Wherefore, my father, should we call him
    hither?
    ŒDI. This winged lightning from the arm of Jove
Must bear me to the shades below. Where's Theseus?
Let him be sent for instantly.
    CHOR.   Again,
Another dreadful clap! It strikes my soul
With horror, and my hairs do stand on end
With fear. Behold, again the lightnings flash!
I dread the consequence, for not in vain
These signs appear of some calamity
Portentous ever, O ethereal Jove!
    ŒDI. Alas! my children, nought can save me now;
The fatal hour of my departure hence
Draws nigh.
    ANT.   Why thinkst thou so?
    ŒDI.   I know it well.
Send for the king immediately.
    CHOR.   Alas!
The thunder rolls on every side. Good Heaven,
Protect us! If to this devoted land
It bodes destruction, let not ruin fall
On me. Oh! let not that be our reward
For pitying thus a poor deserted stranger.
O Jove! on thee we call: protect and save us!
    ŒDI. Is Theseus come? shall he once more behold me,
Whilst yet I live, and keep my perfect mind?

CHOR. What secret hast thou to reveal to him?

ŒDI. I owe him much, and would repay his goodness,
E'en as I promised him.

CHOR.   Oh! haste, my son;
At Neptune's altar leave the sacrifice
And hither fly, for Œdipus, to thee
And to thy country grateful, waits to pay
Thy bounties.   Haste, O Theseus! to receive them.

SCENE IV.

THESEUS, ŒDIPUS, ANTIGONE, ISMENE, CHORUS.

THE. Again this noise, this wild astonishment,
Amongst you all!   Was Œdipus the cause?
Or did the bolt of Jove and rushing hail
Affright you?   When the god in raging storms
Descends thus dreadful, we have cause to fear.

ŒDI. O king! thou com'st in happy hour; some god
Propitious led thee hither.

THE.   Son of Laius,
What new event hath happened?

ŒDI.   Know, my life
At length is verging to its latest hour;
I wish to die, but first my vows to thee,
And to this city, faithful must perform.

THE. But who hath told thee thou so soon shalt die?

ŒDI. The gods themselves, who never utter falsehood,
By signs infallible have warned me of it.

THE. How spake they to thee?

ŒDI.   In repeated thunder
And lightning from th' all-powerful hand of Jove.

THE. I do believe thee, for thy prophecies
Were never false; but say, what must be done?

ŒDI. O son of Ægeus! I will tell thee all
The bliss reserved for thee in thy age—
For thee, and for thy country.   I must go
To my appointed place, and there shall die:
I go without a guide, nor must thou tell

To mortal ear where Œdipus doth lie,
For ever hid. O king ! that sacred place
Shall be thy sure defence, and better far
Than many a shield, or all the social aid
Of firm alliance in the field of war.
What more remains, unutterable now,
Of higher import, thither when thou com'st
To thee alone shall be delivered ; nought
Shall I reveal, or to the citizens,
Or e'en to those, beloved as they are,
My pious daughters. Thou must ever keep
The solemn secret ; only, when thy life
Draws near its end, disclose it to thy son,
Heir of thy kingdom, and to him alone.
From king to king thus shall the tale devolve,
And thus thy Athens be for ever safe
From Theban force ; even the best of cities,
Where justice rules, may swerve from virtue's laws
And be oppressive ; but the gods, though late,
Will one day punish all who disobey
Their sacred mandates ; therefore, son of Ægeus,
Be careful and be just : but this to thee
I need not say.   Quick, let us to the place,
For so the gods decree ; there must I go,
Thence never to return.   Come then, my daughters :
Long have you been my pious guides ; henceforth
I must be yours.   Follow, but touch me not ;
Let me find out the tomb where I must hide
My poor remains : that way my journey lies.
[Pointing with his hand.
Away : thou god of shades, great Mercury,
And Proserpine, infernal powers, conduct me !
O sightless eyes ! where are ye ? Never more
Shall these hands touch your unavailing orbs.
O light and life ! farewell : at length I go
To hide me in the tomb ; but oh ! for thee,
My best beloved friend, and this fair land,
And these thy subjects, may prosperity
Attend you still, and may you sometimes deign
Amidst your bliss to think on Œdipus !   [*Exeunt.*
   CHOR. Goddess invisible, on thee we call,

If thee we may invoke, Proserpina, and thee
Great Pluto, king of shades, oh! grant
That not, oppressed by torturing pain,
Beneath the stroke of death he linger long,
But swift with easy steps descend,
To Styx's drear abode;
For he hath led a life of toil and pain;
May the just gods repay his undeserved woe!
Ye goddesses revered, who dwell
Beneath the earth deep hid, and thou,
Who, barking from thy gloomy cave,
Unconquered Cerberus, guardst the ghosts below,
On thee, O son of Tartarus! we call,
For thou art ever wakeful—lead, oh! lead
To thy dark mansions this unhappy stranger.

[*Exeunt.*

ACT V.

Scene I.

Messenger, Chorus.

Messenger. O citizens! I come to tell a tale——
But to be brief, know, Œdipus is dead.
To speak the manner and strange circumstance
Of his departure will require more words,
And calls for your attention.
    Chor.   Is he gone?
Unhappy man!
    Mes.   For ever hath he left
The path of life.
    Chor.   How died he?—by the hand
Of Heaven dismissed, without disease or pain?
    Mes. Oh! 'twas a scene of wonder. How he left
This place, and, self-conducted, led us on,
Blind as he was, ye all remember well.

Soon as he came to where the craggy steep
With brazen steps leads to the hollow gulf,
Where various paths unite, a place renowned
For the famed league of Theseus and his friend,
Between Acherdus and the Thracian rock,
On a sepulchral stone he sat him down;
Pulled off the filthy weeds he long had worn,
And bade his daughters instantly prepare
The bath and splendid garb; with hasty steps
To Ceres' neighbouring altar they repair
Obedient, bring the vessel, and the robe
Funereal. All things done as custom bids
For dying men, sudden a dreadful clap
Of thunder shook the ground; the virgins trembled,
And clinging fearful round their father's knees
Beat their sad breasts, and wept. Soon as he heard
The sound portentous, he embraced his daughters:
" Children," he cried, " your father is no more;
No longer shall you lead a life of pain,
No longer toil for Œdipus. Alas!
'Twas dreadful to you, but this day, my children,
Shall end your sorrows and my life together.
Never did father love his daughters more
Than I have loved; but henceforth you must live
Without your Œdipus. Farewell for ever!"
He spake, and long, in sad embraces joined,
They wept aloud; at length did clamorous grief
To silent sorrow yield, and all was still;
When suddenly we heard a voice that oft
Repeated, " Œdipus, why this delay?
Where art thou, Œdipus?" The wretched king,
Attentive to the call of Heaven, desired
That Theseus might be sent for; Theseus came,
When thus the dying exile: " O my friend!
Give me thy hand, my daughters give him yours;
Let this, my dearest Theseus, be the pledge
Of amity between you; promise here
That you will ne'er forsake my hapless children,
But henceforth cherish, comfort, and protect them."
The generous king, in pity to their woes,
Vowed to perform what Œdipus desired.

The father threw his feeble arms around
His weeping children. "You,". he cried, "must learn
To bear your sufferings with an equal mind,
And leave this place; for not to mortal eye
Is given to see my future fate. Away!
Theseus alone must stay, and know it all."
This did we hear him utter as we stood
Attentive; when his duteous daughters left him,
And went their way, we wept, and followed them.
Soon we returned, but Œdipus was gone;
The king alone remaining, as if struck
With terror at some dreadful spectacle,
Had with his hand o'er-veiled his downcast eye;
A little after, we beheld him bend
In humble adoration to the earth,
And then to heaven prefer his ardent prayer.
How the poor exile perished none can tell
But Theseus; nor the fiery blast of Jove
Destroyed, nor sea o'erwhelmed him, but from heaven
Some messenger divine did snatch him hence,
Or power infernal bade the pitying earth
Open her peaceful bosom to receive him;
Without a groan, disease, or pain he fell.
'Twas wondrous all; to those who credit not
This strange report, I answer, 'Tis most true.

    CHOR. Where are his daughters, with their weeping
       friends
Who followed them?
    MES.   They cannot be far off;
The voice of grief I hear proclaims them nigh.

SCENE II.

ANTIGONE, ISMENE (*with Attendants*), MESSENGER, CHORUS.

    ANT. Alas! the time is come when we must weep
Our father's fate, the fate of all his race
Long since unhappy. Various were the toils,

The labours we endured, but this is far,
Far above all, unutterable woe.

    CHOR. What is it?

    ANT.   Oh ! it cannot be conceived.

    CHOR. Is he then dead ?

    ANT.   He is; his death was strange
And wonderful, for not in war he fell,
Nor did the sea o'erwhelm him, but the earth
Hath hid him from us; deadly night hath closed
Our eyes in sadness; whether o'er the seas
We roam, or exiles in a foreign land
Lead our sad days, we must be still unhappy.
Alas ! I only wish I might have died
With my poor father ; wherefore should I ask
For longer life?

    CHOR.   Ye good and pious daughters,
Remember, what the will of Heaven decrees
With patience we must bear; indulge not then
Excess of grief—your faith hath not deserved it.

    ANT. Oh ! I was fond of misery with him ;
E'en what was most unlovely grew beloved
When he was with me,   O my dearest father !
Beneath the earth now in deep darkness hid,
Worn as thou wert with age, to me thou still
Wert dear, and shalt be ever.

    CHOR.   Now his course
Is finished.

    ANT.   Even as he wished, he died
In a strange land—for such was his desire ;
A shady turf covered his lifeless limbs ;
Nor unlamented fell; for oh ! these eyes,
My father, still shall weep for thee, nor time
Ere blot thee from my memory.

    ISM.   Alas !
Alas ! my sister, what must be our fate,
Forlorn and helpless, of our father thus
Bereft ?

    CHOR. His end was happy, therefore cease
Your fruitless tears : from sorrow none is free.

    ANT. Let us be gone.

    ISM.   But where ?

ANT.　　　　　　　　　　　　　　I wish——

ISM.　　　　　　　　　　　　　　. Oh! what?

ANT. To see the tomb.

ISM.　　　　　　　　Whose tomb?

ANT.　　　　　　　　　　　　Our father's. Oh!

ISM. But is it lawful? Knowst thou that?

ANT.　　　　　　　　　　　　　　Why thus
Reprove me, my Ismene?

ISM.　　　　　　　　He is yet
Unburied, and without ——

ANT.　　　　　　　　Oh! lead me there,
Then kill me if thou wilt; for where, alas!
Can I betake me?

CHOR.　　　　　　Friends, be comforted.

ANT. Where shall I fly?

CHOR.　　　　　　　Thou hast already 'scaped
Unnumbered ills.

ANT.　　　　　　I'm thinking, my Ismene——

ISM. What thinkst thou?

ANT.　　　　　　　How we shall get home.

CHOR.　　　　　　　　　No more;
Thou hast been long familiar with affliction.

ANT. My life hath ever been a life of pain
And sorrow, but this far exceeds them all.

CHOR. The storm beats hard upon you.

ANT.　　　　　　　　　　　Oh! it doth.

CHOR. I know it must.

ANT.　　　　　　Oh! whither shall we fly?
Great Jove! what hope remains?

CHOR.　　　　　　　　Suppress your griefs;
We should not weep for those who wished to die,
And meet their fate with pleasure; 'tis not just
Nor lawful to lament them.

SCENE III.

THESEUS, ANTIGONE, ISMENE, CHORUS.

ANT.　　　　　　　　Son of Ægeus,
Suppliant to thee we come.

THE.   What would ye of me ?
ANT. Permit us but to see our father's tomb.
THE. It is not lawful.
ANT.   Oh ! what sayst thou, king ?
THE. Know, pious virgins, Œdipus himself
Forbade that any should approach his tomb ;
That sacred spot, which he possesses there,
No mortal must profane ; to me, he said,
If careful I performed his last command,
Should joy and safety come, with victory
And peace to Athens ; this your gods did hear
Confirmed by the sacred oath of Jove.
    ANT. If such our father's will, we must submit ;
But, oh ! permit us to revisit Thebes,
That so we may prevent th' impending fate
Of our dear brothers.
THE.   All that you request,
Or may be grateful to that honoured shade
Whose memory we revere, I freely grant ;
For I must not be weary of my task.
    CHOR. Remember, virgins, to repress your sorrows,
And cease your fruitless grief ; for know, 'tis all
Decreed by fate, and all the work of Heaven.

PRINTED BY BALLANTYNE, HANSON AND CO.
LONDON AND EDINBURGH

www.ingramcontent.com/pod-product-compliance
Lightning Source LLC
Chambersburg PA
CBHW060537030726
47498CB00004B/1224